SHOW ME LOVE

SHOW ME LOVE

A Korean pop fiction novel by

KPOPALYPSE

SHOW ME LOVE

A Korean pop fiction novel by KPOPALYPSE

This book is a work of fiction. Any references to historical events, real people or real places are used fictitiously. Other names, characters, places and events are the products of the author's imagination, and any resemblance to actual events, or places and persons, living or dead, is entirely coincidental, even if such resemblances might take certain well-informed individuals down memory lane...

More information and relevant links at kpopalypse.com

For all the caonimas.

1. MR CHOI

"No paper planes in class, Hana."

"What plane?"

Oh my god, I swear I don't even have a paper plane this time. Can this teacher get fucked?

Ms Kang, my useless math teacher, a tall snooty bitch with no life, reaches behind my left ear and pulls a paper plane out of my hair.

"This one here."

Now I look shameful, not that there's a time at school when I don't. Of course, this teacher is so dumb, she doesn't instantly recognise harassment when she sees it and she's possibly going to think that's my plane.

I bow in my seat. "I'm so sorry Ms Kang, I didn't know that was there!"

The whole class laughs. I can hear the boys up the back giggling loudest of all. I know they're fucking with me again; they must have thrown that plane right from the back of the room into my hair and I didn't even feel it, having thick hair really sucks sometimes. I wonder how long that plane was sitting there stuck in my hair with everyone laughing at me behind my back. Ms Kang fortunately notices the boys giggling too, so she glares at them, walks back to her desk at the front of the class, and then does nothing except sit there and carry on ignoring everyone while she plays with her laptop doing fuck knows what. *That's just great, don't stick up for me or anything you useless fuck-hole of a teacher.* Not that I expect her to do anything, because she's completely useless as a teacher and a human being, but at least she realises it's not my own doing which means that I won't get into trouble for something that's not my fault, for once.

These boys at the back of the class are pieces of shit and I've tried everything I can to get them to stop picking on me, but nothing works. If I sit right up the front of the class where the teacher is, I usually collect their projectiles in my hair, like this one. If I sit in a row nearer to the middle of the class, I have to deal with them reaching out to tap me or poke at me with their stationery, or walking by and trying to shove something down my shirt, or passing stupid notes and so on. If I sit right up the back, right where they are, so they can't do anything from behind, that's by far the worst. I don't want to even think about what happened when I tried that, but that's a mistake I only made once and I learned new things that day about what type of behaviour Ms Kang was willing to completely ignore in her own classroom. Today I'm feeling pretty sensitive and raw and I know I just can't deal with them today at all, so I'm sitting right up the front at the far corner, as far away from them as I can get. Obviously, it's not far enough. I stare back at them and two thoughts occur to me. Firstly, that was a pretty good throw for them to get the plane accurately that far across the room, and secondly, I wonder if I could hurt one of them so much, that they'd have to, at the very least, go to hospital for a while.

What would be the best method to hurt these boys and deliver justice? Obviously, the easiest way would be to shoot them, maybe just shooting one would be enough to get across the message, but more than one probably wouldn't be a bad thing. Unfortunately, I don't have a gun or even know anything about guns or how to get them, South Korean laws being what they are guns aren't exactly easy to get here. I could maybe stab one of them instead, would a knife from the cafeteria be sharp enough to do the job? Probably not, I wouldn't be strong enough to pierce the skin of a boy with one of those dull instruments before he reacted and swatted me away with his fist, and then it would probably be all over for me. At best I would get one or two decent stabs in, it would take multiple stabs to kill a boy unless I got really lucky in the first few seconds. I mean I'm not weak because I don't mind exercise and my gymnastic skills are decent, but I'm also short and female and not going to be able to overpower the boys in the class, there's just no way, I'm only 155cm (not much above five feet) and the guys are huge. Any object used to decimate these boys as they richly deserve would have to be fast to use, something with distance, something that can even the strength imbalance, in and out quickly, plus easy to get and carry. I'm not sure what such an object would be, but thinking about the possibilities makes me feel slightly better.

Suddenly, the school bell rings and kicks me out of my daydreaming. Time for class changeover, gym is next. I'm grateful - gym is way better than math, doing something physical that I'm actually good at will make me feel a little better. Ms Kang folds up her laptop and leaves the room immediately, leaving us students to file out unsupervised. I'm as keen to leave as she is so I get up quickly and move to the narrow exit at the rear of the class. Unfortunately, most of the other students have the same idea, and the aisle between the desks quickly becomes clogged with people. As I push through and try to escape to the hallway outside, I can see that one of the boys in the group who was picking on me is aiming to cut into the line, right behind me, it's Dongjae, a slimy idiotic oaf. I know exactly what will happen next, but I can't deal with it this time, I just can't - so I have to stop him. I can't let him join the queue, not right next to me. There's no way.

"Hey Hana, mind if I *slip in* behind you?" asks Dongjae, although he's not really asking, he's telling.

"Try that shit again and I'll fucking murder you!" I scream back at him.

He smiles. He thinks I'm joking, but I'm not. In fact, I'm not even exaggerating. If this gross pig actually enters the queue behind me, I will do my best to end his life in that moment. I probably won't succeed, in fact it's almost guaranteed that I'll fail, but I would want to see how close I can get to my goal. It's important to have ambition.

He moves along the horizontal gaps between the tables to try and intercept me in the queue. Looking around for some way to obstruct him, I think about sliding the tables together, but it's a bit too hard to do that while also maintaining my queue position, and it's probably more important that I just get away from him. I notice there's a chair between me and him in the gap between the tables so I kick it across in his direction, hoping that it at least slows him down a little. The chair slides across the tiled floor and then falls over before it reaches his feet. I then look on as somehow one of the chair legs bounces up right between his legs, hitting him right in the balls. A lucky shot and definitely not what I expected to happen, I couldn't have planned it better if I tried. He moans in pain and falls to the floor.

"Suck shit, loser!" I yell as I hear Dongjae groaning. I really want to go over there and kick him in the face a few times, because he completely deserves it, but I wouldn't get away with it. He's going to get angry and so are his friends, so it's better that I just try to make my escape quickly before there's a retaliation.

After what seems like way too long, I finally funnel through the door and into the hallway. I make my way down the corridor, past the endless rows of lockers. I've nearly reached the gym when I hear some light footsteps running up to me, closer and closer.

"Hey, bitch!"

I recognise the voice immediately. It's Eunu, Dongjae's girlfriend. I'm not sure how he acquired himself a girlfriend, one of the great mysteries of life perhaps. Eunu is tall and scary, someone not to be messed with. Unlike her boyfriend who is just a typical creep, Eunu is a true *iljin* with a reputation for violence, something that I unfortunately forgot about just before when I kicked that chair in Dongjae's direction. Unlike regular creeps in my class, I can't fight back against *iljins* - the top tier gangs at my school. They can make my life complete hell if I try to mess with them.

Before I can react or even turn around, Eunu grabs a fistful of my hair, right on top of my head near the roots. Her grip is tight and completely controls the motion of my neck, I have no choice but to go where she's taking me. Eunu pushes me to the side of the hallway and pins me in a small gap between two lockers with my face against the wall.

"He had it coming. Tell your meathead boyfriend to keep it in his pants next time." I mumble to her as best I can with my jaw pushed against the cold brick.

Eunu pushes me harder. I try to struggle a bit but there's no room for me to even move my limbs, Eunu is strong and has the positional advantage, I'm completely immobilised. I give up pushing back against Eunu and relax my body a bit, I'm trapped so it's a waste of energy to fight her. Eunu moves her face right up to mine, I still can't see her but I can feel her hot stale breath on the back of my neck. I swear this bitch has never seen a toothbrush.

"Don't worry, he's just kidding around, he's not going to do anything to an ugly dyke like you, he can do better than a *wangtta*. But if you even so much as *look* at him ever again, *I* might."

"So I just get harassed then?" I ask... but there's no response. I notice suddenly that the pressure on my body is gone, and so is the grip on my hair. I turn around and Eunu has already vanished somewhere down the crowded hallway. I breathe a deep sigh of relief; if she considers that little threat to be enough revenge for her boyfriend collecting a chair leg in the ball sack, I definitely got off *very* lightly. It could have been so much worse. I reorient myself, step back out between the lockers and keep moving to the gym, feeling slightly relieved.

The gym is a large open indoor area that's about the size of three basketball courts. The middle space is a combined basketball and netball court, on one side of that is the gymnastics area with floor mats, a trampoline and a high-jump area, on the other end are the offices and a small stage for presentations. I walk over to where the floor mats are hanging up, collect a spare mat and drag it over to an unoccupied floor space away from the other students - as I'm *wangtta*, I'm not allowed to exercise with others. *Wangtta* is the lowest of the low in school social status; I'm not allowed to have friends, I must do all activities alone plus I have to give up all rights to *iljins* and more popular students. I'm just about to place the mat down and wait for the gym teacher to arrive when an announcement comes over the public address system:

"SHIN HANA, PLEASE REPORT TO THE GYM OFFICE IMMEDIATELY. SHIN HANA, PLEASE REPORT TO THE GYM OFFICE IMMEDIATELY."

Hearing my name called out over the loudspeaker is uncomfortable and gives me a jolting sensation. I guess I'm in trouble again, maybe they found out about Dongjae and now I have to explain it all, or maybe it's something else, but school office meetings are never anything good. I slide my mat back across the gym, hang it up on the hook I collected it from just seconds ago, and then walk unenthusiastically over to the office.

When I arrive, the gym coach who is supposed to be teaching my actual class is sitting behind his desk. It's odd for him to keep the class waiting, so I guess whatever this is, it's serious. There's another man sitting on my side of the desk, I've never seen him before. The gym coach motions for me to take a seat on the empty chair next to the other man.

"Am I in trouble?" I ask, as I sit down.

"Hana, I'd like you to meet Mr Choi," says the coach, not answering my question, and motioning to the stranger.

Mr Choi looks maybe about thirty years old; he has slick-backed hair down to his shoulders and he's dressed super sharp in a black suit. He bows and smiles, a really warm smile, which gets me on edge immediately. I'm not used to seeing adults smile at me and especially not at school and especially not like *that*. I wonder who this is - a new guidance counsellor about to give me some bullshit advice that won't help with my problems? An annoying religious chaplain here to try to save my soul? I shiver involuntarily.

"*Mannaseo bangapseumnida*, Hana. I'm Mr Choi, from True Miracle Entertainment."

I bow in return. "*Mannaseo bangapseumnida*, Mr Choi."

"Hana, do you like music?"

Okay, this is really not what I thought I would be getting asked today.

"I don't know. I guess so? Doesn't everyone?"

"You would be surprised. Hana, have you ever wanted to be in an idol pop group?" He's so polite and well-spoken that it's surreal.

"Um... can't say I have? What's this about?"

"Sorry, allow me to explain to you. I'm a talent scout for an entertainment agency. My agency is looking for new talent to train. I'm here to ask if you would be interested in joining a group that we are forming."

I'm not a musician, I know nothing about music. I don't understand why I'm being asked this. Why me? I'm speechless for a moment.

He senses correctly that I have no idea what to say to him. "I have been assessing the school's gym students today and looking at videos of some of their past performances. I think you have excellent potential for our new group. We would be interested in adding you to our team."

This is surreal. What should I even tell him?

"But... I'm not talented? I'm not a singer or anything? I literally can't sing?"

"That does not matter - that is why we have a training process. Singing and dancing can be trained, but genetics cannot." He smiles at me, that really warm smile again. He doesn't seem the least bit bothered that I've just told him I have absolutely zero talent. This doesn't feel right.

"Okay, but... what sort of training? Do I go after school? How does it work?"

"The training is three years long; you would live and train on-site at our agency. You would do training instead of school, there would still be some on-site classes so you can keep up in important subjects but..."

Live and train at the agency. Instead of school.

"What do I have to do?" I ask, cutting him off, just before realising that maybe it's a little rude to do that.

2. MOTHER

I am at home, sitting at the dinner table, with my head bowed. My mother is reading the draft contract that Mr Choi asked me to take home for my parents to look at. Mr Choi will then visit us the next evening at our house, and if agreed, they will sign off on the contract. Not me - my mother's still my guardian, so I don't sign anything, she has to agree. Not my father either, he's been completely out of the picture since I was seven years old, these days it's just my mother at home. They're not officially divorced as far as I know (my mother isn't great at conveying this kind of information) but they might as well be, because he just isn't around anymore. I haven't seen my father in so many years, I don't know what he even does or where he lives now, he could be dead for all I know. Since my mother is the only parent in my life, she will be making the decision alone, and if everything goes well, then I will pack my things and meet at the agency headquarters this weekend to join the group.

I silently watch as my mother reads the contract. I know what's in it, I've already been obsessively reading it earlier today because it was all I could think about after meeting Mr Choi, so as she turns the pages, I know exactly which part she is reading. I study her face for her reactions to each section, specifically the part about me not living at home and not having any contact with her, not even being *allowed* to have any contact with her until the training period is over. I see her eyebrows raise when she reaches this section, but she doesn't say anything about it, and just stares at the page with her ugly bifocals. I continue to wait while she reads the rest of the thirty-page contract, which she does carefully, not skipping anything. Eventually she speaks.

"They don't give you a lot of freedom, do they," she says with a tone of vague disapproval.

Neither do you, I feel like clapping back, but I decide to shut my mouth and just bow more. This isn't the time to get her offside. It's important that I be as respectful as possible if I'm going to get what I want.

My mother puts the contract down and stares at me, with disdain, like she always does. The kind of disdain that is one hundred percent my mother.

"Do you really want this?" she asks.

What a question. I want to say *stop pretending you give a shit about what I want, just tell me if it's something YOU want, or at least will allow.* Instead, I hold my thoughts in and nod. "Yes, mother." I stare down at the dining table, trying to look as humble as possible.

A long pause. "The conditions here are very strict. Can you handle the pressure, I wonder. You're not handling

19

school very well at all right now. How would you handle this?"

"I feel that this is what I need. I know it will be harsh but I will grow as a person to become more mature and your better daughter in the future."

I don't believe the words coming out of my mouth, I'm just saying this because I know how my mother thinks, and this type of grovelling will appeal to her more than *I just want to be away from you forever*.

Another long pause. Then, finally: "Tomorrow, I will talk to him. You had better be sure this is what you want, because once you make this choice, there will be no going back."

Fine with me, bitch. "Yes, mother."

"Go to your room. Let me not see you again tonight." My mother waves me away.

"Thank you, mother!"

I get up from the table, push the chair in, making sure it's perfectly square so she doesn't get upset, and then walk briskly up the stairs to my room. I'm still under a strict curfew for being rude to her a few months back, so I'm not allowed to go outside of my own room after dinner other than to use the bathroom, or anywhere at all outside the home at any time without her present, apart from school.

Once the door of my room is closed, I immediately take my school uniform off, throw it on the floor, and change into my flannel pyjamas. I'm not going anywhere tonight so I might as well be comfortable. I look at the clothes I've just discarded, crumpled in the corner. It seems unreal that tomorrow could be the last day that I ever go to school. I think about what will happen tomorrow, probably nothing much. I should try to keep a low profile, I don't want everyone to know what's happening. If people at school know about this, they'll definitely find a way to use it against me somehow. They always do.

3. HOME GROUP

"Shin Hana, come to the front of the class!"

As far as keeping a low profile goes, I'm not off to a very good start. Ms Moon, my home group teacher, is unhappy about something. I stand up from my desk and walk up to the front of the teacher's desk, facing her, but she motions for me to come further, around to the side, so I'm standing right next to her. When I arrive at her designated position, she looks me up and down.

"You're a disgusting mess this morning, Hana! What's wrong with you? Do you not wash and iron your uniform?"

Bitch, I couldn't give a fuck about you, or my uniform, or this school. This is my last day here, probably. It better be, because if it isn't, I don't know what I'm going to do.

I bow at ninety degrees to show maximum respect.

"I'm sorry, Ms Moon!"

Ms Moon looks me up and down.

"Hana, is there anything that I need to be concerned about?"

You should be concerned about dying of vaginal rot, you old bag. "No, Ms Moon!" I reply, trying to sound as earnest as possible.

"Sit back down, ensure this tardiness is not repeated."

She seems to be satisfied. I move to my seat quickly, hoping she doesn't find something else to complain about.

"And tie your shoelaces!" she booms. No such luck.

"Yes, Ms Moon!"

I quickly crouch down and fix my loose left shoelace before taking a seat.

Home group is a time-wasting class where nothing really happens, it's just for roll call and announcements, so once I'm back in my seat, my thoughts drift to what's happening this evening; the meeting between Mr Choi from the agency, and my mother. The fact that my mother didn't dismiss the contract out of hand makes me feel optimistic. If she really hated the idea, she would have shut it down immediately without even a second thought. Of course, she wouldn't have warmed to the idea for my benefit, because she cares so much about her precious daughter, oh *hell no* - nothing she ever thinks about has anything to do with me, everything is all about *her*. I honestly think she just finds the idea of me being out of the house appealing for whatever reason, and that's fine, because the feeling is definitely mutual.

The contract is pretty strict though, to say the least. I read through it carefully and there's a long list of things that they control. My waking and sleeping hours, when I work, what activities I do when I work, when I eat, what

I eat, how much I eat, the type of clothes I wear, my hairstyle, even when I'm allowed to shower, all of this is under their strict control, I have no say in any of it. There's also no phones, electronic devices or social media during the training period, no dating, no leaving the premises without permission from management, and most of all no disclosure to any outside party about what's in the contract. It's all pretty extreme but honestly, I figure it's not that different to how I'm already living. I'm being controlled all the time anyway, it's just the same thing but in a different place away from the usual people giving me trauma, the contract doesn't put me off like I imagine it would probably put a lot of people off. I really hope that my mother and Mr Choi will come to an agreement. My daydreaming is suddenly broken by the booming voice of Ms Moon.

"Hana, I told you to fix that shoelace!"

I look down to my feet, my left shoelace is completely untied. This is bullshit, I just tied it firmly, seconds ago. Someone is fucking with me.

"I'm sorry, Ms Moon!"

I quickly get out of my chair and tie the shoelace back up before resuming my seat. Although I don't give her eye contact, I can sense her gaze on me, but thankfully she says nothing.

Now that I'm back sitting down and more alert, I can feel something tugging on my left shoelace. It's one of the boys sitting behind me, he's using a ruler to sneakily loop through my shoelace and unravel it. I know this without looking because it's a regular event in this class, so I'm used to the feeling of the plastic ruler sliding over my socks and applying tension to the top of my shoe. I'm not sure who is doing it, but I refuse to look back and give the row of boys behind me any acknowledgement. Why is there always a row of disgusting boys at the back of every class. I adjust my seating position so that the sole of my right shoe is putting pressure on the top of my left shoe and they can't untie it. Then I feel them carefully looping into the right shoelace instead, so I adjust my legs again, this time stretching them out in front of me where they definitely can't reach. Of course, Ms Moon is oblivious to all of this, so if I call them out, I'll probably get in trouble instead, because that's what usually happens, so I just keep quiet. A couple minutes go by and I don't feel the ruler anymore, no more problems hopefully.

"Hey."

The girl on the next desk over waves at me. It's Yujun. Not a friend, because I don't have those, I'm not allowed them, but Yujun talks to me sometimes. It's usually her pretending to be nice to me for as long as it takes to find out information, to then relay to others in the class to use against me, before then reverting back to her bitch self. I fear the worst.

"Hi." I give her a slight nod.

"Hey, I saw you with that guy yesterday."

Oh, here we go. I decide to play dumb. "What guy?"

"You know what guy. That guy in the suit, from the agency. I saw you talking to him in the gym office. Are you going to do it?"

"Do what?" I know what she's asking me but I don't exactly feel like opening up to this bitch, I will make her work for the information.

Yujun rolls her eyes a bit. She knows I'm being obstructing. "Go and become an idol trainee, *stupid*."

I guess I have to tell her something, I can't obstruct forever or this could turn ugly. I try to maintain as disinterested a tone as possible. "I don't know. Thinking about it."

Yujun laughs. "I bet you are! I mean, it's not like you exactly fit in here, is it? Anyway, all the best, I guess! I'll be cheering for you!" She makes sure to say this loud enough so a few people within earshot can hear. There goes my low profile.

Yujun smiles, and then turns away to talk to a friend behind her. This fucking fake skank, I can't stand her. It annoys me that I can't do anything about this.

I try to drift back off into the boredom of home group, thinking about what will happen this evening, but I'm now hyper-aware of everything around me and my brain can't settle down. Ms Moon is distracted, she's reading something, killing time until the end of home group, just like we all are. The chatter in the class is loud as everyone talks and anticipates their next classes. I can hear the boys in the back row snickering, I can't quite hear what they're saying about me, but I know it's about me, that's obvious by how they're keeping their voices just quiet enough so I can't make out a coherent sentence. Then, I feel that ruler again, this time sliding up my ankle, they're trying to lift up my skirt with it. *Oh great.* I reach down my leg and make a grab for the ruler, but whoever's holding it quickly whips it away. I'm becoming increasingly upset, but also determined - I know this creep is going to try with the ruler again, so I wait patiently. Sure enough I feel the ruler creeping up my shins once again, this time I'm prepared. I whip my hand down and grab the ruler, then while still holding onto it, I twist myself around so I'm facing the rear of the class and can see who the culprit is. It's Byunghyun, I should have known.

Most of the guys in the class are creeps, oh wait... most? Sorry, I mean *all*. Anyway, Byunghyun is at least as bad as any of the others, a wiry, weedy guy who definitely didn't win the genetic lottery and compensates for his physical ugliness with even more ugliness on the inside, just an absolute worm. He's not an *iljin*, just one of the popular guys in the class. I'm not sure why he's popular, probably because they're all ugly losers too, and he's always cracking stupid jokes that are just immature and gross and they all like that sort of thing. I hang onto his ruler with the strongest grip I can manage, and so does he, the plastic surface warping and twisting as we fight for possession.

"That's my ruler!"

"Yeah, and those are my legs!"

"Not for long... you'll be public property soon enough! I'm just getting a 'teaser' in before the official release!"

Byunghyun sniggers and so do his shitty disgusting friends sitting next to him. The demoralisation and shock of the insult makes me lose my grip on the ruler just a little, and he quickly pulls on it hard, yanking it out of my grasp. I'm so close to losing my shit and just launching a table across the room at him, but I have to contain myself. I turn back to the front of the class and gather my skirt close to my legs so it can't be easily pulled up. I see that Ms Moon is still reading her fucking book or whatever and of course didn't notice any of this go down. Fucking useless. I wait for the bell that ends home group to ring. I know exactly when the bell will ring down to the second because the clock on the wall behind Ms Moon is always eight seconds slow, I've memorised it. I watch impatiently as the clock's second hand creeps up to the required spot.

At fourteen minutes past eight and fifty-two seconds exactly, the bell rings, and I breathe a sigh of relief. Science class is next, but I have a few minutes to do the changeover so there's no great rush, I'll make it on time if I go slow. I decide to wait for everyone else to leave and go last so I'm not caught in a crush. Predictably, the other students mostly leave as soon as they can. Once they're gone and the way is unobstructed, I follow out the same door and walk down the hall to the science block. I don't get very far when I hear my "name" being called.

"Hey, homework-shuttle! Where is it?"

I turn around. It's Namgil, one of the male *iljins*.

"Homework-shuttle" isn't my name, but I'm used to responding to it as if it is, when Namgil says it. Fear starts rising in my chest, because I suddenly realise I'm in deep shit; I completely forgot that I agreed to write his social studies essay for him last night. I didn't agree because I had a choice, he told me to do it and I said I would do it, I'm his homework-shuttle so I have to comply with his requests for homework. He runs up to me, grabs me roughly by the arm and drags me out of the hallway, through into the male toilets.

"I want my fucking essay, slut. It's due today! Where is it?" he screams, shoving me up against the brick wall and holding my face an inch away from the urinal.

Namgil isn't a weedy ugly nerd like Byunghyun, or a clumsy twit like Dongjae who lets his girlfriend do the fighting, Namgil is huge and terrifying, and his strength commands respect even among the other *iljins*. He's even popular with the *teachers*, I'm not sure how that works, but somehow it does. His only weakness is academic, and I guess that's where I come in, not that I'm any genius but I'm *wangtta* so I have to be whatever he wants me to be. For now, I'm his homework-shuttle. It could be worse. Of course I don't have an essay for him, so I can't do much in this situation right now except beg for my life.

"Please don't hurt me! I'll get it, I promise!"

"You had better! My essay is due at two o'clock. If I don't have an essay by then, I'm dragging you straight back in here and it won't be just to chat." A threat like this isn't idle, Namgil and the other *iljins* will quickly enforce their rules with all types of violence and degradation.

I'm afraid and trembling. "Yes Namgil, I promise! Please let me go and I will bring you the essay!"

I actually won't - it's impossible for me to get him an essay by that time. I could try to write one, or try to bully one of the other *wangtta* girls to do it for me, but I can't even remember what he wants me to write about and I'm not going to ask him to remind me because that will reveal that I've written nothing and that he's probably not going to get one. I could try to download one from an essay website but I'm not allowed to have a phone or computer, and I can't use the library computers because *wangtta* get last priority for school facilities. If I sit at a computer, as soon as a more popular kid wants it, I have to get up, and since those facilities are always in high demand at my crappy school, I'd be lucky to get five minutes on one. So me getting him his essay in the deadline he's set is simply not going to happen, there's just no way it can. Of course, I can't tell him this. I just have to survive this moment, and then work out what to do later.

After holding me up against the urinal for about a minute, Namgil shoves me away and I fall on the dirty toilet floor.

"Go. I need to take a piss, so get your ugly face out of here before I piss on your head."

Namgil starts unzipping himself so I get up and run out of the male toilets as fast as humanly possible. I emerge back into the hallway, right in front of two girls holding little green bottles of *soju*, in the middle of what looks like an alcohol exchange. I don't know their names but they're *iljins* for sure, only *iljin* girls would exchange alcohol indoors openly like that in the middle of a school hallway. They're probably here because Namgil is here, they're likely waiting for him. They both look over at me and give me disgusted stares.

"Ha! Did you just come out of the male toilets?" says one of them, laughing.

"Wow, what a slut! You must really want the dick! Which random cock were you sucking today, can you even remember?" says the other.

I badly want to punch one of these bitches but the consequences of instigating a fight with an *iljin* girl would be fierce, plus two on one isn't good odds, let alone three on one when Namgil gets out of the toilet. I'll also be late for science class if I get held up any further, which I will if I make any kind of scene. I just need to get through this one last day somehow without being destroyed by *iljins* or having any major incident that could hold me back, and then hopefully I'm home free. I take off down the hall, running.

"Dirty skank whore! You dropped your condoms!" one of the bitches yells after me.

"Are these your birth control pills? I found them on the ground, they say *property of wangtta sluts!*" the other screams.

4. AN INTERVENTION

It's lunch time and the line for the cafeteria is long. The school cafeteria food isn't great, but at least it's free, and since I've been on curfew my mother refuses to make lunch for me ever, or even allow me to make my own, so free cafeteria food it is. "Providing food for you is a waste of resources," she says. "I'm not spending any more money on food for you than I have to, until you fix your attitude." That's just *lovely* - I can't tell you the ways in which I hate my mother. Anyway I'm getting bored of standing in this queue and the girl in front of me is Seoah and she's not someone I like. Not that I have anything to actually do with her, but she hangs out with the popular boys that I hate so she's smeared with the same shit-brush as far as I'm concerned because who else except dog trash would give the time of day to those assholes, so I make her life miserable when I can because she deserves it and it makes me feel better. I wait until she has her head turned and then I slip ahead of her and steal her spot in the queue.

"Hey!" Seoah yells.

I don't say anything. Too bad for her, I don't give a fuck about the low-life slags at this school.

"Hey! Fucking Hana you bitch, look at me!"

Seoah shoves me a little to get my attention. I'm not giving her anything, I just remain facing forward in the queue. Fuck her.

All of a sudden, I feel a huge weight on my back, as I get shoved forward. At first, I think it's Seoah, but the force is too powerful; she's not this strong. It must be someone else.

"Hey, idol girl!"

I recognise the voice before I see his face, it's Byunghyun again. He forces his way in between Seoah and me.

"I saw you were having a lesbian fight. Can I join in?"

"I'm not a lesbian, fuck off!"

I do my best to push him away, but it's no use. He's a lot stronger than I am and squeezes his way back into the queue, doing his best to push forward against me and maximise his physical contact with me as he does so.

"Hey I've never been this close to an idol before. Make sure you put this in your autobiography! You'll think of me, won't you?"

Byunghyun laughs as he pushes his weight hard against my back, fortunately I have a backpack on with some books inside which at least gives me a little clearance. I can also feel his hand sneakily creeping down my legs and bunching up my skirt, trying to get underneath it, he's using our close proximity as a way to disguise his groping.

What a fucking gross sneaky turd I swear I am going to murder him but it's my last day and I don't want anything to go wrong, but I'm not going to put up with this disgusting shit either so he can get fucked - I decide in a split second to go on the attack. I grab the only object I can find that I can actually reach, a plastic dinner tray on the bench parallel to the cafeteria line, and immediately start swinging it at his face, edge first. The first swing connects beautifully; the corner of the tray hits him square in the cheekbone, a hit that looks like it would've hurt at least a little. I'm impressed that I managed to swing such a cumbersome item so accurately given how close he is and how little clearance I have to swing anything with him pushed up against me. He instantly backs off from the shock of the impact.

"What the fuck? You fucking mole! You're going to get it now!"

Byunghyun approaches me again. I can see a dull red mark has appeared on the right side of his face. While it feels good that I hit him, I'm not even close to satisfied yet, so I keep swinging the tray at his head, but I no longer have the element of surprise and he's able to push his body hard up against mine in the queue so I no longer have any leverage to swing properly or do anything else.

"You fucking pervert!"

He continues to push right up against me and starts laughing, which of course only angers me further. It's frustrating that he's stronger than me, I want to hurt him even more but I can't, it's like hitting a brick wall with a pillow. He notices how enraged I am and starts laughing. The piece of shit is enjoying this far too much.

Before either of us can say or do anything else, I feel someone pull me harshly out of the queue. It's my home group teacher Ms Moon, who just happens to be here for some reason. She pins my hands behind my back, and frog-marches me out of the cafeteria, through the corridors. I know where we're going, straight to the headmaster's office. I don't resist and I passively let her direct me forward, I know the route pretty well as I've made this particular journey many times. Ms Moon starts giving me some lecture about how I'm a disappointment to the school and my parents or whatever the fuck she's saying I don't know, I'm not even fucking listening, I'm still so full of rage that I can barely think at all. Why is it my responsibility to have to listen to lectures and bullshit when I'm the one getting bullied every day and molested by gross nerds.

We arrive at the headmaster's office. Ms Moon sits me down in the visitor's chair, and then leaves the room, leaving me on my own. The headmaster isn't here, but I can hear his voice behind the door next to his desk, he's talking to someone in the back office or whatever that room is back there behind his main office. This is pretty typical, when students get served up to him in his office, we're never his top priority. I'm so overwhelmed with emotion that I just start sobbing immediately. There's a tissue box on the desk so I start helping myself to bunches of tissues to try and stem the tears. After a couple minutes,

I've gotten most of the crying out of my system and I start to level out emotionally. The headmaster and the other man are still talking in the other room. I notice that my lap is just a big pile of tissues and snot. I'm in the middle of trying to tidy up the mess of scrunched paper and mucus when the door next to the headmaster's chair opens and the headmaster walks in. The other man who he was talking to also enters behind him - it's Mr Choi, the agency staff member from yesterday. I stare at him, feeling absolutely mortified. I'm so ashamed that I can only maintain eye contact for a second before resuming staring at the ground and my tissue pile. Surely, I've just fucked up my chances of getting out of here and into his agency in the worst way possible. There's no hope for me now. I don't even know what to say. What would even do any good in this circumstance? I just want to crawl into a hole and die.

Despite staring down at my lap, I'm conscious of a hand next to me. Mr Choi is reaching out his hand. Does he want to shake my hand? I look up at him, confused.

"Your classes are cancelled this afternoon, Hana. Come with me, I will take you home."

I can barely even talk at this point, so I just nod and bow. I then clean up as best I can, dispose of my tissues in the headmaster's wastepaper basket, and walk with Mr Choi out of the headmaster's office, out of the school hallway and into the parking lot. He holds my hand the entire way, which is kind of weird, but I don't fight it, I just focus on trying to hold back the sobbing. Neither of us say a word to each other or anyone else. Several students notice us leave, and I can hear them talking about me, or maybe *us*, but I don't catch enough of their conversations to know what they're saying. Whatever, at least I'll be far away at two o'clock when Namgil wants his essay, and hopefully I won't ever come back.

We get into Mr Choi's car, a small hatchback that looks a lot cheaper than the suit he has on, and he starts the engine. Only once we are moving, does he say anything.

"Did you think about the offer, and read the contract? Is this definitely what you want?"

I dry my eyes with my school blazer sleeve.

"Yes, I really want this."

I look over at Mr Choi, who keeps his eyes firmly on the road. He nods slightly. For the entire rest of the short trip home he says nothing, but the fact that he didn't ask for directions and already knows the way to my house means that him and my mother have definitely been speaking.

As we pull up to our house, I notice that my mother is waiting for us outside.

"Go to your room - *now*. And don't you dare come out!" My mother sounds angrier than usual.

I quickly comply, racing up the stairs to my room and shutting the door. Once inside, I lie down on my bed and start sobbing again, but more gently this time, as the stress of the day's events pours out of me.

Over the course of the next half an hour, distress gradually gives way to nervousness and then curiosity, and I'm starting to feel more emotionally balanced. I get up from the bed and open my bedroom door just slightly. I try to be as silent as possible so my mother can't hear it open, because an open door for any reason other than visiting the bathroom would be considered by her to be breaking my curfew. I can hear my mother talking to Mr Choi, *loudly*, and while I can't hear exactly what they are saying to each other, what I notice straight away is the tone of their voices. I can't believe it - they're *laughing together*, they sound like they're having a *great time*. I'm not used to hearing my mother speak like this - she's always so cold to me, but she's warm to this person who she hasn't even known for the better part of a single day? Can it be made any clearer how much she despises me? I'd feel like crying if I wasn't completely cried out and dead inside already after the events of today. I also feel conflicted - despite feeling intensely rejected, I'm also slightly elated - they're *getting along*, this means that *I'm probably going to get what I want*. I gently close the door again, sit on the bed and wait.

I try to distract myself by folding clothes and deciding what I might take with me versus what I might leave, if things go according to plan. However, it's hard to get too excited if I don't have certainty, so most of the time is just spent procrastinating on decisions. I end up preparing almost nothing, just underwear, socks and toiletries plus some pyjamas, as I have barely anything else anyway. My mother hasn't bought me new outfits in years other than the school uniforms she's required to get, and I'm not allowed to buy my own clothes, so there's not really anything else for me to take.

After what feels like about three hours, I finally hear Mr Choi leaving. From my window I can see his car pull away down the street. Only once his car has completely vanished from view, my mother comes up to my room and opens the door. She looks me up and down as I sit on the bed.

"Five o'clock in the morning, tomorrow. Be ready."

I try to say thank you, but she slams the door straight away before I can even utter a syllable, and stomps straight back down the stairs. I feel like my heart is stuck in my throat. I have so many emotions, but I feel like I'm not yet safe to express any of them.

5. IT'S ME, HANA

"Hamilton Caitlin?"

The agency gym coach stands in front of us, a lady who I'm guessing is in her late forties, as she looks the same age as my mother. She doesn't look particularly healthy for a gym coach, but then neither does the gym coach at school, they're both kind of fat and frumpy with bloated faces and bodies. I guess to be a coach you only need to be able to yell at people and tell them what to do. She's reading from a clipboard. Myself and the other trainees are lined up in a row in front of her, in our gym clothes, generic purple tracksuits that were provided to us by the agency, each emblazoned with a True Miracle Entertainment logo.

"Caitlin Hamilton," corrects the girl immediately to my right.

"Okay, Hamilton." The gym coach mumbles as she corrects some notes on the clipboard she's holding.

"No... Hamilton's the family name... but it's last. So, just Caitlin." Caitlin smiles awkwardly.

"Caitlin, here's your schedule." The coach accepts Caitlin's correction but doesn't acknowledge it, and passes a piece of paper to Caitlin.

I check out Caitlin as she reads the paper as this is my first time seeing her, or anyone else in this room. She's a fair bit taller than me, with an oval face and attractive soft facial features. She's obviously foreign, or half-foreign maybe, but I can't tell where from. Aside from her name, her long hair is a giveaway that she's foreign as it's naturally brown and wavy rather than dyed, plus she also has obviously natural double eyelids, not the surgically-created ones that I can see the girl on my immediate left has, there's a pretty distinct difference between the two. Caitlin has a really cute but laid-back kind of vibe to her that I feel drawn towards. As Caitlin scans down the page, I see her eyes go even wider and her smile vanish, she's clearly not that happy about what's on her schedule.

"Shin Hana?"

I'm internally jolted a little by my name being called, even though I was anticipating it. "It's me, Hana." I raise my hand from the elbow and wave.

The coach nods, then passes me a piece of paper without a word and I take a look.

SCHEDULE - SHIN HANA

05:00 - wake up
05:30 - morning exercise
06:00 - language

10:00 - break
10:15 - gym
18:00 - dinner
18:30 - gym
20:00 - shower
20:15 - free time
00:00 - lights out

I think about the schedule... that's a lot of gym, it's going to get tough, but only four hours of learning languages, that's it for schooling? That seems like an improvement to me. I smile to myself as I fold up the piece of paper. I look up and notice the gym coach looking at me with an odd look, like she wasn't expecting that kind of reaction. We lock eyes for the barest of moments, and then her gaze moves immediately back to her clipboard.

"Park Iseul?"

"Here," a girl responds a few places to my left. The coach holds out a piece of paper. Iseul is way over at the left end of the line so she walks up to the coach to grab it, then returns to her place while reading it. She only reads the paper for about two seconds but I don't notice any reaction. I check her out; she's about my height, maybe a little shorter, and she has hair cutting off in a bob just above shoulder length. She looks fairly plain to me, like any of the girls at my school, hardly idol material with all that buccal fat on her face. She has double eyelids that are probably the result of surgery but I don't know why, it's not helping. Along with the pudginess she has a real resting bitchstare but also the most upright posture of anyone in the room, a combination which makes her look snobbish. I wonder what special talent brought her to this place because her looks definitely weren't it. Not that I can talk I suppose because I've been called an ugly bitch enough times to know there's at least some truth to it, but I also know I'm not as ugly as *this* bitch. I notice she's only wearing the top half of the agency's tracksuit and she has a school skirt similar to mine on her bottom half.

"Where are your track pants?" asks the coach. It seems I wasn't the only one who noticed.

Iseul shrugs. "I was too warm in them. It's not mandatory, is it?"

I feel immediately unsettled by Iseul's forwardness and slight sassiness, but I'm expecting the coach to go off at her about the track pants and break her down a bit and then I guess I'll see how she really talks. Strangely the coach just ignores everything she says and reads out the next name.

"Jeong Nari?"

"Here," responds the girl immediately to my left. The coach passes a piece of paper to Nari, who immediately grabs it and reads down her schedule, looking thoughtful. As she's standing right next to me, I take the opportunity to check her out closely. Nari is taller than me by a few centimetres, but shorter than Caitlin. Her long black hair has some fake blonde streaks which have grown out a little. There's no way this girl hasn't had tons of surgery on her face, she's had not only the eyelids done for sure but definitely the cheekbones too, at the very least, probably the whole jaw break and reset. She has the carefully chiselled *ulzzang* look that a lot of the girls at my school aspire to, but without any of the "party girl" vibe that often comes with that, but a mature, athletic look, like a real celebrity. She's honestly stunning to look at, much like Caitlin is, but there's a completely different vibe coming from Nari's sculpted features. She studies the schedule written on the paper as if she's trying to decode a puzzle.

"Zhao Shu?" the coach asks.

"Hello!" responds a girl on the other side of Nari. That's a Chinese name, so I guess this agency really are recruiting from everywhere. Shu walks briskly up to the coach, grabs the piece of paper, then just as briskly almost-skips back to her place. She's tiny - shorter than both me and Iseul by quite a margin, not quite down to dwarf level, but not very far off. She also looks like she's been in for multiple face surgeries, but it's a completely different style to Nari's *ulzzang* look. Shu's face style is "first love face", a wide-eyed and girlish look that's popular with Chinese and is supposed to convey youthful innocence. She has short cropped hair to match the shortness of the rest of her, and she really looks like someone who has invested her entire being into looking cute.

"Oh wow!" says Shu, as she reads down the paper. The coach looks at her and Shu immediately puts her hand over her mouth in apology. She has this weird cutesy manner to her that's just as artificial as her facial features, and her voice is really high and grating too. Don't tell me we have a compulsive *aegyo* girl in the group. I can't help but dislike her already.

"So, you must be Park Youngsook," the coach says, holding out the last bit of paper.

Youngsook is on my right, on the other side of Caitlin. She walks up, collects the schedule held out by the coach without a word and resumes her place. Even though she's not standing next to me, I get to check her out fairly clearly just because she's so tall that she towers over the rest of us, she must be approaching six feet. Youngsook looks kind of plain and awkward, not quite as drab as Iseul but not really very pretty either. She has the surgical double eyelids just like the others but apart from this she has really blunt facial features which I wouldn't associate with someone who was trying to be an idol. Her posture is also awkward, like she doesn't look completely comfortable just standing here. Clearly she hasn't been chosen to be in this group for her appearance. I study Youngsook's face and I see her eyebrows raise a bit as she reads her schedule, she looks pretty unhappy... but mainly I just notice Caitlin, who is between us. Caitlin is naturally beautiful and hard not to stare at.

The coach interrupts everyone's studying of their schedules, and my daydreaming. "I will now introduce myself, I'm Ms Han. I'll be responsible for overseeing your gym training, setting tasks and managing your stay here. I'm now going to go through a few house rules. If you have any questions, raise your hand. Firstly, this is already in the contracts you have signed but it bears repeating, there are to be no mobile phones or mobile phone use of any kind on the premises..."

Caitlin's hand goes up immediately, and the coach looks in her direction.

"Why can't we have phones?"

"They're an unacceptable distraction from training, and much of what we're doing here can't be revealed to the public, so there are confidentiality issues. We also don't want to reveal your identities ahead of time. You will be given some time after our induction to message anyone you have to, and then you are to surrender both your phones and SIM cards for the duration of your training. When your training period is complete, these items will be returned to you."

I don't really give a damn about this, because I haven't had a phone for several years thanks to my mother's curfews. She only ever let me have some stupid kid's phone that can't even get on the Internet and is so locked off that it can only call *her*, I threw that useless garbage out immediately and haven't had any electronic devices since. Caitlin obviously has more phone privileges than I do, as she is unhappy with Ms Han's response. "My phone will be out of date by then! Can't I just have it on aeroplane mode or something?"

"No. You can ask questions, but the agency rules are not negotiable. Please do not ask us to change the rules because it will not happen, let me be clear on this point."

I cover my mouth, doing my best to not laugh at Caitlin's pretty stupid question, it's hard to believe that she asked that sincerely. I notice Youngsook is also having trouble keeping a straight face but she manages it. Ms Han gives a slight pause, to give Caitlin the opportunity to say something, fortunately she doesn't because it gives me some time to regain my composure so I don't laugh out loud at her.

Ms Han continues. "Great, let's move on. You do not leave the premises without permission. You only go outside to the outdoor yard area, and nowhere else. You do not enter the administration areas of the building without permission. You do not have visitors. You obey your given schedules at all times. There is only one shower that you will share between you, so showers need to be rotated by all of you within the fifteen minutes of allocated shower time. What you do in the designated free time is up to you, but if you want to succeed, you will use it to train, learn, and catch up on any weaknesses. Yes, Shu?"

I look over at Shu, who has her hand up.

"What is 'language', is that like school?"

I'm not sure what's more annoying, the tone of her voice, or the obviousness of her question.

"Yes, that is school work - learning language skills, reading, speaking, comprehension."

"So, there is no math or science stuff? Just language and words?" Shu has a horribly grating, squeaky voice that is really pissing me off.

"This is correct. You don't need maths or science for your career as an idol, but you will need a full grasp on languages and public speaking."

Shu cheers and pumps her fist a little. "Yay, no math and science! Thank you, Ms Han!"

I'm happy about it too actually, but Shu is making entirely too much of a display about it. Can't she just be grateful in a quiet, non-annoying way? I guess that's too much for the little pipsqueak.

Ms Han doesn't seem to mind Shu's display however and carries on reading out the rules. "You are to comply with weight requirements. You must not eat any food which is not given to you by the agency or not approved by agency staff. You are not to go into food preparation or administration areas without permission. You are not to touch heating or air conditioning controls. You get one day off per month, on this day all training and learning is optional but all other rules still apply. Days off are conditional on performance and may be withdrawn at the discretion of the agency. Are there any questions?"

Ms Han waits. I look through my schedule and then I realise... something's missing, something important. I raise my hand.

"Yes, Hana?"

"I don't have any singing on my schedule? When do we learn to sing?"

"Neither do I," says Nari.

"Your schedules are customised depending on your specific backgrounds and your training needs. Some of you may have slight differences in your scheduling."

Nari holds her piece of paper with her schedule on it out in front of her and I hold mine next to it to compare. They're exactly the same, nothing is different. Caitlin also looks over in my direction, comparing my schedule to hers. "It's the same," she says. I can see Shu and Iseul talking to each other and also sharing schedules. Iseul then looks at Nari and shrugs. It's clear they don't have any singing training either.

"I have singing!" says Youngsook.

Everyone suddenly turns to Youngsook. She holds out her schedule and we all take a look and pass it around. The line we were standing in has now become more of a huddle.

SCHEDULE - PARK YOUNGSOOK

05:00 - wake up
05:30 - morning exercise
06:00 - language
10:00 - break
10:15 - gym
16:00 - singing
18:00 - dinner
18:30 - singing
20:00 - shower

20:15 - free time
00:00 - lights out

"Youngsook... can you sing?" I ask.

"Yeah, I guess so," Youngsook replies.

Ms Han claps three times loudly. "Everyone, stop gossiping and get back in line!" *You rancid bitch. We're not gossiping, we're trying to learn about our role here.* We all stop talking and resume our previous positions.

Ms Han stares directly at me.

"Hana, do you have a problem?"

I guess I must've involuntarily rolled my eyes a little or side-eyed her or something, and she caught a glimpse of it. *Sorry, not sorry.*

"I don't know, I just can't sing, that's all. I mean, since we're here to learn to be *singers*... and I can't actually *sing*, I was just wondering..."

"You're not being trained to be *singers*; you're being trained to be *idols*. There's a big difference, you will learn it."

"Thank you, Ms Han." I don't really know what the fuck that's supposed to mean exactly, but I guess that I'll find out eventually so I decide not to make things harder for myself at this point.

"Any further questions?" asks Ms Han.

Nari shoots her hand up.

"Yes, Nari?"

"Where do we go if there's a problem?"

"What sort of problem?"

"Say we have an emergency, like someone gets injured, or has a medical issue, or there's a fire or an earthquake, something like that."

Everyone looks at Nari, she looks dead serious. I then look over at Ms Han, who looks for the first time a bit uncertain. After an awkward silence, Ms Han responds.

"If there's a medical issue, come and see me. If I'm not on the gym floor I'm in my office in the administration area." She points to a door, in the corner at the front of the gym. "Just go through that door. If I'm not there either, ask the other staff, there's always someone on duty. Anyone will do, just not the CEO. If it's night time, ask the security guard."

"There's a security guard?" asks Nari.

Another uncertain pause. "There are patrols at night. There's also an emergency evacuation plan over by the fire extinguisher on the far wall, so read that later." Ms Han points to the far corner of the gym, where there is a fire extinguisher on the floor plus a small map of the building on the wall. "Any further questions, no? That's great then, you have the rest of the night off, please orient yourself with the area and I'll see you bright and early tomorrow! Oh, and I will be around in fifteen minutes to collect your phones." Ms Han spits all this out rapid-fire in a way that makes it clear that she doesn't want any more questions or at least not any more of the type that Nari just gave her. We all bow, say thank you and file off into the dorms. On the way through I notice Nari stopping to quickly eyeball the fire evacuation plan.

6. LIGHTS OUT

It's midnight, and all the lights in the dormitory room automatically turn off at this time. The dorm room is tiny, one small room with three double bunk beds, one on each wall, and a doorway leading out into the hall on the fourth wall. It's so cramped that I have no idea how the people who made this room even got the beds inside here in the first place. Maybe instead of moving beds in here, they built the beds piece by piece inside the room itself... but once two beds were already built how could they have even possibly had enough room to build the third? Maybe they dropped the beds in here by crane and then put the roof on the building afterward? My brain hurts thinking about it. Not only that but they've crammed tiny bedside drawers in the small corners where the beds meet, it's comical how little room there is to walk. Fortunately, the wooden bunk beds have pull-out drawers built into them where we can stash our belongings, because otherwise there would be nowhere to put all the clothes and bags that we brought with us. I was quick to claim a bottom bunk as soon as we entered this room because I don't like heights, I get paranoid sleeping up high and these bunks don't have a guard rail to stop me from rolling over in the night and falling, an idea that terrifies me. Caitlin clearly has no such fears and has claimed the top bunk above mine. Opposite us are Shu on the bottom bunk and Iseul on the top, and on the right-angled side is Youngsook on the bottom bunk and Nari on the top. We're all under the covers, trying to sleep. Although it's dark in the room, I can see everyone within view fairly clearly, thanks to a combination of the room's one window leaking in some of the ambient light from the street lights outside, and my eyes having adjusted to the darkness, plus the fact that we're all so stupidly close together because of the ridiculously small size of this room. Shu across from me is already asleep, snoring lightly, everyone else is awake as I can hear them all tossing and turning under their quilts.

"Can any of you fucking sleep?" asks Caitlin.

"No," reply Nari, Youngsook and Iseul almost at exactly the same time. They all then notice how they said no at once and start laughing awkwardly together.

"I'm too busy thinking about tomorrow. The schedule is so crazy," adds Youngsook.

I think this is pretty funny because Youngsook has the best schedule of all, I can't resist saying something.

"Hey at least you get singing lessons. How are the rest of us supposed to learn how to sing? I can't sing *at all*, what am I supposed to even do in this group?"

"I'm sure there's a reason why they're only training me in singing. Maybe they'll add you in for training later?" Youngsook replies.

Iseul points at Youngsook. "I think I know why they've done that. Hey Youngsook - sing something, quickly."

"Like what?"

"It doesn't matter... anything, just whatever you want. Sing something that you can do well, something that is impressive. Pretend you're auditioning."

Youngsook spends about ten seconds thinking about what to sing. Then she starts singing a sequence of high notes which is instantly recognisable to all of us, it's the vocal climax to Kim Miya's song "Pure Morning" a well-known hit from the previous decade. I don't know much about singing at all, but even my uneducated ears can tell that Youngsook is an exceptional singer. All of us (except Shu, who is somehow still asleep during this) stare at each other, our jaws nearly hitting the floor.

"Wow. Just wow." Nari sounds astonished.

I hear Caitlin gasp. "Goddamn Youngsook, you can *sing*."

I'm impressed too, but I'm also pissed off. "Well, that's great, but what about the rest of us? It's nice that *you* can sing - I'm happy for you. So why do *you* get the singing lessons and we all get nothing?"

Youngsook seemingly doesn't know what to say, but Iseul cuts in. "I'm sure you don't get 'nothing'. What is on your schedule?"

"Just gym, so dancing I guess."

"So can you already dance?"

"Well, I..."

Iseul cuts me off straight away.

"Yes, you can dance. So, why not shut up?"

I'm really not impressed by Iseul turning this around to be about me. "I was talking about..."

Iseul cuts me off yet again. "No. You, Hana, you are being a bitch. Stop being a bitch now. She has her thing, she's good at it, you have yours, you're good at it. They are training you both to be the best you can be at the things you can already do well." This condescending bitch, like she can talk about being rude.

"But Iseul, I'm going to have to sing *something* at *some* point!"

Iseul laughs. "Do you really think so? Have you heard any idol pop music lately?"

I can't quickly think up a comeback for this, so I decide to complain about something else instead to make myself feel better. "Look at Shu. She slept through those high notes, and us talking. What a lazy cow."

"Well, I guess she wore herself out," says Nari.

"Wore herself out by annoying me."

Shu has an annoying manner that just rubs me the wrong way, I can't explain it. Her presence irritates me, and even now that she's sleeping, I still have to listen to her! I notice that I have two pillows on my bed but I'm only using one to sleep on, so I throw the spare pillow across the room at her face. My throw is excellent, it lands right on her head, but she's dead to the world and the impact doesn't even wake her.

"Hey! Let her sleep!" Nari steps down from her bunk and walks up to where I'm sitting. She grabs my pillow from on top of Shu's head and places it by my feet.

"Sorry but she was already annoying during the day, how can I get to sleep with this bitch snoring in my ear. I'm going to wake her up."

I go to get up and shake Shu a bit or slap her or whatever I can think up, but Nari instantly crouches down into my bunk and blocks my path. "Just go to sleep, Hana. Save your energy for tomorrow, you'll need it."

I push against Nari's arms, but because I'm lying down against a wall and she's sitting up, she's in an advantageous position, I can't get the leverage I need to move past her. "Fuck you. Wake up, Shu, you bitch!" I yell. Shu doesn't wake up.

Nari grabs my wrists, pins me down to the bed and bends over to look me in the eye. Now in close proximity to my face, she whispers at me. "Stop fucking around and shut your hole. We all want to sleep now. Okay?"

The closeness is uncomfortable, but having my movement restricted is worse. I struggle against Nari's grip but it's no use, I can't do anything, she's somehow far too strong. I just stare at her face defiantly instead, and she stares back, clearly not intimidated at all. Nari's stare is really attractive but it doesn't make me hate Shu's snoring any less.

"For fuck's sake Hana, just chill out. You're wobbling the bed around" complains Caitlin, who starts shifting around on the bunk above my head.

Nari's pressure on my wrists starts to hurt. "Can you fucking let go? My hands are turning blue here."

"Are you going to calm down if I let go?"

"Yes."

I'm lying, of course. Nari has pissed me off with this boss woman bullshit and I'm going to clock her right in her pointy *ulzzang* face as soon as I have the opportunity. I wait as Nari gradually loosens her grip on my wrists and as soon as there's no more skin contact, I wind up my right hand to slap her in the head. It doesn't work - I misjudge the amount of room I have to work with and my swing comes out weak. Nari brushes my movement aside easily with one hand while slapping my cheek with the other, then she pins me back to the bed again, much more forcefully than before.

"Apologise," Nari says.

I'm now really angry. "Fuck you, plastic monster!"

Nari releases my left wrist just long enough to crack me in the cheekbone a second time with the side of her hand, then instantly regains her grip before I have time to react. The second hit is much harder, it stings like crazy, and I can feel tears instantly welling up inside, I haven't been hit this hard in a while. Nari pushes my arms down into the bedding and the pressure on my wrists hurts once again, it occurs to me that the first time she pinned me down she wasn't even using all of her available force to do it. She's won and I have no more fight left in me, but I'm also becoming so upset so quickly that it's hard to even form words. It's not so much the pain - although it does hurt, a *lot* - but the humiliation of it, on the first night in the new dorm, being demeaned like this. Tears start running quickly from the corners of my eyes, down to the pillow, I try desperately to hold the emotions back but I can't control myself. Nari's facial expression however doesn't change, she's as stony-faced as before.

"Apologise! Do it!" Nari demands, firmly but calmly.

After about twenty seconds of me quietly sobbing while snot leaks out of my nose, I compose myself enough to whimper "I'm sorry, Nari!"

"And who else?" Nari asks, maintaining her iron grip while I continue to cry.

"I'm sorry, Shu!"

"Good. Now *stay there*, and *shut the fuck up* for the rest of the night!"

Nari finally releases her grip on my arms and moves back to her bunk, seemingly satisfied at having taken me down a peg. I curl up into a foetal position under the covers and silently cry myself to sleep, nursing a newfound headache which reverberates through my entire skull. I notice Iseul staring at me, emotionless and seemingly unimpressed, saying nothing. I also look over at Shu, she slept soundly through all of it. That fucking little shit, I'll find a way to make her pay.

7. THE LEADER

The next morning all six of us are back in the gym, doing stretches. I'm wearing the same purple tracksuit top and pants that were given to us the previous day, it's all I have for gym wear. The other girls are dressed in an assortment of their own clothes, mainly T-shirts and leggings. They worked out from yesterday's events that the provided tracksuit is optional, although Nari and Youngsook both wear the same standard-issue tracksuit pants that I have on, paired with their own shirts. Most irritating of all is Shu; she is wearing her own fresh tracksuit which is bright metallic pink for some reason, it's truly offensive to the eyes. Shu also looks annoyingly well-rested, which pisses me off because I didn't sleep much and I'm still hurting from the slap Nari gave me last night. Ms Han the gym coach is also here, watching us as we stretch.

Suddenly Ms Han claps three times. "Listen up girls! The CEO, Mr Park Jeongmin will now visit. Please stand in a line and greet him. You will call him by the name Mr Park CEO only. Do not speak to Mr Park CEO ever, unless spoken to." Ms Han then diverts attention to her phone and starts typing a message.

We all stand in a line, adopting the same positions as yesterday. After a minute of waiting, which feels like about five minutes, the door between the gym and the administration area opens, and a man walks in. He's about thirty years old, quite tall, with very short cropped dyed blonde hair, and although he's dressed in a very formal looking black suit it's obvious that he's both extremely muscular and slightly overweight. I assume this is Mr Park CEO. I go to bow, as do some of the other girls, but we all stop ourselves mid-movement as the man ignores us all, says something quietly to Ms Han and then stands against the back wall of the gym, facing us. I'm not sure who he is, but he's clearly not the guy. We all continue to stand around awkwardly.

Another minute passes by, which now feels like about fifteen minutes, and the administration door opens again. Another man walks in, he looks about sixty years old, but he's even fitter than the other guy, as he's just as muscular but also leaner. He's quite short for a man, about my height. He wears a casual dark green jumper and track pants similar to the standard issue ones I'm wearing, but black.

Ms Han claps three times. "Please greet Mr Park CEO."

We all bow to him in unison at ninety degrees. "*Annyeong hasimnikka*, Mr Park CEO!"

Mr Park bows slightly in return, and launches straight into a speech. "It is good to meet you all for the first time, in one room. Some of us have met before, but most of us have not. As you well know, you are all here to train to become idols. The training process will take three years, this is necessary as the competition to be a popular idol is very strong. You have been selected because we have seen the potential in all of you, individually, to become idols of great success and great popularity. However, the success of the individual can only be achieved when it is supported by the success of the group."

He speaks slowly and deliberately, like he is measuring each word, like he fancies himself as a philosopher or something, it's so cringe. While talking, he paces back and forth slowly in front of us, and is visibly scanning up and down our bodies at the same time. I do my best to keep my posture as upright as possible as he continues his lecture.

"We are well educated on your backgrounds and individual circumstances, your strengths and weaknesses. You have been selected after careful analysis, with the effective team composition most firmly in mind. As you will be eating, sleeping and working together at all times to achieve you goal, group cohesion is of utmost importance. There will be no corners cut or tolerance for any weakness, laziness or lack of teamwork. Is this understood?"

"Yes, Mr Park CEO!" we all reply in unison.

"Very good. With this group cohesion in mind, it is time for you to decide on a group leader. A leader is responsible for ensuring the group cohesion. She must be..."

Nari immediately puts her hand up, I've never seen anyone put their hand up so quickly in my life, even the annoying teacher's pets at my school didn't put their hands up this fast when they were answering questions. Mr Park immediately notices, stops talking and looks at Nari. We *all* look at Nari. He nods at her, indicating she has permission to speak.

"I'll do it, Mr Park CEO!" says Nari, commencing a ninety-degree bow.

After a few seconds of bowing, Nari resumes her standing position. None of the rest of us say anything, we all just look back and forth between Mr Park and Nari, waiting for something to happen. For some reason I'm expecting him to slap her, I don't know why.

"I see that you are keen."

"I promise to be a good leader, Mr Park CEO!"

"Does anyone else in the room wish to nominate themselves?" Mr Park looks back and forth between all of us. "Raise your hand if so."

About twenty seconds pass and nobody speaks or raises their hand. I sure as hell am not going to, I'm not sure exactly what being a leader of a pop group entails but I don't want the responsibility of whatever the fuck it is, *fuck that*. Not that I'm exactly thrilled with the idea of Nari being a leader after our fight the previous night, but nobody else is stepping up, so I guess it's going to be her.

Mr Park speaks again. "A leader nomination requires to be seconded, and then requires a vote. Will any of you second the nomination of Nari? Speak if so."

Iseul raises her hand straight away. "I second the nomination of Nari, Mr Park CEO. I have a feeling she'll be *quite good* at it." Iseul side-eyes me slightly while she says this. That fucking cow. I think about how satisfying it would be to shove her snooty fat face into a piss-soaked toilet bowl.

Mr Park steps back and smiles a little. "Excellent. All raise your hands if you agree to Nari being appointed as the group leader. A consensus is required."

I watch as everyone raises their hands except me. I think about if I should also raise my hand. I don't want to be singled out, and I don't have any better ideas, nor do I want to get into an embarrassing debate about the issue where people might bring up what happened last night in front of the CEO. Resigned to the inevitable, I also raise my hand, trying not to show too much obvious reluctance.

"Then it is agreed that Nari is the leader." Mr Park beams. He seems genuinely happy about it. "Nari, please follow me. The rest of you, *annyeonghi gyeseyo.*"

"*Annyeonghi gaseyo* Mr Park CEO!" we all say in unison, except Nari, who instead follows Mr Park out of the room and through the administration door. She doesn't look at any of us on the way through. The other man against the wall, who remained motionless the entire time during Mr Park's speech, follows behind Nari and shuts the door closed behind them both.

As soon as the door is closed, Ms Han claps three times, a habit which is starting to annoy me.

"Continue your exercises, girls! It will be time for classes soon!"

We all dissolve our line, move to separate areas of the gym and resume stretching, while looking at each other. It's clear that everyone is feeling a bit unsettled, and so am I. Nobody speaks, but everyone's eyes are saying the same thing. *What's happening to Nari? Why is she being spoken to in secret?* I'm thinking about it also, but I don't really care that much about what happens to Nari, I'm more concerned about what it might mean for me. I try to not think about it too much as I continue my exercises.

8. PLASTIC

"That's it? That's all I get?" Youngsook complains, her eyes welling up with tears.

"Guess so," I reply, munching on my celery stick, our allocated morning break meal. The language teacher Ms Kim has gone, she's finished with our class for the morning which was boring and uneventful, so we're all sitting on our wooden desks in the classroom, while we eat and wait for gym time to start. The desks and chairs here are identical to the ones at my school, wooden with metal poles, ugly and unergonomic. It's much more comfortable to sit on the desk and eat than to sit on the chairs.

Youngsook just stares at the celery stick she was also given. "There's no way I can eat like this! I hate celery!"

Nari is unsympathetic. "Controlling your eating is an important part of being an idol. You'll get used to it, because you have to."

Youngsook reluctantly takes a bite out of her celery stick while grimacing.

Honestly, I don't care much about this. After years of food withholding as punishment at home, I'm used to not eating all that much, but Youngsook is practically crying about it. Our contract goes into specifics about how much our meals are regulated, this shouldn't be such a shock to her. She takes another half-hearted bite out of her celery stick and chews cautiously. It's amusing to see her struggle with this. I can't help but smile as I watch her. Youngsook notices my grinning.

"What are you looking at?"

I can't control myself. I just start giggling at her.

"It's not going to get any better, you know! You read the contract, right?"

"Don't say that, Hana!" she replies, looking defeated.

"What did the CEO say to you?" Caitlin asks Nari, changing the subject. Nari spent about thirty minutes with the CEO this morning, but none of us have had a chance to talk to her about it yet, because we've been too busy taking notes during class, this small break time is the first chance we've had to talk.

Nari sighs. "It really wasn't much of a chat at all. He has a way of stretching out two minutes of information over half an hour. But basically, I'm now responsible for making sure everyone is healthy, is learning things as they should be, and getting along."

What a joke, I can't help but laugh. "What if we don't?"

"It's my responsibility as leader to make sure we all perform to our best."

"Wait... so if *I* don't perform, or if *I* act up in some way.,. *you* get in trouble with the CEO, not me?"

I smile at Nari and start laughing in her face. Nari doesn't appreciate my amusement and her face goes immediately sour. She gets up off the desk she's sitting on, walks over to the table where I'm seated, stands right in front of me and stares me down.

"That's why I'm going to make sure that you *do* perform, and that we all *do* get along, Hana. Whether you like it or not."

I don't appreciate intimidation from this bitch.

"Try and make me."

Nari gives me a dirty look and is just about to say something when Shu suddenly speaks. "Your life would be better if you were happier, Hana. You should just not be so mean and then you would not be so miserable!" Shu says this with a tone of way too much cheerfulness. She smiles at me and I just want to hit her.

"Go play in traffic you fucking dwarf bitch, I'll fucking squash you like a bug!"

"Hmph!" Shu turns her head away from me.

Nari glares at me. "What the fuck is wrong with you, Hana? Do you even want to be here or not?"

Before I can think up a suitable reply, the side door of the classroom opens and Ms Han walks in. "Time for gym," she says, standing by the door.

We walk through the door in single file, down the hallway and into the gym space. While on the way there I quickly cram what's left of my celery stick into my mouth.

As we arrive in the gym, we line up in our usual places and Ms Han stands in front of us.

"Today we are going to start with some dance instruction. The choreography that you will eventually be learning, this is not ready to be presented to you yet, so we will start with something else in order to gauge your synchronisation and to observe how well you move together and work together as a team, and also how quickly you learn. Youngsook, can you finish eating please or I will throw your food out."

Ms Han raises her eyebrow at Youngsook.

"Sorry, Ms Han!"

Youngsook quickly scoffs down the remaining half of her celery stick. I look over at her and watch her wincing while she tries to chew an entire half a celery in her mouth at once. It's funny to watch as it's obvious how much she hates the taste.

Ms Han moves to the desk behind her, picks up a remote control and presses a button on it. A projector on the ceiling flickers to life and then dies again immediately with a sharp pinging noise. She then opens up a laptop computer on the desk and starts doing something, I'm not sure what she's doing as none of us can see the screen, I assume she's trying to activate the projector. After about a minute she sighs in frustration and swivels the laptop around so that we can all see the screen.

"This dance routine is what you're going to be doing. I will leave now and come back in two hours, I'll leave this video on a loop, your goal is to analyse the video and present the dance to me by the end of the two hours."

I look at the screen, the performers are a group of girls and they don't look familiar, but the dance does; it's the routine to the song "Plastic" by Korean idol boy group EB-K (Exceptional Boys of Korea), a huge hit when it came out five years ago. This isn't an easy dance, it has lots of quick, robotic movements that need to be performed precisely. There's nothing graceful about the routine, it's the kind of flashy dance you would do if you wanted to impress someone. It's a daunting task to learn quickly. We all look at the screen and each other while Ms Han leaves the room, and it's obvious that we're all thinking the same thought.

"That's a lot to learn in two hours," says Caitlin.

"Yeah, no shit," I laugh.

"I already know it," replies Nari. Of *course* she fucking does, a show-off type of dance like this would be right up this bitch's alley. "It's really not that difficult in terms of flexibility or stamina, learning this is more about getting the correct sequence of steps in your memory. Once you've got those, muscle memory will take over. Start with the instrumental part where they do most of the dance with their hands and arms, because that's the hardest to remember, so it will require the most practice, the rest is relatively easy and more about positioning."

Everyone just stares at Nari with a mixture of bewilderment and gratitude.

She continues. "Watch the video and start with that. If anyone wants me to help them learn just say so. Don't worry, we'll get it."

Nari exudes confidence while she says all this, it's clear that she knows her shit. I figure that I might as well benefit, so I can make learning this as easy as possible.

"Teach me," I say.

"You?" Nari raises her eyebrows as high as possible.

"You're the one who asked if I wanted to be here." I notice the entire room looking at me.

"Okay. Come with me to the corner of the gym, and follow along. But none of your bullshit, okay?"

"Fine." I'm pretty good at dancing, I'll show this condescending bitch that I'm at least as good as she is.

"Anyone else who wants to learn with me, tag along, and we'll learn together."

All of us eagerly follow Nari into her corner, except Iseul, who ignores us all and stays watching the video on loop, gradually learning the moves in silence.

Nari addresses the rest of the room. "Okay, we're going to start with the hand routine, and the steps for it. I'll do it one step at a time, at half speed, just try to follow along." She starts doing each hand and arm movement in turn, counting up to eight for each group of steps. We all try to mimic her.

"Why are you counting to eight, not four? The music's in four," asks Youngsook, as she attempts to copy Nari's movements.

Nari groans a little. "Dance teachers count in eight. Focus, Youngsook."

The dance isn't that difficult, I quickly have the main section memorised. Nari is actually right, most of the challenge of the dance is memory. Even better, all the individual parts for each member are pretty much the same so I can use the rest of the group to cue off for most sections. I start gradually becoming more confident and speeding it up, doing repetitions ahead of the group.

Nari motions to me. "Hana, stop."

"What?"

"Stay with the group, it helps the others."

I stop and then restart, falling in line with the rest of the group.

Nari notices me locking back into the count straight away. "Hana, for someone with such a shitty attitude, you're actually pretty good at this. Reckon you can hold in your natural ability to be an unpleasant idiot long enough to debut?"

"Maybe I'm better than you."

"Not likely! But... that's a goal. Why not work on it."

I say nothing and keep practising the movements. At least Nari our new leader acknowledged me, it feels good. I reluctantly admit to myself that I'm starting to like this bitch a little.

We all continue practising, diligently trying to learn the "Plastic" choreography with Nari's help. Two hours go by and here's how we're all doing, from best to worst. Obviously, Nari is great, she already knew the dance beforehand so she has a huge advantage, but she's like a machine anyway, I haven't seen her make a single mistake yet. I've got it down, more or less, I think. Next after me is Caitlin, she's picked up most of it pretty well, there's a couple arm movements she keeps forgetting to do, but when she remembers the steps, she gets it every time. Shu is okay at it I suppose although I'm not really too sure because I've been trying not to look at her, her bright pink tracksuit offends my eyes plus she's just annoying in general. Iseul is struggling, after half an hour with the video she eventually joined Nari along with the rest of us because it was clear she wasn't making much progress on her own, but her moves are still hesitant. The worst is Youngsook who is frankly just clumsy, and as we go through the dance, I can see it starting to irritate Nari because Youngsook is holding the group's progress back.

"Come on Youngsook, get your head into it!" yells Nari above the music.

"I'm sorry! I can't keep up!"

"Come on Miss Celery, I don't want to have to slow the dance down yet again."

Youngsook sighs and tries to fall back into the beat, but she's having trouble locking back in, and slips out of time again.

Nari rolls her eyes. "How slow are you? Aren't you a musician? Don't you know what a beat is?"

"I'm a singer, not a dancer! I've never done this type of thing before! Give me a chance!"

"Normal people dance from time to time, you know. Are you fucking normal, Miss Celery?"

I don't know why but "Miss Celery" is hilarious to me. I try to stifle a giggle and only half succeed. I actually do feel sorry for Youngsook, but I can also relate to Nari's frustration. Nari notices my giggling but ignores it.

"You've got maybe a few minutes' worth of chance; the coach will be here soon. Step it up!"

"I'm not the only one who is struggling, you know!" Youngsook complains. Iseul shoots a dirty glare over at Youngsook, but Youngsook doesn't notice as she's too busy staring at Nari.

"So what, you're still the worst," Nari snorts.

Youngsook stares at Nari and seemingly doesn't know what to say. Youngsook has a point; Iseul isn't much good either but she's not copping any flak from Nari at all, I guess it's because Youngsook is slightly worse so Nari is focusing on the weakest first perhaps.

Before anyone can say anything else, the door to the administration room swings open. Ms Han enters the gym floor and addresses us all.

"Okay ladies, let's see your progress - get into your starting positions!"

We all arrange ourselves into the starting positions for the choreography while Ms Han controls the laptop and cues up the song.

"Starting in five seconds. Give it your best."

The song starts a little sooner than five seconds and we spring into action, moving through the opening sequence and into the verses. I do my best to let muscle memory kick in and feel the music. I'm too focused on getting my own moves right to really notice how everyone else is doing, but I figure that they're all trying their best, and I feel like I'm also getting it right most of the time. A brisk three minutes and the song is over, we all hold the final position for a second, and wait for Ms Han to give the signal to stop. She turns off the video, and we take that as permission to stand down. We all exhale in one collective sigh and catch our breath, then look at Ms Han, awaiting feedback.

"That... was *fucking disgraceful*. You girls all need a lot of training, every single one of you. Pathetic!"

Ms Han both looks and sounds furious. She also looks and sounds like a total hypocrite, because she's a fatter bitch than any one of us. We all look at each other quickly, before looking back at Ms Han. We don't have to say anything to each other, we all know what we're thinking: *was it really that bad?*

Ms Han starts walking around the room. She stands in front of Nari. "I will now give you individual feedback. Do not respond, do not bow, do not talk, do not say anything or you will be punished. Just listen. Firstly, Nari, what the *fuck* was that about. Absolutely awful. You dance arrogantly, nobody wants to see your ego on display. You are supposed to be leading a team, not showing off and wrecking the routine. Stick to the actual dance and stop making it about you. It is not your self-expression project. You must serve the song first."

Nari goes to say something and stops herself immediately. I'm shocked - was Nari really that bad?

Ms Han walks over to Caitlin next and addresses her. "Caitlin, your timing is all over the place. Get your shit together."

Caitlin stares straight ahead, obediently. She seems relieved that she got off relatively lightly.

Ms Han then walks over to me. She stands directly in front of my face and stares coldly. I expect the worst. "Hana, try to stay focused, you look like you're a million miles away, I don't know what's going on inside your thick head but you need to stop daydreaming and actually apply yourself, I expected a lot better."

I exhale slightly, feeling relieved. That wasn't so bad.

Ms Han walks in front of Iseul. "Iseul, that was somewhat acceptable, you got it mostly right but you also need to think about the music you're performing to, they're mechanical movements but that doesn't mean you perform them stiffly. Work on looking more like an actual human when you dance."

Iseul doesn't react, she just stares straight ahead. I'm annoyed - Iseul was better than Nari? No way, what bullshit, this gym coach has rocks in her head, surely she wasn't even paying attention. I mean, I was too busy trying to get it right myself to really know who else was good either, but I refuse to believe that Iseul suddenly became way better than Nari, in the few minutes between the last run-through when she was crap and when Ms Han walked in the room, there's just no way that's true.

Ms Han then walks over to Youngsook. I can see that Youngsook already has tears welling up in her eyes, she already knows she's not good enough. I can feel the entire room hold its collective breath.

"Youngsook, you are - legitimately - fucking - *useless*. That was the worst thing I've ever seen, and I'm not young, I have seen a lot. I've taught five-year-olds that dance better than that. If you don't want to be treated like a five-year-old I suggest that you use as much time as you possibly can to practice dancing, otherwise you can pack your bags and get the fuck out of here and your parents can pay the contract termination fee."

Youngsook stares straight ahead. A tear rolls down her cheek, but she keeps it together. I feel bad for her.

Ms Han walks in front of Shu and stares her down. I hope Ms Han really roasts Shu, which would be great. I wait for the inevitable negative feedback. I can see Shu bracing herself for something unpleasant.

"Shu, I don't know what dance you think you were doing but it's not what's in the video, also try to embody the music more, your moves are weak and not punchy enough. This isn't a ballet, it's not just *ahjumma* watching you. Also, if you can not dress like a neon vagina for future gym sessions, I would appreciate that."

Shu doesn't respond, but I can't help but giggle at Ms Han's "neon vagina" comment. Instantly, Ms Han rushes over to me and stands right in my face, her face about an inch away from mine.

"HANA DID I ASK YOU TO FUCKING SPEAK?"

I can smell her breath, it stinks of rotting food, what a fucking gross pig, what the fuck did she eat earlier today. I don't know whether I should say something or not, as Ms Han did tell me not to speak earlier, but she's also asking a question now, so... I don't know?

"ANSWER ME!"

I guess I'd better say something. I go to open my mouth but before I can even form a word, she cracks me across the face with her fist. I try to remain upright and non-resistant but she then hits me a second and third time. The hits aren't that forceful but they still hurt, mainly because my face is still tender from Nari hitting me the previous night. The force is still enough to make me lose my balance as I fall backward onto the gym floor, landing straight on my ass.

"GET UP!" Ms Han screams.

I find my bearings and spend a few seconds getting back on my feet. As soon as I'm standing but before I've really oriented myself properly, Ms Han forcibly grabs me by the arm and marches me out of the gym, through the door to the admin area. We make a left and a right turn through some offices that I don't get a good look at and come to a door. Ms Han opens the door, leads me forward and pushes me inside a small room as violently as she can manage. I lose my balance on something and fall to the floor, my face hitting what is thankfully soft carpet and not another hardwood floor like the gym. I hear the door close and lock behind me, and the sound of Ms Han's footsteps walking away.

After taking a minute to process what just happened, I get back on my feet again and look around. I'm locked inside a room with beige walls and nothing in it, it's completely bare except for one wall with a small wooden shelf running across its length. There's nothing on the shelf except a couple of decorative circles set into the woodwork, little shiny black buttons. There are no windows here and the air smells stale. I'm guessing this room was supposed to be a janitor's closet or maybe a small laundry and the agency are now using it as a punishment room to lock up misbehavers. That's fine, whatever, detention is nothing new to me, I couldn't give a fuck to be honest. Solitary confinement as punishment always makes me laugh, time away from other people is fine with me, if anything I wish I could lock myself away from others more often. I didn't get enough sleep last night thanks to Shu being an annoying snoring little piece of shit plus the pain of getting smacked in the face keeping me up, so I lie back down on the bare carpet and doze off to sleep. I'm exhausted so this time around, it's no problem to fall asleep quickly on the hard carpeted floor.

9. BREATHING

I wake up to the sound of the door of the punishment room opening. I sit up and look over at the door. There's a girl looking at me, I haven't seen her before. She's dressed in a school uniform, very similar to my own with the blazer and skirt, but with stylish black fabric and red trim instead of the hideous greenish-blue and white combination my accursed school uses. I guess she's from a much better school than mine. She looks to be about my own age, and also my height and weight, but she has really smooth facial features. She has that same tapered *ulzzang* jawline that Nari has, but even more severe, I wonder if she's another idol in training or someone else.

She bows slightly. *"Annyeong haseyo."*

I return the bow to what extent I can. *"Annyeong haseyo."* As I bow, I feel a burning sensation and I'm suddenly conscious that my neck is very sore. I'm not sure if it's because I've just been hit and thrown around, or if it's from sleeping on the bare carpet with no neck support, or a combination. I stretch my neck around and try to flex out the stiffness, but this only makes it hurt more.

"Please follow me, Hana."

The girl stretches out her hand. I bow, gingerly stand up and grab hold of it. Her grip is very light, and her hand is clammy and sweating. She leads me out of the punishment room. I notice that there's a concrete lip by the door, this must have been where I tripped over on the way in. We go through some corridors which I assume are the same ones I went through before, it's hard to be sure. We go past some unoccupied open-plan offices, but I'm not focused enough to get a good look as we pass by, however I notice that the office area has windows to the exterior of the building and it's now dark outside, I must have been asleep for quite a few hours. Soon we make it to a door which leads out into the familiar hallway between the gym and the dorms. As soon as I'm in the hallway, the girl stops holding my hand, and disappears back into the administration area without a word or even any acknowledgement. I walk over to the dorms, starting to notice how bruised I'm feeling.

I open the dormitory door and the other five girls are all in their beds. They all stare at me, except Youngsook, who is asleep.

"Whoa. What happened to you? You look like shit!" says Caitlin.

"Oh my god, are you okay?" Shu gasps. Even when I'm feeling this defeated, she can still annoy me just fine.

"They locked me in a room. I'm alright I guess."

I reply to nobody in particular, hoping nobody wants to discuss it too much. I find my bunk and curl up under the covers, not bothering to change clothes.

"What sort of room?" asks Shu.

"I don't want to fucking talk about it right now."

"Did they say anything?"

"Fucking son of a bitch, leave me alone!"

"She's just concerned, Hana. Stop being a rude asshole. We all want to know what happened to you," says Nari.

I sigh deeply and sit up in the bed. I guess if I don't tell them what happened, these bitches will never leave me alone about it and I'll never hear the end of it.

"Okay, okay, fuck. They dragged me into this room, it was just... a bare room, I don't know. Like an old laundry or a janitor's closet or something, I guess. They didn't say anything about it, how long I'd be in there, they just threw me in and locked me up, then just now they got me out and here I am. That's it. What time is it?"

"It's eleven o'clock. You know there's a clock on your bedside, right?" chuckles Nari. I actually knew where the clock was and I immediately feel stupid.

"What did you do in the room?" Shu asks.

"Sleep, *for once*, you annoying snoring little worm," I reply, glaring at Shu.

"It's not my fault you can't sleep!" Shu huffs, turning her head away from me.

"What happened to your face?" asks Iseul.

"You saw her hit me in the gym, that's what happened."

"You look a lot worse than you did in the gym after she hit you."

"She's not kidding. You look really fucked up. Take a look," adds Caitlin. I see a hand extend down in front of my face; Caitlin is passing a small hand mirror down to me from her bunk above my head.

I reach out to grab the mirror and hold it up at eye level. They're right - one side of my face is swollen and there's some purple bruises. I guess I was hit harder than I thought.

"Told you, you look fucked up," Iseul smirks. She's enjoying this far too much for my liking.

"I still look better than you, you snooty little fuck hole." I'm in no mood for her or anyone's shit right now.

Iseul just smirks at me some more. "You're lucky that you've already had your ass kicked today because I actually feel sorry for your stupid bitch face!"

I'm in too much pain to react appropriately and do what I really want to do which is scratch Iseul's eyes out. I lie back down on the bed, saying nothing.

"Cat got your tongue for once? About time!"

"Fuck you," I mumble, turning over in the bed.

"Before you get too comfortable there Hana, can I have my mirror back?" asks Caitlin.

I try to toss the mirror back up above my head to Caitlin's bunk without getting back up, but I miss and it hits the bottom of her bunk instead, and then rebounds, hitting me in the face. "Ah, fuck!" I yell as it scrapes right across where my cheek is the most tender.

"Stop being so rude. Maybe if you weren't so mean, better things would happen to you," says Shu.

"*Fuck off,* Shu!" I yell.

Immediately Caitlin starts laughing. "I'm sorry Hana, I'm trying not to laugh but I can't control it! You've got to admit it, you're kind of funny when you're angry!"

I sigh. Shu reaches over to my bunk, grabs the mirror by the side of my head and quickly passes it up to Caitlin, at the maximum possible speed like she's worried I'm going to try and hit her. A justifiable fear if I wasn't so sore, but I'm in no mood to start a fight with anyone right now, not even her.

"Thanks Shu," says Caitlin, giving Shu way more respect than she deserves.

"Everyone, let Hana rest. She'll need her strength back for tomorrow," says Nari.

"I won't bother anyone," I reply.

Shu, Nari, Caitlin and Iseul all start mock-applauding me. Those bitches.

"Fuck you all, go fuck yourselves assholes! I'll legit stab all of you!"

They all laugh at me, none of them take me seriously. That's just great.

"Hey, can I please sleep?" a new voice - it's Youngsook, who's just woken up from my yelling, or maybe from everyone else clapping, I'm not sure which. I shift my position in the bed to get a better look at her.

"Oh, you're up. *Annyeong!*" says Shu, chirpily. I wince.

Youngsook grumbles something inaudible. It's good to know Shu doesn't just annoy *me*.

Nari laughs. "No sympathy for you - you slept plenty already. You've been out for hours!"

"I had the worst day of my life today, I swear."

"Well try to get over it, because tomorrow you're teaching us singing."

"What?"

"Hana had a point yesterday - you can sing, we can't, and I'm not sure if they're going to train us. So, we have to learn somehow. I assume if we don't do it right, we'll wreck our voices somehow?"

Wow, Nari the girl who slapped me, now giving me credit for something, twice now in one day. That's not a common thing for anyone to do, I guess she likes me, somewhere in there.

Youngsook chuckles. "Well, yeah."

Nari continues. "So, we'll start tomorrow in free time. If we do it any other time we'll probably just get in trouble, and I don't like how trouble looks in this place, let's try to avoid that." Nari glances over at me while she says this.

Youngsook rubs her eyes. "Now that you've messed my sleep up, we could start now if you wanted."

"It's a bit late. Tomorrow is better when we're all focused and we're allowed to be noisier. Think you can survive until then?"

"Seriously, now is the best time to do the first thing - late at night when we're all lying down in bed. It doesn't even require any singing so we won't make much noise.

I'm going to assume that none of you know anything about singing?"

I notice that even though Youngsook has just woken up, she suddenly sounds enthusiastic and perky - a tone I've never heard from her before until now. She's enjoying the idea of teaching us.

"I can sing a bit! La la la!" chirps Shu. I groan internally. It's clear that she can't sing at all.

"I sing... in the shower!" says Iseul, laughing.

I guess I'd better say something about my own total lack of singing ability so Youngsook knows the exact level of incompetence that she's dealing with.

"I can't even do that. I've never sung, at all, anywhere. This singing shit is all new to me."

"Why are you two even here, then? Why even try to become idols?" Youngsook's gaze bounces back between me and Iseul, puzzled.

Iseul sighs. "Family, they really wanted me to do this. Going against the family really isn't worth it for me."

"Beats school," I reply. I could say a lot more on this topic but I'm not feeling talkative right now and I'm curious to see what Youngsook is going to show us, so I just want her to get on with it.

"*Right*, okay then." I can tell Youngsook finds my point of view a little strange. Maybe it's strange, I don't know, but it's how I feel about it. "Caitlin? How about your singing ability?" Youngsook asks.

"My boyfriend says that I can sing okay." Caitlin has a boyfriend? Disappointed but not surprised. I sigh a little.

"How serious is your boyfriend?" Youngsook asks.

"He's serious, he's not joking."

"That's not what I meant."

"Oh, like... how long have we been going out?"

"What does his cock look like?"

Nari puts her hand over her mouth to stop herself from doing a spit-take. Caitlin is silent. I crane my neck around to try and get a good look at Caitlin's reaction, she's the only person here I can't make eye contact with because she's in the bunk above mine. I get a quick glimpse of Caitlin's face hovering over the top of the bunk before the pain of my neck stiffness becomes too much to bear. After about ten seconds, she starts earnestly: "Well, it's..."

Youngsook immediately cuts Caitlin off, laughing. "Okay okay, I don't need to know, really! You didn't immediately answer 'I don't know' so that means he's biased, you can't trust anything he says about your voice."

"But he says I'm good! Really!"

Youngsook laughs. "Of course he does, he's not stupid. Nari?"

"I guess I'm okay."

Nari seems to have an ego, so I think if she actually could sing, she wouldn't be this modest about it. Looking at Youngsook's reaction, Youngsook seems to pick up on this also.

"Right, so none of you can sing that much. That's actually good because it means we're starting you all off at the same level, none of you will be bored. So - I'm just going to give you one thing to do tonight, which is this and it's really easy. Everyone, lie down on your bunks, and place one hand over your stomach." Youngsook lies back down and places her hand on her own stomach to demonstrate, everyone else watches and follows along. "While you're lying down, I want you all to be conscious of the position of your hand. You'll notice that when you breathe in, your hand will rise with your stomach, and when you breathe out, your hand will fall."

"That's it? That's all we do?" asks Nari.

"Yes, that's it. Just do this for tonight. I just want you to be conscious of the muscle and body movement that comes with correct breathing in and out, it will be useful later."

Shu looks puzzled, she gets up off her bunk and walks up to Youngsook. "It isn't working! My stomach goes down when I breathe in, and up when I breathe out!" Shu puts her hand on her stomach while standing and demonstrates with exaggerated deep breaths, the wrong motion. Now that she's out of her bed, I notice she's wearing the stupidest looking pink pyjamas ever. Is everything this girl owns pink?

"You're forcing your breaths. You can just breathe naturally, don't force the breathing or try to take deep breaths on purpose, just breathe as you normally would if you were just lying down relaxing and I wasn't telling you to breathe or even do anything. It's easier to do when lying down than when standing, so lie back down before you try again." Somehow Youngsook was able to resist telling

Shu to go fuck herself and actually answered her question, her restraint is incredible.

Shu scuttles back to her bed. Somehow even the way Shu walks is annoying to me even though the dorm is so tiny that from Youngsook's bed to hers is literally only two steps. Shu climbs into her bunk, resumes the lying down position and tries again. "Okay I'll try this... hey, wait! It's working! Wow, thank you so much!"

I do the exercise for a while. It's dead easy, the correct movement just happens naturally. Youngsook is right - if I think about my breathing too much, I start doing it the reverse way, but if I forget about it, the motion just kicks in the way it should. I'm starting to like Youngsook's intelligence, which hasn't really been evident before now.

Eventually I get sick of the exercise and resume nursing my head. I entertain myself by letting my thoughts wander over to ideas about what I could do about Shu's existence in this group. Obviously, murder is the best option but it's clearly out of the question, as it would be legally problematic, plus who's to say Shu wouldn't get replaced with someone even more annoying, knowing my luck the agency might hire someone even more like her to fill the gap. Chopping off a limb would be funny, but logistically difficult, I mean where would I put the arm or leg in this tiny dorm, it would stink up the place and I'd get caught easily. Torture could be fun but the sound of Shu screaming would probably be the most annoying thing on this planet, it would enrage me enough to want to just kill her to make it stop, and then we're back to the problem with murder. Maybe I could steal something valuable, or destroy it, like that dumb pink tracksuit, once again I'd be caught easily though and it would cause me problems. So there's really only the sneaky options left I suppose, but they might not be very satisfying. I resolve to think on it some more in the future as I drift off to sleep.

10. HOT ROCKS

The next day, we rehearse elements of the "Plastic" dance, trying to tidy up the messy parts. Not that it was even that bad the previous day for a first try if you ask me, but there's definitely room for improvement. Nobody really has their mind on it though, or maybe it's just me who doesn't have my mind on it. I'm thinking about the free time at the end of the day, because I want to learn about singing, it's something I don't know anything about. I'm still puzzled about how I was even hired to be in this group, I was quite open about the fact that I can't sing, but nobody seems to even care except me? I'm not going to question it, anything's better than home and school life right now, but that doesn't mean I don't want to be good at singing, or at least passable enough to not get in trouble. I'm also thinking about my face which still really hurts, although the pain has subsided from a general all-over-one-side throbbing to just some localised aching around the cheekbone, unless I move my jaw quickly and then it spreads out. That's fine because I don't really have anything to say to anyone.

When dinner time arrives, we all file into the dining area, which is actually just the classroom that we do language classes in each morning. We just push the small school desks to the side and there's a long table at the rear of the room that we move to the centre to sit at and eat instead, on the same painful chairs. I missed dinner yesterday because I was in the detention room, so this is my first time having a proper meal since I got here. After two days of only celery sticks, I'm looking forward to having something more substantial in my stomach.

Ms Han walks into the room and hands each of us a small white bowl. Inside each bowl is the same meal - a boiled chicken breast, half a hard-boiled egg, and a few lettuce leaves. It's not much, and it's all cold, but I'm hungry enough for it to smell great. I immediately start eating.

"It's the same meal as yesterday?" Youngsook asks.

I'm expecting Ms Han to backhand Youngsook across the face like she did to me, but it doesn't happen. Instead, Ms Han just stares at Youngsook, then grabs Youngsook's bowl, and without a word, exits the room.

"What the hell?" Youngsook shouts.

Nari laughs. "I think your meal just got confiscated."

"Maybe she'll come back with it."

"There's no way. I saw the look on her face. If you're really lucky you'll get a meal tomorrow."

"Are you fucking serious? I need to eat!"

Nari eyes Youngsook up and down. "You're heavier than the rest of us, you need to slim down, you know."

Youngsook just stares at the empty space on the table where her bowl was, she's clearly annoyed.

Nari continues, not giving a shit. "Take it seriously. You need to be more agile for the dance routines. They're doing you a favour."

"This place is the limit. I'm going to die here, I swear."

"Here, hold out your hand." Shu breaks off some of her chicken breast and gives it to Youngsook.

Caitlin sees this and does the same, breaking off a couple mouthfuls and placing them in Youngsook's bowl.

Iseul then eats the yolk out of her egg and gives her egg white to Youngsook. "I hate egg white."

Nari sighs a bit and doesn't give Youngsook anything. Neither do I, nothing against Youngsook but I didn't eat anything except one celery stick yesterday and today so right now I'm way too starving to even think of sharing my food.

"Nari, show some compassion," says Iseul.

Nari doesn't react to Iseul. Meanwhile Youngsook is speechless, I can see she is nearly about to cry from gratitude, she begins eating quickly.

"*Sillyehamnida...*" speaks a voice, softly.

We all look up from the table. The girl that led me from the detention room yesterday is now standing in front of us. She's wearing the same school uniform from yesterday. She looks at us with a vacant expression.

"*Annyeong haseyo.* I am here to inform you that Ms Han is ill for the rest of the day and will not be continuing gym class. Youngsook is still required for singing class after dinner. For the rest of you, there is no gym coach, so your free time begins from now, please finish your meals at your leisure."

We all bow in return.

"Will Ms Han be back for classes tomorrow?" Nari asks.

"I do not know it for certain, but I believe that she will be," the girl replies.

"*Annyeong haseyo!* What's your name?" Shu asks.

"My name is Ijun."

"I like your uniform Ijun, it's pretty!"

Shu smiles at Ijun. Shu is such a weirdo, why even say that to someone you've just met?

"Thank you!" Ijun replies hesitantly, looking very awkward. Ijun then smiles uncomfortably and quickly leaves through the same doorway as Ms Han, without another word. We all look at each other for a while, nobody is quite sure what to say.

"She's pretty!" says Shu.

"You scared her off by being weird about her clothes" I reply.

"I did not! There's nothing wrong with being friendly. Besides her clothes are pretty."

"Yeah, they are pretty, but you can see how shy she is, you don't have be such a freak, nobody wants to talk to freaks, you fucking weirdo."

"Maybe she liked having someone to talk to. She smiled at me! She didn't smile at *you*." Shu glares at me, like it's my fault she's weird.

I glare back at her. "Don't make me beat you, dwarf girl!"

Nari also stares in my direction. "Hana, stop being a bitch to Shu. I am not fucking having it. I swear I will keep you in line. You've been good so far today - keep it that way."

"Fine I'll try to restrain myself from bashing annoying Chinese dwarf girls today."

"Do you want to get fucking hit? I would love to hit you again. I can tell your face still hurts, I will make sure to hit you in that exact same spot!"

I think about what to say. I don't want to get hit by Nari. Unlike Ms Han, Nari's strikes actually hurt, and I'm certain Ms Han's weak candy blows in the gym only caused so much damage because Nari softened me up the previous night. I want to know how Nari is able to hit that hard. I wish I could cause more damage when I hit people with my bare hands, it's a skill worth learning. I think perhaps I should study up by pissing Nari off more, and then analysing what she does when she hits me, how she moves her muscles. My cheek still hurts however so I'll go the peacemaker route for today, but if Nari thinks I'm intimidated by her, she's dead wrong.

"I'm sorry Nari. I mean it, I'll try to be good." I try to sound somewhat sincere.

"What's your fucking problem, anyway? I want to know."

Nari doesn't sound completely satisfied with my apology, but I really don't want to have *that* conversation.

"Does it matter what I say? I mean, there's no response that would make it acceptable to you, is there?"

Nari falls silent and just gives me a stink-eyed glare. Thank fuck for that. I eat the last of my chicken breast, and then watch Youngsook eat her donated food, which she finishes off quickly.

"Thank you all so much, you are lifesavers," she says.

"They will punish you by withholding food here, so if you like to eat, be careful about what you say," Iseul replies.

Youngsook groans. "Oh great, guess I'd better be an angel then!"

"Really? That's a normal thing?" Caitlin asks.

Iseul just stares at Caitlin and raises an eyebrow.

"I'm going to get some fresh air." I'm fed up with everyone being bitches so I get up from my seat and wander off to the gym so I can go through to the yard area and check it out, I haven't had a chance to even look at the yard properly yet.

Nari yells after me. "Dinner time's not over yet, you'll get in trouble."

"Ms Han is sick, nobody else is going to say shit. Who else is there, Ijun? She's not going to do anything." I keep walking out of the room, Nari can go fuck herself.

I go through the gym, open the sliding glass door that leads to the small yard area and look around. There's nothing out here except a few trees, a metal bench and an iron fence with barbed wire on the top that surrounds the entire area. I guess they really don't want us climbing the fence and getting out, or maybe they don't want others getting in, who the fuck knows. It's evening and the sun is low, a street lamp on the other side of the fence provides a little illumination in the dusk. I lie down on the bench and try to relax in the cool evening air. The metal bench is not very comfortable against my back, but the breeze across my body feels soothing after a day of dance practice.

After about five minutes of lying down on the bench, I'm interrupted by a voice.

"Hey."

I turn around, it's Caitlin.

"Hey." I sit up on the bench. Caitlin is still in her tracksuit and has her gym bag with her as well. which she wears on one shoulder. She looks relaxed and radiant in the night, with the light from the gym interior behind her.

"Much happening out here?" she asks, as she starts reaching around in her bag for something.

I sigh, starting to actually feel relaxed. "Nope. Nothing is happening. Nothing is good, I like it out here."

Caitlin keeps fishing around in her bag. "Hey, have you seen these night patrols or whatever? Do you think there really are any security guards?"

"Maybe they're on the outside of the fence to drag us back in if we escape. But there sure aren't any anywhere else."

"That's convenient." Caitlin pulls a water bottle out of her bag and places it on the bench, then keeps looking in her bag for something else.

"Why do you want to know? Are you planning a heist or something?"

"Not quite! Do you smoke?"

"No way, cigarettes are gross."

Caitlin pulls out a plastic bag and smiles as she places it on the bench.

"I don't mean cigarettes."

I look at the bag, it's plastic and transparent. Inside is a brass pipe, a cigarette lighter and a few scraps of green material that takes me a few seconds to recognise, just because I really wasn't expecting one of the other trainees to pull *that* out.

"Are you fucking serious? No way - how did you get that shit in here?"

Caitlin winks at me. "I know the tricks. Want some?"

"I've... honestly never tried it. I'm a bit afraid."

Caitlin laughs out loud. "What - *you*, of all people? Are you for real?"

I suddenly feel a bit stupid, but it's true, I've never tried it and I *am* pretty hesitant about it.

"I only ever see the total trash bags at my school smoke this stuff, the boys who go around in gangs beating people up. It turned me off the idea. Nobody who spoke to me was ever into it."

"Honestly, you could use it, you're so highly-strung and angry, you could do with some mellowing out. Seriously, it's not that scary, you'll like it, I think. Are you okay to give it a shot?"

I sigh. I suppose I don't have anything better to do. "Sure... fuck it, why not, let's try it."

Caitlin smiles.

"Okay, I'll get this ready for you."

She starts prepping the pipe, unscrewing part of it and putting a small piece of the marijuana inside.

"What's this about gangs at your school, is that really a thing here?"

I say nothing. I appreciate Caitlin being friendly but I do *not* want to talk about this, especially with someone I've known for like two days. I'm hoping she changes the subject without me prompting her.

Thankfully, Caitlin gets the hint. "Your school sounds fucked. Couldn't you go to an all-girls school, wouldn't that be better?"

"Oh, my mother wouldn't allow it. 'You have to learn to associate with the opposite sex' she says. Such fucking bullshit."

"Okay, so this is ready. Do you know how to smoke it?"

Caitlin waves the pipe and a cigarette lighter in front of my face.

"No fucking idea."

I gingerly take the pipe and the lighter out of her hand. I put the end of the pipe into my mouth and Caitlin reaches over and takes it away immediately.

"No, not like that. If this is your first time, you'll burn the back of your throat doing it that way. Angle the pipe more towards the roof of your mouth, like this..." she holds the pipe at a downward tilted angle, and the cigarette lighter underneath it. "I'll hold the lighter. When I light the flame on the bottom, draw the smoke in and hold your breath, okay?"

I nod and Caitlin ignites the lighter as I carefully get into position, but when I go to draw in a breath, I can't do it; I'm too tensed up and I've already inhaled to my maximum before I start so there's nowhere for the air to go. Smoke leaks out everywhere from both sides of the pipe and Caitlin laughs.

"You're so stressed! Here, I'll grab that for a second, you've probably got hot rocks in there now because this weed is pretty dry, so I'll have to prepare this for you again or you'll burn yourself." Caitlin takes the pipe away from me and starts unscrewing it.

"I don't know why that was so difficult." I feel a bit stupid. How can it be this hard?

"You need to take some deep breaths, and get yourself relaxed before you try again. There's benefits to learning about the opposite sex, you know." Caitlin says, smiling while she prepares the pipe again.

"Bullshit. All boys should be murdered." It occurs to me straight after I say it that maybe this statement came out a little too quickly and too bitterly to sound normal.

"Well, just don't murder my boyfriend yet, okay? I'm not sure where I'll get a new supply from when this bag runs out now that I'm locked in here, I have to work that out. If I can get the supply going again from somewhere else, maybe you can kill him after that."

Caitlin's trying to lighten the mood with some humour and that's nice, I appreciate it. Maybe she's smarter than she looks, at least about some things. I can't help but smile a little. Caitlin looks at me and smiles back, and I feel my heart melting a little, I'm really not used to this kind of interaction.

"Okay this is ready again, are you ready? I'll hold the lighter again, just breathe out deeply first, okay? Don't rush it, there's no hurry."

I nod, while Caitlin holds the lighter low in front of my face and positions the pipe at the same angle as before. As she ignites the lighter, I inhale. I have some emptiness in my lungs this time, so it works. Instantly my cheeks fill up with smoke. I hold the breath in for a few seconds, unsure if I'm supposed to be inhaling even further or just holding it. It's uncomfortable as the smoke is hot and has a foul odour, also I'm conscious of a rising metallic feeling at the front of my mouth, I'm not sure if it's the metal pipe or something else. After a couple seconds it feels way too uncomfortable to continue and I exhale, coughing everywhere as smoke comes leaking quickly out of my mouth and nose, burning my nostrils a little on the way through.

Caitlin laughs. "You did it! How was that?"

"Fucking gross! I hate it! I don't feel any different either. Aren't I supposed to feel high or something?" I start spitting everywhere, trying to extract the awful metallic taste from my mouth.

"You're cute. You're not going to get stoned off just one toke, you have to do it a few more times to get any effect. Try again?"

Caitlin holds the pipe up, meanwhile I keep spitting, the residual taste of the smoke is really bothering me.

"You mean I have to do this again? More than once? Yuck, no thanks! Can I steal your water bottle?"

"Sure."

Caitlin takes the pipe back and starts smoking it herself, which she does with the ease of an experienced smoker. Meanwhile I grab the water bottle, remove the cap and drink several mouthfuls of water before spitting each one out, trying to wash my mouth clean.

"This fucking tastes like someone shat in my mouth! Yuck!"

"You know, for such a violent delinquent you really are a total square. You don't smoke weed, you don't smoke cigarettes either, you don't even like boys - do you drink?"

"No."

"You're so angry and you haven't even experienced life! What do you even do for fun?"

I sit and think about Caitlin's question, while she continues to smoke. I'm not even sure I know how to answer it. I guess I like gym I suppose, and I'm pretty good at it, but I'm not an athlete or anything, it's not a "passion". Do I even have one of those? What do I even want to do? What do I really enjoy? I've been allowed to do so little with my life so far that I really don't even know what I like. I don't even know how to answer this question, so I just sit in silence, feeling stupid while I watch Caitlin create smoke clouds.

"It's okay Hana, you don't have to answer, I was just curious. You know, I'm really starting to regret giving

Youngsook some of my chicken. She'd better give some good vocal lessons."

11. WANGTTA

"Okay, that's time, let's swap over quickly."

It's annoying, two and a half minutes isn't long enough to have a proper shower, but there's not really anything any of us can do about it. The showers are on a timer - there's only one shower alcove and the water only works between eight and quarter past eight, so if we don't all complete our showers in the allocated fifteen minutes, we don't get to wash. I quickly step out of the cubicle, deliberately leaving only the hot water running. I wrap a towel around myself, scoot out of the bathroom area, and then out into the hallway. Nari is waiting here, with a towel wrapped around her torso as well, she enters the shower area immediately as soon as I exit.

"All yours, I left it running."

I watch her from behind as she walks past me into the shower area and turns the corner into the cubicle. I check out her arms and back muscles, and can't help but swoon a little. Nari is absolutely ripped, very lean and muscular, she must body build or exercise for a ludicrous amount of time per day to get a figure like that. Now I can see where all that strength to hit me so hard came from, she has more muscle definition than a lot of guys I've seen.

A few seconds later I hear a scream from Nari. "Ahh! Fuck!" That's the hot water hitting her bare skin for sure.

"Sorry if it's too hot! I was cold!" I yell, loud enough so Nari can hear over the running water. I'm laughing inside though.

I walk down the hall and into the dorms. Caitlin, Youngsook and Shu are here. Caitlin is dressed in a T-shirt and shorts, Youngsook and Shu both wear loose fitting pyjamas. I don't know where Iseul is but she should be here, she had her shower just before me.

"Where's Iseul? I ask.

"Getting changed in the toilets, I think." Caitlin replies.

"That's a good idea," I say as I grab my school uniform, minus the stupid tie, and walk off to the toilets to get changed. I never plan to wear this thing again in an actual school or anywhere in public, but it's comfortable so it can officially now become my lazing around in the dorm clothes during free time when I don't want to wear pyjamas. I'm not too worried about intruding on Iseul because even though there's one shower cubicle, there's two separate toilet cubicles so we can both change in privacy. It doesn't end up mattering anyway, as just when I reach the door to the toilet area, Iseul walks out, wearing dark blue pyjamas. As she walks away, I turn to look at her. She also turns around to look at me, at the same time, staring me up and down in a weird way.

I stare back, feeling massively uncomfortable. "What are you looking at?"

Iseul starts sniggering at me. "Get changed, I'll tell you when you come out!" She turns around and walks off.

"What's so *fucking* funny?" I yell after her, but she just keeps walking away, ignoring me.

I really want to get changed quickly as I'm starting to get cold walking around wearing just a towel, so I try not to think about it as I enter the toilet space. There's nobody else here so I look in the mirror above the sink, throw my school uniform in the basin and examine the towel I'm wearing, turning around, looking for a "kick me" sign or a place where I've accidentally exposed myself or anything else that might produce laughter from someone. I can't find anything amiss. *Surely this bitch is just fucking with me*, I conclude as I take off the towel, and put my school uniform on. A couple minutes later I re-enter the dorm. I see that Nari has also finished her shower and is sitting on her bed, in pyjamas already. Iseul sits on her top bunk, grinning from ear to ear. I notice for the first time that Iseul has a missing tooth. Some idol!

Iseul points at my chest. "I thought so! You're from *Kyemdongshin!*" She's pointing at the logo on my school jacket, Kyemdongshin is the name of my high school.

"Yeah... so?" I reply.

Iseul lifts up her own school jacket, which is sitting on her bed. "*Chungbong!*" she says. I look at her school jacket, it's Chungbong High's jacket. It's the neighbouring school, it's where the richer kids in the neighbourhood go. The poorer ones go to my school.

"It's the school a few blocks away - so what?"

I look around at everyone. Nari and Youngsook are both staring at me oddly. Shu and Caitlin on the other hand just look confused. Iseul continues grinning at me.

"You don't know? You didn't hear?" Nari says.

"Hana, it was all over the Internet for months!" Youngsook adds.

I sigh. I didn't want to tell people this, but here we go. "I don't get to use the Internet at home, or watch any television. Sometimes I do at school, but not very often, only for classes."

"You don't have friends at school, who you talk to, who talk about current events?" asks Youngsook.

I hesitate. *Can we not go here.* I can't deal with this topic and I don't want people to know. I just stand there in silence, trying not to get emotional. How do I even tell them that I'm *wangtta*, the lowest of the low, and I literally don't have a single friend, because it's forbidden? What do I even say?

After a few seconds Youngsook figures it out anyway by my reluctance to answer. "Okay, that's a dumb question... I'm sorry, Hana." She's sharp, my respect for her goes up, but our interaction means that now the others are probably going to figure it out too.

Nari sighs. "Who wants to tell Hana what happened at Chungbong?"

Iseul raises her hand. "I will!"

Iseul is going to tell me something bad that happened at that school or whatever but I don't care about it. That's not why I'm getting upset. I'm upset because Youngsook asked about friends at school and I don't have any and now my social status as dirt is almost definitely going to come out in front of the whole group. This is terrible for me; it could mean that I get treated as *wangtta* within this group just like I was at school, I'm terrified of this possibility. It's a hard label to shake once you have it, *wangtta* can follow people for life. I can't live like a *wangtta* my whole life. I desperately don't want anyone to know, but it might be too late.

Iseul puts on her Chungbong jacket, wearing it over the top of her pyjamas. "Fine, stand there, I don't care. Hana, your school, Kyemdongshin is full of delinquents. You know that much, *clearly*." My heart sinks in my chest. Iseul's hinting that she knows. "Did you know that they don't just pick on you, they also pick on students from other schools? Did you know that they bully Chungbong High kids all the time? Did you know that Chungbong High retaliated and beat some of the Kyemdongshin kids up to teach them a lesson, so then two months ago, Kyemdongshin *iljins* firebombed a building at my school, and a girl died? And another girl went to hospital with burns all over her body?"

Shu gasps. "Oh my god!"

I guess Shu's fresh off the boat and is as unaware of local news and events as I am. I couldn't care less though. I point my head downward, trying to keep my cool and not start crying. Iseul knows for sure, but can she just shut her mouth now?

"How would I even know what the fucking assholes at my school do? I'm not part of that!"

Iseul laughs. "I'll bet you're not! Like they would even tell you! You're acting all bitchy in front of us but you're just a fucking *wangtta* and you don't want us to know!"

I can't control myself anymore, I start sobbing.

Nari sighs. "Iseul, we still have vocal lessons to do and I don't want another night of drama. Go easy, don't wind Hana up."

Iseul stops laughing. "Fine, Nari."

Youngsook speaks. "I'm not doing any lessons with *any* of you until Hana calms down."

The pain of having Iseul bring this out in the open in front of the whole group is overwhelming. My sobbing becomes a lot louder, and I start shivering. Caitlin climbs down from her bunk and takes my hand. "Everyone, I'm going to take Hana outside to talk, someone needs to calm her down. Youngsook, when we get back, we'll do vocals, okay?"

Youngsook nods. I silently follow Caitlin out of the dorm, through the gym and to the yard. Caitlin sits me down on the bench carefully and looks into my eyes.

"Hana, what the fuck is *wangtta?*"

Caitlin is foreign, so it makes sense that she wouldn't know what this is, she probably went to school in another country where they don't have it. I'm not even sure how I could exactly explain it so she could understand it, even if

I wasn't upset, I don't think other countries even have something like this. I try to say something anyway but nothing comes out except air. I break down even more, howling and crying and shaking, I can't stop myself. How can I explain that I am tainted, and I thought I could escape it in this place, and it's now coming back to haunt me?

Caitlin immediately tries to wrap her arms around me, and a reflexive reaction triggers inside me, I instinctively push her away and slide away from her on the bench. Taken by surprise, Caitlin jumps back. She looks into my eyes, with a sincere, concerned expression that I've never seen from her until now.

"Can I do it slowly? Is slowly okay? I'm not going to hurt you!"

I stare at Caitlin. I don't know what to tell her, and I can't stop crying enough to say anything coherently anyway, but I want her to try again. I try to convey this with my eyes somehow even though I'm just sitting there crying and shivering. She seems to get the message, as she very, *very* slowly moves closer to me and wraps her arms around me. It feels threatening at first, but after a while I adjust to the feeling and it starts to feel warm and comforting. I'm thankful that Caitlin is perceptive.

"There. It's okay, right?" Caitlin whispers.

I continue to do nothing by cry and howl and shiver. Although I desperately want to, I do not attempt to hug her back. I keep my arms fixed by my side; it feels safer this way.

Caitlin increases the pressure of her embrace just slightly. "It's fine, Hana. Let it out. It's better to let it out this way, right?"

After about fifteen minutes I run out of steam and my breathing gradually starts to return to normal. Caitlin loosens her grip but remains holding me. It feels beautiful to be held, but also threatening.

Caitlin whispers. "It's okay. Just tell me when you're ready to move, and we'll go inside. No pressure. No hurry."

I draw in some breath to try to say something, but the words don't come out. Caitlin notices this and she backs up her embrace and looks at me, waiting for me to speak. I take a few more breaths and try to calm down some more.

Eventually I manage a whisper. "I'm sorry about this. That has never happened to me before."

Caitlin's eyes widen. "Really? Nobody's ever given you a *hug?*"

I shake my head. "Not like this. I'm so sorry! I just... react... it's difficult..."

"Oh my god, Hana. Who hurt you so much?"

"Who *didn't?*" I reply, starting to tear up again.

Caitlin exhales deeply and reaches forward to hug me again, but I instinctively back away, again.

"Okay, sorry. Slowly."

She reaches out a second time, much slower. This time I'm anticipating the movement towards me, so I let it happen, allowing her to embrace me and put my head on her shoulder.

"I'd really like to know what this *wangtta* business is all about, but you're not really in a state to talk about it, are you?"

"Ask any of the others, that's fine. Just don't ask me about anything. I don't want to talk about it."

She might as well ask them now that the whole group knows anyway, saves me having to explain it, which I just can't do.

"They'll all know?" she asks.

"Not Shu. The rest will know."

"Why not Shu? Is it because you don't like her?"

"No. It's because she's foreign, like you."

"Shu's not Korean?"

"She's Chinese. She won't know what it is."

"Your snot and tears are seriously gross, Hana. I just changed into this shirt, and now I'm going to have to change it again. I won't forgive you for this, you know."

I laugh a little at Caitlin's cute attempt to lighten the mood.

"Thank you for not making me talk about it."

12. CONTROL

Half an hour later, all of us are standing in the gym in our usual standing positions, except Youngsook, who is pacing around in front of us, examining our posture. I'm still pretty fragile from earlier, but I've calmed down enough to handle being with the group.

"Shu, that's good, shoulders back a bit. Iseul, you are perfect. Caitlin, you are kind of hunched over, can you stand straighter?"

Caitlin adjusts herself a bit.

"How's this?"

"That's not actually straight, you're just craning your neck more. It's fine though, I'm not Ms Han, you're allowed to suck a bit, I'm not going to beat you to death for it. Just try to get better at it!"

Caitlin nods and tries to correct her posture a bit more, she's just naturally a bit slouchy though.

"Teach us properly or there's no point," says Nari.

"Nari, your shoulders are too far forward and too high. Push them back and down to get maximum space in your chest cavity. Also, your chin needs to be parallel, not upward. You're also not completely straight." Youngsook smiles a little, she seems to be enjoying telling Nari she's not doing it right.

"Surely being completely straight doesn't matter that much, after all we have to move in all sorts of ways while we sing," says Nari.

"You want to learn properly, this is properly. Don't say you want the correct method and then ask me to bend the rules for you, pick your side."

Nari rolls her eyes a bit and adjusts her position. I see Youngsook's gaze falling on me so I do my best to be as upright as I can.

"Hana... okay, that's not bad. You're doing okay."

I feel a bit wobbly but I suspect Youngsook is being lenient with me because half an hour ago I was bawling my eyes out. It's nice to know she's human.

Youngsook then addresses everyone. "So, remember what we did last night, we're going to do this again, but standing up this time. However, this time, every time you exhale, you're going to clench your teeth and blow the air out through your teeth, like a hissing sound, like this, at this volume - *sssssssssssssssss* - your goal is to keep an audible hiss going for thirty seconds at a time, at the same steady rate, without running out of air, and without losing the volume of your hiss. If you're filling up your lungs properly, from below, using your diaphragm which is the muscle above your stomach, after the thirty seconds are up you should still have a little air left. If you do it the wrong way, by puffing your chest out and sucking your stomach in, you will run out of oxygen and become dizzy and pass out and die and then we will have to dispose of the body but at least once we've finished digging your grave, we can all shower for thirty seconds longer. So, I'll start, I'll just do it on my own."

Everyone laughs a bit at Youngsook's joke while we watch her demonstrate the exercise. Even Nari can't help but crack a smile, although I think she's trying to hide it, or maybe all that plastic in her face just doesn't smile easily.

"Okay, now it's your turn. Remember; big breath from the diaphragm, don't compromise your volume or your amount of air. In three... two... one... breathe in... now exhale."

Youngsook watches the clock on the gym wall while also listening to our exhalations. At the end of the thirty seconds, she starts laughing.

"Actually, none of you did that right. Let's do it one at a time and I'll tell you where you're going wrong. Iseul, I'll start with you, when you're ready."

Iseul takes a big breath and Youngsook immediately raises her hand to stop her.

"You're not using your full capacity. Start with the stomach, fill up the air from the bottom first. Imagine filling a glass with water. The air, like water, starts from the bottom. Only once your stomach is filled, then you start filling your lungs. Try again."

"Is that how singers really do it?" Iseul asks.

"Yes and no. That's not really how it works, I mean your stomach doesn't fill up really, it's just a bit of a mental game, to get you doing it the right way. See how you go."

Iseul takes another deep breath and then slowly starts exhaling over the next thirty seconds.

"That's... significantly better. Shu, your turn."

Shu also takes a big breath and starts exhaling, she runs out of air after only about ten seconds.

"I'm sorry, I'm short! There's only so much air that can fit into me!"

Youngsook laughs. "That's got nothing to do with anything! You're just expelling air too fast. You don't need that much air to get the volume. Do it again and the hand that isn't on your stomach, put it this far away from your chin." Youngsook takes Shu's hand and moves it a fair way out in front of her face. "This is your warning indicator. If you can feel your own breath hitting your hand all the way out to here as you exhale, you'll know you're pushing the air out too hard. Try again."

Shu tries the exercise again and manages to get about twenty seconds out of it. "That was better, wasn't it?"

"Getting there. Just adjust the position of your hand to find the sweet spot. Nari, your turn, let's go."

Youngsook walks over to where Nari is standing. Nari takes a deep breath and Youngsook immediately stops her by raising her hand.

"What's wrong with that?" says Nari.

"I thought your chest was going to explode. I don't want to be killed by ribcage fragments over here. You don't have to fill up your lungs at light speed."

"Won't we have to quickly take in breaths to sing lines in songs?"

"Yes, but we're just doing exercises for now. It's more important to take time so we can feel the muscle motions and get used to how the correct breathing is supposed to feel, we can speed it up to performance level later. Do it again but just go slower."

Nari seems annoyed. "I can already do it quickly though."

Youngsook lets out a big sigh. "Fine, *whatever*, I don't want to have an argument about it. If you want to take shortcuts that's *fine*, just don't blame me when your singing's off. Hana, you're next, go ahead."

I do the exercise, inhaling a big breath and then exhaling through my teeth slowly. Running out of air doesn't seem to be an issue but I'm finding it really difficult to regulate the amount of air flow so it's a steady stream. I hear the hissing fading in and out, I know it's not good enough. At the end of it I look at Youngsook with a defeated expression.

"You get a pass for that, honestly." Youngsook says, smiling a little.

"Stop being soft, I know you want to be nice, but she needs to know that was bad," Nari gripes.

Youngsook turns to Nari with a pissed off glare. "Do I tell you how to fucking teach dance moves? Do I? Even when you're insulting me and telling me how shit I am at it?"

"But you *are* shit at it. You're letting the team down with your fucking sloth moves. That's just facts."

"I do my best and I don't complain, so you can do your best at this and not tell me how to run it."

Nari starts laughing. "Don't complain, my ass! You've been griping about food ever since your first meal, Miss Celery!"

I can practically see the steam coming out of Youngsook's ears. "Let's not change the subject. When we're singing, or doing singing exercises, we're using muscles. Hana was out there in the yard howling for the last half an hour, doing all that weird breathing that comes when you cry and scream for a long time, that's a lot of movement that is putting a strain on all those internal muscles and mechanisms which support the voice. She's not going to be able to come in here straight after something like that and breathe consistently because her muscles are already physically worn down and need recovery time, and *that's* why she gets a free pass, not any other reason."

"Fine, then. Just keep going." Nari sighs, grudgingly accepting Youngsook's observation.

Youngsook turns to Caitlin and nods. Caitlin does the exercise, but stops halfway through and just sighs.

"What's wrong?" Youngsook asks.

"Sorry but the amount of fucking hostility and emotion here is stressing me the fuck out. I've been dealing with it all night. It's fucking with my breathing. I'll try again."

Caitlin tries the exercise a second time and seems to complete it okay.

Youngsook observes Caitlin's breathing. "You seem to naturally slouch a little, it's getting in the way of your lung capacity. I think if we can fix your posture up, the rest will sort itself out."

"Okay" says Caitlin, raising her eyebrows a little and smiling slightly. She then glances over at me, but I'm not sure why. Suddenly Caitlin bursts out laughing for a few seconds, before swiftly trying to control herself.

"I'm sorry, Youngsook! It's not you! Just... a private joke!"

Youngsook looks at me, as if I'm in on the joke somehow. I'm not, so I just shrug.

"Private with who?" Youngsook asks Caitlin.

Caitlin looks at me, seemingly waiting for something. I'm completely confused. If there's a joke, I don't get it.

"Me and myself, I think!" Caitlin says to Youngsook, smiling awkwardly.

13. I'M ASLEEP

We're all in the dorms in our beds, with the lights out. Shu is asleep already, as usual, somehow. The way this bitch can sleep, how the fuck does she do it, I'm so jealous. The rest of us are still awake. I'm lying down with my eyes closed, trying to sleep but not having much success. I'm too emotionally exhausted to talk, so while I wait for my brain to become tired, I just listen to the others.

"Where are you from, Caitlin?" asks Nari.

"What do you mean, where was I born? Or what nationality I am? Or where did I live before I came here?"

"All three, I guess!"

"Okay. I was born in New Zealand. My dad is from there, but my mother is Korean. I don't remember that much about New Zealand though, I've been living in Oakland since I was five."

"Where's Oakland?"

"It's near San Francisco."

A short pause. "Where's San Francisco?"

Caitlin snorts. "Yeah, I should have just said I was living in the United States, right? San Francisco is on the west coast, it's the same coast as LA, but further north, so it's colder."

"Okay, I know where LA is. That's like Hollywood, right?"

"Yeah, that's it!" Caitlin sounds amused.

"So why come to Seoul to be in a group? I'd die to have an opportunity to pursue my career in LA! Isn't everything happening over there?"

Caitlin takes a deep breath. "Well, I didn't plan it like that, honestly. I didn't even plan to be in entertainment at all. I was actually down in LA from Oakland, visiting some friends, and I was scouted. Dude comes up to me in the mall, just right off the street, and just interrupts me while I'm shopping and starts talking to me about this group, and how I've got the perfect look for it, that they needed a 'visual member' and 'you're just what I'm looking for' and so on... I honestly thought he was a pick-up artist at first, it sounded like such bullshit!"

"Maybe it is!" laughs Youngsook.

"It was honestly like, *so super weird*, because he didn't even want to talk about whether I could sing, or dance, or anything like that, like the red flags were a mile high on this dude. I was pretty sure he was shady, but he was persistent, he wouldn't leave me alone, so I got his business card just to get rid of him. A few days later I checked everything out with my parents because I started thinking about it, like what if it's real, you know. They looked into it and worked out it was actually a legit guy from a real legit company in Korea, like everything totally checked out as the real deal which was not what I expected *at all*, so I decided to go for it. I mean I didn't know what else I was going to do except continue to fail at school back in Oakland so it seemed like an opportunity I might as well take, you know? If this all fails too, I haven't lost anything really."

"So you're not that ambitious, then."

If Nari is trying to wind Caitlin up, it doesn't work. Caitlin just flips Nari's question around.

"Nari, how did you get into this?"

Nari answers quickly. "I travelled to Seoul from Daegu and got in through a dance audition. I beat out hundreds of people to get this opportunity. Don't tell me I'm the only one who did it the hard way and you all got snatched up straight off the street, because if so, I won't be happy..."

Youngsook laughs. "I auditioned!"

"Not a dance audition, I bet."

"Singing, of course. You know, that thing *singers* have to do." Youngsook sounds a little pissed off.

"How about you, Iseul? I know your family wanted you here?" Caitlin asks.

"I'm the CEO's niece. There's no way my father was *not* going to make me join this group."

"Ha! I knew it!" shouts Nari.

"You didn't have any say in it?" Caitlin sounds confused.

"Yes and no. It's kind of a family obligation. I could have refused, but it would have caused problems with the family, it would not have been worth it. It's hard to explain, I'd rather not go into it."

"What about you, Hana? How did you get here?" Caitlin asks.

I say nothing and keep my eyes closed, pretending to be asleep. Nothing against Caitlin, I just am over talking to people in general today, I have no energy left for anybody, I just want my day to be over.

"Hana?" Caitlin asks again.

I'm not saying shit. I do my best to keep completely still.

After about ten seconds of me not replying, Caitlin speaks.

"Okay, I think she's asleep. Hey, who can tell me what *wangtta* is all about? She was really upset over that but she didn't want to tell me what it meant."

Oh, here we go. I knew this would come up.

"I'll bet she fucking doesn't't!" laughs Iseul.

I hear Youngsook speaking. "Are you sure she's okay with you even asking us? That stuff's kind of raw for people who are in it."

"She said it was okay for me to discuss with anyone, she just didn't want me to ask *her* about it."

I stay silent and continue to do my best being asleep impression. Honestly, I'm okay with them talking about it, because Caitlin was obviously going to ask about it sometime. Better that they talk through this stuff now when they think I'm not listening, than later when I'm asleep or not around and actually not listening, or even worse, when they know I'm fully conscious and they want to ask me a bunch of fucking questions about it. Not happening. This way is best.

"Wait a second everyone," says Iseul, before addressing me directly. "Hana, you are worthless. You are a human toilet. Disgusting *wangtta*. You get bullied all day and night. In this group we will bully you more, you will never escape. You will be our slave. You will be bullied until the day you die!"

I know what Iseul is doing, I don't move or react.

After a few seconds Iseul laughs. "Yeah, she's asleep for sure! I think we can safely discuss it now!"

"*Wangtta* is a bullying victim," says Nari.

"Yeah, I kind of picked up on that just now. Did you really mean those things, Iseul?" asks Caitlin, sounding concerned.

"No, not at all. I'm just checking she was really asleep. Anyway, *wangtta* is not just as simple as being a bullying victim, there's a bit more to it."

"It is that simple for me," says Nari, sounding very disinterested in the topic.

I hear Iseul take a deep breath. "Caitlin, if you're a *wangtta*, you're singled out as a person on the bottom rung of a whole social tier, you're considered an outcast. You don't speak to those on the higher tiers. Nobody is allowed to be your friend, or they are punished by joining you on the *wangtta* tier if they do - so they don't. You also have to obey the *iljins* and do anything that the *iljins* demand."

"Oh wow, that's like hardcore. It sounds like prison back in the States."

"Don't tell me you've been to prison, Caitlin. You don't look like the type!" Iseul laughs.

"No, not me, but my older brother did a little time when he was my age. He was only in there for a few days, but he told me that the people in there who've done the worst crimes, like the rapists and child molesters, they have to keep to themselves, the other prisoners won't talk to them or touch them, or use the same cutlery even. What's *iljin*, I guess those are bullies?"

"Not all bullies are *iljins*, but all *iljins* are bullies, more or less. But *iljins* also are respected in the school, because they are organised, and violent, they have power, it's like a gang. They rule the school, more than the teachers in some ways. They can even bully teachers, and ruin their careers."

I hear Caitlin gasp a little. "How does it even get like that? Can't the teachers do something about it?"

"Teachers here care more about their job and their reputation. If a teacher points out that there is a bullying problem then not only does it gets the *iljins* upset but it reflects badly on that teacher themselves for being ineffective at discipline. Even if the complaint goes higher, it just gets hushed at the higher level anyway because then the school principal doesn't want to suffer the bad reputation from the education department. On top of that there can be retaliation from the *iljins*. So, nothing gets done."

"Can't the *wangtta* just stick up for themselves?"

"Impossible. Hana is an aggressive little mole, so I bet she's tried it, but she would have lost those fights. Bullies will respect strength, but standing up to an organised gang who will always have higher strength in numbers is just suicide. Once someone is designated *wangtta*, they just do what they are told and act compliant if they know what's good for them, because there is no limit to what an *iljin* can demand from a *wangtta*. No limit at all."

Don't I know it. Iseul's description, aside from the insult directed at me, is upsettingly accurate. I can feel tears starting to flow down my face. I'm hoping that in the darkness nobody can see that I'm silently crying.

"I'm so glad I didn't go to school in Korea. How do people here even live."

"The way to get through it is to just ride it out, do what you're told, and hope your status doesn't follow you from the end of school to your workplace or wherever you end up."

Nari starts speaking, sounding cross. "Well, we have to get along, it's important. This will *not* become part of our group dynamic. We all have the same status here - except me, I'm the leader. Iseul, you dump this shit *right fucking now and do not pick it up again, not now, not ever!*"

I wait. Iseul eventually sighs.

"Fine."

"We're here to train to be a successful group, and that's it. No more or less. I want *nothing* getting in the way. Not this, not anything!"

"Just don't blame me when Hana gets out of hand."

"I can handle Hana. If she gets out of hand, I will deal with it."

I'm silently grateful for Nari's leadership at this moment. She's still a bitch, but if she's going to ensure my *wangtta* status is erased while I'm in this group, that means so much to me. I suddenly want to do something nice for Nari, but I'm not sure what. I continue to silently cry myself to sleep.

14. LINE UP

All of us six girls are lined up in our usual positions in the gym from my left to right: Iseul, Shu, Nari, me, Caitlin, Youngsook. Ms Han is here, standing in front of us.

"I don't like this positioning. You always line up the same way. Why do we have all the tall people on my left, and all the short people on my right? Do you realise how stupid that's going to look in photographs when you debut? Have you ever seen a photograph of an idol group where they are lined up shortest to tallest? It looks moronic!"

We all look at each other. We're not *exactly* shortest to tallest, because I'm shorter than Nari by a little, and Shu is shorter than Iseul, but it's true that we have a bit of a jagged diagonal slope going on, and we're all so different in height so it's noticeable. I don't think any of us ever considered this, we just stood where we wanted.

"Caitlin, go and stand on the end, by Iseul, so we have the two tallest people at each end. Shu, move to the other side of Nari, you're the shortest so you need to be closer to Youngsook's side to balance her out."

Caitlin walks over to the left end, and everyone on my left shuffles around. Now from my left to right: Caitlin, Iseul, Nari, Shu, me, Youngsook.

Ms Han doesn't smile, but she seems at least satisfied with the change. "That's better. This can be your order from now on."

I have to stand next to Shu every fucking day? *Oh great.* This can't be permanent, I have to say something about this, I wonder if can do it without making it obvious to Ms Han why I'm asking.

"We have to stay in this standing position all the time?"

"Yes. Is there a problem?"

I can feel everyone's heads turn to look at me. I struggle to think of what to say, so I come up with the first thing I can think of.

"I just think... some variety would be good? Shouldn't we get used to standing next to different people?"

Ms Han stares at me flatly, she isn't impressed.

"Variety is not good, consistency is. You need to learn your positions so you can lock into them each time in an organised manner. We don't want to have you all shuffling around randomly during line-ups for photo shoots and appearances, being a disorganised rabble and holding up proceedings."

Well, I tried. I say nothing, and look sideways over at Shu, she's glaring at me uncomfortably. Shu certainly knows why I asked, I think the others do as well, but Ms Han doesn't, so that's fine.

"I'm not comfortable standing next to Hana!" Shu pouts annoyingly. There goes my attempt to be subtle about it.

"Why?" Ms Hana asks.

"Because she's *mean*!"

Ms Han stares at Shu, she clearly isn't any more impressed with her reasoning than with mine.

"I'm meaner. Stay in your positions, and that's final."

Shu glares at me, and I glare back. I want to smack Shu in her stupid "first love face" so badly but I can't do it right now as Ms Han is watching us.

"Today is the first day of the week, so we're going to do our weekly weigh-in. Everyone line up in front of the scales and I will call out your weights. Caitlin, you are first. The rest of you, line up behind Caitlin and retain the order you're in now."

We all shuffle over to the left side of the gym in front of the scales and form a queue. The gym scales are on a small platform which is on wheels. Caitlin steps onto the scales and Ms Han glares down at the digital readout by Caitlin's feet, disapprovingly.

"You're 51.3 kilos, that's too heavy. That's ridiculous for an idol. Get off, you'll break those. Iseul, get up."

Caitlin steps off and exits the queue, returning to her original position. I look at her face, expecting her to be annoyed by Ms Han's reaction but she doesn't seem to register any emotion at all. Iseul gets on the scales.

"48.9 kilos. Barely acceptable, get off. Nari, get up."

Iseul steps off, looking unbothered. Nari steps on the scales.

"50 kilos exactly."

"It's because I have muscle tone," Nari retorts.

"We're not bulking here, Miss Universe. Just see that you don't put any more on. Get off. Shu, you're next."

Nari steps off and moves back into our normal line-up. Shu steps up.

"Yay, I'm 47.5!" Shu yells.

"You're short, you should be under 45. Get off those scales. Hana, you're up."

Shu seems a bit shocked and just kind of stands there. I move forward and get on the scales, giving Shu a satisfying little push with my arms so she gets the fuck off them a bit more quickly. Shu stumbles a bit and glares back at me as she scuttles back over into the line-up, unfortunately she doesn't fall flat on her face but then it's hard to tip over something that short so I won't be too hard on myself about it. I steady myself carefully on the scales, and don't even bother to look down at the digits as I know Ms Han is going to tell everyone what they are anyway. I really don't like looking down when I'm on scales, just the small amount of height difference between the scales and the floor is enough to trigger my fear of heights if I look anywhere but straight ahead. It doesn't help that these scales are chunky, and on wheels.

"48.1 kilos. Not great, but I'll tolerate it. Try to slim down a bit, fatty. Youngsook, you're next."

Whatever, bitch - I don't give a fuck. I step down from the scales and return to my normal line-up, next to Shu, who gives me a mean glare and flinches away from me a little, but doesn't say anything - just the way I like it. I hear Youngsook step onto the scales behind me.

"Holy hell you are one fat bitch!" Ms Han screams. "56.4 kilos! What kind of fat are you carrying around? Don't tell me you're pregnant?"

Youngsook seems shocked by Ms Han's outburst, she just stands on the scales, not saying anything.

"Get off those scales immediately! Get off *now*, unless you want to replace them, porky!"

Youngsook quickly steps down from the scales and re-joins the line-up. Ms Han yells after her.

"Don't run too fast there, wouldn't want you to have a miscarriage before you've named the baby!"

"It's not my fault I'm tall!" Youngsook says, audibly trying to hold back her tears.

"Some advice for you, your jaw muscles are a small muscle group, flapping them around doesn't burn a lot of calories! Try exercising something larger, like an arm or a leg! I want you under 52 kilos by this time next week, make it happen!"

Youngsook just stands there, saying nothing and wiping her eyes.

Ms Han addresses the entire group. "You are all a bunch of fat slugs, there's no way we can debut you, our van doesn't have strong enough suspension to take you to your schedules. I expect improvement from each and every one of you. Next weigh-in had better get some results. I don't want to see any of you sloths today, you all disgust me. Go do your exercises, practice your dance routines and do not ask me for anything."

Ms Han leaves the room and slams the door to the administration area. We all stare at each other.

"What's up her ass?" says Caitlin.

I start laughing at Caitlin's comment. At the same time, Youngsook suddenly starts bawling and rushes off into the dorm. Caitlin and Shu both go running after her.

"Fuck, why does someone have to cry here every fucking day," Nari sighs.

I ignore them all and stay in the gym, starting my stretching for the day, thinking about how I'm going to lose my next kilo, if I could even be bothered.

15. SHOPPING

We're all in our morning language class and I am nearly falling asleep. I didn't get anywhere near as much sleep as I would have wanted. Today we're learning about verb conjugations, not very exciting stuff. The language class teacher is Ms Kim, a dopey woman who doesn't seem to care about anything and hardly even talks to us. Ms Kim gives us exercises from a book, we do the exercises, not much else happens, she just leaves us alone basically. I've had teachers like this before in school, usually relief teachers. It's clear that Ms Kim is like them, I think she's just waiting until retirement age. It's a nice break from gym but it's also boring and it's hard to stay awake.

All of a sudden, I feel that something's stuck in my hair. I reach back with my right hand to grab whatever it is, and I immediately recognise the *very* familiar feeling of a paper plane. I take the plane out of my hair and look at it... there's something written on the inside. I unfold it and take a look.

The note says: *I'm going 'shopping' - what do you want? Anything at all, dream big. If I can get it - you owe me.*

I turn around. From the back row, Iseul is staring at me. She nods.

I turn back to the note and keep reading. The others have all written stuff down. Nari has written *salted sunflower seeds in their shells, resistance bands*. The fitness gear is typical Nari, I'm surprised that she's asking for a contraband snack though. Shu has written *books (fiction - horror, mystery, fantasy)*. Shu likes horror fiction? There's no way. Youngsook has written *propolis lozenges*, I have no idea what that even is. Caitlin has drawn a picture of a flower in a flower pot, the number *420* is written on the pot. She can't want a flower pot, that doesn't make sense. This request must represent something else but I don't know what, I'll have to ask her about it.

I immediately write on the paper: *pocket knife*. I refold the plane and fly it back to Iseul, it lands neatly on her desk. I go back to not really reading my exercise book, thinking instead about how the hell Iseul is actually going to get any of these things when she can't even leave the premises.

Thirty seconds later, I feel the same plane land in my hair again. Is my hair that attractive a target? Why not just aim for the desk or something. I open the plane up.

Iseul has crossed out my knife request and has written underneath: *GET REAL, FUCKHEAD. Pick again.*

I write on the paper: *poison that only works on Chinese bitches - p.s try to land the plane on the desk instead next time*. I refold the plane and fly it back, glaring at Iseul as I throw it, doing my best to throw it straight at her ugly face this time. I aim well but unfortunately she catches it before it pokes her eye out.

A couple minutes later, the plane hits my hair, harder this time. I grab it and unfold it.

Iseul has written underneath my text: *I'm trying to do something nice for everyone, try not to be WORTHLESS for once in your life. No wonder you were bullied, you surely deserved it. Last chance, wangtta.*

This note pisses me off, but I don't want to make a scene in language class. I try to calm down and hang onto it for a minute, thinking about what I want. Honestly there's nothing that I want right now that desperately. Eventually I write *something that I can get on the Internet with p.s call me that again and I will murder you in your sleep*, fold it up and send it back.

A couple minutes later, thankfully before the paper plane has a chance to bounce back in my direction, the side door of the classroom opens and Ijun walks in, dressed in her usual red and black school uniform. Ms Kim departs without a word as Ijun stands in front of the classroom.

"*Annyeong haseyo.* Morning break is cancelled, it is time for gym class. However Ms Han will not be holding gym class for today as she is preparing your new routine for tomorrow, and morning food is also not ready yet. Please practice at your leisure without supervision and we will bring food out later this morning. Tomorrow, you will have the new routine to practice."

"Thanks Ijun," says Iseul.

Ijun vanishes into the admin area without another word. We all file into the gym. I take up my new line position out of habit, before remembering that we're unsupervised so it doesn't really matter. Youngsook is next to me and does the same. We stare at each other for a moment, feeling silly.

"Since Ms Han isn't here, and we're getting something new tomorrow anyway, I don't see any point in going over 'Plastic' today." says Nari.

Youngsook sighs. "That's a relief! Those dance moves were killing me!"

"What should we do instead?" asks Shu.

Nari thinks for a moment. "Never mind dance practice, we lack basic group cohesion. There's too much tension and everyone's crying all the time, I'm sick of it. We can't perform as a team if you all hate each other. You all need to learn about conflict resolution."

Shu nods. "That's a good idea, I support this! But how do we have conflicts without upsetting each other?"

Nari takes a deep breath. "Well, it's important that people feel like they are heard, but without other people feeling accused or put down. I've heard that a good way to make sure that people can still express themselves without having to worry is to use a *you-I* statement rather than just a *you* statement. So instead of saying *you make me feel bad*, because that's very accusatory, you can say *when you do a certain thing, it makes me feel bad*. This is supposed to work better, because it's phrased so it makes the other person understand that it's not an accusation, but just a statement of how it makes you feel."

Caitlin shrugs. "Makes sense, I guess?"

Nari looks over at me. "Why don't you try it, Hana. It's no secret that you don't like Shu. Tell her why, but try to use non-accusatory language. And without swearing. Then maybe we can resolve it peacefully. Think you can do it?"

I think for a moment, and then look at Shu.

"Okay... Shu, when you do that forced *aegyo*, which is like, all the time, it makes me feel like I want to punch you in the head."

Shu looks at Nari. "That doesn't feel very nice. I don't like this!"

I keep going. "Shu, when I see your ugly plastic face, it makes me feel like I want to melt it off with a blowtorch."

"HEY!" yells Shu.

Nari holds out her palm to me, a signal to stop talking. "Okay Hana, fucking shut your hole now, this is not an excuse for you to bully Shu. Obviously, this isn't going to work, there are some loopholes here that you are exploiting. I might need to think about this a bit more."

Caitlin looks at Nari. "What about apologising and taking responsibility? Isn't that supposed to help resolve conflicts?"

I can't resist. "Shu, I'm sorry that I get easily annoyed by you and I feel like beating you up all the time. If I were to beat you up, technically I would definitely be the one responsible for it..."

"Shut the fuck up, Hana!" Nari yells, raising her hand in preparation to slap me. "Say *one* more fucking nasty thing about Shu, and get hit!"

I flinch back as Nari's hand comes up. I really don't want to get hit by Nari, so I stop talking.

"In fact, Hana... *do* apologise to Shu, right now. But do it properly, and *sincerely*."

"This is like a trap!" I complain.

"WHY?"

"I don't actually *like* Shu, so I'm not sorry! So, if I'm apologising, I'm just doing it out of fear of getting hit. That's not sincere... is it?"

"Why are you so mean, Hana?" Shu complains.

Nari glares at me. "Do you like having a bruised face, Hana? Because you're about to get one!"

I sigh. "I can't be sincerely sorry when I hate this fucking Chinese dwarf bitch..."

Before I can say another word, Nari's hand connects to my cheek. The slap isn't that painful but it's enough to knock me off balance, I collapse onto my right side and land on the gym floor. I look up at her, she starts screaming at me.

"I don't want to keep doing this to you Hana, but violence is the only language you understand! We all *have* to get along! You *have* to be respectful to your other members! There is no other way! I don't *want* to have to beat basic decency into you by force, but you don't give me any other choice! *Get the fuck up!*"

Nari sounds exasperated rather than angry. After a few seconds of getting my bearings back, I gradually stand up.

"Apologise to Shu!" Nari yells.

I guess I'd better go along with Nari. I turn to Shu.

"I'm sorry, Shu, for my behaviour."

"Hmph! As if I would accept! You just don't want to get hit again!"

I turn to Nari. "See? Even Shu agrees with me!"

Nari says nothing, but approaches me slowly and threateningly, with her arm wound back, clearly getting ready to hit me a second time. I know how hard Nari can hit and that first blow was weak, she was deliberately holding back. I get the feeling that if she has to smack me a second time, she will use full force. I try really hard to think quickly of something to say to Shu that's actually sincere, but also honest, and isn't just about me wanting to bully her. It's hard to do, and a little upsetting for some reason. Nari then stops approaching me and freezes in position, indicating that I'm on my last chance. I'd better think of something good.

"Shu... it's pretty obvious... that I have issues, right? I don't mean issues with you, I mean issues with myself, yeah?"

"You sure do! You just said a smart thing!"

Suddenly, I feel tears coming up. I'm not even sure why, but this topic upsets me for some reason.

"I don't know what to do about it. I really don't!"

"Do you think I deserve to be hit by you?"

"No!" I reply immediately, starting to sob. "It's not about what you deserve. I just... can't control my own emotions. You push my buttons and... I don't know why. I really don't." I bow at ninety degrees in front of Shu. "Please forgive my failings as a human being!"

Nari talks to Shu. "That was barely an apology. You don't have to forgive a damn thing."

I look back up at Shu, who looks me in the eye and holds her nose in the air.

"I will consider how to feel about it. Words are easy for you to say, if you start to behave better, I may forgive you in the future."

What a fucking pathetic display from this pipsqueak, I just want to slap this fake arrogance out of her so badly. She's lucky she has Nari to protect her. What's even worse is that even when she's talking to me like this, Shu still has that trace of *aegyo* in her voice, which aggravates me so much. Knowing how much I will get in trouble for hating her doesn't make me hate her any less.

Nari speaks. "Hana, go immediately back to your bed in the dorms, and stay there. Don't come out until dinner. Nobody else go with her, let her reflect on her actions, alone."

Without another word, I walk quickly to the dorms, get into my bed and get under the covers. I can't help it that I hate Shu so much, but how can I realistically stop hating her, I can't see a way. Maybe she doesn't deserve my hate, but what the hell else am I supposed to do about it? I guess it's not her fault that she was born annoying, but is it mine? I think about it but I can't come up with any solution other than hitting Shu a lot to make myself feel better, I don't know what sort of fucking amazing revelation Nari wants me to reach. I guess I'll just have to be sneakier about bullying Shu until I can find another way to deal with things. I realise this isn't very smart, and that I'm obviously a hypocrite, but I can't just snap my fingers and not feel this way, can I? I think on this for a while until I exhaust my brain enough to fall asleep.

16. SUNFLOWERS

"Hana, why are you wearing your school uniform? We're not at school, you know."

The rest of the group all look at me.

"It's comfortable, I get cold."

Youngsook waves her arm, motioning for me to join the others at the dinner table.

"But it's not even cold. Sit down."

I don't know what Youngsook is talking about, it's fucking cold. Also, I just feel more secure in it. I sit down at the table next to her. Nari slides a bowl in front of me.

"Here's your dinner, eat up."

I grab the bowl and silently start picking away at the chicken breast and salad with my hands. I'm amazed my dinner is intact and nobody stole any when I wasn't here.

"Have you had a chance to think about anything and reflect today?" asks Nari.

"I mainly slept," I mumble in between bites.

"Well do you think you can at least promise to not be a bitch for the rest of today? I'm really trying to make you get along with the rest of this group, but you're making it very difficult, you know."

I'm eager to change the subject. "What's that stuff in that bag?" I ask, looking at a clear plastic bag on the table with some weird stuff in it that looks like cockroaches or something, I have no idea what.

"Answer me and I might tell you."

"Fine, then. I'll stop being a bitch, okay, happy? I don't promise to enjoy it. I don't even promise to not complain about it."

Caitlin laughs. "So, you're going to be a bitch about not being a bitch, then?"

The entire group starts laughing at me. Oh my god, can a meteor just hit the planet and kill me in this moment. I'm now even more keen to change the subject.

"Hey! I made my promise, Nari. Tell me, what's that weird stuff in the bag? Dead bugs?"

"The most *shit snack* you've ever had in your life," says Youngsook, rolling her eyes.

Nari takes one of the things out of the bag and holds it up so I can see it. I swear it looks just like a dead baby cockroach.

"These are sunflower seeds. You have to break open the husk, and you eat the seed inside, like this." Nari twists and splits the shell in half with her fingers, pulls the seed out and eats it.

Youngsook continues, in a sarcastic tone. "Seriously, this snack is the dumbest thing I've ever seen. The seed in there is so tiny, you spend more energy just trying to break

143

the shell to get the seed out than you actually get from eating the seed. You might as well not even eat them. Even worse, half the time when you're twisting the husk you break the seed by mistake and it just falls into bits and then you can't easily separate the bits of the husk from the bits of seed so you just end up throwing it out because the entire thing mixed together tastes like a bunch of wood chips."

Nari looks at Youngsook. "You're missing the point - that's exactly why this snack is so good. If you have a snack craving, you eat these and you don't put on any weight because it's so much work to get the seeds out and they're so tiny. Since we're supposed to be cutting, I think it's *perfect* for us, especially *you*. Feel free to have as many as you want."

Youngsook rolls her eyes massively. "Trust you to use the opportunity to be naughty and sneak in contraband to actually just be even more of a discipline freak."

Shu reaches out into the bag and pops a seed into her mouth. "You know, if you suck on the husk without breaking it, it's really salty, it tastes good. It also makes the husk easier to break later after the salt is gone."

"You're literally sucking on a wood chip with some salt on it." Youngsook laughs.

"You can't shame me! You eat bee poop!"

"They're good for your throat."

"Propolis is poop from a bee's butt! Having an insect poop into your mouth is yucky!"

144

I can't let this go on. Shu is talking - it must stop. "I think Youngsook would know best, she's the singer."

Iseul points at me. "Hey, Hana! I have something for you!" Iseul has a backpack on the chair next to her, she unzips it, pulls out a computer tablet and waves it in my direction.

What the fuck, Iseul actually got me a device for Internet browsing? I go to reach for the tablet but Iseul yanks it away immediately.

"Not so fast, Hana. You have to be nice to Shu first. For a whole *week*. Not just tolerant, but actually *nice*. Then you can have this. Do you think you can manage it?"

Shu stares me up and down. "I don't know if I want Hana being my friend and stuff. It's pretty clear she hates me."

Iseul turns to Shu. "Don't worry Shu, you two don't have to be best friends or anything terrifying like that. We all know that won't happen. Hana just has to be polite, not push you around, not insult you - for a week. Until then, this is mine."

Shu smiles. "That looks like a pretty nice tablet! Maybe Hana will be good!"

Iseul puts the tablet back in her backpack and stares at me. I don't say anything. *A whole week? Really Iseul, you bitch? I don't think I can do it. You can keep the fucking tablet.*

Iseul then turns to Caitlin. "I don't have what you want, yet. That's going to take a little longer."

Caitlin nods. "I was being optimistic. I didn't think you could get what I wanted, but your note said to dream big, so..."

Iseul smiles. "Oh, don't worry. I can get it. It'll just take some time to organise."

Nari looks at Iseul. "I don't see the point. Where are we even going to put a flower pot?"

Caitlin suddenly bursts out laughing.

"What? What's funny?" Nari asks, looking confused.

Caitlin does her best to stop laughing, not very successfully - she puts a hand over her mouth but it doesn't really help. Iseul stares at Caitlin trying to keep a straight face, but gradually loses it and starts laughing as well, unable to control herself. Then the penny drops with me, I start to laugh also. I still don't quite understand the exact significance of the picture Caitlin drew but I'm slowly learning that if something's making Caitlin this amused there's generally only one thing it could mean. Shu and Youngsook both stare at the three of us, looking a bit puzzled by how much we're laughing. Nari however isn't impressed at all.

"Hana?"

Nari looks at me, probably because between me, Caitlin and Iseul, I'm the one controlling my laughter the best. Caitlin falls off her chair and starts rolling on the floor, continuing to laugh. Iseul starts clutching her stomach, wheezing.

"I don't know, I'm just laughing because they're also laughing!"

I don't want to have to be the one to say it, and seeing Nari this clueless is honestly hilarious. She'll probably lose her shit when she finds out what Caitlin's request means because she's such a hard-ass, so I'll let someone else break the news.

"Oh shit! I think I actually pissed myself!" Caitlin gets up and rushes out of the room. I can hear her laughter echoing down the hallway as she scrambles clumsily to get to the bathroom while presumably attempting to make a minimum of mess. Iseul follows her a few seconds later, not saying anything but also laughing continuously, still clutching her stomach.

I look at Nari and shrug. It's best that she doesn't know.

17. SHOW ME LOVE

We're all lined up in the gym, waiting for Ms Han. Usually, she opens the door to the language class at quarter past ten on the dot, but this time she didn't come and neither did Ijun, so we just filed out there anyway.

Nari bounces back and forth on the balls of her feet, looking eager to get started on something. "I'm not going to wait lined up like this forever, I could actually be doing something."

"I'm sure we all could," I reply, stretching out my legs one at a time. The hours of being sedentary during language class are also making me keen to get moving.

The door suddenly opens and Ms Han walks in. She's carrying her usual clipboard and also some plastic sheet folders.

"Everyone please take one and pass the rest down."

She passes the folders to Youngsook, who passes the rest of them along until everyone has a folder.

Ms Han paces back and forth on the gym floor. "We are going to be fast-tracking your debut process. The initial planned training period was three years, but the company has decided that this is far too long. Therefore, we aim to debut you as soon as possible. An exact date is not yet fixed, the outcome will depend on your success and achievements within the training process, so we will continue to monitor your progress carefully. However, we wish to prepare you for the debut as completely as we can, as quickly as we can, so we are now sharing the information about your debut song and concept, so you can memorise your words and dance parts."

I look through the folder. On the first page, is a lyrics sheet to what is no doubt our debut song.

SHOW ME LOVE

Verse:
When I see you looking at me
I don't know how to tell you how I feel
You don't know the feelings inside my heart
The secrets I keep buried deep inside

Pre-chorus:
I can't explain everything away
I just want to make you understand that my feelings
are real

Chorus:
I just want you to show me
Show-show-show me love

Will you ever know me
Know-know-know my love for you

Rap:
You think you know how I'm feeling
But you don't understand the meaning of my lies
I wish I could tell you everything
But there are some things
That boys can't understand

[Pre-chorus repeat]

[Chorus repeat]

Bridge/middle-8:
Show-show-show me love, ah
Know-know-know my love, ah
Ah-ah,
I can't tell you how I burn so deep inside
I want you to understand that my feelings are real

[Chorus repeat]

I didn't expect much, but I'm still taken aback by how cheesy these words sound. It's hard to imagine them put to music of any kind. I look over at Youngsook, who is having trouble keeping a straight face. It's obvious to me that she thinks it's ridiculous too.

"The song words are cute!" says Shu. I groan internally. Of course she likes them.

I continue flipping through the folder. A few pages are devoted to dance steps, I flip over them as I figure Ms Han is going to show us those in person anyway. There's a page with sheet music, that's nice but I can't read sheet music so I just flip that over as well. Then there's a page with the costumes. The costumes for all six members are shown, and they're all slightly different, all variations of strapless dresses with low backs. Mine looks pretty, a long dress in blue and purple, but I'm not sure if this will suit me, not that I really care. Obviously we have to get dressed up somehow so I'm sure someone will find a way to make it work. It's not my problem.

Iseul opens her folder to the dress page and points to her dress. "I am not wearing this."

"What?" responds Ms Han.

We all look at Iseul.

"Sorry, I'm not wearing this." Iseul is stony-faced and stares straight at Ms Han.

"You do not have a choice, Iseul! You are wearing this, and that's that!"

"I do not mean disrespect. I cannot wear this." Iseul stands firm, her gaze not wavering.

" Listen you little tramp, I won't stand for this attitude! You are wearing the costume as shown! This is not negotiable!" Ms Han goes to grab Iseul by the ear but Iseul fights back, swatting Ms Han's grip away with her forearm. I can't believe that this is happening.

"No, I won't wear it!" Iseul shouts. "If you do not accept this, get Mr Park CEO!"

"YOU'LL BE SORRY!" screams Ms Han as she storms out of the room, slamming the door behind her.

Nari looks at Iseul. "What's the problem? The costumes are okay, I thought?"

Iseul straightens herself up and adjusts her tracksuit top. "She will be the one who is sorry, shortly."

"Our contract says that we have to wear their stuff. We can't push back like this, that's crazy! You'll get kicked out of the group!"

Iseul goes to say something but stops as the door opens and Mr Park walks in, with Ms Han following behind him. We all bow.

"Iseul?"

Iseul bows a second time at ninety degrees. "Mr Park CEO, may I please have a word with you privately, alone."

"Come with me." He motions for Iseul to follow him.

Iseul bows a third time. "Thank you, Mr Park CEO."

Iseul follows Mr Park as they walk towards the doorway into the administration area. Ms Han goes to follow, but Mr Park raises his hand to stop her.

"Please mind the other trainees. I'm sure our meeting will be very quick."

Ms Han stops, looking frustrated. We all look on awkwardly as Ms Han doesn't seem to know what to do with herself.

"We will wait for Mr Park CEO's return. Please familiarise yourselves with your folders in the meantime."

I stare at the folder, wondering what could be wrong with Iseul's dress. It's honestly quite pretty, one of the better dresses in the group, with a cute "princess" styling, blue and high-cut at the front with white frills and plunging to the waist at the rear. It's certainly not overly revealing compared to the other dresses, in fact it's actually one of the *least* revealing dresses of them all, Nari and Youngsook have much more revealing cuts and Caitlin's even has a window at the front which would surely reveal cleavage. I look at the others, who are staring at their folders, looking like they're deep in thought.

After about five minutes, Iseul walks back in through the administration door, and joins back up with the group. She looks straight at Ms Han and smiles.

Mr Park emerges behind Iseul from the doorway. "Ms Han, please come with me."

Ms Han gives Iseul a filthy look, and then she and Mr Park both disappear into the admin area. Mr Park gently closes the door. We all look at each other.

Nari turns to Iseul, her eyes wide. "Iseul, you *have* to tell me what is going on here! Why the *fuck* did you do that?"

"I just didn't want to wear it. Is it that big of a deal?"

Nari raises her eyebrows a mile high.

"I think you are going to get your butt seriously kicked over this one."

"We'll see what happens, won't we."

We remain lined up and wait. After about a minute, we all start to hear a noise gradually building, it's the sound of Mr Park, yelling from somewhere in the office area. I can't hear exactly what's being said, but I don't need to, it's plainly evident that he's absolutely tearing shreds out of Ms Han. The yelling continues for a couple of minutes.

"Are we going to get to do any gym today or what. I wouldn't mind being shown these new dances." Nari stares down at her folder, holding it open in one hand while trying to step through the positions with the rest of her body.

I laugh. "I just want to see Ms Han eat shit, personally. She's so rude. She's even ruder than you, Nari."

"I'm not rude, I just care."

"Bullshit!" Youngsook coughs, with her hand up to her mouth. I look for a reaction from Nari but she doesn't respond, I don't think Youngsook's insult was clear enough for Nari to hear.

"Oh no, here she comes!" exclaims Shu, completely unnecessarily because we can all hear Ms Han's footsteps stomping up to the administration doorway.

The doorway flings open and Ms Han walks up to us, looking very unimpressed. Her face is bright red.

"Return the folders *now*."

We all pass the folders along to Youngsook, who holds them in front of her. Ms Han snatches the stack of folders out of Youngsook's hands aggressively, and then walks briskly back out the door, slamming it behind her as hard as possible.

"That's annoying, I wanted to learn something new today," sighs Nari.

A couple of seconds later, the doorway opens again, slowly.

Ijun walks in and bows softly to us. *"Annyeong haseyo.* All classes are cancelled for today. You have free time, please still attend dinner at the usual time. Thank you."

"Cancelled again?" complains Nari.

"Ijun, are you okay?" Iseul enquires.

I notice that Ijun is shaking, and looks upset.

"Everything is fine. An administrative error."

I notice a tear running down Ijun's left cheek. Perhaps it wasn't just Ms Han who the CEO was angry at.

"Ijun, is it just the gym that is cancelled, or singing also?" Youngsook asks.

"Everything. Classes will begin again tomorrow, thank you."

Ijun shuffles back through the door without another word, and closes it quietly.

Nari stares at Iseul, who stares back.

"What?" asks Iseul, smiling.

18. PROTEIN

We're in the dorms, it's late. Nari, Shu and Youngsook are all asleep. I'm trying to get to sleep but it's just not happening for me tonight. Iseul and Caitlin are sitting up, talking to each other about something very quietly, I'm not sure what but I'm trying to tune it out. Caitlin's tracksuit-clad legs hang down from her bunk above my head. I stare up at them, hoping their swaying motion helps me drift off to sleep.

"Hey Caitlin, catch!"

It's Iseul's voice. I look over at Iseul, she throws something gently from her bunk over to Caitlin's. I peer out the side of my bunk and watch Caitlin reach forward and catch it with both hands. It's a large black plastic tub, the type that bodybuilding supplements come in.

"What's this?" Caitlin asks.

"Special delivery!" replies Iseul.

Caitlin unscrews the tub and takes a look inside, then quickly screws the lid back on again. "Oh... wow, I'm impressed! Thank you so much, I definitely owe you one now. Hey Hana, are you okay down there?" Caitlin notices me peering up from below her legs.

"Yeah, sleepy but not," I reply. I've been tossing and turning for the last ten minutes trying to get a good sleeping position, I'm sure Caitlin has been feeling the vibrations from my restlessness travelling up to her bunk.

Caitlin jumps down from her bed, holding the black tub in one hand. "Follow me if you want, Hana, I'm going to the yard to digest some *protein*. You should try some, it might help you get to sleep."

She walks off quickly. I can't sleep anyway so I might as well follow her. I put my school uniform jacket over my pyjamas and trace Caitlin's steps out of the dormitory, through the gym space and out to the yard through the sliding doors. When I get there, Caitlin is already sitting on the bench and has the plastic tub open in her hands.

"Wow, Iseul really came through, this'll do me for a few weeks at least!" Caitlin smiles as she lifts a clear plastic bag filled with marijuana out of the tub.

I stare at the green bag. "I'm not sure if I want to do this. Last time was pretty gross."

"I'm determined to get you stoned. I know it's yucky at first, especially if you don't smoke - but you just have to push through it. It gets better, I promise."

"This shit makes you sleepy, right?"

"Usually. Depends on how good it is." Caitlin pulls a pipe out of her tracksuit pocket and starts unscrewing it.

"Fuck it. I need sleep, let's see if I can do this."

"Alright!" Caitlin smiles, doing a cute little fist pump. She packs some marijuana into the pipe, screws it up again and points it at me. "Do you want me to hold it? Is it easier if I do it?"

I grab the pipe. "No, it's okay, I'll hold it but if you can hold the lighter that would be good, at least until I get the hang of this. I'll probably just burn my fingers off."

"Okay so when the flame hits the bottom, you've got to inhale, suck the air into your mouth, and then down into your lungs, and try to keep it there a while." Caitlin holds her cigarette lighter directly under the pipe. "Are you ready?"

I nod. Caitlin lights the lighter, and I cautiously start sucking through the pipe. I don't really feel anything happen. After a few seconds it tastes too disgusting and metallic to continue, so I stop.

Caitlin laughs. "You're afraid of it. You've got to suck the air in a bit harder than that."

I spend a few seconds spitting air, trying to get the horrid metallic taste out of my mouth. "This is really disgusting... but let's go again. I want to see if I can do it."

I ready the pipe up to my lips and Caitlin lights the lighter again. I start sucking in air, making an effort to get as much air in as possible. I feel hot smoke filling my cheeks, I try to hold it there as long as I can, but a gradual burning sensation in my nostrils gets the best of me after a few seconds and I exhale, smoke leaking out of my mouth and nose at once.

Caitlin smiles, she seems impressed. "Hey, that was better! You need to try and get it down more into your lungs though, but you inhaled enough of it this time to actually do something! Another seven or eight times and you'll be on your way!"

"Are you serious? I have to do this another seven or eight times before I even feel anything? It's hurting my nose! I don't think I can stand it that long!" I clutch my nose, hoping that if I pinch it, it will stop hurting.

"You're going to get metal mouth anyway, all smokers get that, but your nostrils won't burn if you exhale properly through your mouth. Don't hold it in your cheeks, you've got to get that smoke down into your lungs properly. Let's go again."

I ready the pipe and Caitlin lights up the bottom again. My nose still hurts from last time, and I'm nervous about it, I don't want to make the pain worse. My sucking isn't too bad this time but once I have the smoke in my mouth, I can't work out how to get it further down. The smoke gradually leaks out of my nose again, causing a much sharper burning sensation on the way. I exhale and then clutch my nose again, trying in vain to numb the burning.

"I'm sorry Caitlin, I can't continue. This is hurting too much!"

Caitlin takes the pipe away from me. "I guess we'd better stop, but that was a good effort."

I'm still pinching my nose. "How the fuck do I stop this burning?"

"Just wait it out."

"I'm just not built for this. Isn't there a better way?"

"Well, if we had access to a kitchen we could bake it into some brownies, but the agency would probably have a fit over that because of the diet we're on. I'm sure they'd much rather we just smoke it!" Caitlin starts laughing, repacking the pipe for herself this time.

I smile a little also, I guess that is pretty funny. "I guess I just don't have the discipline to do drugs properly."

"You know, we really need to up your delinquent points. You being such a ratbag and not even doing drugs, that's just slacking, you're missing out. Have you even had sex yet?"

I'm taken aback by the total bluntness of Caitlin's question. I don't know how to answer it. Only gross boys ever ask questions like that, but although Caitlin seems super forward she actually also seems sincerely interested. I don't know what to tell her though, I'm not even slightly ready to talk about something like this. I just sit there, trying to think of something to say.

Caitlin draws on her pipe and exhales with the ease that I definitely don't have. She then looks at me and senses my awkwardness. "Okay, that was the wrong question, sorry. You don't like boys though, do you?"

"I should legally be allowed to kill boys."

"Yeah, I feel that, but... do you like them... you know, anyway?" Caitlin looks at me, expectantly.

This topic makes me feel like there's a gaping chasm of confusion in my chest. "I can't even think about that. I don't know, they're just gross and disgusting all the time.

Even when they're not gross, they're gross. I just want boys to leave me alone."

Caitlin draws in more smoke from her pipe. "Okay, so do you like girls?"

"I hate them a little less than boys, sometimes."

Caitlin laughs and it interrupts her smoking, she coughs heavily and smoke shoots out of her mouth.

"Oh, come on, Hana! You know what I mean!"

I think about it, trying to come up with a coherent answer. I'm not sure if I have one.

"Well, girls are pretty sometimes, so I don't know. Maybe? I'm a bit confused."

"You haven't figured yourself out yet?"

I look downward. "I'm sorry. I don't know... I'm not any good at talking about this."

Caitlin puts her pipe down and gradually shifts closer to me on the bench. I sense that she's inviting me to hold her, but she keeps her arms by her side. I lean my head into her shoulder and she slowly wraps her arm around my back, it makes me jump a little bit but not too much, the school jacket is thick and gives me a layer of protection so I feel safer. As far back as I can remember at school I've been isolated, long before the *wangtta* status, the others at school already knew what I was - tainted, not to be touched or associated with. I'm only to be touched for violence, or to take something away from me, whatever the others wanted, food, money, or anything. How am I supposed to even know what I like? I know I hate it when I'm hurt by others, and I like it when I hurt others back, whoever they are. I wish I could be hurt by others less, and hurt others more. Is that wrong? Does it matter? Caitlin's embrace feels so warm and new. I don't know how to respond to this feeling but I wish I could get closer to her, she's so beautiful and kind. I silently cry into her shoulder, feeling her breath against my head, thinking about answers, discovering nothing.

19. GOOD LUCK

"51.8 kilos. Caitlin, how did you get heavier this week?"

Caitlin shrugs at Ms Han.

"If you've got nothing to say, get off, fatso. Iseul, get up here."

Caitlin gets off the scales and returns to our line-up. On the way back she makes a little face at the rest of us with her tongue hanging out sideways, clearly indicating that she thinks Ms Han is stupid. Iseul walks by her and gets up on the scales, giving Caitlin a subtle mock congratulatory fist-bump on the way through.

Ms Han stares down at the reading. "49.4? You might think you're a princess just because you got yourself a new dress, but you're not wearing it yet, so there's no excuse for you to be any heavier. What do you have to say for yourself?"

Iseul stares at Ms Han. "What do you want me to say?"

"Get the fuck off those scales before you void the warranty on them. Nari, you're next."

I sigh. Ms Han being a rude bitch during our regular weigh-ins is tiresome, and she's not exactly the picture of health herself so she can get fucked, she's easily twice the weight of any of us. I stand in line and try to keep my cool, but seeing the hypocrisy is infuriating. I watch Nari get up, Iseul raises her eyebrows at Nari and nods a little as they walk past each other.

Ms Han looks down at the scales. "50 kilos exactly. At least you didn't fatten up. You're the leader - any thoughts on why you're leading a bunch of fat frumps over to the fried chicken wagon?"

Nari speaks completely flatly, with zero emotion: "Your teachings are so valuable, and you're such a good coach, I think it's because you haven't been around much lately... I think we struggle without your expertise and skill."

It's absolutely clear that Nari is shading Ms Han's lack of attendance at our classes, which has been increasing lately. These last few weeks Ms Han has only been at about half of them before always having to leave early for some bullshit reason or other, not that I mind because she's a hateful bag of a woman and the less of her I see the better. Ms Han can't really say much against this obvious shade disguised as a compliment, but her face says it all as her expression screws up angrily.

"Bullshit, get off my scales! Shu, you're up!"

Nari walks off and Shu runs up to the scales. I don't really want to watch Shu do anything at all, so I turn to my right and I notice that Youngsook already has tears running down her face, no doubt anticipating torrents of abuse from her upcoming weigh-in result.

My attention is immediately diverted back to Shu as she shrieks: "Hey, that's not right! 48.4, there's no way!"

"You're so tiny, how do you even store all that fat in there?"

"I don't know..." Shu says quietly, rocking back and forth on the scales, trying to act cute or something.

"I guess it's your stupid fat head that's the problem, get the *fuck* off my scales you piece of shit! Hana you're up!" With the word *'fuck'* Ms Han simultaneously slaps Shu across her head, knocking her back. It's hilarious, I start giggling, fortunately Ms Han doesn't notice.

"Ow! That hurts!" Shu squeals as she hurries off the scales and back into our line-up. I make eye contact with Shu as I walk past her and up to the scales, just to see if she's crying, but sadly, she isn't. *Oh well, hit harder next time Ms Han.*

I adjust my feet on the scale as Ms Han glares at me. I look down. The scales read 48.4 kilos - how?

"Got anything to say for yourself, fatty?" Ms Han grimaces, trying to look scary or whatever. She's pathetic, the only reason why I don't slap the shit out of her is I know how much trouble I will get into. I don't want to be kicked out of the group for giving this idiot what she deserves, so I just stare at her.

"I've hardly eaten all week. I think your scales are broken. You should check them."

"They will be if you don't get your chunky elephant legs off them, Hana."

This bitch, I know I shouldn't lose it at her, but I'm so close. I stand there for a few seconds just looking at her up and down, hoping she understands that I'm judging her fat fucking face.

"GET THE FUCK OFF!" Ms Han yells.

With incredible restraint, I slowly step off the scales and start to move back to my line position, being careful to maintain eye contact so she doesn't deliver a surprise clip to my head like she did with Shu.

"What are you glaring at, MOVE! Youngsook, you're up!"

I walk past Youngsook on my way back, mouthing a quick "good luck" to her.

Ms Han then steps in front of the scales, blocking Youngsook's path.

"Wait. No, no way. Get the fuck back in the queue Youngsook. I can see the fat on your bones. I can feel you absorbing fat from the atmosphere with every breath and converting it into fat on your disgusting body. You're not even getting on these scales you fucking pig, you're not ruining my precious scales which are worth way more than you will ever be, just go back to the line-up. Don't walk too fast either, you might have a cardiac arrest, you fucking walrus."

Youngsook starts sobbing as she returns to her spot in the line-up.

Ms Han keeps yelling. "You are all a bunch of fat filthy pigs! Never in my life have I seen a line-up of such fat sons of bitches!" She then walks straight up to Youngsook.

"What the fuck are you crying for? Who gave you permission to cry? I know you're trying to lose weight but I don't think the weight of your tears is going to be enough to compensate for the fat on your pig body! Hurry up and dry up!"

"I'm sorry..." Youngsook sobs as she tries to get herself under control.

This isn't good enough for Ms Han, who starts yelling and slapping Youngsook in the head repeatedly with each syllable: "YOU - DO - NOT - CRY - IN - MY - GYM - YOU - FAT - FUCK!" Youngsook starts bending down and cowering, trying to be compliant and at the same time protect herself from the blows.

I feel someone pushing me aside, it's Nari. She takes my place next to Youngsook and then reaches out in front of Ms Han, stopping her blows from connecting with Youngsook by blocking them with her arms. Nari then slowly walks forward a couple of steps, forcing Ms Han carefully backward. Nari is a lot stronger and fitter than Ms Han, who can physically do nothing about her movements being controlled. Nari pushes Ms Han back until she can't reach Youngsook anymore, and then lowers her arms.

"I'm the leader. This is my responsibility. If you want to hit someone, you can hit me."

Ms Han winds up and slaps Nari across the cheek as hard as she can. Nari turns her head slightly and just absorbs the blow like it's nothing. Ms Han then hits Nari a few more times, faster, but weaker hits, seemingly in frustration. Nari seems even less bothered, just absorbing the attacks with her face.

Nari stares at Ms Han with a blank expression. "Are you done? Are you going to actually coach us now?"

Ms Han winds her hand up and hits Nari one more time, this time with a closed fist. This takes Nari by surprise as she is knocked back a little, but remains standing. Nari then just raises her eyebrows a bit but doesn't react further. Ms Han suddenly walks away and storms out of the gym, slamming the door as usual.

"Are you okay?" I ask Nari.

"Little bird hits. She hits even weaker than you!" Nari turns to face me, she's smiling but I notice that she has red bruises on her cheeks and her nose is bleeding.

I point to my own nose. "Some blood there."

Nari puts her wrist up to her nose and catches a drip. "Thanks, I'll go and take care of the bleeding, won't be long. Look after Youngsook." Nari pinches her nose and wanders off in the direction of the bathroom.

I look over at Youngsook, she seems to have calmed down now that Ms Han is out of the room. She looks back at me and takes some deep breaths.

"Placing bets on how long before we see Ijun arrive to give us time off for the day!" laughs Iseul.

We all laugh a little. Ijun suddenly announcing Ms Han's absences has become a routine event.

"Less than thirty seconds!" says Caitlin.

"Hey everyone..." I look over at Shu. She's stepping on and off the scales, while looking at the reading. "Hana's right. These are broken! I weigh different each time I'm on these! 48.4! ...47.6! ...48.1! ...48.7, oh no!"

A couple seconds later, the doorway opens again, slowly. Ijun walks in and bows softly to us.

"*Annyeong haseyo.* All classes are..."

"I WIN! Yes!" shouts Caitlin, fist-pumping the air and jumping up and down.

We all start laughing while Ijun looks at us, perplexed. Even Youngsook manages a little smile.

Ijun then continues. "Classes are cancelled. Free time for the rest of the day, except Youngsook, you still have singing lessons at the usual time. Please take a folder each, they are all the same, I will leave them here."

Ijun is holding a stack of plastic sheet folders, which she leaves on Ms Han's desk at the rear wall of the gym near the scales, before quickly exiting the room.

Shu is closest to the desk so she grabs the stack, leaving only one folder behind for Nari. Shu starts distributing the folders to each of us. She hesitates a little when she comes up to me and looks at me warily.

"Thanks," I mumble, snatching the folder out of her hand, hoping to grab it quickly enough to hurt her hand somehow. No such luck. I open the folder up and take a look, it's the same one that we were given before for the "Show Me Love" concept. I flip immediately over to the dresses and I notice that the designs have all changed. The backs of all the dresses are much higher than before, showing skin only down to shoulder level. The fronts of the dresses have changed less, they're the same as before from memory.

"Wow, the new dresses are even more pretty!" gushes Shu.

I look over at Iseul, who's staring at the dress plans intently. She doesn't seem upset by the changes but I can see something's ticking over in her mind, she has the faraway look of someone who is trying to do a math problem in her head.

"Satisfied with that?" asks Nari, who I didn't notice has just re-entered the room. I turn to look at her, she's holding some tissue paper up to her left nostril. She's staring at Iseul.

"I think... this will be fine."

"That's great because now that we finally have these again, I'd actually like to learn the damn dance now without the reference material being snatched away." Nari dabs her nose with the tissue, checking to see if the bleeding has stopped.

Iseul stares back at Nari, flatly. "There's no rush to learn it. We're not debuting next week, you know."

"The sooner we learn it and get good at it, the sooner we can debut though. Where's my folder?"

Blood suddenly resumes pissing out of Nari's nose and starts making a mess of her tracksuit and the floor. I look at Nari and point to my nose again. "Hey Nari, just letting you know that you're bleeding everywhere."

"Fuck! Back in a minute..."

Nari jams the tissue paper back in her nostril and runs off in the direction of the toilets again.

"Who wants to hide the folder from Nari?" I say to everyone as she's walking out.

Nari yells at me while she's running off. "FUCK YOU HANA, I HEARD THAT! IF I DON'T SEE THAT FOLDER WHEN I COME BACK, I'LL BEAT YOU!"

I giggle a little. I guess I won't hide it. Nari is no fun.

20. PRIVACY

"Show-show-show me love, ah... Know-know-know my love, ah..."

Shu is playing with her plastic sheet folder, singing various parts of the song to herself. All of us are in the dorms sitting on our beds, except Youngsook, who is in another room somewhere having singing lessons. I wince as Shu grinds her way through the melody. Is it possible to beat someone to death with a plastic sheet folder? I don't know, but I want to try it.

"Shu, why are you trying to sing it? We don't even know how the music goes yet!" laughs Caitlin.

"Yes, I do! I can hear Youngsook through the walls. Listen!"

We all stop talking for a moment. Shu is right, when everyone is silent it's possible to hear Youngsook quite clearly through the building walls. She sounds good, certainly better than any of us are likely to.

"Wow, her voice is powerful," says Caitlin.

"It's amazing what someone can hear when you shut the fuck up for two seconds, Shu," I laugh.

"Hey!" Shu yells at me.

"I'm sorry, your singing is just annoying."

"Hana..." Nari says, threateningly.

I don't feel like getting destroyed by Nari today, so I walk back my statement. "Okay! Okay! I'm sorry Shu. I'm just... easily annoyed by singing, I guess."

I wait for Nari to say something, but she doesn't, however Shu actually gets the hint and shuts up. Even though the silence is awkward, I'm grateful.

"Hey Shu, how does the chorus to 'Show Me Love' go again?" asks Iseul, laughing. Oh my god, that troll.

"It goes *I just want you to show me, show-show-show me love, ah...*"

"Okay, toilet break!"

I get up out of my bunk and walking into the hallway. If I can't beat Shu to death or at least insult her a lot, I'll just have to leave the area until she shuts the fuck up. I don't exactly feel like going to the toilet either, but it seems like a good place to go just to get some guaranteed privacy. I walk into the toilet area, open one of the two cubicles, sit on the seat and latch the door closed. It's not so uncomfortable in here, the toilets in this building are nice seats that seem to get cleaned on a regular basis unlike the horrible dirty squatting toilets at school, plus I can't hear Shu from in here. I start to wind down emotionally a bit and feel relaxed. I slouch back on the seat diagonally and lean my head against the cubicle wall, thinking pleasant thoughts, like how to murder Shu and get away with it. I wonder how hard it would be to get my hands on some rat poison. I've heard rat poison has no taste or smell, so it's easy to slip into food. I guess I would be a prime suspect though, but maybe that's not a problem,

I'm sure the *aegyo* gets beaten out of people in jail so there would be nobody as annoying as Shu in there. After a couple minutes of thinking, I start to become drowsy and lose track of time.

I'm in a semi-sleep state when I'm woken up by someone else opening the door to the toilet area. I hear someone's footsteps come up to the cubicle and stand outside the door.

"Hana."

I look down, I can see Iseul's feet in the gap between the toilet door and the floor. What the fuck does she want?

"What?"

"Can I come in?"

"What? Fuck off! What the fuck for?"

"Nari asked me to check on you. I'm just making sure you're okay."

I groan. "Yeah, I'm fine, I promise I'm not slitting my wrists in here or anything."

"You've been nearly a whole hour on the toilet!"

"Yeah, I just want some privacy from certain annoying bitches, is that okay?"

"No, it is not! Open up, I need to actually see that you're okay."

Opening the door to Iseul, I don't think so.

"Leave me alone."

"I'm not leaving." I can see Iseul tapping her foot under the door gap.

This is too much. Can't she just fuck off?

"Stay out there then, I don't give a fuck."

Iseul doesn't say anything further. I just sit there and do nothing; she's eventually going run out of patience surely. I'm much more patient than anyone when it comes to being confined in small spaces, I can wait the entire night if I have to. I hear Iseul moving around, and I see Iseul's knee on the floor instead of her foot. She must be going to poke her head under the cubicle, I get ready to kick her in the face.

"*Annyeong*!" she says in a stupid *aegyo* voice as her head appears in the gap.

I immediately thrust my foot out in her direction but she's too far away for it to connect. "GET LOST!"

Iseul's head disappears from my view, she's probably getting back up. Is she going to leave me alone? I don't hear footsteps walking away so I guess not. I don't hear anything else either, I guess she stood back up and is just waiting there. Then I notice that the privacy latch of the toilet door is turning very slowly - somehow, she's turning it from outside.

"No, you don't!" I yell, as I quickly stand up and grab hold of the latch to keep it in the locked position. I can't apply enough strength; the latch keeps turning anyway. How? Iseul isn't a weakling but I wouldn't think she's this much stronger than me, I even have the advantage of the latch handle on my side. After a few seconds of struggle the latch pops open and Iseul swings the cubicle door out, then immediately steps forward right in front me so I don't have any leverage at all to swing the door back in her face.

"Easy!" Iseul says, grinning at me. She waves her right hand, which holds the tool she obviously used to force the privacy latch - a pocket knife.

I instantly flinch back as far as the tiny cubicle space will allow, hitting my head on the rear wall. The cubicle is small and having Iseul this close up in my personal space is upsetting and gross because I really don't like this tramp, but the knife is a lot *more* upsetting. I stare at it, breathlessly, not knowing what to think. My thoughts start racing, I can't control it. *Is this going to be like that time when Namgil told me that I had ten minutes to get him a warm pastry for recess but the store he wanted it from was a ten minute walk so I had to run there and back and by the time I got back his pastry was cold and he dragged me into the toilet to punish me and I remember the feeling of the metal blade against my collarbone and the cold tiles on my face and him asking me if I liked how it felt and if I brought his food back cold on purpose it's not going to be like that is it?*

Iseul sees my gaze fixated on the knife and how I'm completely freaking out. She rolls her eyes. "Relax, idiot. I have brains, I'm not a dumb psycho like *you*."

She folds the blade into the handle. Thank fuck for that, she just was using it as a tool to open the door up. I feel really stupid suddenly. I slide back down onto the toilet seat, relaxing just enough to become conscious that my body is shaking and my legs are now really weak.

Iseul looks at me up and down. "You seem really messed up. I'm sorry, I had no idea. You could have said something?"

"I was just fine until YOU turned up!" I scream at her.

Iseul backs up out of the doorway and raises her hands. "What the fuck did *I* do?"

I'm not in the mood to explain anything to this bitch. "FUCK OFF!" I scream, slamming and latching the toilet cubicle door closed as hard as possible now that Iseul has backed up enough to not be in the way. The sound reverberates through the building, I'm sure everyone else can hear it. A few seconds later, I hear someone come rushing into the toilets, judging by the determined-sounding footsteps, it's Nari. Nobody else in the group walks quite like her.

"Iseul, what happened?" Yeah, it's her.

"I didn't do anything! I just opened the door and she flipped out!"

"Better not have."

"I didn't do shit, I swear it!"

Nari raises her voice a little as she talks to me through the door. "Hey Hana, are you okay in there?"

"I'm *just fucking fine*, I just want some privacy, that's all. Can everyone just fuck off and go mind their own business for a while?"

I hear Iseul sighing. "She's fine, really, I saw her. She's just being a cow, as usual."

"Yeah okay. Scream if you need anything, Hana."

Nari sounds like she believes Iseul, that's fine with me if it means she's going to leave me alone. I hear Nari and Iseul walking out of the toilet area together, so I start to relax a little bit more. I become conscious that I'm breathing really heavily. I try to slow down my breaths a bit and think a little about what just happened. I guess it's not Iseul's fault that she's an insensitive dipshit who doesn't understand that maybe breaking into someone's toilet cubicle holding a knife might be an issue, dumb silver-spoon bitch, I guess. How the fuck did she actually get a pocket knife in here though. That fucking snob must be well-connected if she can get drugs and weapons as easily as the bullies at my school can. Guess she's in deep with something or other so I'd better not fuck with her too much and attempt to at least be a little nice to her. It's a goddamn shame because I'd really like to bash that ugly bitch. She's kind of short and not too tough, I think I could take her, she only was able to overpower me and open the latch on the cubicle because she had the knife as leverage. It would be neat to get that knife off her one day, I could find a few uses for that. I can feel myself becoming drowsy again, hopefully I can doze off uninterrupted this time. I feel myself gradually sliding off the toilet seat so I slide myself completely off it and sit beside the seat on the floor instead, in the small space between the toilet s-bend and the tiled wall. I feel secure in the confined space, so I lay my head on the toilet seat, and allow my mind to drift off again.

21. DISCIPLINE

"*Hanahanahanahanahanahana...*"

I wake up. I realise I'm still on the toilet floor. How long has it been? Also, what the fuck is that noise?

"*Hanahanahanahanahanahanahanahanahana hanahanahanahana....* ah, you're right! It worked!"

Shu's voice. Of course they would use *her* to wake me up. I look from where I'm sitting towards the door and I can see Shu's head peering at me, in the gap between the door and the floor. Unfortunately, from this position she's nowhere near in reach of my feet. She has a huge grin on her face.

"Go kill yourself, Chinese dwarf!" I yell at Shu.

"I told you it would work!" I hear Caitlin laughing.

"Get out of there Hana and stop being a bitch while you're at it, it's time for morning exercise," says Nari.

I hear them all walk off as I squeeze up from the gap I'm in, and slowly unlatch the door, which swings open. Nobody's left here, they're all obviously in gym, so I make my way out to the gym area. When I get there, the others all stare at me.

"Well, you look like shit. How did you sleep?" asks Youngsook.

"Best night of sleep since I got here, I think. No Chinese bitches snoring in my ear."

"Why aren't you in your gym clothes?" asks Nari.

I shrug. I completely forgot that I'm still in my pyjamas. I turn back around the way I came. I'm just about to exit the gym when Mr Park comes in.

We all bow. "*Annyeong haseyo!*"

I walk briskly back to the middle of the gym space with the others, feeling a little embarrassed about my attire. The CEO did have to come in at right this moment, on the one day when I'm dressed like this, didn't he?

Mr Park addresses all of us. "It is good to see you all. Thank you all for your diligence and patience with us so far during the training process. You may have noticed Ms Han's lack of attendance in recent training sessions. Ms Han will no longer be joining you as she is no longer an employee of the company."

I immediately turn to Youngsook to gauge her reaction, as Youngsook was the one who got along the worst with Ms Han, even worse than me. I notice that Youngsook is trying very hard to hide her own smile.

"We are yet to determine a replacement gym coach. We will begin..." Mr Park suddenly stops talking. I look at the rest of the group and Nari has her hand raised. Mr Park motions for Nari to speak.

"Let me do it."

I roll my eyes. How typically Nari.

Iseul starts talking. "Mr Park CEO, you might as well. Ms Han did nothing. All she did was yell at us, she didn't even know half the steps..."

Mr Park puts his hand up, his way of saying he wants Iseul to be silent. Iseul shuts up immediately. *Oh, to have that kind of power.*

"Nari, Iseul - please come with me."

Mr Park walks out of the room through the office door, Nari and Iseul follow. After the door shuts, the rest of us look at each other.

"Do you think Mr Park is going to start screaming at them?" asks Caitlin.

"Probably not. I mean, Iseul's his niece. I'm sure he'll be nice... oh... wait, never mind I guess..." Youngsook's voice trails off as we start to hear Mr Park's voice getting louder and louder from the other room.

"Glad it's them and not me!" Caitlin grins.

We all stand and wait. We can't tell what Mr Park is saying but he's obviously upset about something. After a few minutes, Mr Park's voice gets quieter again and we all stop listening in fascination.

"This is a good day. Whoever our new gym coach is, it can't be anyone worse than Ms Han," Youngsook says.

"I know, she was a fucking slug." I laugh.

"I know, right? She's there all like 'do the damn dance properly or I'll smack you', like, you do it first, you know? Here I am, fifty-five kilos and super tall and she's twice my weight and she's tiny, it's not fair. She was so trashy. I can't believe she punched me in the stomach!"

"What? When was that?"

"You don't remember?"

I have no idea what Youngsook is talking about, but I have no doubt that it happened. It's the sort of thing Ms Han would do.

"Oh right, you might've been in detention or asleep. Anyway, I hope she enjoys her new job picking up garbage in the streets or whatever. What a trash person. Who knows, I might even get better at dancing now." Youngsook smiles and stretches out her calves while she waits.

"She never got those scales fixed either," adds Shu.

I realise that Nari and Iseul both aren't around, and neither are any instructors. Time to hurt Shu while I can get away with it.

"*Jjangkkae* shouldn't speak," I hiss.

"*Gaoli bangzi!*" Shu responds, glaring at me.

That fucking bitch. I instantly take a swing at Shu's face with my hand, but she's ready for it and ducks the blow. I go to wind up and hit her a second time but something is stopping me, my hand freezes in mid-air, I look behind me and Caitlin has grabbed my forearm. I struggle against her control but I wasn't expecting this, so I don't have a very good position. Caitlin tightens her grip.

"Hey, let go! I thought you were my friend?"

"I am! I like you enough to stop you! We're a team, so can't you just chill?"

"You sound like Nari."

"Well, she has a point. She's not telling you off all the time for no reason, you provoke it. All of us would appreciate it if you could find a way to relax that didn't involve shitting on Shu or trying to sneakily beat her. She's a nice girl, she doesn't deserve your crap."

Shu gives me a smug look. Before I can struggle out of Caitlin's grip and smack the plastic out of Shu's jawline, I hear Mr Park.

"Hana, come with me!"

Oh shit, he's back in the gym and I didn't even notice. I was clearly trying to slap Shu, there's no hiding it. Caitlin releases my arm, and I walk towards the door and follow Mr Park, into a corridor and then an office. Nari and Iseul are both sitting at Mr Park's desk. There's a spare chair in between them. Mr Park motions for me to sit, so I do.

"So, you are the rotten seed that is poisoning this group."

Mr Park's talks calmly but his gaze is intense and terrifying. I stare downward. I'm not sure exactly what the others have and haven't told him, but he just caught me red-handed so there's no point denying anything.

"Yes, Mr Park CEO."

"Do you have anything to say for yourself?"

"No, Mr Park CEO. I am sorry, Mr Park CEO. I know I have been immature..."

Mr Park laughs, cutting me off. "You don't even know exactly what you're in trouble for, and you're already admitting it. You must be a real ratbag in need of some discipline. I shall not waste any more words on you. At half past eight o'clock tonight, if you wish to remain an employee of the agency, you will meet me here, again, at this desk."

"*No!*" shouts Iseul. I look at her, she's... upset? Why does *she* care so much about me? I look over at Nari, who seems confused by Iseul's reaction as well.

"Silence!" Mr Park responds, glaring at Iseul, grimacing like a vein on his forehead is about to pop.

Iseul bows and doesn't say anything further.

Mr Park redirects his attention to me. "It seems that polite requests don't work, firm requests don't work, and even Ms Han's discipline has had zero effect... but I know what will definitely work. All three of you, no more talking, get out of my office."

We all bow and then file out of Mr Park's office.

"Hana, I am really sorry," Iseul says, looking shaken as we re-enter the gym. I don't know what to think. Sorry about what?

Nari stands at the front of the gym, where Ms Han usually stands. "Alright everyone, I have a couple things to say. Firstly, they're not hiring another gym coach, the agency doesn't want to spend the money. That means it's me, I'm now our new gym coach, I'll be showing you all the routines."

Everyone cheers. Even I can't resist cheering a little.

Nari continues. "Don't be too happy, we still have to work. But I promise to be fair."

"Even to me?" Youngsook asks.

"I'll try to be as nice as I can be about it but you really do have to lift your game a bit. Seriously."

Youngsook mumbles something under her breath that I don't quite catch.

Nari then stares directly at me. "Secondly, Hana - is going to be very nice to everyone from now on."

"Yay!" exclaims Shu.

Nari walks up to me. "...because Hana, if you're not nice... I have been told to not punish you anymore, but immediately just hand you over to the CEO."

"Hana called me a racist thing and tried to slap me just before!" Shu squeals.

"Is that true?" Nari looks back and forth between Caitlin and Youngsook.

"Yes," they both say in unison.

Iseul looks at Nari. "Hana is going to get punished enough tonight."

"Are you sure about that, Iseul?"

Iseul looks me up and down in a weird way, I don't know how to interpret it. She then looks back at Nari.

"Yes, I'm sure."

22. THE THREE CLUBS

I'm in the yard alone, sitting on the bench in my tracksuit. I've just had a shower and normally I'd be feeling relaxed but I don't know what's going to happen when I see the CEO shortly. I know it's not going to be pleasant though. I stare up into the night sky, thinking about nothing.

After a minute I hear the sliding glass door open and I turn around, it's Iseul.

"Hey, not much time. How are you feeling?"

Iseul sits down next to me on the bench. I instinctively slide away from her a little.

"Do you care?"

"Listen up Hana, I know it's in your nature to be an unpleasant *wangtta* bitch, but just because we don't exactly love each other like true soul mates doesn't mean I think what's about to happen to you is right. Girls look after girls, okay? So, listen to me, there's a lot I need to tell you, and not a lot of time. I'm doing you a favour you don't deserve and certainly have not earned, so try and be grateful for once."

Iseul is trying to help me, although I'm not sure why. I guess I'll force myself to be nice, because she obviously knows something that I don't.

"I'm sorry Iseul," I mumble, looking downward.

Iseul smirks. "Great, keep that not-being-a-bitch thing up, it suits you better than your usual look. Now, first thing - do you drink?"

I shake my head to indicate no.

"Wrong answer. You drink as of right now. If the CEO asks you if you drink, yes, you drink."

"What's the CEO going to do, force me to get drunk?"

"He's not that type to get someone drunk and take advantage, he has a reputation. But you need to be able to drink. You don't drink *at all*? Never been drunk?"

"Never."

"Wow, okay. I guess I should have expected that."

I stare at Iseul, feeling hurt. I know what she's implying, that because I've been *wangtta* my whole life, I wouldn't have ever had an opportunity to share alcohol with anyone. She's right of course, but that doesn't make it any less hurtful.

"Anyway, here's what's going on. Our CEO is a *businessman*, let's just call it that, and he doesn't just own this agency, he also owns some... clubs. When he gets really shitty at his female staff, he sometimes sends them to work at one of the clubs, I've seen it happen to people before who are disrespectful to him. Since he wants to meet you at eight thirty, that's probably what's happening, because the clubs open late."

"Doesn't sound so bad, working at a club... what do I do, pour drinks?"

"If only! So if he says you have to work at a club, ask him the name of it. American Juice is the name of the easiest one. If you get any sort of choice, you want to work there, not the other two. It's a whiskey bar, what you do there is people pay money to drink with you. It's easy work, you just have to put up with men talking and be nice to them, make conversation, and so on."

"What do I talk about?"

"It doesn't matter, just whatever they want to talk about, literally anything. You're keeping lonely rich people company, basically. The guys who go there are creeps and will probably try to pick you up, of course say no but be polite. The things you have to really watch for are people slipping stuff in your drinks, and people trying to feel you up. Like, some of the guys might try to touch you."

I cringe. "Oh, gross. Can I hurt them?"

"You don't have to put up with any touching that you don't consent to, security will come and take them outside, just scream and make a fuss if it happens, they will notice. Also, drink as slow as possible, you don't want to get drunk so take baby sips. I assume you don't know your alcohol tolerance because you don't drink, but I doubt you have much. You'll probably be drinking whiskey or other hard spirits; these are strong drinks. Your goal is to get them to drink as much as possible, while you drink as little as possible. Just put the drink up to your lips and don't sip more than a single drop of it if you don't have to. Got it?"

I nod my head.

"Okay. There are two other clubs that I know about, maybe he has more than that but if he does, I don't know about it. They're called Club Soap and Blue Tower. I don't know exactly what goes on at either, I've only ever been inside American Juice. But whatever it is will be something unpleasant, you won't like it. If the CEO says you have to work at either of these other two clubs, *beg him* not to make you."

"Do you think it's likely?"

Iseul pauses for a few seconds. "No. It'll be the whiskey club. It's your first time, and you're not in enough trouble to justify the other two. However, if you *keep acting up like you have been...*"

I cut Iseul off. "Okay, okay, I get the message."

"The last thing is, be nice to *everyone* while you're there. You must be polite at all times to everyone you see. I know this isn't in your nature to be a polite and nice person so since you have zero social skills or common sense, I'm just making special mention of it that you should act like a human being for once. Anyway, go and get dressed quickly, I suggest your stupid school uniform that you love so much is appropriate here because you're going to want to be wearing layers, and customers will probably find it cute anyway, it won't piss them off. Go now."

Iseul waves me away. I don't appreciate being insulted but I do my best to let it go. I get up off the bench and walk towards the sliding doors, my mind churning over.

"Wow, not even a thank you or anything. You really are an ungrateful bitch!" Iseul remarks as I walk away.

I turn back to Iseul. "I'm sorry..."

"Ha! Too late now, get out of my face, *wangtta!*"

There isn't enough time for me to argue about this with Iseul. I turn back around and run off to the dorms to quickly get my clothes, and then into the toilet cubicle to get changed because I'm not changing in front of the others. Once I'm in my school uniform, I walk through the gym into the administration area and sit down in Mr Park's office. Nobody is here. I sit and wait for a few minutes, expecting Mr Park to arrive at any second, but nothing happens. A few more minutes go by and I become bored, has he forgotten that he wanted me to see him? I start looking around his office for something to occupy my mind. Mr Park's desk is wooden and has a black plaque with his name written in raised gold text, it looks fancy. The wall behind his desk is frosted glass. On one side wall are some grey filing cabinets, on the other is a large bookshelf, filled with books. I walk over to read the spines, it's all boring-looking stuff about management, accounting and so forth, huge books, how can anyone read things like this without falling asleep? I guess this is the kind of thing people who run businesses need to read, what a life. I think about stealing a book and taking it to my room to help with my insomnia, when I hear the door behind me open gently. My heart jumps - I don't want to get caught looking at his books, it might be seen as disrespectful, could I get in trouble for that? I turn around, it's Ijun standing in the doorway. I breathe a massive sigh of relief that it's not Mr Park.

"*Annyeong haseyo.* Mr Park CEO is occupied with another matter and will not be seeing you tonight. Please re-join the others, you have free time for the rest of the evening."

"Thank you," I reply.

I'm just about to ask if I'm still in trouble when Ijun quickly closes the door and disappears.

I walk back to the dorm and open the door. Everyone's sitting on their beds, they all stare at me.

"That was quick, what happened?" asks Nari.

I look at Nari and shrug. "Nothing, he wasn't even there."

Iseul looks me up and down, that weird look again.

"He probably forgot all about it. Very lucky for you, Hana."

Nari makes an exasperated face. "Wow, us girls really are the lowest priority for our own agency, aren't we."

I look at everyone in the room, nobody says anything, they all just stare at Nari.

23. VIDEO

We're all in our line-up in the gym, in our matching purple tracksuits, we've been asked to dress in these for today. Since Ms Han no longer works for us, we've reverted to our original formation, from left to right; Iseul, Shu, Nari, me, Caitlin, Youngsook. Mr Park is also here.

Mr Park switches on his laptop. "Please assume your starting positions, so I can set up the video capture."

We all move to the opening positions of the dance for "Plastic", the song by EB-K that was the first thing we learned when we arrived at the agency. We're not perfect at it yet, but we're a lot better at it than the "Show Me Love" dance, which is still a bit too fresh for us to do a perfect top-to-bottom run through of, so we're recording a dance video for "Plastic" today so the agency can use it to analyse our technique.

Mr Park starts playing with a tripod on the gym desk, trying to clip his phone into it. He seems to be having a lot of trouble making it happen. I look over at Nari, she looks like she really wants to offer help, but something's making her hesitate, I guess she doesn't want to put Mr

Park in a position where he looks stupid. We all sit and patiently wait in silence while Mr Park fiddles around with the tripod mechanism. After about three minutes of fumbling, he finally figures it out and manages to assemble the tripod, lock his phone into the holder and position it on the gym desk.

"When I start the music on the laptop, begin the routine."

Mr Park backs away from the tripod, moves to the laptop and starts up the song, which begins blasting through the PA system on the gym floor. I move through the motions of the song's dance routine, starting off with the arm movements for the intro which I've done enough times for them to be in muscle memory. I don't look at anyone else, I've done this dance enough to know my place in the formation. I move into some of the broader sweeping movements for the chorus, it feels good. Then suddenly, the music stops just when the second verse begins. I freeze in position.

"What happened?" Nari asks.

I hear laughter behind me and turn around. Caitlin and Youngsook are both lying on the floor. They've had a collision mid-dance somehow. I can't help but laugh also.

"Fucking *ouch!*" Caitlin howls while rocking back and forth, clutching her ribcage, although she can't be that badly hurt as she's laughing at the same time.

Youngsook looks embarrassed as she sits up on the floor, supporting herself with her hands. "I'm sorry about that! I just thought we moved the other way there for some reason."

"Youngsook, this isn't good enough! You should know this routine off by heart by now!" Nari scolds.

Youngsook stands up. "I do... I just got mixed up, that's all."

Caitlin stands up gingerly and pokes a finger into the area of her ribcage where she was hit. She winces in pain. "That's pretty tender now - please remember to go the other way next time, that hit was pretty brutal."

Youngsook's face is red. "Sorry! I'll be more careful!"

Mr Park motions for us to move back to our starting positions for the dance.

"Okay, let's try again, from the top. This is for the cameras, so don't forget that you need to smile, it's part of the performance. Remember that you're so much prettier when you smile."

Mr Park plays the song again and we go through the dance movements. The second time feels better than the first, I feel like I'm really gelling with the song. That is, until the end of the second verse where I notice Shu is slightly out of position. While pushing her back to where she's supposed to be would be a good idea, I don't want to ruin the video by nudging Shu back, so I just adjust my space accordingly and keep one eye on her, which makes it harder to also follow along with the song. Eventually Shu notices she's out of alignment and pulls herself back into formation. The rest of the routine goes by without incident. Once the song finishes, we all freeze in the final standing position.

"And... that's it! We're done." Mr Park presses his phone on the tripod, turning off the recording.

Instantly we all relax. Youngsook, Caitlin and Iseul all immediately collapse on the floor to regain their breath. The rest of us remain standing but we're all about equally exhausted, the routine is physically demanding.

"Hey Hana, come here... how bad am I bruised?" Caitlin beckons for me to come closer, and she lifts up the side of her tracksuit top enough for me to see her ribcage.

I sit on the floor next to Caitlin and crouch down so I can see better. I don't notice anything odd.

"Where am I looking? Looks okay, I think?"

Caitlin grabs my hand and pushes my fingers between her ribs, slightly higher than where I was looking.

"Here, that's where it hurts the most."

I'm not sure if I can see anything at all, but it's weird to have someone directing my touch like this.

"As far as I can tell you're okay. I don't see a bruise or anything." I become aware that even though we've now stopped doing the dance routine, my heart is still racing.

"Thanks, Hana." Caitlin lets go of my hand, pulls her tracksuit top back down and lies down on the floor. "Fuck, it hurts though!"

"I'm so sorry, Caitlin!" Youngsook repeats her apology.

Caitlin smiles. "It's fine, I'm not gonna die. I'll just try to go easy with my body today, I guess."

I look over at Mr Park, he's busy trying and failing to collapse the tripod stand. Eventually he just gives up and walks out of the room and into the admin area with the tripod stand still assembled. I can't help but laugh a little.

"What are they going to do with that video? I don't think I danced too good," Shu says.

Nari looks down at Youngsook on the floor. "You danced better than Youngsook, at least you managed to stay upright. Youngsook, we really need to work on how we can make you more agile. Your skills are lagging so far behind the rest of us. It also doesn't help that you're too heavy."

Youngsook looks at Nari. "Can you not remind me of that every single second of every day?"

"If you want to stop hearing the reminders, lose some weight and get better at dancing. You should practice more than you do."

"I have to do singing practice though. Someone has to carry your failing vocals." Youngsook sounds bitter, she's getting pissed off.

"Listen Miss Fried Chicken, there's machines that can fix my vocal. Nothing can fix your thunder thighs except losing some weight."

I start involuntarily giggling. I cover my mouth to try and stop it, but it's difficult to control myself. Youngsook notices me giggling and gives me a dirty look, I hide my face in shame. I'm not trying to make her feel bad, but I'm sure that she does, and I'm sure that I'm not helping.

Youngsook turns her attention back to Nari. "This is bullshit. You're always on Hana for bullying Shu, but you're bullying me all the time!"

"The difference is that Hana bullies Shu because Hana feels like it because she's a socially maladjusted idiot. Whereas I tell you that you're letting the team down because you're letting the team down. If you don't want me to be so harsh, try putting in some actual effort!"

"You could be nicer, is all I'm saying."

"Yeah, I'll just reward you for being bad, that'll work. I don't think so. Do you really think the results you're getting are good enough? Do you?"

Nari waits for Youngsook to reply, but no reply comes. After about ten seconds, Youngsook gets up and walks out of the room.

"Oh great. So, what now?" asks Iseul.

I feel bad about laughing at Youngsook being insulted, so I get up and run after her. She's easy to find, as soon as I enter the hallway from the gym, I can hear her sobbing coming from the toilet area. I walk there and she's sitting on the toilet seat with the cubicle door open. I stand in front of her, in the space outside the cubicle.

"Hey," I say.

"Hey," Youngsook replies, drying her eyes with toilet paper. "I'll be back out shortly. I just need a few minutes."

I feel so awkward, but I can't not say anything. I try to find the right words. "I'm sorry for laughing at you. I don't mean to, it just... comes out."

"I wasn't that upset about it, I'm more worried about Nari shitting on me all day and night. You laugh at some weird stuff though. I don't really get why you do that."

"Neither do I, I just find things funny that I shouldn't. I promise I'm not trying to be mean."

"I wish I could laugh like that, sometimes. Think you can teach me that skill?" Youngsook smiles a little.

I start thinking about laughter. *One time the group of iljin girls in my science class blocked the exits to the room after everyone had left except me and Haneul, one of the other wangtta girls. They said they wouldn't let me go anywhere if I couldn't make them laugh, so I grabbed Haneul by her hair and slapped her in the head. The girls thought that was funny enough and they let me leave the room, but they made Haneul stay, I don't know what they did to her before she was allowed to leave but it was half an hour before she was let out.*

"I'm sorry. I don't think I can help."

24. DO RE MI

"So this is the scale, it's a five-note scale, and we go up, then down. Everyone listen carefully. *Do-re-mi-fa-so-fa-mi-re-do*. Got it?"

Youngsook is sitting on her bed in the dorms, she scans the room to check our understanding of the vocal exercise. We all nod.

"Okay, great. Let's all now do it together, slowly. On the count of four. One... two... three... four..."

We all sing in unison, except Shu who starts early for some reason. "*Do-re-mi-fa-so-fa-mi-re-do*."

Youngsook looks at Shu. "You were a beat too early. It's the one of the next bar, not the four of the count."

Shu looks puzzled. "But you said *on* the count of four?"

"I guess I meant *after*, rather than *on*. It's a musician's habit, we always say 'on the count of four' but it doesn't mean that it's literally *on* the four in this case."

Shu scowls a bit. "That's confusing!"

"You'll get used to it. Let's do it again. Everyone ready?" Youngsook looks around and everyone nods.

"One... two... three... four... *Do-re-mi-fa-so-fa-mi-re-do*." We all sing in unison this time.

"Okay, so everyone's timing was fine then. However, some of you aren't pitching it right. Let's just go around the room and check everyone. Shu, you go first. I sing, then when I'm done, you sing and try to hit the same notes, in your own time, okay?"

Shu smiles. "Okay! *Do-re-mi-fa-so-fa-mi-re-do*!"

Youngsook holds her hand up. "Stop. Me first. Listen closely. *Do-re-mi-fa-so-fa-mi-re-do*."

Shu repeats Youngsook's phrase. "*Do-re-mi-fa-so-fa-mi-re-do*." I wince, she sounds so painful.

"That was good, your notes are fine. Just, don't attack it so hard. You don't have to project your voice out so much." Incredibly, Youngsook finds Shu's vocals to be tolerable. Maybe she's just being nice.

"Don't people need to hear me though?"

"Shu, you're going to have a microphone *right here*." Youngsook moves her hand about thirty centimetres in front of her face. "That's the maximum you ever need to project your singing voice, it just has to get to the microphone. Try to imagine that the listener is this close to you. Push any harder, and you're just overworking yourself for no reason."

Shu nods. "Okay!"

If this is a clever ploy from Youngsook to make Shu quieter and less annoying, I hope it works.

"Right, Iseul, it's your turn. Repeat after me. *Do-re-mi-fa-so-fa-mi-re-do*."

Iseul watches, takes a deep breath and tries to copy Youngsook. "*Do-re-mi-fa-so-fa-mi-re-do.*"

"Your fifth note is flat. Sing *so* again. *Soooooooooo.*"

Iseul repeats Youngsook's note. "*Soooooooooo.*"

"Still not quite there. It's close. What if we move the entire sequence down a bit? Try singing it lower. *Do-re-mi-fa-so-fa-mi-re-do.*"

Iseul tries to copy Youngsook again, with the new lower sequence of notes. "*Do-re-mi-fa-so-fa-mi-re-do.*"

"Not quite right. It's not your range, you definitely have the range for it. You just need to get that last note higher. I'll come back to you and we'll work on it. Caitlin, you're next. Repeat after me. *Do-re-mi-fa-so-fa-mi-re-do.*"

Caitlin takes a deep breath and copies Youngsook. "*Do-re-mi-fa-so-fa-mi-re-do.*"

"Not bad, pitching is good, but don't forget to open your mouth. The notes will have trouble getting out if your vocal channel is too closed up."

Caitlin sighs. "Yeah sorry. I guess I'm just worried about looking stupid. People don't want to see my tonsils, do they?"

"Don't worry about it. Watch the top singers, they all look stupid when they sing. Just open your jaw up and let it rip, it's okay as long as you keep it relaxed and don't tense up or push too hard."

"I'll work on it."

"Hana - your turn, repeat after me. *Do-re-mi-fa-so-fa-mi-re-do.*" Youngsook looks at me, ready for me to try and sing the passage of five notes, up and down the scale.

I take a deep breath and do my best. *"Do-re-mi-fa-so-fa-mi-re-do."*

"Okay, that's not quite right. You're starting from the wrong place. Just try to sing this one note. *Dooooooooo.*"

I do my best to copy Youngsook. *"Dooooooooo."*

"No - higher. *Dooooooooo.* Can you make it like that?"

I try again to match Youngsook's pitch. *"Dooooooooo."*

"Not quite right. You're having a pitching problem. We'll work on it later. For now just try to practice getting the notes out smoothly. Nari, your turn."

"Do-re-mi-fa-so-fa-mi-re-do." Nari spits out the notes immediately.

"Wait for me first, Nari."

"Why? I can already do it."

Youngsook takes a deep breath. "You're using me as a reference pitch, if you go first, you don't have the reference, so you lose the advantage of something to gauge your relative pitching against. You don't have perfect pitch, do you?"

"How do I know if I have perfect pitch?"

"Sing E5." Youngsook stares up at Nari, who is sitting on the bunk above her.

Nari waits for a few seconds. "Aren't you going to sing it first?"

"No. If you have perfect pitch, you'll know what E5 is without me having to sing it first. That's... like, the *point* of perfect pitch."

"Fine, then."

Nari immediately sings a random high note and Youngsook starts laughing.

"You... don't have perfect pitch, Nari. Trust me on that. Please just... do the exercise. *Do-re-mi-fa-so-fa-mi-re-do.*"

Nari sighs. "*Do-re-mi-fa-so-fa-mi-re-do.*"

"You're incredibly tense. You need to loosen your jaw a lot, you're holding all the tension there. Try again."

Nari tries again. "*Do-re-mi-fa-so-fa-mi-re-do.*"

"Okay, I think we've found our designated rapper."

The entire room laughs.

Nari looks unimpressed with Youngsook's observation. "You're just bitter that I'm actually trying to make you dance properly."

"Here we go yet again," sighs Caitlin.

The door to the dorms swings open. Ijun stands in the doorway.

Ijun bows. "*Annyeong haseyo.* Hana, Mr Park CEO wishes to see you personally. Please be in his office in five minutes."

I bow back to Ijun and she leaves immediately without another word.

"Guess you're getting punished after all," smirks Iseul.

"I guess so."

25. BUYER'S MARKET

"So what's your name?"

"Hana. What's yours?"

The man declines to tell me who he is, instead changing the subject. "You look lost, Hana. Is this your first time here?"

I'm sitting in one of the alcove tables of American Juice, the CEO's "whiskey bar", in a basement somewhere in one of Seoul's red-light districts, which isn't that far away from the dorms. Everything is dark with low light, deep red carpet, and the same shade of deep red on the furniture upholstery. Neon pink, purple and red strips light up various parts of the walls and ceiling. The alcove tables are placed around the edge against the walls of the venue, with plush restaurant-style bench seats on either side of each table. In the centre is the bar, with high wooden benches highlighted in neon and dozens of bottles on shelves out of reach. Some music is playing, old style *trot* ballads, I don't recognise them. There are only two customers here, the one who is opposite my table talking to me, and another one who has just arrived and is currently ordering a drink at the bar. A lone security guard, a massive man who looks well over six feet tall, stands by the customer entrance, playing with his phone. I've been told by the bartender that my job is to circulate between the customers and make polite conversation until agency staff pick me up later in the evening and take me back to the company dorm. The man talking to me looks like he's in his fifties or maybe even sixties, it's hard to be sure in the low light. He is wearing a brown suit. He has thick-rimmed glasses and a kind expression. He keeps both hands on his drink, a small whiskey glass which is nearly empty. I have an identical drink in front of me that I'm not touching until I have to.

"I've never been inside a bar that serves alcohol before."

"How did you get here?"

"I'm on a punishment shift. When I do something that my company doesn't like, they send me here for a while, apparently."

"What do you do?"

"I'm training to be a pop idol."

The man smiles. "What's the name of your group?"

"We don't have a name yet. If we do, they haven't told us what it is. We're just trainees at the moment."

"I've heard the training system is very harsh, is it true what they say about it?"

"I don't know. It's not so bad."

The man looks at me like he doesn't believe me.

I continue. "I mean... yeah it's harsh I guess, there's not much food and I get yelled at a lot, but school is way worse if you ask me."

The man looks down at the logo on my blazer. "Your school was on the news recently. I'm not surprised that you had a hard time there."

"I don't have anything to do with what's going on there now. I haven't been there for a while."

"What does someone have to do as a pop star in training to get sent to this place?"

"I can't control my emotions well. Sometimes I hurt people. You know how sometimes you meet someone, and they are just so annoying and you just want to hit them every time you see them? It's like their face is just so punchable?"

The man nods. "If I am to be completely honest, that feeling is not foreign to me."

"You feel this way too?" My eyes widen.

The man adjusts his posture and sits further forward in his seat. "I run a company that deals in logistics. Our staff have to coordinate driver schedules and shipments of goods. Sometimes things go wrong, and staff do not always act appropriately to fix the situation at hand. I want to remove some of our staff due to their repeated mishandling of important contracts, but the job market for the niche where we employ is a buyer's market right now."

"What's a buyer's market?"

"It means that supply exceeds demand, so those in the market can be choosy. There is more work available than there are people looking for work, so those who have the right qualifications in our field can pick and choose between available jobs. It's not so easy to get qualified staff with experience to replace someone who leaves, and when we do get them, we still then have to train them to work with our specialised systems, which is an expensive process that is time-consuming. So while I wait to find the right people, I have to tolerate existing staff and existing situations that no man should have to endure. It can become frustrating."

"Okay." I try to hide my confusion, because I honestly don't understand at least half of what he just said.

He smiles. "You'd better go and see to the other gentleman at the bar. I'll be here when you return. Take your drink, you can bring another for me when you come back."

I bow. "Thank you."

I slide over on the plush bench seat, get up from the alcove, and walk over to the bar with my drink in my hand. The man sitting on one of the barstools at the bar looks like he's in his thirties, he's immaculately dressed in a black suit and tie and has short cropped hair. I carefully sit down on the barstool next to him.

"*Annyeong*," I say.

"*Annyeong*," he replies. I watch his eyes as he scans me up and down.

I sigh internally a little. I guess I'd better do the making conversation thing. "What's your name?"

"Joon."

"Hi Joon, I'm Hana."

"You look kind of young. Are you a virgin?"

The question startles me with its bluntness.

"What?"

"Are you a virgin?"

"I can't tell you that. Why does it matter anyway."

This son of a bitch, I despise him already.

"Aren't you supposed to entertain me?"

"Nope."

Joon immediately becomes pissed off, I see the expression on his face tighten.

"Bullshit! I'm paying for you with these overpriced drinks; I expect some entertainment!"

"If you're not entertained it's not my problem."

"That's pretty fucking pathetic for a talk bar. I guess I'll be telling your boss that I won't be coming back here."

"That suits me, go home and masturbate!"

"You're an arrogant little shit, aren't you."

Joon grabs my arm and pulls me towards him, then grabs my waist with the other hand, pushing me into his lap, trapping me between his legs while he sits on the barstool.

"Are you crazy? Do you wanna die?"

"Isn't this cosier? You're definitely not a virgin, you have a slutty body. How about we go outside and you show me what you can do with it." Joon shoves a hand under my blazer and starts touching the front of my shirt. I try to pull away from him but there's no point, he's way stronger than I am.

"How about you go fuck yourself, retard?"

Joon tries to get a hand under my shirt and I do my best to fight him off, fortunately it's difficult for him to maintain his grip on me with one hand and navigate my clothing with the other at the same time, so despite his superior strength I manage to force him into a stalemate where I can't escape but he also can't get under my clothes. Suddenly I find myself on the floor next to the bar and Joon is nowhere in sight. What the fuck just happened? I sit up and see that the bar's security guard has knocked Joon down and is dragging him outside by his neck, leaving a row of toppled barstools in his wake.

"Oh, fuck yes!" I yell.

I get up straight away and follow the security guard out of the front door and up the stairs. I hear the bartender say something to me as I'm heading out but I don't quite catch it, I think he's telling me to stay inside but I'm not missing seeing this piece of human garbage getting thrown out for the world, I don't care how much trouble I get into. The guard drags Joon up the stairs with one hand and launches him out onto the concrete footpath outside the venue without a word, like it's nothing. Joon moans and rolls around on the ground, clearly in some serious pain.

"Hey, you piece of fucking shit!" I scream at him.

Joon looks over so he can see my face. As soon as we make eye contact, I repeatedly spit into his eyes. After about five spit gobs I go to kick him and stamp on his head but I only get one swift kick into his ribs before the security guard grabs me by the shoulders and calmly directs me back inside the venue without a word.

When we get back in, the bartender isn't happy. He's about to say something to me when the security guard beckons to him and motions for me to sit back in the alcove with the older customer I was talking to before. I pick my drink up from the bar and then resume my seat in the alcove.

"Are you okay?" the older customer asks.

"Never been better."

I turn back and see that the security guard and the bartender are having some sort of private conversation. The bartender suddenly looks less angry and doesn't seem to want to talk to me anymore, which is a relief. The security guard then looks over at me as he moves back to the front entrance. I give him a wave.

"You're the best security guard ever, mister!"

He gives me a silent nod and resumes his position by the door, casually playing with his phone like nothing even happened.

26. SECURITY

It's late. Caitlin and Iseul are sitting on the bench in the yard, with the protein supplement tub and a big plastic bag of marijuana between them. There isn't room on the bench for three people plus all Caitlin's marijuana gear so since I'm not smoking any, I'm sitting on the ground, leaning my back against the trunk of the closest tree that grows in the small yard area.

"Are you alright after last night?" Caitlin asks me while packing her pipe.

"Yeah, I'm okay."

Iseul raises her eyebrows. "You've been more than okay since you got back. You've been... actually in a good mood. It's not like you, you're usually such a miserable, sour little shit. What happened?"

"It's not much fun talking to creep after creep trying to pick me up, but the security guy there is amazing. He sure took care of business!"

Caitlin passes her pipe and the lighter to Iseul. "Want some?"

Iseul nods and takes the items from Caitlin. "Thanks!" She then lights up without any hesitation, sucking up the smoke with ease. Iseul is at least as good at Caitlin at smoking marijuana.

"Did you just get hit on all night? Is it that bad?" Caitlin asks.

Iseul exhales and coughs slightly. "Caitlin, it's a talk bar. That's what it's for. Disgusting men go there to pick up girls. Hana was one of the girls."

Caitlin looks back and forth between me and Iseul. "So, it's sex work?"

Iseul takes another drag of the pipe and then slowly lets out a cloud of smoke. "Sort of. Not exactly. Well... not really. But kind of."

Caitlin laughs. "What do you mean? Is it sex work or not?"

Iseul passes the pipe and lighter back to Caitlin. "You don't strictly *have* to have sex with anyone, but the guys are hoping."

"That just sounds like anywhere!" Caitlin chuckles as she lights up the pipe.

"It's not quite the same thing. The difference is that you - well, in this case Hana - is hired by the bar, to sit with the guys, and give the nice ones some company and the disgusting ones some company plus the hope that they might get something more out of the deal. Meanwhile the bar charges the customers overpriced drinks and that's how the money is made. So, the guys are basically paying extra money for the bar to provide company and even the odds of them getting some action that night. It's a place for guys with no game, insecure men who don't know how to talk to a girl, because the girl is required to make conversation with them even if the guys have no personality."

Caitlin exhales a massive smoke cloud. "So how does the sex come into it?"

"Some guys just go there because they're lonely, but most want a little action. Guys will negotiate terms and then offer money. While the girls aren't *required* to do anything sexual, most will if the money is good, there's no limit to how much some people will offer. There's an area outside around the back of the venue where those things happen. However, it wouldn't have happened in Hana's case, because she's on punishment shift. They said no money because of our contracts, right Hana?" Iseul looks at me while motioning for Caitlin to pass the pipe over.

I nod. "Why would I do anything with those fucking gross pigs?"

Iseul laughs as she takes the pipe from Caitlin. "Exactly. The agency gets the money, so Hana has no reason to do anything, so she can just say no to everyone, and the guys have to respect it. Someone else in that situation, who actually wanted to make some money, they would pick and choose who they take outside, and for how much, and also how far they go. It's not a bad system, you don't get that kind of choice in many other places."

Caitlin looks at Iseul as she lights up the pipe. "You know a lot about this. You've been there, obviously? Did you work there?"

Iseul winces as she holds her breath and then exhales smoke. "No. Definitely not. I know all the staff though, I used to do deliveries there so I know all of what goes on. My uncle has owned that bar since before I was born."

"Who's the security guy?" I ask Iseul.

Suddenly I'm interrupted by a loud voice. "HEY! What are you guys doing?"

All three of us turn around, it's Nari, standing right in front of the bench, none of us noticed her come through the glass doors. Caitlin jumps a little.

"Oh, hi Nari" says Iseul, lighting up her pipe again.

"Guess we're busted now!" giggles Caitlin.

"What the fuck is that shit? Is this drugs?" Nari looks absolutely livid.

Caitlin and Iseul suddenly start laughing, Iseul has to interrupt her draw on the pipe halfway through and smoke starts coming out of her nose. Nari looks at me, I just shrug at her. I'm not saying anything.

"'Is this drugs'... oh my god I think I'm dying..." Caitlin starts laughing so hard that snot is coming out of her nose. "Oh shit, gross..."

Nari paces back and forth, furious. "*It's not fucking funny!* I can't fucking believe it. Are you trying to ruin our careers? Do you know what will happen if people find out you do this? Are you *all* doing this?"

Iseul looks up at Nari, and holds the pipe out, smiling. "Want some?"

"Fuck all of you, I'm telling the CEO about this *right now!*" Nari storms off back through the glass doors in the direction of the admin area.

"Go right ahead, have fun!" Iseul yells after her.

Nari turns back around and stares at Iseul from the doorway, seemingly confused about Iseul's lack of concern.

Iseul stares back, giggling. "Go on. Off to the CEO you go. What are you waiting for? Don't let me hold you up!"

Nari storms off a second time into the admin area, this time making it all the way through.

"How long do you think before she's back here?" Caitlin asks.

"Not straight away. Give it a few minutes to sink in. Hana, do you want some?" Iseul holds the pipe out in my direction. I shake my head to indicate no.

Caitlin also shakes her head. "Hana doesn't smoke, she doesn't really like it."

"A pity, Hana - you could sure fucking use it."

"Yeah, that's what I tried to tell her. She gave it a go."

I shrug. "I tried it, it's gross, I can't stand it."

Iseul hands the pipe and lighter back to Caitlin. "Right. Well anyway, the security guard... you want to know who he is?"

I nod. "Yeah. He was so great."

"There's a few that rotate. Describe him."

"Six feet tall at least, muscular."

"That doesn't narrow it down at all. Was he Korean or foreign?"

I think about it, it was dark in the club, I only remember a few details. "Korean. Can't remember if he was bald or just had really short hair. Very quiet, didn't say much at all to me, just nodded a lot."

Iseul nods. "Ah. That's definitely Sunghun. You saw him beat up people?"

"Did I ever! He was fucking amazing."

"Well, he's being paid, you know. That's what he's supposed to do, help if you're in trouble."

Help if I'm in trouble. Where has that been all my life.

I look over and see Nari coming back to the yard through the gym area.

"Fuck *all of you*, seriously, you are all fucked." Nari rudely pushes Caitlin's marijuana gear off the bench and sits in the cleared space, right between Caitlin and Iseul. She then puts her head in her hands and starts sobbing.

"What happened, Nari? I know you want to tell me!" Iseul smiles cheekily.

Nari looks up, with tears in her eyes. "Okay, so I go into his office and he's *right there*, and I say to him 'do you know that Iseul and Caitlin and maybe Hana are all *getting stoned* outside in the yard and they have *a massive bag of drugs* that would put them in prison for like three years at least and our careers are totally *fucked* if we do a drugs test or the cops come here or anything like that' and you know what he says to me? *Do you know what he fucking says to me?*"

Iseul cheekily smiles at Caitlin, winking. Caitlin covers her mouth trying to control herself from laughing again.

"He says *what, bigger than this?* and he opens up the drawer of his and pulls out *another* massive bag of drugs!"

"YES!" Caitlin starts laughing hysterically. Iseul and myself also start laughing.

"What the fuck crazy shit have I gotten into?"

Nari's anguish at this is just priceless.

"Welcome to the agency, I guess. Don't worry, we'll still debut!" Iseul says.

"We'll just have a lot more fun than other groups while doing it!" adds Caitlin.

Nari continues to sob. "This is such *fucking* bullshit. I'm taking this shit seriously, but am I the only one? How the fuck did I wind up here? I didn't sign up to be part of some criminal... thing! I'm changing agencies the first chance I get, I'm serious!"

"You really think it's all that different anywhere else?" Iseul says. "You should be happy you're at least with a legitimate agency that is going to try and debut us and push us out there for real. They're not all like that."

"You promise me this is a legit agency and not some money laundering scheme and I'm not wasting my time?"

"Other agencies are much worse than just a money laundering scheme. Oh, Nari. You are so naive; you have no idea. It's kind of cute."

"Just answer the question."

Iseul puts her arm around Nari. "Relax, it's legit. Or at least, as legit as it gets. I wouldn't be here if it wasn't.

Remember I'm family, they wouldn't put me in the group if it was a scam. I know you work hard and this shit isn't your speed but..."

Nari grabs Iseul's arm and pushes it away. "Damn right it isn't. I should report you all to the police!"

"...and based on your conversation with the CEO just now, how do you think that's going to work out for you?"

Nari just stares at Iseul, looking bitter and not saying anything.

Caitlin looks at Nari. "Hey Nari, you forgot the most important part of your story."

"What?" Nari snaps back.

"Was the CEO's bag bigger than ours?"

We all start laughing again, while Nari goes back to holding her head in her hands.

"I *can't fucking believe* you people..."

"You're upset about this, aren't you?" Caitlin asks.

"YES of *course* I am!"

Caitlin puts her arm around Nari.

"Hey, I'm sorry you're upset, Nari... I really am, but... I think I'm just a bit too stoned to give a fuck!"

Caitlin and Iseul both collapse in laughing fits.

27. STUDIO

For the first time, all six of us are lined up in the recording studio. It's a small set of rooms at the other end of the hallway from the gym, that is always locked. Youngsook is here often for vocal lessons, but the rest of us don't get those, so we've never been allowed to set foot in this part of the building until now. We're standing in the big group recording room, a large area with thick beige carpet on both the floors and the walls. There's a music stand and a large microphone in the centre of the room, and big wooden double doors leading out into the hallway plus another big door that goes out to a control room with huge double-glass windows. Mr Park is here in the recording room with us, and standing next to him is Mr Nam, a weird short piggish man, he looks maybe sixty years old. He has a full head of hair but something looks wrong about it, I'm pretty sure he's wearing a wig.

Mr Park smiles. "Now I will leave you all in the capable hands of Mr Nam, who will oversee the recording of your vocal parts. You will have no other schedules today apart from this, Mr Nam will determine your breaks and when he needs you, so please follow his direction for today and resume normal schedules tomorrow. Good luck!"

Mr Park then exits the room through the large hallway door and closes it shut. Mr Nam walks up so he's standing in front of us.

"I've only seen Youngsook before, I haven't seen the rest of you. Welcome, ladies! The others besides Youngsook, please step forward and say your names, one by one, so I can remember you! We'll be working together closely today!"

"I'm Iseul." Iseul steps forward one step.

Mr Nam looks Iseul up and down carefully. A little too carefully for my liking, this guy is already giving out gross disgusting pig vibes. Don't tell me I have to spend the entire day with this creep.

"Ah, Iseul, I will be sure to remember that name! Are you looking forward to singing today, Iseul?"

"Yes. We haven't been able to do much singing yet. I'm keen to try it out." Iseul is clearly bullshitting; I can tell by her tone which always gets really snooty at times when she has to impress someone. I can't stand her upper-class act, but I still feel a bit sorry for her because it's clear that this creep likes her and she can no doubt sense it.

Mr Nam smiles. "Wonderful! Please step back and the next person please step forward."

Iseul moves back into the queue and Shu steps up, taking a couple steps. "I'm Shu! Happy to meet you!"

Mr Nam smiles again, only slightly. "Hello Shu! Please do well today! You can step back in the queue." I guess he doesn't like Shu much, guess I can't blame him for that.

Nari then steps up. "I'm Nari."

Suddenly I hear a loud vibration. Mr Nam's phone is going off, he has it rested on a music stand in the middle of the room, it rubs loudly against the metal of the stand.

Mr. Nam grabs his phone and switches it off. "I'm sorry about that. Nari, you can step back." He doesn't even give Nari eye contact.

It's my turn. I step forward a couple steps. "Hi, I'm Hana," I say, doing my best to sound unenthusiastic.

"Thank you, Hana, please step back now." Mr Nam says this while barely even looking at me. he's still so preoccupied with his phone. I shiver as his gaze scans across my body very briefly, fortunately he doesn't seem that interested in me, that's a good thing.

"You're the last one, please step up." he says motioning to Caitlin.

"Hi, I'm Caitlin!" she says.

Mr Nam spends a good ten seconds just standing there and ogling Caitlin before speaking.

"Caitlin, we'll start with you today. Can you please help me set up the microphones?"

"Sure, I'd love to! Just tell me what to do!"

Mr Nam turns to the rest of us. "Ladies, the rest of you can wait over in the control room. There are some large couches there against the walls behind the control desk, please take a seat on those, there'll be enough room for all of you to relax comfortably. I only need one person in this room to help me do microphone positioning. The door is soundproofed, please shut it once you go in."

We all file into the control room. There are four huge leather couches on one wall, plus a water dispenser with some glasses underneath and a small glass coffee table in front of each of the couches. In the middle of the room is a big office chair, a couple mixing desks, huge metal panels lined with hundreds of knobs and three big computer screens, plus some mysterious rectangular boxes with blinking lights and a ton of cables coming out of them. A few sets of speakers line the walls. On the other end of the room beyond the desk is a huge window, allowing anyone in this room to see clearly into the recording room. Everyone quickly claims a couch, since I'm the last person to file in, I have to share one with someone else. I shut the door behind me as instructed, and notice the soundproofing immediately; I can't hear a thing that Mr Nam and Caitlin are saying in the recording room as soon as the door is closed. I'm thirsty so I grab a conveniently already-full glass of water from by the dispenser and decide to take a seat on Nari's couch.

"Can he hear us?" Iseul asks.

Youngsook looks at the mixing desk and then through the window at Mr Nam. "Probably not, I think we have to hit a button on this desk to be heard. I don't know which one but I've seen him do it before. We can test it. Everyone, while his back is turned, scream on the count of three! One... two... three..."

We all scream at the top of our lungs. Mr Nam doesn't react to the sound; however, Caitlin catches us screaming out of the corner of her eye and gives us a strange look.

Youngsook laughs. "They can't hear us. Caitlin saw us though, she thinks we've all gone mad probably."

Iseul relaxes a bit and sinks into her couch. "How long have you known this Mr Nam guy?"

"He's the one who's been giving me vocal lessons."

"Right. What's he like? Is he weird to you? I'm getting really weird vibes from him. I think he might be a huge pervert."

"I've never had any problems with him. He's never been inappropriate or anything like that. We just do exercises and run through the song?"

"I thought he was polite?" Shu says.

Nari watches Mr Han carefully through the glass. "You two are just not his type. No offence, I'm not either, and neither is Hana. He acted like all of us weren't even in the room, but he stared at Iseul and Caitlin like he was trying to melt their clothes off with his eyeballs. You noticed it too, right, Hana?"

I nod. "I sure did. He's a creeper, ugh."

"Look at him with Caitlin now, what the hell is he doing?" Nari gets up from the couch and walks forward so she has a better view through the glass. I also get up to take a closer look, Mr Nam is making Caitlin adjust the microphone stands and is just very obviously staring at her ass the whole time.

"I don't think Caitlin knows what she's dealing with, we have to tell her," I say.

"How can she not know?" Iseul asks.

I think about it for a few seconds while drinking the water in my glass. "I guess she's just really keen to be doing something new. I mean, we all do the same shit every day. Maybe she's not noticing because of that."

Nari sits back down on the couch. "Don't worry, as long as this guy is in the room with any of us, I'm going to be watching him like a hawk, no matter what. It's my responsibility to make sure that you are all safe."

"That's good because I can't handle watching this gross pig any more. I swear I will murder him. By the way this water tastes like crap, don't drink it, the tap water in the bathroom is better." I sit back down and put my glass down on the glass coffee table, now half-empty.

Nari laughs. "You're just jealous because you're lesbian for Caitlin, you don't want this guy cutting in."

I look at Nari and lie down on the couch, stretching out. "Actually, I'm just as lesbian for you."

"Ha! What bullshit! You called me 'plastic monster' on the first night here, you bitch!" Nari smirks at me a little.

I can't believe that came out, how did I just say that? I might as well roll with it. "It's fascinating though, your face. I admire the craftsmanship, it's so pretty. Like when you look at some nice architecture, and you think to yourself, someone had to take their time building that just right, and they did a good job, you know?" Nari doesn't have to know that I'm not completely joking. It's a good way to shade Nari that she can't really do much about because it's also a compliment. Finding ways to make Nari feel weird or self-conscious is fun, it feels righteous, because she makes me feel bad often when she disciplines me too hard. It's a form of revenge I can get without getting into a fight, which I'll definitely lose. Also, I'm finding her really pretty at this moment, for real.

"What work have you had done?" I ask.

Nari looks me up and down. "You shady bitch!"

"A whole lot, I'll bet. Eyelids for sure, jaw shave for sure, also nose job definitely. It looks hot. I'm getting hot and bothered over here." I mock-fan my face with my hands a little, before I suddenly realise that I *am* feeling a little heated. Am I really into Nari this much?

"You're an idiot, shut up." Nari diverts her attention back to the window.

"I like your muscle tone too. Look at those ripped back musc..."

I'm interrupted by Iseul screaming. "Holy shit guys! Look at these two!"

"Oh no..." Nari says. "We've got to find an excuse to go out there."

I get up from the couch to get a better look out of the window. I watch as Mr Nam is slowly massaging Caitlin's shoulders. It's fucking nauseating, watching as his gross hands paw at her, that fucking shithead, looking at this sight fills me with disgust. I start feeling nauseous all of a sudden.

"Oh hey, I think I'm actually going to vomit, for real. There's no toilet in this studio area, is there?"

"Nope, you've got to go out to the hallway and use the toilets opposite the dorm," says Youngsook.

"Right, I'm going there, bye now."

I walk briskly out of the studio control room, opening the door as fast as I can, which is pretty slowly as it's a heavy door that feels about three times heavier than the last time I used it for some reason. When I emerge into the recording room, I'm not feeling particularly balanced. I stagger through the recording room, bumping into Caitlin on the way through while mouthing a quick "oops" and then out into the hallway in the direction of the toilets. Once I'm in the hallway the waves of nausea become too much; I double over onto my knees and throw up all over the hallway floor.

"Are you okay?"

Nari crouches down next to me. I guess she was right behind me.

"Yeah, I'm fine, I..." my sentence is interrupted by a second wave of queasiness as another spray of vomit exits my mouth and nose.

"It's fine, get it out of your system."

I groan under the weight of the nausea. "I'm sorry. I don't know why seeing that affected me so much."

Nari says something but I don't hear it as the sound of her voice is drowned out by a third spray of vomit from my mouth onto the hallway tiles.

"Do you think there's any more in there?"

I wait for about twenty seconds before answering.

"Okay, I think that's it."

"Looking at that really hit you hard, hey?" Nari asks.

"I'd like to hit Mr Nam hard."

I spit out the last few chunks onto the floor, before realising that my vision is getting blurry.

"Hey, Nari... I feel really strange."

Nari puts a hand on my forehead.

"You're burning up. Come with me."

Nari puts her hands under my body, and I'm suddenly conscious that I feel a bit like I'm floating. Nari is carrying me, I think. I'm too disoriented to be sure, but I feel like I'm not in control of my own movements. I don't know where I'm going, so I just let myself be led down the hallway. After a few seconds of floating, I'm gently placed in my bed in the dorms.

"Rest up, I'll be back in a moment."

Nari aligns my legs on the bed and pulls the covers over my body.

I want to say something back to Nari, but I don't know what? "I'm sorry?" No, that's not really right. "I love you?" Definitely not. "Hey, how are you so strong and perfect?" Maybe, but I'm unable to speak anything coherently. Nari is so pretty. Nari leaves the room and I gradually lose consciousness, unable to focus any thoughts at all.

28. A PROPER RUN

"Hey, wake up, Hana."

I open my eyes. My eyelids feel heavier than usual. I'm in my bunk. Youngsook is here, she's sitting on my bed, shaking my shoulder gently.

"Wake up Hana, it's time for you to go and record your parts now. Everyone's waiting." Youngsook stares down at me.

"Oh. Hi there. Okay. Move back a bit so I can get out of bed." I gradually sit up and stretch my arms.

"Sure, sorry." Youngsook shifts back so I have some room to stand.

As I stand up, I realise my entire body feels sore and weak. I walk towards the door, but I feel wobbly like I'm about to fall over. Somehow, I manage to stay upright. I become aware that Youngsook is holding my arm, and that this is what's keeping me balanced.

"It's okay, I've got you. Let's walk slowly to the studio, okay?" Youngsook squeezes my arm a little.

"Sure, sounds great."

I make my way with Youngsook out of the dorms, and down the hallway, passing the spot where I vomited before, which looks like it might have been cleaned up, it's difficult to tell as my vision is still in a semi-awake state where everything is blurry and too bright. We move through the heavy door into the studio area. There's a music stand here with headphones hanging off them, and a microphone on a stand, with a weird circle thing in front of it, all in the middle of the room. Youngsook walks me up to it.

"Stand here, behind the circle, and look this way."

Youngsook turns my body so I'm facing the microphone, and behind that, the control room window. I see Mr Nam at the desk in the control room, and behind him I can see the other girls. My vision refocuses and gradually starts to clear up.

Youngsook lightens her grip on my arm. "Hey Hana, I'm going to let go now, are you okay to stand on your own?"

"I guess so, won't know until I try. Don't go too far."

"Put these on." Youngsook hands me the headphones and I place them on my head. Instantly I can hear voices... it's everyone in the control room.

"Hey, what's up! Can you all hear me?"

"Yes!" all the girls in the control room say in unison.

"Are you okay, Hana?" asks Mr Nam.

I wish people would stop asking me this. "Fucked if I know. I feel kind of weak. Should I even be doing this?"

Mr Nam seems unconcerned. "It will be fine. I'm going to roll the song, and you just have to sing along to all the parts. If you can get through it, you probably only need to do this one time."

"Yeah right, okay. What's the circle thing? It's in my way. Can I move it?"

"That's a pop shield, it stops the wind from your mouth hitting the microphone. Just sing right through it, toward the microphone. Don't try to sing around it."

Youngsook opens up a folder on the music stand, which has the words for "Show Me Love" written on it. Suddenly a backing track starts up in my headphones.

Mr Nam talks again, over the top of the music.

"I'm not recording you yet, just try and sing along, we'll do a practice run. You'll hear a guide vocal on the backing track, that's Youngsook's voice. Try and match hers, but don't worry if you get it wrong or miss parts, just do what you can do."

I give Mr Nam a nod. Suddenly Youngsook's singing appears in my headphones, and I try to follow along. I'm already familiar with how to sing the song. I've been hearing Youngsook's voice leaking through the walls of the building enough over the last few weeks as she's been practising it to get a good enough idea about how it goes. Actually singing the tune myself however is another matter.

When I see you looking at me / I don't know how to tell you how I feel / You don't know the feelings inside my heart / The secrets I keep buried deep inside

The first part of the song is easy because it's all pretty comfortably in my vocal range.

I can't explain everything away / I just want to make you understand that my feelings are real

I have no hope of doing this pre-chorus section, I'm not sure how Youngsook is even singing this part, but I can't replicate it, I just sort of warble through it and hope for the best. I try to make eye contact with Mr Nam to see if he hates it, but he doesn't even look up, he's too busy looking at his screens back there or whatever it is.

I just want you to show me / Show-show-show me love / Will you ever know me / Know-know-know my love for you

The chorus has a chanting kind of feel that seems okay to do, I'm not sure if I'm hitting the right notes though. Oh well, he said it doesn't matter so I guess I don't care.

You think you know how I'm feeling / But you don't understand the meaning of my lies / I wish I could tell you everything / But there are some things / That boys can't understand

This stupid fucking rap section is so cringe. I don't know anything about rap, I just try to talk in time to beat. That's all rap is, isn't it? Fuck, I have no idea.

The song then repeats some sections. I think I do them slightly better the second time over, but then I realise the worst part of the song is coming up.

Show-show-show me love, ah / Know-know-know my love, ah / Ah-ah, / I can't tell you how I burn so deep inside / I want you to understand that my feelings are real

What am I supposed to do here, make sex noises? This part is gross, it's so obvious a guy wrote this. Youngsook's guide vocal sounds a bit comical here, I try and be sultry or whatever the fuck I'm supposed to do with it. I guess it works okay.

The recording then stops, I expected it to keep going because there's still a whole chorus to go, but it doesn't.

"Isn't there another chorus?"

"No need, for the final chorus we just cut and paste the vocals from the chorus before. That was good, you didn't miss any sections! How are you feeling about it?"

"That was good?"

I don't know much about music but I know enough to know that it was shit, what the fuck is he talking about.

"It'll be fine. Ready to do a proper run?"

Wow, you literally just don't give a single shit, do you.

"Sure. I'm ready to do it for real."

I notice that my dizziness has mostly left me at this point, I'm standing upright a lot more securely. I take some deep breaths, and I hear the backing track start up again. I move through all the sections, singing everything, but I don't do as good a job, my voice starts cracking and I get nervous. It's different when I know that I'm being recorded. The track stops again just after the weird moaning breakdown part.

"How was it?" I ask.

"I think you can do it better. Let's do it one more time. Don't worry so much about accuracy, just try to do it with energy."

"Alright."

I look up at Mr Nam and I notice Nari and Iseul are both giving the finger to Mr Nam behind his back. I start laughing.

"When you're ready." Mr Nam says.

I give him a nod and he starts the track up. I sing through all the parts again, Nari and Iseul's stunt puts me in a good mood and it helps me focus on the track, I feel like the result is better. Eventually the recording ends at the same place as before.

"That was great, Hana!"

Mr Nam smiles at me from behind the control desk.

"Yeah, I'm happy with that."

"Come in and listen to it!" shouts Nari.

"Fuck, I hate hearing the sound of my own voice. Do I have to?"

"What, don't you want to hear it?" Nari asks.

"No...? Why the fuck would I?"

I look at Nari through the window, who is throwing her hands up in frustration.

"Hana, you do realise that you're going to be a pop singer and you have to get used to hearing your own voice from time to time?"

Iseul looks at me from the control room. "Hey, if I had to hear my own voice on this thing, you do."

I sigh, take off the headphones and walk into the control room, with Youngsook behind me. I feel steady on my feet now, so I don't need her help. When I arrive, everyone cheers.

"You did it!" Caitlin exclaims.

"Well done Hana, only two takes!" says Nari.

Mr Nam nods at me. "I'll play you the track with just your voice alone and not the others."

Mr Nam plays the backing track over the huge control room speakers. The volume is loud and the bass response thumps through my chest. I hold my breath, waiting for my singing voice to appear, getting ready to cringe super hard. When the vocals start, to my surprise they sound clean and on-pitch.

"This is *me?* That's what I sound like?" I ask. I guess it really is my voice, but there is no way I sounded this good.

Mr Nam smiles. "I may have made a few adjustments."

29. TRUST

It's night. We're all lying down in our bunks. Across from me, Shu is reading a book of some sort, and Iseul is playing with her tablet. The others are all lying down trying to sleep. but nobody is having any success yet.

I stare at Iseul's tablet. I wonder if maybe having an electronic device to while away some time would help me sleep. I should try to get it off Iseul.

"Iseul, you told me that if I stopped bullying Shu, you would give me that tablet."

Iseul dials up her snootiness to the maximum. "Yes, this is correct. I did in fact say this."

"So can I have it?" I ask.

"You locked me in the toilets yesterday!" Shu whines.

"That's not true."

Shu puts her book down and glares at me. "Only because Nari saw you doing it and stopped you."

"I was just checking the latch wasn't loose. I wasn't locking anyone in anywhere, I promise."

Nari laughs at me. "Funny how you waited until Shu was in the toilet to do that actual checking. I'm sure that's just a coincidence, right?"

I groan. "*Fine then*, Iseul can keep the tablet another week, see if I care."

Nari looks over at Iseul. "Iseul deserves an award for tolerance anyway for putting up with Mr Nam last week for four hours straight."

Iseul sighs while continuing to play with her tablet. "Do I ever. He made me do that sex-noise part like thirty times, everyone else only had to do it three times at the most. What was he doing, recording multiple takes for his own personal use? He's disgusting, it's so obvious he likes me and Caitlin."

Youngsook looks up at Iseul. "Are you sure? He works with me a lot. He's never been weird like that."

"I think you're reading too much into it, he was a bit touchy-feely but he really wasn't that bad," Caitlin adds.

Iseul raises her eyebrows at Caitlin and Youngsook.

"You two are so naive, I swear. The guy is awful, watch yourselves around him. He gave you those business cards, right?"

Caitlin leans over the top of her bunk. I look up at her as she talks to Iseul. "Yeah. He said they were contacts that could help with my career."

"Not likely. Throw those things out. I threw mine in the bin, you should do the same."

"But isn't this an opportunity?"

"An opportunity for *them*, not you! Get rid of them!"

"Fine then. Hey Hana, I can't reach the bin from here, take these."

Caitlin reaches down from her bunk to mine, holding a handful of business cards. I stretch up and grab the cards out of Caitlin's hand.

"Ah, my cards now, thank you Caitlin, I shall *enhance my career* with these" I say jokingly.

"Throw those out, Hana!" Iseul warns.

I lay back down and start flipping through the cards. "Not yet. I want to know who these people are. Don't you want to know who we need to look out for?"

"That's easy. Everyone male."

Iseul's response stops my brain dead in its tracks. I look over at her. She didn't even look up when she said it, she's still playing with her tablet. *Like what she just said is nothing, it's just how it is.* She's so right, I have to tell her.

"Iseul, if you keep hating men this much, I might start liking you a whole lot more."

"Steady on there, psycho. I don't hate all men, just the ones around here. Anyway, I am not sure if I want you liking me that much. Don't you have enough lesbian relationships to maintain in this place?"

Oh, for fuck's sake, Iseul you bitch.

"I'm not a lesbian, fuck off!" I yell.

"Could have fooled me in the recording studio the other day," laughs Nari.

I don't like where this conversation is going.

"That's not my fault, I was sick!"

Nari snorts at me. "Sick in the head, clearly."

Wow, Nari, what a shock that you're so intolerant. Who would have picked it.

Iseul clears her throat. "Okay. To be fair to Hana... I don't think Hana was sick; I think she was *drugged*. Hana, I saw you take that water from by the cooler, that was already poured and prepped ready to go, probably for me or Caitlin. You drunk it instead and then started saying some crazy lovey-dovey shit which is *very unlike you*, and then became sick shortly after that. I bet that sick bastard Mr Nam had some date rape drug in there and was just waiting for his moment to give it to one of us later."

"Vomiting isn't a normal reaction to being drugged though, is it?" Nari asks.

"No, but it doesn't mean it can't happen. Maybe Hana was allergic to that stuff. Maybe her system couldn't handle it. Who knows."

"You don't know that for sure though, do you?"

"No, I don't... but that doesn't mean I don't believe it. You have to understand what some of these people are like." Iseul sits up to make sure the whole room can hear. "If you're ever offered drinks by anyone, in any setting around here, and that means *any* type of drink, for *any* reason, no. If you didn't pour it yourself from the mains water supply, or open it yourself from a factory-sealed bottle, or buy it from a bar where you watched the bartender like a fucking hawk, forget about it, you're not drinking it."

I'm speechless. Iseul's explanation makes sense to me. Saying what I said to Nari in the studio - in full view and earshot of the others - that's not something I'd normally feel comfortable about doing. It was so awkward when I was talking to Caitlin *alone* about that stuff, so perhaps something was lowering my inhibitions. After that I had trouble walking, too. It adds up.

Shu puts down her book and looks up at Iseul's bunk. "Wow, we really have to be careful! Who do we trust?"

"Each other."

Shu sits up on her bed and looks directly at me.

"Gosh, I think that could be tricky!"

Well, this is awkward. What do I say? I honestly really do hate Shu a lot, but there are degrees of hatred. I'd slap Shu in the face for some fun, or maybe daydream about her getting hit by a train, but I wouldn't do anything seriously creepy and harmful to her, that's just disgusting, I could never. How do I explain this?

Nari looks at me. "Well, there's a question, do you have anything to say about that, Hana?"

"Can I trust you, Hana?" Shu pleads annoyingly. The whole room is looking at me, I can feel their judgement. I'd better come up with something that's honest. Fuck. I take a deep breath and sit up on my bed.

"Okay. Just, hear me out. Shu, I know that we really don't get along..."

Nari suddenly snorts.

"Nari, let her speak!" says Shu.

I keep going, feeling even more awkward. "In fact, I really don't like you. I... *so* don't like you. I don't know if I *ever* will like you. But..." I pause for a moment, trying to think up a good way to continue. "I don't *want* to not like you. I don't actively sit here thinking about how I can hate you more. I mean, if I liked you, my life here would probably be a lot easier, right?"

"Yes, it would," chuckles Nari. Everyone laughs a little, and although I'm a bit offended, I involuntarily laugh a little too.

"Put it this way... Shu, I can't promise what I can't promise, but I can definitely promise this. If I was in a room with you, and one of the guys in my high school classes was also there in the room with us, and I had a gun, you would be totally safe. You would have nothing to fear from me. And if that guy even so much as looked at you the wrong way, let alone touched you or slipped something in your drink or whatever else fucking shit guys do, he would be dead. In fact, he may not even have to do anything like that to be dead, I might just kill him *anyway*, just for *being there*, just because I might *want to*, if I could get away with it. The hate I have for you isn't that big. It's... recreational hate."

"Whaaat?" exclaims Shu.

"Okay, maybe that's the wrong word. What I mean is that it's not serious hate. And I'm trying to control it, I really am."

"Wow, you're so *weeeeeird...*"

"I'm sorry. I know I'm a bad person."

"Still, that's probably the sweetest thing you've ever said to me! Thank you!"

Shu grins at me. I shiver a bit.

30. LOVE LIGHT

"Some special deliveries today! Everyone please collect a box and a folder!"

We're all in the gym, practicing the "Show Me Love" dance steps individually when Mr Park walks in. He's carrying some plastic sheet folders, behind him is the man with blonde hair that I saw back when I saw Mr Park for the first time, I guess he's Mr Park's security guy or his assistant or something. The man is carrying half a dozen cardboard boxes. Mr Park points to a space on the gym floor and the man dumps the boxes there and leaves. Mr Park then places the folders on top of the table at the front of the gym and waves to us.

"Have fun and take good care of the clothing! Don't forget to hang everything on the portable hangers when you're done, so nothing gets ruined! It's very important that we look after the clothing!"

Mr Park leaves the room and shuts the door behind him. We all stop what we're doing and pick a box.

"Who owns which box?" asks Caitlin.

"I can't see a name on any of them - I think we just open them up and see!" says Shu, attempting to open a box with her hands.

Nari notices Shu struggling and rips open the top of her cardboard box. She then distributes the other boxes randomly around the gym floor and rips open the top of each one. I find the closest box to me and look inside. There are some items in here, I start pulling them out - a dress and some shoes. I recognise the dress instantly from the big white frills in the costume design pictures we were previously given, it's Iseul's "Show Me Love" costume.

"Hey, Iseul, I've got your dress here."

"Thanks. I think I've got Caitlin's. Doesn't Caitlin's have the hole in the front?"

Due to being given the plans in advance, we all already know roughly what everyone's clothing is supposed to look like, so we all gather in the middle of the gym and swap our box contents around until everyone has the dress and shoes that they should have.

Nari holds her dress up. "Okay, let's try these on."

Iseul disappears in the direction of the toilet and bathroom to get changed, everyone else strips down to their underwear right there in the gym. I feel super awkward standing around with everyone getting their clothes off and I definitely don't want to be in my underwear in front of the others, so I let the more confident people do their thing and discreetly carry my dress and shoes into the dorms for some privacy. I spread the dress out onto my bunk and take a good look at it, it's actually much prettier looking than in the planning pictures, with a cute princess design and deep blue and purple hues, a subtle style that's not too crazy. I take off my tracksuit and put the dress and matching purple shoes on, everything seems to fit well but then I realise that the dress fastens high at the back with corset-style latches that I can't reach once I have it on. I can't do this myself; I'm going to need some help.

I walk out into the hallway, and I hear Iseul shout "fuck!" from the direction of the bathroom.

"Are you okay, Iseul?"

"Come here Hana, I need some help." Her voice echoes out from the bathroom. No doubt she's realised the exact same thing that I have; we can't get into these dresses on our own.

I walk into the bathroom area. Iseul is standing right in front of me, facing me.

"This fucking dress, I can't do it up from the back myself. I need some help with it."

"Yeah, I'm having the same problem. I think all the dresses are like that."

"I'm so pissed off; I didn't even think of this - I'm so fucking stupid! Hana, can you keep a secret?"

"What secret?"

"I need you to do up this dress for me. Don't tell *anybody* about what you see while you're doing it. Especially not Nari, she will *freak*. Got it?"

I guess I owe Iseul. "I promise. I'm good with secrets."
Of course I am. Why would I even bother to tell people stuff?

"Thank you. Turn around. I'll do yours first."

I turn around and hold up my hair so it's not in the way. I feel the back of the dress getting tighter as Iseul hooks up the metal loops, a process that gets trickier for her as she moves upward. The dress starts to fit snugly, I'm pleased to discover that the size has been cut correctly and it doesn't feel too tight or too loose.

Iseul taps me on the shoulder. "You're done. Now turn around and do mine."

I turn around, Iseul is facing away from me with her back exposed. I look down in amazement. Across her entire back is a huge tattoo, that spirals from between her shoulder blades all the way down to the base of her spine. The tattoo is an outline only, it isn't filled in, so it's hard to even see what the picture is supposed to be, but this is not the type of tattoo that is in any way normal. Not even celebrities have tattoos like this, not female ones anyway.

"Wow, that's some skin art. What is that?"

"You don't know?"

I squint at it but I can't figure it out.

"I don't know anything about tattoos, it's also a bit hard to tell from this angle. But I guess now I know why you wanted high-backed dresses."

"That's fine, it's better that you don't know what it means. Just do up my dress and don't say shit to anyone about it. It's bad enough that Nari knows about the drugs now. I'm sure she'll find out about this too eventually, but I'd like to delay that for as long as possible."

"How is this worse than something that's already illegal?" I ask, gradually doing up the loops on Iseul's dress.

"Just... do the dress up please."

I do the remaining loops up to the top, which is easy to do, I don't struggle with it as much as Iseul struggled with mine. After about ten seconds I'm done.

"You're fastened up. How does it feel?"

Iseul turns around. Her dress looks great on her, deep blue with pretty white frills everywhere, the dressmaker really did an outstanding job compensating for Iseul's visual blandness. "I like it, it's comfortable and it's not too tight. They measured us up right. Yours looks good too, I like the colours. Does it feel okay?"

"Yeah, it's fine. I actually feel a bit special in this thing. Let's go and re-join the others."

We walk out into the hall and back to the gym area, everyone else has their dresses on, and are proudly showing them off to each other. They all look amazing. Caitlin's is the standout, a yellow and white dress with a smart businesslike look and a transparent mesh window in the front that shows the barest hint of cleavage, sexy but not cheap looking. Nari's dress has green silken fabric and is softer and more flowing, the lightness of the fabric means it clings to her and shows off her muscle tone when she moves, it seems like it was designed with exactly this in mind. Youngsook's dress has detailed gold and green leaf style patterns and a bit more of a loose, summery vibe than the others. Shu's dress is red with gold binding, she looks a bit like a spoiled Chinese princess crossed with

Santa's little helper but I'll admit it's a look that works for her. Whoever designed these outfits clearly put a great deal of thought into the best look for each of us.

Youngsook picks up one of the new plastic sheet folders that Mr Park brought in.

"We have a new song!"

I grab one of the folders from the gym table as well and open it up. On the first page, is a lyrics sheet.

LOVE LIGHT

Verse 1:
You came into my room, and gave me your heart
I know why you're here, and what you want to do
Time is precious, and I can feel your soul aching
Let's make the most of us, let me take care of you

Pre-chorus:
There's no need to rationalise our love
The meeting of our hearts is its own reward

Chorus:
I'll turn the switch
I'll shine the love light
It's automatic, fantastic
We will always be together
As long as you wish it
As long as you want it

Verse 2:
You came into my heart, and stole my soul
Now you're gone, and I don't know what to do
Time is precious, and I can feel my heart yearning
For the time that we next meet, let me take care of
you

[Pre-chorus repeat]

[Chorus repeat]

Bridge/middle-8:
There's no need to explain your feelings
I know everything that happens in your heart
I'll turn the switch
I'll shine the love light
Walk in and take what's yours
And I'll take what's mine
Until the next time

[Chorus repeat]

I'm not sure which song is worse, this one or "Show Me Love" but there definitely isn't any kind of lyrical genius happening here.

"Oh wow, I love it!" pipes up Shu. Of course, she has to say something inappropriately positive as usual. I do my best to ignore her.

Youngsook does a little cheer. "Hey everyone - there's no dance steps to this one!"

I flip over to the next page, she's right - there's nothing. I guess this song doesn't have any dancing, maybe it's a ballad. Instead, the pages go straight to sheet music which I still can't read because nobody has trained me, so I skip over that, and then onto the costumes. There are two sets of costumes indicated for each group member, one set is exactly the same clothes set from "Show Me Love", no changes at all as far as I can tell. The second set are some slinky black dresses, all extremely similar for each of us, just slightly different straps and neckline cuts. Mine is really high at the neck with a bow tie attached, it looks cute. The dress fabric looks a bit drab in the photos but the photocopied black doesn't come out very well on the page, so maybe they'll look better when they're delivered.

"How are the dresses, Iseul?" asks Nari, with just a hint of hostility.

I turn to Iseul's page of the dresses. Hers is similar to mine, high at the front, high at the back, but she has a bigger bow with a big black and silver brooch.

"It's fine," Iseul replies.

Suddenly the door to the administration area opens. Mr Park walks through.

"Nari, Iseul... can I see you both in my office in five minutes. Change out of the stage costumes first, please." He then vanishes back into the administration area.

Iseul beckons to me. "Hana, I guess I'll need your assistance getting out of this thing now."

31. PUBLIC

I'm in the yard, Iseul is here, after having had the meeting with Nari and Mr Park. She's back in her tracksuit, but I'm still wearing my costume dress, which makes me feel a bit weird, but at least it's not too uncomfortable. Iseul has her tablet with her.

"Sit down with me on the bench, Hana. You're going to want to be sitting down for this. I'm just trying to find the right page."

Iseul scrolls through her tablet as I sit down on the bench.

"This isn't good, is it?"

"Ah, here it is! Just scrolling down... there, take a look."

Iseul puts the tablet in my lap. It's a video... of *us*, from a Korean video portal site. It's the video of the dance practice that we recorded of EB-K's "Plastic". Iseul presses play on the video. Everything is there, including the part where Caitlin and Youngsook run into each other, which the video replays multiple times over, including a slow-motion replay. The video title reads "TRUE MIRACLE ENTERTAINMENT NEW TRAINEES EBK DANCE PRACTICE FAIL".

I look at Iseul. "I wasn't told this was going online?"

Iseul shakes her head. "Yeah, it wasn't - it leaked, somehow. It's a bit shameful to have this public, but that's not the issue. The issue is in the comments. Scroll down a bit."

I scroll down with my finger and take a look. The first few comments are just people being mean or crude about Caitlin and Youngsook's accident.

Look at these clumsy bitches, the standards for pop music are so low now. Plastic isn't even that hard a song to dance to. What are these girls doing with their lives.

This is the group that's going to make us forget about Redshift? Good luck, nugu.

Not another girl group, there's already way too many, why don't they just give up. Agencies need to stop debuting groups, focus on the groups they already have.

Clumsy girls clogging up my feed with their lack of talent, where do they find these people?

That tall girl can't even dance. And why are we importing foreigners into our music. There's plenty of Koreans who can't get jobs in entertainment.

None of them can dance for shit but that girl who gets hit in the ribs is a fucking babe, I would smash that.

However soon the comments start talking about me.

The girl the camera zooms up to at 1:36 is Shin Hana, I'm from her school. She's a crazy bullying bitch. Every day she would force me to do other student's homework assignments. If I didn't do them, she would drag me into the toilets and punch and kick me. She would often extort me for money, she also tried to make me eat my own vomit once.

Shin Hana is in this group, she's a misogynist. She will pick fights with anyone just because they're a girl, she sent a girl in my class to hospital once. She also hates animals. Someone brought their puppy to school and she kicked it just because it was barking a lot and it annoyed her. What puppy doesn't bark? I hate her, she's a trash person.

Hana pulled a knife on me once and demanded that I masturbate in the school hallway right in front of the other students. I thought I was going to die, so I did it. She then started laughing at me and calling me a dirty bitch. I hate her, she should be locked up and the key thrown away, there's no chance for people like that to reform and be productive in society.

I used to be friends with Hana but then I started dating a foreign exchange student and she threatened him that she was going to stab him if we kept going out. So he stopped going out with me. Two weeks later, she stabbed him anyway, I don't even know why. The guy changed schools to get away from her and eventually suicided, I miss you Hamil RIP

Hana is just so random, she will lash out at anyone. One minute you're minding your own business and the next minute she's pushing you out of a queue or pulling your hair for no reason and you're like "why me, what did I do", she has serious anger issues. How did she even get into a pop group. Those other trainees must be going through hell having to deal with her.

Look at Hana living the good life in a pop music agency after the legacy of bullying she left at our school. So many people went to therapy because of her, scars that won't heal for the rest of our lives. Her gang members still run the school too. I detest this bitch, we need to make sure this group doesn't succeed and they're forced to kick her out.

I can't read this without crying, I have to stop reading.

"I know you were *wangtta* at your school, so a lot of this seems like bullshit. But is there any truth here? If there is, we need to know."

"It's not true! None of it's true!"

"*Absolutely* none of it? I must admit, some of this stuff... does kind of sound like you."

"It's not true... mostly! There were reasons!"

Iseul isn't convinced. "Right then. Let's go through these comments one by one. You tell me how true they are, individually. Let's start off with forcing others to do your homework. Did you do that?"

"Maybe a little."

"Really?" Iseul seems shocked.

I look at Iseul through my tears. "Only a couple of times, because the *iljins* at my school would force me to do *their* assignments, and I sometimes couldn't get them done on time so I would have to force another *wangtta* kid to do them who was smarter, or I would... get dragged into the toilets and punished, as the post says. But I never beat anyone up for that."

"Extortion?"

I shake my head. "That's a lie, never did that."

"Did you ever get extorted yourself?"

252

"No. My mother wouldn't let me have money, so there was nothing to extort out of me."

"What about extorted for other things?"

"Can we move on?"

"Okay - did you make someone eat their vomit? That can't be true surely." Iseul's trying her best not to laugh.

"That's a lie. How gross."

"Yeah, I really can't picture you doing that. Next - you were a misogynist who would target girls?"

"That's complete bullshit. I'm... what's 'misogynist', but for boys, not girls? Is there a word for that?"

"Misandrist."

"Okay, then that's me. One of those. I would target the guys, but only because they were being gross."

Iseul starts laughing again. "Yeah, I can see you doing that! Did you really send one to hospital? A guy, I mean?"

"Yes. A guy was harassing me, trying to feel me up so I cut his head with a metal ruler that was in his bag. It went deep, he had to have stitches and everything."

Iseul backs up a little and holds her palm up next to her face. "Okay, stop there. High-five, please."

I'm still really upset but I manage to crack a smile. I limply give Iseul the high-five she wants.

Iseul continues going down the list. "Right, next one... animal cruelty?"

I shake my head. "No, never. We're not even allowed to have animals in school, that shit is just straight bullshit, they're just trying to make me look bad."

Iseul looks down the comment list. "Um, that next one, I don't even want to say it..."

I look at the tablet. I start shaking my head to indicate it's false and then I start sobbing uncontrollably. I can't even speak about this and what the truth is. Iseul looks at me. I think she understands exactly what I want to say but can't.

"Hana, I'm just going to hold your hand for a moment, is that okay?"

I nod. Iseul grabs my hand and squeezes it. I start crying and howling even more.

Iseul keeps her grip on my hand and lets me cry for a couple minutes. She doesn't seem to know what else to do though, I miss Caitlin's more affectionate nature, I wish she was here right now and not Iseul who is trying to be nice but still kind of is a bitch.

When I finally settle down, Iseul lets go of my hand and continues. "That foreign exchange student comment - there's no way, right?"

"Of course I didn't do that. Do you really think I would do something like that over a *guy?*"

Iseul pauses for a moment.

"Okay, but what if it was over the girl, not the guy?"

"I'm not a lesbian, fuck off. I would never."

"I don't mean to be overly cynical, but I'm not wildly convinced about that, Hana."

"I didn't fucking do it, okay? What else do you want me to say? Are there any more of these?"

"Only a couple. One comment says that you're just randomly violent. You don't have to say anything Hana, I know that one's definitely true!"

"I have to fight back sometimes, don't I? If I don't lash out, I get victimised even more! The *wangtta* at my school who don't fight back have it even worse than me!"

"There's something about 'your gang' here, too. I know you don't have a gang, that's blatantly obvious. You barely even have control over yourself, I really can't see you controlling anyone else, let alone a whole gang of people. So that one's nonsense, we can cross that off."

I just hang my head and don't say anything.

"Okay, so while there is maybe some truth here and there, there's also a lot of bullshit mixed in and it's obvious that you're the target of a hate campaign. Let's talk about a solution now. Do you know who these people are, the ones commenting?"

"Yes. I know exactly who would have written this. Not which person exactly, but I know which *group* of people, definitely."

"That's good, because we have to make this issue go away before it gets bigger, something like this could sink our group if we don't find a way to stop it. That's what our meeting was about, the boss is very concerned. He knows this could blow up in a big way once we debut. I told him not to worry and that I have an idea on how to squash it, though. Are you interested in knowing more?"

I nod my head.

"Hey, Iseul..."

Iseul puts her hands over her lips.

"I know what you're going to say. You're sorry for being such a bitch to me, you didn't realise I could be this much in your corner, and you'll also try to be nicer to Shu as well. Don't make promises you can't keep, Hana. I'm doing this for all of us, not just you. Your repentance is appreciated, but actions speak louder than words, so I'll be more grateful when I see those, rather than your empty tear-stained bullshit and then back to the same old behaviour - got it?"

I nod humbly.

Iseul slides a little closer to me. "Right, now... what about if the plan involved a little violence? Do you think that you would be okay with that?"

I look at Iseul. "I can't fight these people? There's way too many, and they're way stronger?"

"I'm not talking about *you* fighting. Some people owe me a favour. What if I told you that I could enlist a little outside help? You would be okay with that?"

"I would be *very* okay with that."

"It'll take a while to organise, maybe a week. When it's time, I'll let you know."

32. A LITTLE VIOLENCE

"Ride should be here soon. Let's go outside, Hana."

I walk through the hallway, to the front door. Iseul is here, in her Chungbong High uniform, the first time I've seen her with the entire outfit on. It looks stylish, better than my own school uniform, which I also have on. I walk with Iseul out of the front door of the agency building, and down the small footpath to the street. I haven't walked along this footpath even once since I first arrived at the agency months ago. It feels strange to be out in public, even though there's not many people around.

"Why are you wearing your school uniform?" I ask.

Iseul smiles and does a little mock-curtsy. "If we're going to school, I think it's important to dress the part."

"But it's my school, not yours! Why do you even have it at all? Why even bring it with you to the dorm?"

Iseul laughs. "You're such a hypocrite! Hypocrisy just runs in your blood, doesn't it? Not only did you *also* bring your uniform from home, and not only are you wearing your uniform *right now*, you even wear it *all the damn time* when you're not training!"

"You told me not to wear agency gym gear? This is the only other outfit I have that isn't pyjamas."

Iseul's eyes widen. "Are you serious right now? You didn't bring any other clothes here?"

Iseul goes to say something else but stops herself as a black SUV-style limousine with blacked-out windows rounds the corner. The limousine pulls up at the edge of the footpath and the door opens.

"We will continue this conversation inside the vehicle. Ever been inside a limousine before?"

"No, of course not."

"Stupid question I guess. Mind your head."

Iseul ducks into the limousine doorway and stretches a hand out for me to follow. I get in and sit next to Iseul on the rear seat. The interior is dark and lit with neon, and the tinted windows allow visibility to outside, but not much brightness. One side of the limo is a long couch and there's a minibar on the other side. Four huge, well-built guys are also here, all dressed in black suits, they are all sitting on the long couch part together which barely has enough room to contain their bulging torsos. I start to get a little nervous.

"Everyone, please pay your respects to Hana."

Iseul motions to me. I notice that Iseul has switched to her more grating, pretentious snooty accent.

"*Annyeong haseyo!*" The four men bow in unison.

"*Annyeong haseyo,*" I reply softly, bowing back.

Iseul smiles. "Hana, forgive me if I don't introduce you to any of these gentlemen by name, but I really can't do that, it could cause problems. However, I promise you that they will look after your needs during our journey. Would you like anything from the minibar?"

"I don't drink," I reply, calming down a bit now that it's established that the men in the vehicle are friendly.

"That's right. I should have remembered that. I don't know if I have much that's non-alcoholic here. Soft drink? Water? Milk? I think we might have orange juice here as a mixer as well..." Iseul opens one of the minibar doors and starts rummaging through beverages.

"Milk is fine, thank you."

Iseul pours a glass of milk and hands it to me.

"You're easy to please."

"I haven't had milk in a long time. I really miss it."

Iseul calls out to the driver. "Okay let's get going."

I feel the car accelerate as Iseul then turns back to me.

"Don't worry, he knows where to go."

I sink back in the chair, it's really comfortable and squishy, like a lounge chair. I look out of the windows and drink my glass of milk as the limousine moves slowly through the urban streets.

Iseul switches back to her informal manner. "Okay, Hana, so what's the deal? How did you not bring any proper clothes to a place that you knew you were going to be living at for three years?"

"I don't have any. My mother won't buy them for me. She only buys uniforms for school, that's all I get."

"Come on. You're not a child, can't you buy your own... oh, you don't have money, that's right."

I keep staring out the window. I notice pedestrians and other drivers turn their heads and look at the car as we pass by. "I haven't had casual clothes that fit me in years. Not since my father was around."

"You know, the next time I go shopping for everyone, don't stupidly ask for weapons you moron, just remind me that you need clothes. I can't believe you didn't put that on the list before."

"I guess I've just grown used to not having them, I don't know. Anyway it's not like we ever go anywhere."

"Don't you watch television or read the Internet and miss not being able to wear what you see others wear?"

"I'm not allowed to watch television or read the Internet. Except when we have to for school."

"Okay... but what about when you're not at school and you go out of the house?"

"I'm not allowed to go..."

Iseul interrupts me. "Oh my god, are your parents even more psycho than you? What was your life, seriously? You just go to school, get bullied, and, what else... sit in your room at home? Eat and sleep? And that's it?"

"I don't know, what else am I supposed to do?"

"I'm beginning to really start to understand why you're so fucked in the head, and how you became *wangtta* so easily."

"Gee, thanks."

"I mean it in a nice way. It's not even your fault that you're such a stupid psycho bitch. You've been forcibly made to be stupid and psychotic. I bet this agency seems like a paradise to you."

"I don't mind it here. It's a bit boring and I don't like the discipline sometimes, but it's not that bad."

"Speaking of school, we're arriving at your school in a moment. Where could we park the vehicle for maximum attention?"

I feel the car slowing down, we're arriving at the drop-off point at the school's main entrance. "Not here. Weird cars at the front are no big deal, we won't get noticed much. There's a parking lot around the rear that the students use. A few of the *iljins* own cars, motorcycles or scooters, they're usually there at around this time stroking themselves over the fact they own a vehicle, trying to impress others, such losers. If we park this thing there, we'll be noticed straight away, and then others will show up, this huge thing will be like a douchebag magnet. The idiots always come to the car park when someone shows up with new wheels."

Iseul speaks a little louder so the driver can hear. "Did you catch that? Rear car park please."

The limousine drives around the edge of the school and eventually comes to a stop in the rear car park. There are only a few students here but I watch them and they notice the car immediately.

"Okay Hana, you're our spotter. Stay in the car, and keep an eye on everything, just don't get out of the car, whatever you do. Just point people out for the guys."

I nod and then wait. For a while there's nobody around, and the few people who were milling around the car park all clear off. After a few minutes, more people walk by the area and notice the black limousine, including a teacher.

Iseul points at the teacher. "Do you recognise her?"

I have to squint a bit because the windows are so dark, but as she walks closer to the car, I can make her out. "That's Ms Kang, she's my math teacher. Don't worry about her, just ignore her. No matter what happens she's not going to do anything."

"Are you sure about that? She seems a bit concerned by our presence."

"Trust me, she's a useless bitch. She might act curious now, but as soon as anything bad goes down she'll pretend she didn't even see us. If she gets in the way of what we're doing, just slap her out of the way, she certainly deserves it. But you probably won't have to, she's allergic to any sort of responsibility."

Iseul squints through the tinted glass at Ms Kang. "I'm not so sure, she looks like she's getting her phone out."

"Hey... never mind that, they just showed up!" I point to a group of kids coming down the concrete stairs to the carpark. "All of that group of six there, that big guy, the other guy, the four girls - they're the ones, for sure. Target the big guy first, he's the ringleader."

Iseul nods to the men in suits. "Do your thing, please."

The men put surgical masks over their faces, then two of them reach down under their seat and pull out wooden baseball bats. They open the doors and exit the vehicle. As soon as they get out, Iseul slams the door shut.

"Feel free to steal one of their seats if you want a better view of the action. Driver, can we move a bit closer?"

The limousine rolls forward slightly so the vehicle is perpendicular to the stairs and I can get a good view of what will happen next, but I stay in my current seat because it's comfortable. I watch with glee as the men go to work. The two guys with bats start smashing Namgil the *iljin* ringleader multiple times with solid hits across the face, torso and legs. I watch with astonishment as I see blood and teeth go flying. The guy who he's with, I don't recognise him but he scatters immediately, and so does one of the girls. The other three girls however come to Namgil's defence, and that's where the unarmed guys get to work, keeping the girls away from the bat-wielders and slapping them down with little effort as they repeatedly approach. I recognise Eunu as one of the girls, it's a great pleasure to see her continually try to fight and get tossed around like a ragdoll. While this is happening, more and more students start appearing and crowding around. A few of them try to stop the fight, and also get quickly tossed aside and bruised. The parking lot soon becomes filled with the sounds of crying, screaming girls, blood on the concrete and people moaning while they roll around on the ground. I start crying with joy, it's beautiful. Predictably, Ms Kang must have run because I can't see her useless face anywhere. With Namgil barely conscious and groaning on the footpath, the men with the bats have done their job, they re-enter the vehicle. Iseul applauds them as they enter the car and sit down, meanwhile the other two are still fending off attacks from upset bystanders with little effort.

"We need someone who can convey a friendly message to the others about correct social networking use. Can you pick someone out as a messenger please, Hana? Preferably someone popular that people will listen to?"

I watch the men crush random students into the concrete with their bare hands for a while, until I notice that one of the spectators who hasn't gotten involved is a face I recognise. I point him out to the two men in the limousine.

"See that guy there, that tall, weedy, ugly piece of shit? Get him, bring him in here, unharmed! If you have to force him to come here, do it, but make sure he stays conscious! Hey Iseul, I'll send a fucking message alright, do you have that pocket knife?"

Iseul's eyes widen. "Are you fucking serious?"

"You have no idea." I turn and look at Iseul directly in the eye, I try to keep a straight facial expression but I know I'm tearing up a bit.

Iseul takes a deep breath, produces her pocket knife out of her blazer and hands it to me.

"Girls look after girls. Just promise me you won't kill him; we're not really prepared for something like that."

"Thanks. I'll be good, I promise."

I put the pocket knife inside my own blazer.

The men exit the car, and grab Byunghyun, who definitely wasn't expecting it. He struggles a little but he's easily overpowered and unable to resist, he's brought to the vehicle with no major violence necessary. The men drag him inside and sit on the couch with one of them on each side, holding his shoulders down so he can't move. I immediately squat down in front of the minibar so I'm directly opposite him.

"Hello Byunghyun!"

"Hana?"

"Drop your pants, your dream is about to come true."

He looks nervous as hell, as he should. He doesn't have much choice, so he complies and drops his school trousers.

"You can leave the underwear on. I can work around it. This won't take a moment."

I produce the pocket knife and hold it up to his crotch.

"WHAT THE FUCK?" Byunghyun screams and tries vainly to struggle against the men holding him down.

"Settle down - you're not going anywhere just yet. Hey, I know this might be a bit of an ask, but is it okay if I get an apology? It might affect certain outcomes." I was just going to cut him, but the feeling of having power over Byunghyun is intoxicating, I want to drag it out.

"I'm so sorry, Hana! I'm so sorry, please believe me! Please don't hurt me! Please!"

"Not sure if you're very sincere there. I mean, it would just be in your rational self-interest to apologise when someone has a knife up to your balls, right? I think if I took this knife away, you might be less polite."

The other two men suddenly enter the car, they're a bit bloodied up, but it doesn't look like it's from their own blood, so it's fine.

Iseul taps me on the shoulder. "We might have to move soon, Hana."

I turn my attention back to Byunghyun. "So, since I doubt your sincerity, here's something to remember me by, so you know that at least *I'm* sincere." I push the knife against the side of his crotch deep enough to draw blood, and make a shallow cut, not on, but right alongside his genitals.

He screams in agony. "Hana, I'm sorry! I'm sorry!"

After making the cut, I hold the knife up to his face, with his own blood on it. "There you go, you piece of shit. Now every time you jerk yourself off, you won't be able to help but think of me! Isn't that what you've always wanted?"

"You're fucking crazy!"

"Oh, and if I have any problems and hear about this later from police, or see anything about this or anything else about me or my group online, anywhere, from you or anyone else at this school - and trust me, I'll know *straight away* - I'm coming back, and I'll be cutting deeper, and I'll be sure to take a trophy next time. You had better get out there and spread the word quickly, before I see anything that I might not like."

I turn to the men holding Byunghyun down.

"He offends me, can you please remove him?"

The two men who were holding Byunghyun open the doorway and toss him out of the limousine, throw his discarded pants after him, and slam the door. I then feel the limousine pulling away.

I give the knife back to Iseul. "Thanks for that. It means a lot. I didn't want to have to use the milk glass."

Iseul holds the blade with shaking hands and rinses it in the minibar water tap. "You're freaking me out, Hana. I did say a *little* violence."

"Come on, your boys weren't exactly gentle out there."

"I am not going to ask what he did, but I assume he deserved that."

"I was holding myself back. Thank you, everyone. I definitely wouldn't have been able to do that on my own." I bow to the men on the couch, and they bow back.

Iseul flips the blade down and puts it back in her blazer pocket. "Oh my god. I sure hope that cleans up the comments section, I don't want to have to see the more extreme version of that."

"Do you think Nari will be upset if she knew exactly what we did?" I ask.

Iseul thinks about it for a few seconds before replying.

"I... do not think she would appreciate the violence, no, but she *is* pretty career-driven, I think she would still be more upset if we did nothing. She will be shocked for sure, but as long as I don't go into too much detail, I think I can get her to see it as the lesser of two evils."

"What evils?"

33. ONE ON ONE

"You know, Nari, I really like this way of doing our assessments better."

Shu, Iseul, Caitlin and Youngsook are all at the back of the gym, working on their routines separately. I'm up the front, with Nari.

"Doing this one-on-one allows me to give better feedback. Hop on the scales."

"Are these fixed yet?"

I step up on the scales and steady myself cautiously while Nari looks down at the reading.

"48.4 kilos - no change. Get off them, and then get on again. That's how Shu found out they were broken. I want to see if they've been repaired yet."

I step backward off the scales and then back on them a second later. Nari looks at the readout a second time and laughs.

"48.9 kilos. Okay, get off and then get on again, another four times. Then we'll just go with the average. That'll have to do until they fix the scales."

I jump back off and on a third time and look at Nari.

"48.4 again. Hmm, actually this isn't going to be reliable enough. I mean, how do I know whether it's broken at the low end or the high end of the average. They just need to get these fixed, forget the weigh-in for now. Let's go through the 'Show Me Love' dance steps. Move to the centre, you have it all memorised by now, right?"

"I've been practising a lot."

I adjust myself into the starting position for the dance, trying to visualise my position as if the other girls were around me.

"Okay, I'll count to eight, then start. Sing along as you do the moves if you need to cue yourself, but don't worry about if the singing is any good or not for the moment, it's just to keep your place without the backing track playing, because we don't have one handy right now. Let's go, five... six... seven... eight..."

I move through the movements of the song, to the best of my memory. Nari has the plastic sheet folder for the song with her, but she doesn't refer to it, I'm sure she already has it memorised completely. I get through the first verse and pre-chorus fine, it feels good. The verse and pre-chorus are the parts that I'm told I'll most likely be singing on the final cut of the song, so I've practiced my synchronisation for these the most so I don't get jumbled.

Nari puts her hand up as soon as the chorus begins. "Stop. You need to step right, not left, in that step coming into the 'one' of the chorus. Pick it up again from the middle of the pre-chorus. Ready?"

I nod, and move back to the position that I was in at that part of the song.

"You're doing good so far. Let's start it up again. Five... six... seven... eight..."

I pick up again when Nari reaches the 'one' count, and this time, I move in the right direction. The chorus has some tricky steps that I need to synchronise with the others, but I feel like I get through it okay. Then the song goes to the rap part which is pretty much just me standing around in different poses while someone else does the rap. there's really nothing to it. From there it's back into the pre-chorus again and then the chorus. I nearly make the same mistake as before coming into the second chorus, but I catch myself in the act and quickly move back in the correct direction. I look at Nari, she's smiling at me, she definitely noticed.

"Good pickup - keep going!"

Once I'm locked into the right motion for the second chorus, memory takes over and I'm fine. From here the song goes to the breakdown and then a final chorus, once again the breakdown doesn't have much motion and I'm not really that involved. I finish off the third chorus with no mistakes.

"That's good - now move to the finishing pose, ending fairy!" shouts Nari.

I drop down on one knee and put my hands up to my face with a victory sign, the "ending fairy" pose that's designed to look good on television should the cameras happen to zoom in on my face in particular at the end of the song. I wouldn't consider that likely in reality as I know I'm far from the most attractive person in the group, but I guess it's good to be prepared. I throw on a cheesy fake smile to top it off. Nari seems pleased.

"That's it! You can stop now! Good work!"

I let go of the pose and flop down on the gym floor to catch my breath. The entire routine doesn't seem like it should be as exhausting as it is.

"Just watch those chorus starts, other than that, there was really nothing wrong with that at all. You've picked it up well. Catch your breath for a few moments."

"Hey, Nari!" I hear a voice shout. It's Caitlin, I look over as she comes running up to Nari.

"What's going on?"

"It's Shu. She just collapsed!"

Caitlin points to the other side of the room, where the rest of the group were practising. I sit up on the gym floor and look at the others. Shu is lying down on the floor at the other side of the gym, on her side. Youngsook is bent over her, she looks like she's feeling Shu's temperature, or maybe doing something else, I'm not sure. Iseul's doing something with her tablet.

"Caitlin, go into the admin area, tell whoever is in there about it."

Caitlin nods and quickly runs off through the door to the administration area, while Nari rushes over to where Shu is. I follow Nari to see what's going on.

Youngsook looks up at Nari. "She's breathing fine, but she's looking really pale."

"Good that she's breathing." Nari rolls Shu onto her back. "Go to the break room, grab a chair and bring it here. We'll use it to prop her legs up while we wait for an ambulance."

Youngsook runs off to the break room while Iseul types something into her tablet.

"We don't need an ambulance. I've messaged some people, I've got a car on the way."

"What fucking car, Iseul?"

"Just a car. Ambulance will take forever. Car will be here in five minutes, maybe less."

Nari turns to me. "Fine. Hana, can you go into the admin area and make sure Caitlin doesn't get anyone to ring an ambulance? I guess we won't need it now."

"Sure, I'll do that!"

I get up, run over to the admin area and open the door. On the other side of the door there's a hallway with a glass divider and a bunch of open plan offices. Nobody is here. I take a right turn, and open the door to Mr Park's office, the only one that has actual solid walls. Caitlin is here, but nobody else. She jumps a little when she hears the door open, and turns around.

"Oh, hi Hana! You scared the crap out of me! I can't find anyone to call an emergency for us, are you looking for someone too?"

"Actually, I was looking for you. Nari said to make sure nobody calls an ambulance, because Iseul's sending a ride around to pick Shu up and that'll be a lot quicker."

"Oh, right." Caitlin thinks for a few seconds. "Can you wait here? I'll be right back."

"Sure, I guess."

Caitlin runs past me and out of the office, back through to the gym. I wait in the doorway to Mr Park's office, and look around. I wonder how come the other offices are always unoccupied. I've never seen any of the other staff at the various computer terminals. Before I can think about it any longer, Caitlin comes running back into the office.

"Everything okay?" I ask.

Caitlin takes a few breaths after running. "Sure. I just needed to check something. I told them that you found me anyway, so they know I'm not calling an ambulance. I think Shu will be alright. Like, I know you don't *care*, but... it's still pretty bad that she collapsed, right?"

"It's pretty funny if you ask me! I'm sorry, I know, I'm terrible..."

Caitlin walks around Mr Park's desk and sits in his huge office chair. "I know you don't like her, but she tries really hard, and she never complains. She's so hassle free, compared to, I don't know, Youngsook, who's always complaining about food and being miserable, or Nari, who's always complaining about Youngsook complaining about food and being miserable. This is the only drama we've even had with Shu. I hope she's alright, I guess she's been pushing herself a lot." Caitlin senses my disinterest. "You don't give a single shit, do you?"

273

"I'm sorry. I mean, what can I say? I really find her so irritating. I get that she's not a bad person though. Just... bad for me. Bad for me to be around. And I have to be around her all the time, you know? From when I wake up to when I fall asleep, she's always there, even when she's asleep I have to listen to her snore. Maybe if we didn't have to be in the same room day in, day out, perhaps I could like her more then, but it's hard when you're forced to be with someone you don't like constantly, you know? I mean, it's different if it's someone I like more and actually *want* to be with... like you."

As soon as the words leave my mouth, my heart jumps a little in my throat, I realise how I must sound. I look at Caitlin nervously. Caitlin just stares at me for a while and reads my nervous gaze. She's figuring me out. *Uh-oh.* I feel awkward and self-conscious, I can't help but lower my head in shame.

"Sit next to me. Pull up a chair."

I nervously grab one of the chairs that face Mr Park's big office chair, drag it over to Mr Park's side of the desk and sit next to Caitlin.

Caitlin looks at me, concerned. "Wow, you're terrified, aren't you?"

I nod.

"You like me, right?"

I nod again.

"Like, you *really* like me, right?"

I try to nod a third time, but I just kind of end up standing there being awkward.

"You've been through a lot of shit. Have you ever been touched by someone, who you actually wanted to touch you?"

I shake my head to indicate no. I've been trying to hold in my sadness but I can't do it with this question. I do my best to talk while tears form in the corner of my eyes.

"Does when you held me in the yard before, does that count?"

Caitlin smiles. "I don't know. Does it?"

I don't really know what to say to this, so I don't say anything.

Caitlin moves a little closer to me on the chair. "I know this is really weird for you. I don't want to hurt you, so I'm not going to touch you. But you can touch me, if you want to."

I'm hesitant. I don't even know what to do. What if I do something wrong?

"Don't you have a boyfriend?" I ask.

"If we had a good relationship, do you think I would have packed my bags and come to Korea for three years? Trust me, he's a dick. He doesn't even have good weed."

I smile a little at Caitlin's observation, but I can't get over my nervousness about the imminent threat of intimacy. I need an excuse to not act.

"I just feel like it's wrong, maybe?"

Caitlin gives out a little snort. "The other week you took a ride with Iseul and stabbed a guy while she watched and you high-fived and bonded over that shit like you were going to the amusement park. But *this* feels wrong?"

It's pretty funny when Caitlin says it like that. It makes me feel a little better.

"I'm sorry. I'm just scared."

"Okay, how about I go first. Have you ever been kissed by a girl?"

"No."

"Would you like me to try?"

I nod.

"Don't worry, I'll go slow. You just tell me if you get freaked out, okay?"

I nod again.

"This chair is huge and way more comfortable. There's enough room for two here."

Caitlin stretches out her right arm, and very slowly wraps her hand around my back, pulling me off my own chair and onto hers, I feel a hesitant jolt as her hand moves around my ribcage, but only for a moment, then I start to feel more secure. I gradually slide forward, as Caitlin brings her lips up to mine. I feel like I'm surrounded by warmth, I want to get closer. I wrap my arms around Caitlin's waist and press myself against her body.

"So... you're okay with this, then?"

Caitlin brushes my hair away from my face with her other hand. I squeeze her waist tighter.

"Yes."

"So much for going slow, I guess."

34. CHARITY

"It would be nice to have something else to eat, just once."
Youngsook groans, while picking at her chicken breast.

Nari stares at Youngsook. "If you don't want it, give it
to Shu. She fainted yesterday, she could use the nutrition,
whereas you on the other hand still need to cut."

Youngsook doesn't say anything. She continues eating,
staring at her food and looking gloomy.

I look over at Shu as she ravenously wolfs down her
food. She went to hospital yesterday and they fed her
through an intravenous drip for a couple hours, then sent
her back here. Since then she's been looking pale and
withered, not her usual self. I think to myself that Caitlin
likes Shu for some reason, and I like Caitlin, so maybe I
should make an effort to be nice to Shu a little. I guess I'll
never be rid of this annoying Chinese bitch, and we're all
stuck in this group together, so I might as well try to learn
how to at least live with her. I'm not that hungry because
I've been a little distracted mentally over the past day
thinking about Caitlin and how we're going to next meet
away from the others, so I push my bowl in front of Shu.

"Thank you, Youngsook," says Shu, without looking up.

Everyone else around the table looks at me and gasps. Shu then looks up as well, probably wondering what the fuss is. Her eyes practically pop out of her skull as she realises that it's me who gave her the extra food.

"Hana...?" Shu says, her mouth gaping open like someone cut her jaw tendon, which is an appealing thought but sadly probably not one I'll ever realise.

"I said that I would try to be nicer. I meant it. You need to eat."

"Thank you, Hana!" Shu beams, as she grabs my bowl and spoons the contents into her bowl, then gives it back.

"You didn't spit on it or anything, did you?" Nari asks.

I smirk a little at the thought of that. I wish I'd thought of it a few seconds ago but my mind was elsewhere.

"We're probably going to debut sooner than expected. What if Shu collapses during a performance and we have to cancel something important? Also, we have to look good for next week's photos. I'm trying to think of everyone."

Nari raises an eyebrow. "It's kind of... not like you, to think of everyone. What brought this on?"

I look around at everyone's reaction. I can see that Caitlin and Iseul are both desperately trying to keep a straight face. Caitlin would surely know my motivation, and I know she told Iseul what happened, because they get along and talk a lot, especially when they smoke weed together, so Caitlin would have said something to Iseul about me and her getting closer. Nari, Youngsook and Shu on the other hand just look confused. That's fine, it's not their business.

I try to keep my expression neutral. "I don't know, I'm just trying to be a more mature person. I'm not going to lie and say it's easy, but I know it's something I should do."

Shu looks up from her food bowl and smiles at me. "Your efforts are appreciated! Thank you!"

Nari stares at me. "You've got a pretty long track record of bullying Shu, so you're not off my radar yet - not by a long shot. However, I also appreciate the effort. Keep it up, and I'll see how much I can trust you in the future."

I look at Nari and don't say anything, then I look over at Iseul, who can no longer keep a straight face and starts grinning like an idiot.

"I'll see you in the gym, Hana. Enjoy the company of your new best friend!"

Iseul laughs as she gets up from the table and walks out into the hallway. I look in Iseul's food bowl, I notice that she's left the egg white in there, which is pretty normal for Iseul, she only eats the whole egg when she's absolutely starving.

"Do you want it?" asks Youngsook. "I'll have it if you won't."

Nari immediately grabs the egg white and puts it in Shu's bowl, then glares at Youngsook. "You're cutting, stop sabotaging yourself."

Shu quickly picks up the portion of egg and eats it in one bite. "Thank you, Nari!" she says with her mouth full.

Youngsook shoots Nari a dirty look back. "I'm fucking sick of this shit, Nari! I didn't pick on anyone, and I get picked on all the time!"

Nari is unsympathetic, as usual. "I'm not picking on you. I'm trying to get you to adhere to your diet. I'm the leader, that's my job!"

"All I do is try my hardest! Where's my medal for not bullying the other members, huh? When do I get a break? When do you have something nice to say to me?"

"You don't get any medals, you don't get anything, what do think this place is? What do you think we're working towards? Do you think your voice is enough? You don't work on the dances, you let this team down *constantly* with your sloth dance moves, you don't do *any* extra dance practice and just bum around during free time, you don't even *try* to curb your eating, so until you make some fucking minimal form of actual effort Miss Pork Chops..."

"I've fucking had enough of your insults!" Youngsook interrupts. All of a sudden Youngsook stands up, grabs Nari by the hair and pulls her off the chair onto the floor. "You fucking bitch!" she screams.

Nari tries to slap Youngsook but it doesn't connect, however Nari does manage to grab Youngsook by the scruff of her tracksuit top and pull her down onto the floor as well. Both of them slide around on the dining room floor trying to slap and kick each other, with neither of them connecting blows or getting the upper hand. Nari is strong, but Youngsook is just a lot bigger, so they're about evenly matched, there's no clear advantage that either of them have. Meanwhile half the chairs have gone flying across the room and the table has tipped over. I notice Shu has scattered to the far corner of the room, she looks terrified, while Caitlin just stares blankly, looking as stunned as I am at what's happening in front of her. All of a sudden, I hear Iseul running back into the room, she immediately runs up and dives onto the floor between Nari and Youngsook to try and break up the fight. Instantly she starts absorbing blows from both Nari on one side and Youngsook on the other as they try to reach each other.

"I need some fucking help here!" Iseul yells.

I quickly dive onto the floor to grab Nari and try to pin her onto her back. I can't hold her down, I'm not that strong, but I'm still in the way enough to stop her from hitting Youngsook effectively. I look quickly over at Youngsook, Caitlin is trying to restrain her, also with limited success.

"Fuck you, you fucking bullying trash! I fucking hate you!" Youngsook yells.

"Are you crazy? Stop justifying being a lazy bitch! How badly do you wanna get hit?" Nari screams back.

Youngsook is furious, I've seen Nari this angry before, but not Youngsook. "You don't intimidate me! You think you're so superior and can throw your weight around but that won't work on me!"

"That's only because you're a fat disgusting lazy slag who doesn't exercise, doesn't practice, doesn't do shit! You're sabotaging the dreams of not only yourself but everyone in this room! You have no respect for anyone else's efforts! I'm supposed to be the leader, but I can't lead you to anything! What do I have to do to get you to lose a kilo, you fat slut?"

I do my best to try and pin Nari down to the floor, but I'm not strong enough to keep her held in one position. "Get the fuck off me you lesbian," Nari scowls as she kicks me in the legs, not enough to hurt but enough to push me off her, away in Youngsook's direction.

Before I can even tell her to fuck off for calling me a lesbian, Youngsook screams something that I don't quite hear and gets up, knocking Caitlin aside easily and trampling right over Iseul. As I lay on the floor, I see Youngsook's feet coming straight for me.

Suddenly, a noise. "*Hanahanahanahanahanahana...*" it's Shu's voice?

I awaken to Shu humming my name like a mantra. Something wet and cold is rubbing my face.

"Yay, she's awake!" Shu exclaims.

I open my eyes and wait for them to adjust to the light. What just happened? I'm looking up at a ceiling. Caitlin and Shu are both standing over me, Caitlin has a towel in her hand.

"Hey, how are you doing?" asks Caitlin.

I groan and slowly sit up. I become aware that my head really hurts. It feels like no time has passed at all. "What happened?"

Caitlin laughs. "Nari got the shit beaten out of her! Her and Youngsook are off with the boss somewhere, getting lectured probably. You've been out cold for about five minutes."

I look around slowly, trying to ascertain how much I've been injured. My neck doesn't feel too stiff, but my head is throbbing. I notice that the furniture in the dining room has moved about and is strewn all over the place.

I stand up gingerly. "I don't feel so great, I think I'm going to go and lie down." I start walking off in the direction of the hallway, when I notice I'm a bit wobbly. I feel someone grab my arm.

"Hey, I'll walk you."

It's Caitlin. We walk slowly together out into the hallway and then across to the dorm room. I enter the dorms with her guiding me and notice Iseul is here, lying down on her bunk. Caitlin moves me over to my bunk and releases my arm once I'm in a safe position.

"Iseul, how you holding up?"

Caitlin reaches up to Iseul's bunk and taps her on the shoulder.

Iseul looks over at us and groans. "Careful, I'm in so much pain right now! Why did I try to break up the fight, that was so dumb, I should have just let those two idiots kill each other. Then we could have had a nice peaceful four-member group."

I sit down gently on my bunk and fall on my side, letting my head slowly rest on the pillow. The wobbliness gradually subsides, it feels good to be lying down on something soft.

Caitlin sits on the edge my bed at looks over at me. "You'll be okay, Hana?"

"Yeah," I mumble. I don't really have the energy for a conversation right now. The pain in my head numbs my ability to think straight, so I just lie there and let my attention wander. I'm dimly aware of Caitlin playing with my hair as I drift off to sleep.

35. PHOTO

"Are we done yet?"

"Just hold still, please."

I'm sitting on a chair in the gym, in my "Show Me Love" stage outfit, getting my makeup done. The makeup lady was introduced to me half an hour ago as Marie, some foreigner. I don't know where she's from but I wish she'd go back there. Marie waves some fluffy brush thing in my face, which is making me squint and flinch back.

"Can you be a bit gentler with that fucking brush, fuck."

"Don't swear at me." Marie scolds me in her annoying accent. I really want to hit this woman but all of us girls are here dressed up for the photoshoot, Mr Park is here, and there's a photographer here as well, so I can't do anything too overt to make myself feel better about having to sit in a chair for ages and get poked and prodded by this bitch because it might fuck things up.

"Just do the fucking makeup and be a bit gentle, is it that hard?"

"You are really rude, you know. Other girls would be grateful to have the kind of opportunity that you have in this company. You will have to have your makeup done all the time so you had better get used to having some gratitude, and also... holding still. Especially since you haven't even had any work done. You are going to have to be in the makeup chair a lot to compensate for that. You should at least consider getting your eyelids done like the other girls. You are so ungracious."

And make your job easier? Like I give a flying fuck, just do your job, bitch.

Marie grabs my head harshly while she touches up my eyeliner, pushing on my skull right where I got hit the other day by Youngsook's foot.

"Fuck! It's sore there!"

"Stop complaining, the less you complain the sooner we're done."

After a few seconds, Marie finally releases the pressure on my injury. She then reaches into her makeup toolkit and pulls out a hand mirror.

"Take a look."

I reach out to grab the mirror when suddenly I feel some hands touching my shoulders from behind. I nearly jump right out of my seat.

"You're looking radiant."

It's Mr Park, complimenting me on my appearance.

Don't you dare touch me you fucking creep. "Thank you, Mr Park CEO."

Mr Park remains holding my shoulders for a few seconds, just long enough to drive home how unsettling and inappropriate it feels, and then lets me go. I exhale deeply, and then angle the mirror in my hand so I can see my face. I'll admit it, this ugly annoying foreign bitch has done a pretty good job of my makeup, significantly better than I could do myself given how out of practice I am with makeup in general. I move the mirror around to look at myself from another angle and I notice Mr Park is still behind me, checking me out. It would be great if he would stop being gross but I guess that's probably not going to happen. I hand the mirror back to Marie.

"Hana, please go to the photographer" she says.

I don't respond, but I'm happy to finally be done with this annoying slag and her makeup so I walk over to a space against the rear gym. The wall area has been cleared and a green sheet has been taped up behind where I'm standing. The photographer is here, playing with some equipment doing something, I don't know what. Behind him, the other girls in the group and the CEO gather around to watch me get my photos taken.

"So, what do you want me to do?" I ask. I stretch my legs out, which are stiff from sitting in the makeup chair.

"I'm not ready for you yet, just relax for the moment," the photographer says.

I keep stretching my legs and then bouncing on my heels, trying to work the stiffness out of them. Meanwhile I also check out the photographer. I'm guessing he's about thirty-five years old and he's slightly overweight and kind of scruffy with long scraggly hair, I guess when you're the one behind the camera and not in front of it, you don't have to look good. After about a minute he seems like he's finally getting his shit together.

"Okay, it's all ready. Make a pose for me."

"What sort of pose?"

"Just anything. I'm testing."

Great, now I have to think of something on the spot. Caitlin notices that I'm looking a bit awkward so she points at me and does a fancy elegant ballet style pose, so I just copy her pose. I hear some clicks from the camera.

"That's fine. Now try and do something cuter."

"Like what?"

As soon as I say the words, Caitlin and Shu both start doing cringe *aegyo* poses. I try to copy them as best I can. The photographer stops taking photos, gets his head out from behind the camera and looks at me.

"Use your face a bit more. You're looking glum, try to smile a bit. You're so much prettier when you smile."

Fuck you, I hope you get murdered. Why do you men always have to say shit like that. "I'll work on it."

I'm not really feeling like smiling right this minute. All of a sudden, I notice Caitlin sticking her fingers up at the photographer's back while he can't see. Alright, that's pretty funny. I can't help but laugh a little.

"That's it! Keep that energy going!" the photographer shouts.

I go through as many cute poses as I can while I've got the smile going. Each time I see the flash, I move to something slightly different. I start to get into the rhythm of it and I gradually feel slightly more confident. After a few minutes, the photographer seems satisfied.

"Okay, that's it for Hana's solo shots, now we need some group poses. Can everyone line up please and look at the camera. Cute poses please."

We all gather in our usual formation and do a bunch of cheesy poses while the photographer snaps away. Fortunately, he doesn't care as much about the height difference as Ms Han did, so we stick to our preferred formation. It's a relief, as seeing Shu do cute poses right next to me might be enough to make me cutely throw her under a bus.

"Okay, can we get a more serious sexy vibe now."

We all look at each other awkwardly, except Nari who pouts and does some pose where she lifts her legs up and turns her ass around a bit, it looks pretty silly. The photographer seems happy with this.

"That's it! The rest of you, join in!"

We all start doing variations of what Nari is doing. The flashes from the camera start increasing in frequency, clearly this is what the photographer wants. A minute of this nonsense goes by, and then the flashes stop.

"Okay, I think I've got all the group shots I need! Caitlin, can I do a few more solo shots with you please. The rest of you are dismissed."

Mr Park smiles and claps. "Okay the rest of you girls, good work, you're done for today! You have free time for the rest of the evening, we'll pick training back up tomorrow."

We all file out of the gym except Caitlin. I see Nari whisper something in Caitlin's ear on the way through, and Caitlin nodding.

"Hana, please help me get out of this thing," Iseul says.

I nod and follow Iseul into the bathroom, while Youngsook, Nari and Shu all go straight to the dorms to change there.

Once we're in the bathroom together, Iseul turns around so I can unclip her dress. "Trust Caitlin to score the extra photo round with the creeper."

"Yeah, typical. I hope she's alright," I reply.

I quickly undo Iseul's clips, a process which has now become routine, and then turn around so Iseul can return the favour.

"I don't think it's new territory for her, I think she can handle it. I wouldn't worry."

I feel the tightness at the back of my dress gradually loosening as Iseul works my clips loose. We both extract ourselves carefully from our very pretty but cumbersome dresses, and get back into our tracksuits. After this we hang the performance dresses up in the gym space on their designated hanger and walk through the hallway in the direction of the dorms.

"Look down." Iseul points at the hallway floor.

I look down. What's Iseul talking about?

Iseul looks at me, and notices my confusion.

"You don't see it? There."

Iseul points to a specific spot on the tiled floor. I look closer at where she's pointing. There's a thin trail of blood.

"Someone's bleeding?"

"Guess so. The trail goes to our dorm, so it's one of the other girls. Let's find out who." Iseul walks through the hall and into the dorms, pointing out with her hands some more light blood splatches as she passes by them.

"Hey, you finally made it, you two introverts!" Nari laughs as Iseul opens the door to the dorm space. Nari, Youngsook and Shu are all sitting on their beds.

"Yeah, we did. Hey, who's bleeding? There's a trail of blood in the hallway leading here."

Shu, Youngsook and Nari all look at each other.

Iseul points down at Youngsook's feet. There's a small puddle of blood there.

"It's you. Are you okay?"

Youngsook looks down and puts her hand over her mouth, looking absolutely horrified.

"Oh shit, excuse me! I'll go clean up!" She gets up and runs off out of the dorms in a panic.

Iseul looks at the blood puddle, and then at Nari. "That's more than a period stain. You didn't do anything weird to her, did you?"

"No, since the CEO spoke to us, I've been strictly hands off Youngsook. Something else is going on. Does someone want to check on her? I don't want to be the one to have to do it, it might cause problems."

"I'll go," I reply.

"Thanks, Hana."

I walk out of the dorms. Where would I be, if I just found out that I was bleeding? Probably the showers. I walk over to the bathroom door and open it. I guessed correctly; I can hear Youngsook is in here.

"Hey Youngsook, you're in here, right?"

"Yeah, I am."

"Can I talk to y..." I round the corner to the shower cubicle. Youngsook is in here, with her blood-stained pyjama pants down to her knees. There's a single deep gash on the front of each of her two thighs, the left one looks like it's healing but the gash on the right thigh is weeping blood.

Youngsook removes her tracksuit pants completely and turns on the shower tap. "Fuck, I didn't think this would open up again. I need to run some cold water on it." Youngsook turns the tap but the shower tap doesn't produce any water.

"It's not shower time yet. The shower taps won't work outside of the pre-set time."

Youngsook screams in frustration. "Oh my god, *fuck this place!* Why can't we have showers like normal people? I'll just have to use the sink water I guess."

She hobbles over to the sink, runs the tap and starts splashing cold water on her wound. I stare awkwardly. I have no idea how to handle this when it's somebody else.

"Can I do anything to help?" I ask.

"No, you can go. I'll be fine, I just have to stop the bleeding, it'll be okay. Cold water will do it."

"Okay..." I turn around to leave.

"Hana, you understand, right?"

I turn back to look at her, I can see her eyes looking at me with a pleading expression. I can't really find the words to say to her, so instead I roll up the sleeves of my tracksuit top, and show her my forearms, criss-crossed with tiny faded scars from years of cutting. I want to tell her: *I would cut every time my mother would beat me for whatever the reason of the day was. Every time I was humiliated again and again by teachers who only cared about belittling me. Every time the boys assaulted me while the girls looked on and laughed, or just ignored it altogether like my predicament was scenery. I never knew why, but it felt better, to be the one in control, to hurt myself in a controlled fashion. A few months before I came to the agency, I stopped cutting myself, and started hurting others when I could get away with it, it seemed like a better way, and it felt more comforting. It didn't always work out how I wanted, but it's the only way I could become less of a victim. I enjoyed the feeling of hurting people. They've only ever hurt me, so isn't it fair? I should be allowed to hurt anyone I want.* How do I explain this to someone else. I can't do it, so I just stare at Youngsook, the tears welling up. She nods at me, and I feel like in this moment, we understand each other somehow, at least a little.

36. MICROPHONES

"I sound weird in these, Mr Nam. Like, the echoes are all boxy or something, I don't know how to describe it."

"Stay there Caitlin, don't move. I'm going to put some overhead microphones up."

Mr Nam walks out of the control room of the recording studio, and into the large recording space, where Caitlin stands in front of a microphone, wearing headphones. The rest of us girls watch him from inside the soundproof control room, through the large double-glass window. Mr Nam grabs a couple of the smaller microphones at the side of the room on long stands and positions them near Caitlin so the microphones extend way above her head, pointing downward. I keep watching as he then positions a ladder right by Caitlin and climbs it to make finer adjustments to the microphones.

"Wow, those microphones are really high! What's that for?" asks Shu.

Iseul watches this and looks annoyed. She walks over and closes the door between the control room and the recording room, so Mr Nam can't hear us talk to each other in the control room.

"Now that's suspicious, right there. He could have lowered the stands and fiddled around with the microphones at ground level, instead of putting them in position and climbing up on a ladder. It's so obvious he's just trying to get up there to stare down Caitlin's top."

Youngsook shakes her head. "I don't see anything wrong. The microphones need to be pointing to an exact position. You can't really gauge how accurate your positioning is until you're actually looking down the microphone's angle of sight once it's on the stand in the correct position."

"Why does he need overhead microphones anyway? He didn't do that for any of us, only Caitlin!"

"Well, she's the only one complaining about the echoes sounding funny. A microphone further away from the singer's voice will catch some of the sound bouncing around the room, you can then push that sound into the singer's headphones to get a more natural acoustic effect. Sometimes artificial reverb sounds too dry, like it's coming from a machine, which of course it is. Natural reverb sounds more... well, natural, so it stops that strange machine-like echo feeling that you can get."

I don't really quite understand what Youngsook said just then, but it sounds like she knows what she's talking about. That doesn't mean Mr Nam isn't a creep though.

Iseul shakes her head. "Okay but why does it have to be above her head, at prime staring angle? Why not just the other side of the room? And why does Caitlin have to stand right there?"

"He has to aim the microphone at her mouth, that's a bit hard to do if she's not standing in the right spot. Also, there's different reflections from different positions, look at the acoustic baffling on the ceiling, it's not the same as on the walls. It's all about the space to the nearest hard reflective surface. You see, if you get the height of the room and divide it by..."

Iseul cuts Youngsook off. "Stop it, I don't want to hear it! You're just making excuses! Look at him, he's *still* adjusting those microphones, taking his sweet time, wow. He must really care about the sound *so much*. Oh, wait he's coming down now... about time. Let's see how legit this is."

Mr Nam descends the ladder and re-enters the control room. Iseul and Youngsook do their best to act innocent like they weren't just talking about him behind his back. Mr Nam then sits down and talks to Caitlin through the small microphone protruding from his mixing desk.

"Say something, Caitlin."

"Er... something?"

"More than that, please. We need to test your audio."

"Okay. Monday, Tuesday, Wednesday, Thursday... oh wow, that's so much better, thank you! It doesn't sound so weird anymore!"

Youngsook glares at Iseul with her best "told you so" look. Iseul gets the message and crosses her arms.

"Okay, let's try another run-through. Don't worry about being perfect, just try to get the emotion of it." Mr Nam starts playing "Love Light" again. I hear the click track which sounds four times to cue the song, and Caitlin starts working her way through the singing parts. I'm no singer, but even I can tell Caitlin is struggling to hit the correct notes in some places. She does her best, until the end of the bridge, when she suddenly collapses in a laughing fit.

"I'm sorry, there's just no way I can hit that note! It's like, *way* out there!"

Mr Nam stops the recording. "It's fine, just pick a random note that sounds near it. I'll start it up again a few bars back and then punch you in, just try to sing it with confidence, don't stop."

Caitlin nods. "Okay, I'll try! Just expect this to be pretty bad, just being honest here."

The song starts up again, from just before the bridge section where it slows right down. Caitlin does her best to sing along to the bridge's guide track, she misses the note completely, but Mr Nam gives her eye contact through the glass window, gesturing to her to keep going. Caitlin nods back and awkwardly pushes her way right through to the final chorus. I can tell that she feels uncomfortable with it. Once all the vocal sections are over, Mr Nam stops the song.

"That was great! You can come back into the control room now."

Mr Nam then swings around on his chair so he's facing us. "Iseul, can I get you to go out there now? I just need to tidy up a couple of your parts."

"Again?"

"Yes, there's a couple sections I think we can do better."

Iseul gets up off the couch she's on and exits the control room, mumbling something under her breath, passing Caitlin in the doorway. Caitlin comes in and sits next to me on the couch and we watch Iseul ready herself in front of the microphone.

"That was shit, wasn't it?" Caitlin asks me quietly so Mr. Nam can't hear.

I giggle a little. "That high note wasn't the best. I wouldn't worry though, we all messed it up. He'll do some computer magic to it, I guess."

I look back over to Iseul who is now in the recording room, she puts on the same headphones that Caitlin left hanging on the music stand and looks through the window at Mr Nam.

"Do you want me to adjust the room microphones on the high stands for you?" Mr Nam asks.

"I don't care about it; can we just get this done. Please. I've been doing vocals way too long."

"Okay, I'll roll the recording just before the bridge. Try to make it sound sexy."

Iseul pulls a face like she wants to punch someone. Mr Nam starts the recording and Iseul tries to sing along in a breathy kind of manner. It sounds awkward and she's clearly not comfortable with it at all, it's actually so hard to watch. Before the recording even gets to the impossible high note that nobody in the group except Youngsook can do, Mr Nam stops the music.

"Not really what I'm looking for, can it be a bit more feminine please."

Iseul groans and the recording begins again. Iseul runs through the vocals a second time. It's not sounding any less awkward than before, I honestly feel sorry for Iseul. Halfway through the track, Mr Nam cuts the recording again.

"Can't one of us do it? She's clearly not comfortable with the part. I don't mind doing it," Nari offers.

Mr Nam turns around. "Nari, I already have enough of your voice on the track."

Girls look after girls. I put my hand up. "I'll do it, Mr Nam. Really I don't mind."

It's different for Iseul because this gross son of a bitch has the hots for her, but he's made it clear enough that he doesn't like me at all so he probably wouldn't try to get my voice on the track fifty times so he can jack off later.

"Hana, no. I need Iseul's voice. I know you all mean well, but no more offers please." He turns his attention back to Iseul. "Let's try again."

The track starts up again. Iseul tries to sing it again, but she's upset and it's starting to affect her voice. Halfway through the part, Mr Nam stops the recording.

"That's a bit better, it's more feminine, but your voice is too weak, try to make it stronger."

Caitlin nudges me in the ribs gently and then clears her throat. "Hey Mr Nam... can I ask you something?"

"Yes, what is it, Caitlin?" asks Mr Nam.

"You know those cards you gave me last time? Once we're done here, can I talk to you about those, in private? I was just really curious about a couple of things."

"Sure Caitlin, I'd be happy to help you with any questions." Mr Nam turns back to Iseul. "We'll make this the last one. Please do your best."

The recording starts up again. Iseul, looking relieved that she won't be tortured again today, gives it her all and tries to do some sort of 'sexy' thing, I don't know. It just doesn't work coming from someone like Iseul. However, it seems to satisfy Mr Nam, who has a big grin on his face all of a sudden.

"Okay, that will do for today! You all can relax now! Caitlin, please stay and I will help you now."

I can see Iseul breathe a massive sigh of relief as she hangs the headphones back up on the music stand. The rest of us all file out of the control room, except Caitlin, who remains seated. I look at Caitlin with my best "are you really sure you know what the fuck you are doing" expression but she just stares back at me blankly, I'm not sure if she understands my meaning. Nari whispers a quick "be careful" to Caitlin as she walks by, Caitlin just smiles a little like it's no big deal.

"Hey Iseul, we're all done. Let's go back to the dorms." says Nari as we all emerge in the recording room.

Iseul looks worried and starts walking with us, out the door and through to the hallway. "Why isn't Caitlin coming?"

"She wanted to ask Mr Nam some questions - about those business cards."

Iseul looks horrified. "Really? Damn, that's not good." I feel my heart sinking, I don't think it's good either.

Youngsook laughs. "It'll be fine. Caitlin might not be the brightest sometimes, but I reckon she knows how to handle guys."

Iseul sighs. "Yeah, that's exactly what I'm worried about, she might be about to give Mr Nam a little too much handling."

Suddenly, Caitlin appears out of nowhere, jumping on Iseul's back and tackling her to the ground, laughing. "What did you just say about me, you dipshit?"

Iseul squeals as she's taken by surprise and collapses onto the hallway floor under Caitlin's weight. "Where the fuck did you come from, you bitch? Aren't you supposed to be in the control room with Mr Nam?" Everyone backs off and looks down at Caitlin and Iseul, bemused. I breathe a sigh of relief.

"I was getting you out of jail, stupid! After everyone cleared out, I just told him I'd forgotten what I wanted to ask him and left! You should have seen the look on his face!"

Iseul groans. "Oh my god. You clown."

I can't help but smile at the thought of Caitlin pissing off Mr Nam like this. I look at the others, they all seem to be amused. After the ultra-long and boring studio sessions I don't think any of us like him all that much, even those of us who aren't suspicious of his intentions.

"Hey, he would have made you do that vocal part a hundred more times and you know it." Caitlin starts poking Iseul in the ribs for fun.

Iseul puts her arms up to her sides to defend herself. "So you agree that he's a pervert then?"

Caitlin stands up and catches her breath. "He's not that bad, you just weren't getting the part right... but I could see you were having a bad time recording it over and over. Just needed to give him an incentive to wrap it up quickly!"

Iseul gets up from the floor and reorients herself. She looks at Caitlin with a deadly serious expression.

"Caitlin, from the bottom of my heart, you're a complete whore. But thank you, for using your whore powers for good."

Caitlin smiles smugly as we all file into the dorms.

37. THE NIGHT

I wake up. I'm lying in my bed, on my side, facing the wall. It's after midnight. It's not uncommon for me to wake up during the night, I don't sleep that well. Something feels different though, there's something large and warm right up against my back. I roll over in bed and nearly have a heart attack. It's Caitlin, sitting on my bed, in her pyjamas.

"You're awake. Hi there."

"Hi" I reply, feeling a bit freaked out by waking up to someone in such close proximity.

"Just checking up on you. You were making some strange noises. Like you were having a bad dream. Like, *really* bad."

I think about it and try to remember what I was dreaming, I can't. After years of trying to actively forget all dreams, I now very rarely remember anything about them. I can't recollect the last time I even tried to remember a dream deliberately.

"I thought I'd better wake you up. You alright?"

"Yeah."

Caitlin bends down so her head is right next to mine.

"You look sad. What's going on?"

Her proximity makes my heart rate increase.

"I just have a hard time with sleep. I just can't switch my brain off some nights."

"I know the feeling. I sleep terrible when I'm not stoned. Want me to try and make your night better?"

Caitlin smiles at me and my heart nearly jumps out of my chest. I don't know what to say. "Yes" is of course what I would like to say, but it seems too casual somehow for an offer like this, and "oh my god yes" feels too tacky and desperate, like I'm a weirdo or something. How do people in these situations even know what they're supposed to say? I just stare at Caitlin's eyes and pull the bed quilt down very slightly. Caitlin understands, and slides slowly under my quilt, gradually pushing herself against me and enveloping me in her body heat. She wraps an arm slowly around the back of my neck.

"Is this alright?" Caitlin whispers while nestling her head in between the side of my neck and the pillow.

"Yes," I reply, in between extremely heavy breaths.

"Do you think the others will wake up?"

Caitlin starts kissing me along my jawline, working her way up to my lips.

I shoot a glance over Caitlin's head. Shu is fast asleep, as usual, an earthquake couldn't wake that bitch up. I can't see the others but I don't hear any movement.

"Willing to risk it."

Caitlin pulls her leg gradually up to straddle my body and climbs on top of me. She cradles my head in her hands and envelops me with a long, passionate kiss. I feel drawn to the warmth of her mouth, it's enough to overcome the nervousness of having someone, anyone, this close to me. I wrap my arms around Caitlin's waist and lose myself in a few minutes of kissing.

"Hana, it's too hot under this quilt."

"I guess we should remove it?"

"No, the others will see. I have a better idea." Caitlin starts undoing the buttons on her pyjama top.

Suddenly Youngsook groans and noisily rolls over. I start panicking.

"Is she awake? I don't think I can do this if she is."

Caitlin quickly does her top buttons back up.

"Damn. Not sure. Let's find somewhere to go."

We both exit the dorm in our pyjamas and creep quietly out into the hallway. Caitlin walks in the direction of the gym.

"We can use the CEO's office again, nice comfy chair and nobody goes in there. What do you think?"

I think back to the good memories of what happened last time we were in that chair.

"Okay."

"Wait in the gym. I'll check it first; it might be locked up at this hour. If I get busted, I'll just say I was looking for cleaning product or something. Cool?"

I nod. We both creep into the gym. I sit on the gym floor while Caitlin walks up to the administration area door and gives it a slight push. It opens. Caitlin looks back at me and smiles.

"Won't be long!"

She gives a cheeky wave and vanishes into the doorway. I wait for about a minute, and nothing happens. She was just going to check if the CEO's office was locked, it should have taken a few seconds at most? I stand up, creep right up to the administration door and open it just slightly. Caitlin is on the other side, looking at the CEO's office. She hears me come through and immediately turns around to look at me.

"Shhh! He's in there!"

I listen closely. He's not only in there, someone else is in there with him, talking, someone female. I can't hear what's being said, but I recognise the voice that's talking immediately.

"That's Ijun! What are they doing in there at this hour?"

"Who knows but let's get the fuck out of here, we'll go someplace else before we're caught."

Caitlin motions for me to go back towards the gym. I comply and she follows behind me and shuts the door after us. I walk out to the middle of the gym floor.

"That was just strange."

Caitlin opens the sliding glass doors and beckons for me to follow her, out to the yard.

"Come with me, maybe we can get some privacy out here."

"Nope, sorry!"

It's Youngsook, smiling and waving at us. She's in the yard, smoking a cigarette by one of the trees. She must have snuck by us while we were distracted by the goings on in the CEO's office. I follow Caitlin out to the yard and we both sit down on the bench.

Caitlin looks surprised. "I didn't know you smoked?"

Youngsook sighs and blows a jet of smoke up into the air. "I'm trying to quit, but it's hard. I thought I could quit for good when I came here, but honestly this place makes me want to smoke more than ever. The fact Iseul can get literally anything doesn't help."

"How have we not been noticing? Do you only do it at night?"

"I try to not smoke at all, but I sneak out here and have one at night if I'm stressed or I can't sleep. Since you two woke me up, and since I'm also pretty fucking stressed at the moment thanks to pre-debut assessment coming up soon, I thought now's a good time. Sorry if I messed up whatever lesbian thing you two have got going on."

"I'm not a lesbian, fuck off!" I yell.

Youngsook and Caitlin both laugh at me.

"What? I'm not!"

Youngsook shakes her head. "Hana, I'm not sure if you actually know what a lesbian is."

Caitlin grins. "You don't like boys, right?"

"You know how I feel about that."

"Yeah, I guess I do. And you like girls, yeah?"

"Some of them." I can't help but look Caitlin up and down a bit as I say this.

Youngsook and Caitlin both start grinning at me again.

"What? Fuck off!" I hold my head in my hands, this is embarrassing and I'm not ready for it.

Youngsook laughs, smokes the last of her cigarette, then drops it on the floor and treads on it, before then picking it up again a few seconds later.

"Right, I'm done. you two lovebirds have fun."

Youngsook walks off back to the gym and closes the glass door behind her.

"Thanks Youngsook!" Caitlin yells after her.

Youngsook does a little unenthused wave, without looking behind her, as she wanders off back to the dorm.

I sigh. "Fuck, she totally caught us!"

"There's really nowhere we can do anything without a high risk of getting busted in this place. Someone's always going to come and check on us if we're away too long, regardless of where we are or when it is."

"What can we do about it? We all live pretty much on top of each other, all the time."

Caitlin looks at me. "I don't know. I'm sure something will come up."

38. ASSESSMENT

"You need to smile more. You have such a pretty face. Don't forget to smile!"

The entire group is sitting on the gym floor, except Shu, who smiles as she comes to a standstill and does her ending pose for the "Show Me Love" routine. Everyone in the group applauds, and so does Mr Park, who is sitting on a chair off to the side of the gym. I do the bare minimum of clapping required that I can get away with.

"That's better!" Mr Park beams. Oh, how I still can't stand Shu, and watching her do "ending fairy" poses makes me want to break her face. I hate it even more that Mr Park is clearly completely happy with her. How did he not notice that she just danced like shit? I know I have to ignore my feelings so I just take a deep breath and try to emotionally level myself out. It's not easy.

Mr Park motions for Shu to sit down on the lone "pretend interviewee chair" at the front of the gym space, a chair that's been stolen from the dining room. "Now it's time for your interview assessment. Please take a seat."

Shu bounces over to the chair and sits down, smiling.

"Shu, I will now ask you some interview questions. Please answer with the most appropriate response as per the interview training guidelines."

Shu nods diligently with a determined face. She's actually taking this seriously.

Mr Park looks down at his clipboard notes. "Shu, how do you feel about finally debuting?"

Shu beams a huge smile. "I'm so excited to finally meet all our fans! I love all of you very much!"

"What can we expect from your debut stage?"

"Our debut song is called 'Show Me Love'! It's all about the love that we feel, but that we can't always express! Please enjoy our performance, I hope to surprise you with my cute charms!" Shu grins like a shithead and does a heart shape with her hands. It's so cringe, I can barely watch.

"Do you have anything to say to the fans who have waited so long for debut?"

"We have trained extra hard for you to deliver the most perfect performance of our career, please expect us fondly!" Shu bows in her chair.

"Can you tell us about your training regimen? How much do you get to eat per day?"

Shu raises her right hand. "Next question please!"

Mr Park smiles and nods. "Excellent! That's all the interview questions for your assessment."

"Yay!" Shu bounces up and down in her chair.

"Your final result is a pass, you have performed well in dancing, singing, charms and interview style. Your weigh-in results are acceptable. Just please remember to smile more, especially during dance routines."

"I'm sorry Mr Park CEO, but sometimes when I dance, I concentrate so hard on the dancing that I forget to smile! I will work on it, Mr Park CEO!"

"Just remember that your smile is your ace card, so play it every chance you get. Your success depends on the public falling in love with you. You're so much prettier when you smile." Mr Park motions for Shu to stand up. "You are dismissed now, please take a seat with the rest of the group. Youngsook, you're up, please get on the scales."

I'm annoyed. Shu did not deserve such a positive assessment. I watch as Shu walks over and sits down on the floor with the rest of us, while Youngsook gets up and approaches the scales. Youngsook looks hesitant and fearful, I don't blame her. These assessments never go well for her, and as our debut date approaches, they're getting harsher and harsher. Youngsook gets on the scales and stares down at the reading. I watch her mouthing "oh my god".

Mr Park gets up off his seat and walks over to the scales, not all the way, just close enough so he can see the numbers. He stares up at Youngsook. "51.7 kilos? Why are you still so fat?"

Youngsook gets off the scales and doesn't say anything.

Mr Park continues. "Have you actually seen yourself in the mirror? You have too much thigh fat, and a fat face, surely you are not blind and can also see this. Our job is to sell you to the public, this means you are supposed to be liked by the public, but nobody is going to fall in love with you if you don't take care of yourself."

"I'm sorry Mr Park CEO sir." Youngsook says as she bows at ninety degrees.

"Obviously you are a failure in this aspect. We will summarise later. Move onto the singing. Please now sing the 'Show Me Love' chorus, unaccompanied."

Youngsook takes a deep breath and tries to compose herself, then starts up with the chorus.

I just want you to show me / Show-show-show me love / Will you ever know me / Know-know-know my love for you

Youngsook sounds shaky, but still way better than the rest of us. Mr Park clearly knows it as well, he claps as soon as Youngsook finishes. "Very good, Youngsook. At least you can consistently do this part right."

"Thank you, Mr Park CEO."

"Now please move onto the dance routine. You are to do the 'Show Me Love' dance, only from the bridge section, through to the last chorus and the end of the piece, unaccompanied. Please start when ready, you can also count or sing if you wish, but remember to sell the dance to the audience." Mr Park points towards the rest of us sitting down on the gym floor, indicating that we represent the audience. He then walks back to his chair and sits down, watching Youngsook closely.

Youngsook starts the dance routine from the bridge section. She doesn't choose to sing the words but instead hums the melody quietly as she moves through the various sections of the bridge and then into the chorus. At the end Youngsook holds her final pose and gives a weak smile. It's obvious that she's upset and it's affecting her performance.

"What on earth was that? You move like a disgusting slug, it's not acceptable for you to move so slowly. The song requires fast, snappy movements. Also you made no effort whatsoever to sell the song to the audience, despite me specifically reminding you of this. You're not charming at all, you're pathetic."

Youngsook starts sobbing as she bows at ninety degrees again. "I'm so sorry, Mr Park CEO! I will try harder!"

Mr Park raises his hand for Youngsook to stop. "I do not even want to discuss it further. Please take a seat in the chair and we will do some interview questions."

Youngsook quickly moves over to the seat and sits down.

"You ran over to that chair quicker than you did any of the dance routine. You must be in a hurry to rest your lazy bones." Mr Park glares at Youngsook and then reads from his clipboard. "We will start with the questions now. Youngsook, please describe your sleeping routine."

Youngsook thinks for a while and then answers. "Well, at midnight..."

Mr Park abruptly cuts Youngsook off. "Wrong answer! Surely you know that you are not to answer any question like this that asks for training specifics. You merely raise your hand and the representative from our company will direct the interviewer to move onto the next question."

"I'm sorry, I forgot, Mr Park CEO." Youngsook bows in her chair, I can see her tears falling into her lap even from where I'm sitting.

Mr Park is unmoved. "Youngsook, please now describe what individual charms you bring to the group."

Youngsook goes to say something but whatever it is doesn't come out properly, instead she bursts out crying in her chair.

"Why is this company wasting our time and money on you? Do you not understand that this is a business? Do you even want to debut at all? Can you even get through a simple assessment? Do we have to debut this group as five?"

Youngsook bows repeatedly as she continues to bawl, it's hard to watch her break down like this.

"You are clearly in no condition to continue an assessment with this pathetic emotional display. Do you think you are permitted such displays in public once you debut? I assure you that you are not! If you think being able to sing is enough to compensate for being so useless at everything else, you are wrong! Homeless shelters all across Seoul are filled with excellent singers who are also fat and ugly and show no charms! I consider you a failure on every level until you can show improvement! GET OUT OF MY GYM!"

Youngsook runs off through the exit door, sobbing and bowing as she moves across the gym floor to the exit.

"Nari, stand up!" shouts Mr Park.

Nari is sitting next to me. She stands up quickly.

"You are the leader of this group! If Youngsook is not performing, that means you are not performing! You haven't been giving Youngsook adequate motivation to improve her performance, I consider you negligent for this! It is a dereliction of your duty as a leader!"

Nari bows. "I am sorry, Mr Park. I have tried..."

"Bullshit! You have only tried to decorate your own ego; your leadership is non-existent! Where is the proper mentoring? What have you done to give constructive feedback to your team? Where are the results? The other members of this group who are performing well are doing so in spite of your leadership, not because of it! You are so busy preening and posing, dreaming of your own success, thinking you are something, but until the entire team performs, you are nothing! Do you understand this? You are wasting the time of everybody in this room, including yourself! Get out of here immediately, go and find Youngsook and give her the motivation she needs to succeed! I don't want to even see your plastic face in an assessment again until Youngsook can deliver a proper performance! NOW GO!"

Nari bows and exits the room without another word. It's obvious she's upset but she can contain it a lot better than Youngsook can.

"Hana, get up!" Mr Park yells.

Great, it's time for my assessment and he's already pissed off before I start. I stand up and walk over, up onto to the scales. I don't bother to look down, Mr Park will look at it.

"What do the numbers say, Hana?" he asks.

I really don't want to look down while I'm on the scales. "You can't see them?" I ask.

"Don't you care what your results are, Hana?"

I remain looking straight ahead. I don't want to look down, I know I'll get dizzy and start freaking out.

Mr Park sighs. "Okay, get off. Come over here."

I breathe a sigh of relief and get off the scales. I walk over to Mr Park.

"Hana, I have no doubt that your weight results are good. You are one of the few in this group who is meeting the weight requirements. However that is not the concern I have with you. Let's move to the singing for now. Please sing the bridge section of 'Love Light', unaccompanied."

Oh wow, he really did have to pick the hardest section of that piece didn't he. I take a deep breath and do my best to squeak, strain and mumble through the impossible vocal line, that starts with the whispery "sexy" section and ends with that ridiculous high note.

There's no need to explain your feelings / I know everything that happens in your heart / I'll turn the switch / I'll shine the love light / Walk in and take what's yours / And I'll take what's mine / Until the next tiiii - oh fuck

I finish up and look at Mr Park, feeling shameful that I bombed the last note, although I knew I would, because I've never sung it correctly before, not even once.

"Good enough!" he says, smiling.

Really? I can't believe that was anywhere near good but at least he's happy so whatever I guess, I'm not going to argue.

"Please now do the 'Show Me Love' dance, from the same section, through to the end."

I nod and start going through the movements from the bridge section. This is easy, I've done this so many times that I don't even have to think about it. Once I get the motions going, the muscle movements just happen near-automatically, one after the other. I progress to the end, pretty good as far as I can tell, and smile a bit when I finish up because I know that's what he wants.

Mr Park claps. "Good! Just remember that you also need to smile more, and not just at the end, try to have a lighter expression during the dance as well. You're so much prettier when you smile." Please sit down and we will now do the interview questions."

Yeah whatever, you creepy dickhead. I walk over to the interviewee chair and sit down.

"Hana, how does it feel to realise your dreams of debuting on the world stage?"

I think for a while. "I'm sort of numb to it, I guess. I don't know."

"Hana, you're supposed to sound happier than that."

"But what if I'm not?"

Mr Park doesn't respond. "Next question - abortion is a controversial issue, are you pro-choice or pro-life?"

"I'm pro-abortion. There shouldn't be a choice, and there shouldn't be any life either. If you're pregnant, get an abortion. Any other choice is the wrong choice."

"Wrong answer! You're not supposed to answer questions like these. Just put your hand up and the manager will tell the interviewer to move on."

I shrug. "I'm sorry Mr Park. I've just been trained all this time to be honest, so it's weird to suddenly be holding back."

"The only time where you can safely be honest is in this room."

"But I *am* in this room?"

"Do you understand that this is a roleplay exercise?"

"Yes, but I'm just roleplaying as myself, aren't I?"

"Yourself, if you were in a public interview situation, where there are limitations on what you can and cannot say, as we discussed in training. We need to discuss this point."

I don't know if any response is required so I just stand there and look at Mr Park. I've learned from experience that when Mr Park is talking, if I don't know what to say, saying nothing is often a good option.

He continues. "I am concerned that you don't care about your image in this group, and that you don't have any pride in your accomplishments. You don't appear to be emotionally invested at all in our activities, I sense this because..."

I stop listening at this point, he's starting to ramble and when he gets going, he doesn't stop. Why should I listen to him, it's just going to be the usual half an hour of prattle. I just stare straight ahead at his mouth as it moves. I'm sure he thinks that whatever he's saying is terribly important but to me it's just mouth noises. I'd rather think about my own thoughts, I don't like listening to old men in charge. They all talk as if their opinion is so important on everything, I don't think it's important at all. Just get to the point and tell me what you want to do, because we both know I'm going to have to do it anyway.

"...you don't even seem to be fully engaged in what I'm telling you, like your emotions are switched off..."

Oh shit, I just caught that bit, he's realised that I don't want to listen to him, that I'm not even paying attention. I guess I'd better look like I care so this fucking bastard doesn't catch on. I suppose I'll cry or something, that'll work. It always feeds the egos of teachers and bullies and parents and other trash when they make you cry, it makes them feel like they're really doing something. I'm sure I can think of something that'll make me cry.

"...you need to be fully engaged with the group, it's a team effort..."

I know. *One time I was at school and one of the girls passed me a note, I opened it and it said "someone has a crush on you and wants to meet you, meet at nine o'clock at the west end of the carpark". I turned around and it was Harin who is like one of the prettiest girls at school and she even talked to me a couple of times even though I'm wangtta at huge risk to her own popularity. I'd never had someone like her pass me something like that. Was it really from her or someone else? Sure it was probably bullshit, but what if it wasn't? So I went to the carpark after school because I really wanted to know, and there was nobody around, and then all of a sudden, she was there, it was Harin. She said "come with me" and we walked down between a couple of cars and it felt a bit weird like something was wrong because why are we going here and then like five or six guys got out of one of the cars and I immediately panicked like I knew this wasn't right straight away even before they said "let's get her" that son of a bitch Harin wasn't my friend she was just pretending so her boyfriends could get what they wanted luckily I realised in enough time to get a head start I just started running and thankfully they couldn't catch me, I'm used to running away from trouble so I run pretty fast.*

"...Hana, are you there?"

Anyway I ran straight to my home and told my mum about what happened, she just stared me up and down like the creeps in my class do and said "your skirt is too high no wonder you got that kind of attention from boys perhaps you should dress more like my daughter would instead of a harlot" and I just went off screaming at her like "I'm your daughter, how dare you judge your own flesh and blood I just nearly got fucking raped you cunt" and then she just totally ignored what I said and just said "how dare you, you're disgusting, you're a filthy tramp, how dare you talk to your mother like that" just because I called her a cunt and I was like "if the shoe fits, cunt" and so she grounded me for a whole six months because of that and she enforced that curfew every fucking day until I came here, like am I supposed to hate my mother this much what's wrong with me why can't I have a normal mother why is it like this why am I stuck with you and these walls I can't even have a normal life with you I can't go anywhere or do anything or have anything I'm not even allowed to have things or have friends I have nobody why am I your prisoner I can't live like this I hate you I hate you I hate you I hate you I hate you I hate you I hate you I HATE YOU I HATE YOU I HATE YOU I

39. HELP

"Hanahanahanahanahanahana..."

I wake up. Oh, for fuck's sake.

"Hanahanahanahanahanahana.... ah yes! She's up!"

I gradually open my eyes. Caitlin and Shu are both sitting on Shu's bunk, the one opposite mine. They're staring at me with what feels like an undue amount of interest.

Caitlin pats Shu on the head. "You're a really good alarm clock, you know."

"I do my best!"

I'm still a bit too tired to get truly mad. I rub my eyes and stretch out.

"How long have I been out?"

"Since Nari put you to bed yesterday."

"Nari did what?"

"You don't remember that?"

"I don't remember anything. I remember I was doing the assessment, and then I woke up... here?"

Caitlin looks at Shu. "You tell her."

"Okay, you were doing the interview with Mr Park CEO, and he started asking about how you were sort of not listening and stuff, and then you started crying, and then you started *really* crying, and then you started *really really* crying, and then you cried so hard you fell off your chair and couldn't get back up, and you were just sort of shaking and crying on the ground a lot, and then Nari and Iseul picked you off the floor of the gym and carried you here and put you into your bed. And you've been here ever since!"

I close my eyes. They still hurt a little.

"Oh. What time is it?"

"Time for morning stretches! You need to get up now!" I open my eyes again a little to see Shu staring and grinning at me way too cheerfully, like a tiny weapon of *aegyo* designed specifically to torture me.

I look around. "Where are the others?"

"In the gym, silly!"

"Except Youngsook," adds Caitlin.

Shu nods at Caitlin. "Oh, that's right! Youngsook isn't here. We don't know where she is."

"She'll turn up, I guess."

I get up and grab my tracksuit from the edge of the bed. It's not unusual for Youngsook to be late for gym, seeing as she hates doing anything physical. Sometimes she skips the morning stretch routine altogether unless Nari makes a special effort to go and get her. I head into the bathroom to get changed, nobody's in here so I can change into my tracksuit quickly. A minute later I emerge in the gym, the other girls are all here, except Youngsook.

"Hey Hana, glad you could join us, are you alright?" asks Nari, while she sits on the floor doing splits.

"Yeah hello." I find a space on the gym floor to stretch my legs out on. "Thanks for looking after me yesterday. I don't remember much of it but the others told me what happened."

"It's no problem, it's what we do for each other. You haven't seen Miss Chicken Wings by any chance?"

I giggle a bit and shake my head. "Haven't seen her."

"I'm going to check on Little Miss Fried Potatoes, she's probably still in bed absorbing carbohydrates from the atmosphere." Nari bounds up from her sitting position, scoots out of the gym area and off to the dorms to check up on her. I stifle another giggle at her remarks and keep on doing leg stretches.

"We just came from there, she's not there," Caitlin says, but Nari's already too far away to hear her.

"Hey hamburger, wake up!" I can hear Nari yelling from the dorm area. Then I hear her come running back.

"She not there?"

Iseul shrugs. "She didn't sleep with us last night either. I just assumed that she was here in the gym."

Nari scratches her head. "I took her back to the dorms, and sat with her for a while because she wasn't feeling that good. Then I came back to watch all of you do the assessments. That's the last I saw of her."

"What did she say?" asks Iseul.

"She was worried about being thrown out of the group for not measuring up. She didn't say she was going to leave though."

Just then we all hear the front door of the premises open. Shu goes over to check it because she's closest, and Youngsook limps through the entrance. We all stop what we're doing and run out of the gym, over to the entrance area, and look at Youngsook.

Youngsook is clearly injured, she looks like she's been in a car accident or something similar, there are bruises all over her face, arms and legs. Nari grabs Youngsook around the shoulders and leads her to the dorm, and we all follow. Nari gently guides Youngsook over to her bunk and lies her down, then sits down on the edge of the bed next to Youngsook's head on the pillow.

"What happened to you?"

Youngsook just lies on her back and stares at the ceiling, saying nothing but she's clearly in a fair degree of pain. She's not noticeably bleeding or anything but her bruises look intense and her gaze looks like it's an eternity away.

Nari takes a deep breath. "Fuck this derelict company for not giving us phones. I'm getting management to call the hospital." She runs out of the dorms and off down the hall to the offices. I take Nari's place sitting by Youngsook.

Iseul sighs. "How many times do I have to tell Nari that I can get a car here quicker than she can get an ambulance here. Caitlin, do you want to go after Nari?"

Caitlin nods and leaves the dorm area to chase after Nari.

Iseul turns to Youngsook and squats down beside her on the bed. "Youngsook, do you want to say anything?"

Youngsook says nothing, but raises her left arm slowly. In her left hand, is a business card. Iseul takes the card.

"Shit... this is one of the cards that I was given from Mr Nam. Hana, I threw my cards out, Caitlin gave hers to you... do you still have them?" Iseul gets up from by Youngsook's bed and goes over to her own bunk. She picks up her tablet to message for a ride.

"Yeah, I think so."

I open my bunk drawer and look at the corner where I kept the cards. They're not there. I look back over at Youngsook. She smiles weakly, and for the first time since she walked in, she says something.

"Don't worry. I refused."

Youngsook smiles weakly. Me, Iseul and Shu all look at each other. Nobody says a word.

Iseul starts using her tablet to write a message while holding the business card wedged between two of her fingers, I take the card out of Iseul's hand and read it. It's not a card for Mr Nam himself, but someone else.

MR LEE YEONG GI
EXECUTIVE DIRECTOR
APEX PERFORMANCE
CONSULTING AND MANAGEMENT

Never heard of him or whatever this company is. Who even knows what a company like this does, but he's one of that asshole Mr Nam's "business associates" I guess. There's an email, phone number and address for an apartment complex. I look over at Youngsook, and she looks back at me.

"I didn't know what else to do. I thought my career was maybe over. I just wanted... some help?"

Looking at her condition is infuriating. I'm filled with an overwhelming rage. I might not get along with or even like everyone in my group, but even the ones I don't like are still the closest I have to any kind of friends or family. Youngsook's nice anyway, sure she's annoying sometimes but she's been through so much and she definitely doesn't deserve this shit. I won't let her be treated like this, and especially not by some creep.

"Don't worry - I'll help."

40. SUPERMARKET

I'm in language class, just doing nothing basically. We've been given some exercises to go over and read silently but I couldn't be fucked with any of it and my mind is wandering. As usual Ms Kim is just reading a book at her desk, basically ignoring us, she just babysits the class and does fuck all else and that's fine. Nothing is better than something bad. All of us are here learning, except Youngsook who is still in the hospital. I haven't heard any recent news but last I heard she was stable, the fractures from the three ribs where she was hit the hardest fortunately hadn't punctured any of her organs, and the collarbone break was only very minor, so she's looking good to re-join the group once she's had a few weeks to heal. She'll have to take it easy for a while though, no strenuous dancing. She should be happy with having a legitimate excuse to not do dance routines, actually.

All of a sudden, I feel that something's stuck in my hair. Even though I know what it is, I can't help but flinch a little every time I feel a paper plane in my hair. Maybe I should consider shaving my head one day, I wonder what that would feel like. I take the plane out of my hair and look at it... as expected, there's something written on the inside. I unfold it and take a look.

At the top of the page: *The supermarket is open. Don't forget to dream big.*

Underneath, the others have all written stuff down. Nari has written *vape* - Nari smokes? Surely not, she's such a health nut - why would she even need a vape? I refuse to believe Nari smokes, even secretly. Shu has written *more books please - any genre except romance. Fiction only - thank you!* Caitlin has drawn a picture of... I'm not sure what? It looks a bit like the beakers I used to use in science class for experiments, but it's not symmetrical, it's kind of lopsided. Underneath it, the number *420*. I never did ask her what this number means, obviously it's related to marijuana somehow but exactly how, I have no idea, I remind myself that I have to ask her. Next to it, Caitlin has drawn another picture, of a square box. Two stick people are inside the square box, both identifiable as female due to their triangular skirts. There's a love heart between them. On one wall of the box that contains the stick figures is a locked padlock. I smile to myself - I know exactly what Caitlin is asking for here. I hope Iseul can come up with something.

I immediately write on the paper: *1. clothes. 2. revenge* and because I'm bored and feeling artistic, a picture of a gravestone. I refold the plane and fly it back to Iseul, she's ready for it and she catches it mid-air. I turn my attention back to my book. It's not long before I feel the paper plane stuck in my hair again, I pluck it out and unfold it.

Iseul has written next to my note: *how serious are you - choose a method*.

I think about it for a while. *Don't forget to dream big*. I write on the note *100% - bang bang, let's kill men dead* and next to it, a picture of a gun firing a bullet. I refold the plane and fly it back to Iseul, she's waiting for it and tries to catch it but it flies over her head and lands against the far corner of the room. I watch Iseul creep up out of her chair to retrieve the plan from the corner, and then skulk back to her seat. Fortunately Ms Kim is too engrossed in her own reading to even notice.

I get back to looking at my exercise book, but I can't concentrate on the words. I'm too busy thinking about avenging Youngsook. I don't know what happened to her exactly, none of us have had the chance to talk to her directly ever since she entered hospital, but I know what men are like and I have no doubt how things would have generally played out. She would have gone to that guy asking for advice, he would have met her and tried to make some kind of advance, Youngsook being too intelligent for such creep moves would not have been okay with it, and so he took it out on her when he couldn't get what he wanted. I start fuming at the thought of this injustice when suddenly I see something flash by my head, it's Iseul's paper plane, which whizzes right by me and lands on Ms Kim's desk. I look on in horror as Ms Kim picks up the paper plane.

"Who threw this?" she asks, as she grabs the plane and holds it up.

I look back at Iseul, she has her hand raised. "I did it."

Ms. Kim must have noticed the writing; she unfolds the paper plane. "What is all this?" she asks as she reads through what we've all written.

"I get bored, I like to doodle. I'm sorry, Ms Kim!"

"What an imagination," says Ms Kim disdainfully as she scrunches up the paper into a ball and drops it into the wastepaper bin by her desk. "Be mindful that you entertain yourself only with study in future."

"It is a character flaw. I will work harder in future to be more mature and less imaginative."

"You do that."

Ms Kim returns to reading her book. I breathe a sigh of relief, as I realise Iseul's diversion tactic is successful, Ms Kim hasn't really understood the context of the notes.

I look over at the other girls. None of them are happy with Ms Kim, Nari in particular looks like she's about to punch someone, but she doesn't say anything. We all resume reading and watching the time pass.

A while later, language class ends, and Ms Kim packs up her things and fucks off. As soon as she leaves the room, Iseul rushes over and retrieves the ball of paper from the wastepaper bin. She hands the paper to me without saying a word and I open it.

World population is 50.4% men, 49.6% women, doesn't seem right to me. Could use some adjustment?

41. THREE HYDRAS

It's late and we're all in our beds, waiting for the lights to automatically go out at midnight. Shu is already asleep, as usual. Nari is reading one of Shu's books. I'm not sure what Caitlin is doing because she's in the bunk above mine. Iseul is playing with her tablet that really should be mine, not hers. I decide to say something about it, again.

"You know Iseul, I haven't said anything mean to Shu in at least two weeks. I've been good and restraining myself. You should be giving me that tablet."

Iseul laughs. "Nope! You've had enough chances. After your many instances of bullying Shu I have decided that you don't deserve this tablet, ever. Anyway it's too useful for me. I need it to keep track of things."

"Fine then, I'll just go and slap Shu some more seeing as I have nothing to lose."

"And I'll slap *you* some more, and I'll thoroughly enjoy doing it too," shoots back Nari, not even looking up from her book.

"You know, it's almost worth it."

Nari jumps down from her bed and walks up to me aggressively. "Is that right, Hana? I guess that just means I have to hit you harder so it isn't worth it. You can then have a bed right next to Youngsook in her ward. How about it?"

Iseul waves her tablet at us. "Hey you two lesbians, stop flirting with each other and have a look at this."

"I'm not a lesbian, fuck off!" I instinctively yell back.

I look past Nari, over at the tablet Iseul is holding, it shows a video. The video title reads "TRUE MIRACLE ENTERTAINMENT NEW TRAINEES UPSKIRT AND CLEAVAGE". What? How? I keep looking at the tablet in disbelief as Iseul taps the screen and the video plays. Nari has also turned around, and Caitlin pokes her head down from the top bunk to see. It's video footage of Caitlin, taken from the studio recording room. The camera angle is way above her head, it's obviously the position where Mr Nam put those microphones. The camera lens zooms into the gaps in the neckline of Caitlin's clothing. Iseul is furious.

"That son of a bitch! I *knew* something was wrong with that bullshit!"

The scene then changes to something else. At first, it's all black, but after a while the light exposure adjusts. It's footage of Iseul, sitting on the studio couch directly behind Mr Nam. The angle of the camera shows that it's positioned right under Mr Nam's big control desk and the angle goes right between Iseul's legs. Iseul stops the video.

"*Great*, we're in a fucking *molka*. I've seen enough, I'm going outside, Hana come with me please."

Iseul gets out of her bed and I follow her out to the hallway, through the gym area to the yard. Iseul sits down on the bench and motions for me to sit next to her. She looks at me in the eyes, clearly upset.

"Hana, you were serious, with that note?"

I nod. "One hundred percent. Just like I wrote."

"I guess you've been through some shit with guys beyond just regular *wangtta* stuff, huh?"

I nod again. I try not to think too hard about Iseul's question, because if I do, I'll start getting upset, so I don't say anything else.

"I'm feeling a little vengeful right now myself, but I'm not so good at getting my hands dirty. You like it though, don't you?"

"I can't compete against a man's strength, but if I ever work out how, you'll know because you'll see a lot of dead men."

"Meet me here again tomorrow at this time, and we can discuss it some more. Hey Hana, I want to change the subject, just a little. I'll show you something cool." Iseul turns her back to me. "Lift up my top."

"What the fuck, Iseul? I can't do that!"

"Relax, I'm not Caitlin. I'm not asking you to take the whole thing off, just slide the back of my pyjamas up."

I do what Iseul asks and gradually lift the back of her pyjama top up, trying to be as modest as possible about it. I see her tattoo design again, it's no longer an outline. It's been partially filled in since I last saw it. Now that there's some colour and shape to the drawing, I can see what it is - it's a picture of some mythical creatures, some dragons but each one has multiple heads. The tattoo work is huge, colourful and intricate, like a painting. I've never seen anyone with a tattoo like this before.

"Okay, you can put my top down now, you pervert."

I release her top and the fabric falls down over her back, Iseul turns around and smiles at me.

"Pretty cool hey?"

"What does that tattoo mean? It's kind of pretty, but what's the point of having something like that?"

"Three Hydras," says a voice behind us. It's Nari.

Myself and Iseul both turn around, she's crept her way out here without us noticing.

"I saw that, Iseul! How are you in a fucking *gang?*"

"Nari..." Iseul starts to say something but she's interrupted by Nari screaming.

"Fuck! *Fuck!* I can't fucking believe it! Since you're his niece, I suppose the CEO is part of it too? I mean, that would explain the drugs, right?"

"Detective genius Nari, on the case I see."

"This is bullshit! I just want to debut in pop music and be an idol, I don't want to be part of some organised criminal bullshit! Why can't I just pursue my dream like a normal person? I'm changing agencies the very first chance I get!"

Iseul starts laughing. "Hey Nari, what agency would you prefer to be in?"

"A big one, so I can actually be successful and not involved in this bullshit! Maybe TN Entertainment, they have lots of big stars, unlike this place where they can't even afford proper staff." Nari starts pacing back and forth, I can almost see the heat rising from her face.

Iseul thinks this is hilarious. "Oh, TN Entertainment, the pop agency owned by Five Star Clan, that one? Or maybe XF Entertainment, who 18C triad run all their gambling and prostitution business in Korea through?"

I watch Nari's face turn white as a sheet.

Iseul keeps going. "Okay maybe not those two then, fine. What's the other big agency right now, the one that's been buying up a lot of other small independent companies recently, HIVE? Yeah, they're part of Songyemi Family's operation, in fact I have an issue with one of the CEO's daughters that I need to sort out sometime, luckily for her I kind of got distracted by this whole being in a pop group myself thing..."

Nari looks at Iseul with an exasperated stare and tears running down her cheeks. "Oh come on! There has to be *one* agency out there that isn't part of some crime bullshit?"

It takes a lot to make Nari cry, but Iseul has somehow managed it. I'm impressed. Iseul on the other hand can't stop smiling.

"Exactly what industry do you think you're in, Nari?"

I watch as Iseul starts laughing in Nari's face.

42. SAFETY

It's about one o'clock in the morning and I'm waiting where Iseul has told me to wait, on a bench a couple of blocks down from the front of the agency building. Traffic is light and there's only a few people wandering the streets. I watch each car as it drives by, to see if it's my ride. Eventually a black van pulls up a few metres in front of me and then gradually reverses back. The side door of the van slides open, there's a man and a woman inside, peering out at me, both of them are wearing all-black tracksuits and black face masks.

"Hana?" asks the woman.

I stand up and wave. "It's me, Hana."

I'm relieved to see her. I asked Iseul to make sure the van wasn't all men, because there's no way I'm getting into a van full of strangers that are all men. That is so not happening.

"Get in, quickly."

I step up inside the van. It's a small minibus style van with about ten seats. I pick a random empty seat and sit down.

"Driver let's go," the woman calls out. I feel the van starting to move forward.

The man takes a seat opposite mine and looks at me.

"You're a schoolgirl?"

"Not anymore. I just don't have a lot in my wardrobe. It's this or a tracksuit with agency logos on it. I'm sure you understand why I can't wear that for this meeting?"

The man doesn't seem that interested in my wardrobe predicament. He lifts a long metal case up onto his lap, and opens it up so the contents are facing me. Inside is a selection of four handguns.

"Okay, let's get to business. You selection has already been paid for; the question is now just what do you want."

"I don't know. What's going to do the job the best?"

"Have you ever shot a gun before?"

"No."

"Well, you've got two types of choices here, revolvers and automatics. These two are revolvers, they're easy to use and the shots are powerful, but they only carry six bullets each." He indicates the two pistols on my left, they are large and look kind of old style, like the ones in old movies.

"What if I miss? I might need more than six bullets."

The man motions to the other two guns, which look more modern. "These other two are automatics. They both carry fifteen shots each. Each bullet is a little less powerful, but with so many shots in a magazine you get more chances to hit. They also fit silencers better so they can be quieter."

"What do you mean by less powerful? Can I still kill someone with one of these?"

"Yes, the bullets will go through most things easily, including people. Since you're not shooting an armoured target, you should be fine."

"What's an armoured target?"

"A target wearing body armour."

"Oh."

The man takes out one of the automatic guns, a silver gun with a black handle. "If you want an automatic, since you're completely new to this, I'd recommend this one here. It's very reliable, it also has a safety, which the other automatic doesn't have."

"What's a safety?"

"It's a switch to stop the gun from shooting."

"Isn't the point of having a gun to shoot the gun, not to not shoot the gun?"

"Yes, but it's easy to discharge a gun by accident if you've never used one before. If you keep the safety switch on until you need to use it, then it won't go off when you don't want it to." He points to a small lever on the side of the gun. "Push this lever down, like this - and it can't be fired. Push it again and it flips up, and you see the red dot right there? That means the gun is activated and can be fired."

I watch all this carefully and try to remember it.

"Okay. If you think this gun is good then I trust you. To fire it I just point it at the thing I want to die and pull the trigger, right?"

"You need to make sure the gun is loaded, and also that there's a bullet in the chamber. You can check if there's a bullet by sliding back this part halfway." He pulls back a sliding part of the gun at the top to reveal a hollow space inside. "If you see a bullet there, you're good. Since there's no bullet there, we slide back all the way, like this." He then pulls back the sliding part further and the gun clicks. "That puts a bullet from the magazine down below, into that space. Now let's check again." He pulls the sliding part back a little again, showing a bullet in the space that wasn't there before. "Now, when you shoot, each time a new bullet will come up into here automatically to replace the previous one, so you don't have to keep sliding it, that's why it's called an automatic. Do you know how to aim a gun?"

"I think so. Look down the sights at the top and line them up, right?"

"Yes, they have to line up. This one here, has to line up so you can see it in the gap here." He points at the two sights at the front and rear. "Do you need a silencer? If so, I'll install it for you."

"Having a silent gun seems like a good idea. Can I have one of those please."

"It's not exactly going to be silent. Guns are very loud, it can be surprising how loud they are even if you've shot one before, let alone if you haven't. A silencer only makes the gun a little less loud."

"Why do they call it a silencer if it's not silent?"

"Well, that's why technically they call it a suppressor."

"Okay. Is it still worth having on there?"

"Yes. The noise from guns is very loud, trust me that you will damage your hearing from firing even one shot, you will want it to be quieter. Especially as a musician."

I can't help but laugh. "To be completely honest with you, I'm not sure if I'd call myself a musician."

"Aside from less noise, there's also less flash, so it's a bit easier to hit multiple shots because it's easier to see your target once you start shooting. The downside is that attaching one of these makes your gun longer, so it's going to be harder to conceal."

"That's okay, I have a big bag to store it. Easy shooting is good shooting."

"Okay, now I will tell you some other basic gun safety information because you're new to guns."

"What do I have to learn about safety for? If I wanted this person to be safe, I wouldn't be buying a gun to shoot them with?"

The woman starts laughing. "She's a live wire, this one! Iseul did warn us!"

The man clears his throat and continues. "Safety for *you*, not for them. The first thing to remember is, always treat guns like they're loaded. Which it will be anyway in this case, because I'm going to give you this one loaded and ready to go, but with the safety on. So no stupid crap like looking down the end of the barrel where the bullets come out."

"I realise that I'm only fresh out of school but I'd like to think I'm not that stupid."

"You would be amazed if you knew some of the stupid things people three times your age do with guns. I was told you only need one magazine?"

"Yeah, one will do, I don't think I'm going to need more than that. If I can't hit someone once in fifteen tries that's a bit shameful."

"Okay, so you don't need reloading instructions. Second thing is, be sure that you don't point the gun at anything you're not willing to destroy."

"Oh, so I can point it wherever I want?"

The man and the woman both look at each other. Suddenly the woman starts laughing again.

"What?"

"Hana, if being a pop singer doesn't work out for you, let us know through Iseul. I think we could probably find you other work to do."

43. THE BRICK

When was the last time I actually made a phone call? I don't remember. Maybe never?

It feels weird to have a phone in my hand, even if it's a phone from the previous century. This strange brick-shaped thing has chunky circular buttons and a small monochrome screen that I can barely even read, I have no idea how to operate it. I've seen people use phones on television shows and I've seen other people make calls, so I know basically what to do, isn't there supposed to be a call menu or a contact list or something, fuck. I should have asked Iseul how to use it. There's a button on it with a phone handset so I guess I press that to bring up the call menu, but when I press it, nothing even happens. I press it over and over again in frustration and it just beeps at me. I'm not convinced this thing is even working, trust me to get a phone that doesn't even work. But if it's making a noise, it can't be dead, can it?

I think about the last time I used a telephone. *I remember when I was very young, my father would let me talk to people on the phone, but I wouldn't make the calls myself. He'd dial the number, and then he'd put the phone up to my ear, and I'd listen to the dial tone, and then a click as the call connected. It was always my grandmother on the other end, she lived in Busan in an aged care facility and couldn't afford to come up to Seoul, and my father couldn't afford to go down there often either. My grandmother always liked hearing my voice, she said it made her smile. Those days are gone now.*

I look down at the phone, feeling sad. Even the phone my father had looked more modern than this piece of shit, it was one of those flip-up things. I don't know what else to do with this brick phone here, so I just start hitting random numbers on it, and one by one the numbers pop up on the tiny screen, each one giving a weird beep as I push it. It occurs to me that maybe I have to press all the numbers first, and then press the handset button to make the call once I see all the numbers. I pull the Apex Performance business card out of my tracksuit pocket and place it on the bench in the yard. In the darkness it's hard to read the numbers. I do my best to read them carefully and press the numbers on the business card with the grey plastic buttons, until the row of digits on the screen matches the digits on the business card. I double-check the numbers to make sure they match, then I press the handset button, and put the phone up to my ear. It's working - I can hear the same dial tone that I used to hear when I was a child. The sound fills me with sadness, but also a sudden rising panic because I realise that I haven't rehearsed what to say if someone answers.

After a few dial tones, I hear a deep male voice. *"Yeoboseyo?"*

Shit, how do I even start. I've never done this on my own before, but it should be simple, right? I look at the business card. *"Yeoboseyo...* is that... Lee Yeonggi, from Apex Performance?"

"Yes. How can I help you?" He sounds young.

I try my best to sound dumb, which isn't hard because while I'm not naive about the potential of the situation, my lack of confidence on the phone is probably showing, so I try to channel that energy into the conversation itself so I sound as stupid as I feel.

"Hi. So, my name's Hana, and um... I'm in this pop group, and we're in training. I'm worried, like, about my career, you know. I was speaking to my producer Mr Nam and he um... said that I should give you a call. He said you could help me..."

"Ah. Yes, I know Mr Nam well, I'm glad to hear that he referred you. He only refers the very best of talent to us."

"Wow, that's good. I guess it means I'm talented! So what do you do?"

"Apex Performance is a consulting and management business. I meet with people in all walks of life who have joined the entertainment industry, and counsel them on how to achieve the most effective results. Sometimes we just give advice, sometimes we operate in a managerial capacity and take talent on board to work with them closely. What concerns you the most about your career at this moment?"

"I just don't know if my management really has my best interests at heart. They don't seem to completely know what they're doing. I feel like they're not giving me the direction I need to succeed."

"How so?"

Fuck, what kind of a fucking question is that. I think for a moment. What would someone in this position even say? What would Youngsook have said?

"I feel like... I'm a good singer, you know, I've worked really hard on my voice, but my agency doesn't prioritise singing, they only seem to be interested in dance, which I'm not good at. They're so mean to me in assessments, even after I sing my heart out. How do I get them to recognise my talents?"

"Do not worry. I specialise in one-on-one counselling with trainees in situations that are just like yours. We should schedule a meeting."

"You would be willing to meet with me?"

"Absolutely."

"Where should we meet?"

"Can you come to my apartment?"

I sure can.

44. THE APARTMENT

I'm travelling up the elevator to Lee Yeonggi's apartment, and feeling more nervous than I've ever felt. Is this really what I want to do? Can I really do it? It's one thing to wish it, and I've probably wished such a fate on boys a thousand times over, but it's another thing to actually carry out the act. I start thinking about Youngsook's bruises. Who knows what could be waiting for me in there, but it's certain that Yeonggi deserves what's shortly coming to him. I'm doing the right thing, I know it. In any event I've set enough of my plan in motion that I can't really go back now. What am I going to do, go back to the gun guy and say I had a change of heart? Fuck that. I do my best to put any concern out of my mind.

I made sure to dress appropriately for a meeting with an important person who wants to enhance my career. I'm wearing my dress from the "Show Me Love" photo shoot, it's quite a pretty dress, I think it should make a very good impression, even if it's only me wearing it. Around my shoulder I'm also carrying my clothes bag, which is just like a big gym bag, I emptied the clothes out of it back at the dorm so I only have the gun in there plus the chunky brick phone and a couple of towels that I stole from the agency bathroom to put on top so that's what he sees if he pokes his head into the bag. I was told that the bullets in it would shoot through most things easily, so the towels being there shouldn't be a big deal, I should be able to shoot right through them if I have to.

The elevator stops and I get out, I'm in a hallway. I ready my right hand on the gun in my bag, just in case Yeonggi is wise to what I'm up to and there's an ambush or something, I need to be ready. I start walking down the hallway looking for the door with the right number on it, but none of the doors have numbers on them or anything really. I wonder if a lot of the apartments up here are even occupied, maybe not. Good for me because it means no witnesses. Eventually I come across a door that's very obviously the right one - not only does it have his name on the door in gold and black lettering, but there's a copy of his business card right underneath the doorbell. That's a nice touch. I look down into my bag and move the towel aside so I can check the gun. I push the sliding thing on the gun back halfway like I was shown, yes there's a bullet in there, that's good. I should be ready for when the action happens. I tuck the gun back into the depths of my bag but keep my hand on it, as I ring the doorbell with my other hand. Who knows what will happen when he opens the door. After a few seconds, the door swings open.

"*Annyeong haseyo!*" says Yeonggi. He's a young man, maybe about thirty years old, maybe younger than that.

He's dressed in a black and white suit and has neatly cropped hair. He looks sharp and athletic.

"*Annyeong haseyo!*" I say back, bowing.

"Please come on in, Hana."

Yeonggi motions for me to walk into his apartment. I enter through the doorway, discard my "Show Me Love" dress shoes on the shoe rack and enter his apartment living space. I'm in a spacious lounge room with big plush sofas, a large television and beyond this, a kitchen that extends around a corner that I can't see. There doesn't seem to be anyone else around, and he's behaving himself for now, so I take my hand off the gun in my bag so I don't look suspicious.

"Make yourself comfortable on the sofa, and I'll get you a drink."

I walk to the sofa and sit down. Yeonggi walks over to the kitchen area and starts preparing a drink of some sort around the corner.

"What do you drink?"

I'm not sure what to say here. I guess it doesn't really matter, because I'm not going to be drinking it anyway. I remember Iseul's words to me about drink spiking - if some guy connected to the agency in some way that you don't know, or even that you do know, offers a drink, it's almost certainly drugged.

"Surprise me."

I hear the sound of a bottle opening and pouring, and eventually Yeonggi enters the lounge with a drink in each hand. He places mine in front of me, some fizzy urine-coloured substance in a tall, thin glass. I don't know what it is exactly but it's clearly alcoholic. He holds an identical drink in his own hand and starts sipping.

Yeonggi looks me up and down. "You are looking very pretty tonight, Hana."

"This is the dress I'll be wearing for my debut."

"I didn't mean the dress, I mean *you*."

A shudder goes down my spine. I've been in his apartment less than two minutes and he's already trying it on. I don't say anything.

He notices that I haven't picked up the glass. "You're not drinking?"

I'd better make up some bullshit. "Not yet. I just got here. I want to let it sit. Good alcohol should sit for a while first, you know?"

Fortunately for me, he doesn't sit down next to me, but instead sits on a sofa chair that's at right-angles to the one I'm sitting on. I move my bag so it's next to me, on the opposite side of where he is, so when it's time to reach for the gun, he doesn't see it coming.

"Now Hana, about your career predicament, firstly I just want to give you this advice based on how I saw you walk in here this evening..."

I instantly tune him out, I'm not even listening. I've got bigger things to worry about, like how this execution situation is going to go. I figure I probably don't have a lot of time; he's going to start to get increasingly pissed off when he realises that I am not drinking his probably-drugged drink. At that stage, he could get violent, and if it comes to a physical fight, he's going to win, I can tell this just by looking at him. One thing I've learned over and over again at school is that being a short, skinny girl matters - I really can't do much about it if someone bigger or stronger attacks me physically.

"...there's many different factors that contribute to the success of each individual idol, but it helps to have a personal advantage, if you know what I mean..."

This is why I took to gym so much at school, it wasn't just the satisfying feeling of doing something physical, I wanted to get tough enough to even the odds just a little. Not that I was going to start winning fights, especially if it was two or more on one, which it usually was, but I wanted to be able to at least struggle free if I was pinned down, or run fast if I had to. However there's only so much I have to work with genetically. Even after all these months of training as an idol, devoting hours to it every single day, this guy who probably spends most of his life on his sofa masturbating, is way stronger than me. It's unfair if you ask me, but that's okay, that's what the gun is for. That's why I wanted a gun for this. I've always dreamed of having the kind of power where I can destroy people that I hate, and now I have it. I just have to make sure that I act at the right moment.

"...and I know training to be an idol is a hard life, but you must apply yourself in many new directions, including getting to know others who can help you..."

Anyway, I don't have much time. I'd better start shooting at this guy. I'm procrastinating though - why? I should be filling him full of holes right this instant, but it's so difficult to make that final step. Can I really do this? What if I called the plan off, could I get out of it now? What would happen if I just excused myself and ran out the door, would Yeonggi forcibly stop me? Would I end up like Youngsook, or even worse? Or do I have him all wrong? He certainly at least looks sharp, what if he's actually a nice guy and I'm...

"...you're not drinking, Hana? Your drink has been sitting there long enough..."

Okay, he's a guy, and he's really trying to get me to drink that fucking drink, so he's probably not nice. Given that he's male, the chances that he deserves death just for existing alone are sky high. I shouldn't have any empathy for this piece of shit. But why can't I do it? What's wrong with me?

"...you seem upset. Don't be sad, you're such a pretty girl. Why don't you smile? You're so much prettier when you smile."

Okay, that's it. That's fucking it. I can do it now.

I pull the gun out of my bag and point it at him and immediately start pulling the trigger. Nothing happens, the trigger doesn't even move at all. Fuck - why the fuck not? Yeonggi doesn't seem to realise straight away that I'm pointing a gun at him, I guess he didn't expect something like this. I suddenly realise why the trigger isn't moving – that stupid safety switch is still on. I should have trusted my instincts that a safety switch was a stupid idea. I get my other hand and flick the switch up like I was shown, and then start pulling the trigger again. This time it's working, the gun kicks back as a bullet flies out and hits the chair behind Yeonggi. He starts freaking out, trying to dodge my aim and reach for the gun, I just keep shooting as fast as possible in his direction. It's hard to control the gun's exact aim because of the kicking motion but I figure if I shoot quickly enough before he can really react, eventually a bullet is going to hit. After only a couple of seconds, the gun just makes a clicking noise and no more bullets come out, I've expended the full magazine. I feel like the gun shouldn't have run out of bullets that fast, I feel a bit unsatisfied honestly, like there should be more in there. Did I really just shoot the gun fifteen times in a row? I guess I must have, but for some reason it doesn't feel like it.

I lower the gun and look over at Yeonggi, who has fallen back into his sofa chair. I've mainly just put holes in the sofa, but I definitely also hit him at least twice. Maybe I hit him more times than that, but it's really hard to tell and I don't exactly want to inspect his wounds too closely, that would be yucky. His head is hanging down, he's got a patch of red leaking through his clothes around his stomach area, and I think I hit him in the shoulder too because there's a red patch there also. There's some blood on his legs as well, but I don't know if that's from bullet holes, it might have just dribbled down from higher up. He looks like he's still breathing though, which isn't ideal or really what I want, so I stand up and start stomping on his face. This feels better and much more satisfying, it reminds me of when I met Harin the afternoon in class after she tried to get me gang-raped by her douche friends, I just grabbed her while she was sitting down at her desk, pulled her to the ground and started stomping on that bitch's fucking head, over and over. I was just about to get metal chair legs involved when her classmates and the teacher stopped me, typical useless teachers are blind when I get molested right there in the classroom but as soon as I turn the tables, there they are, protecting the guilty, it's so disgusting. Anyway the difference here is that nobody is around to tell me when to stop, so I can kick this guy's head in as hard as I want, for as long as I want. I keep kicking him until my foot hurts and I can't do it anymore, then I give myself some time to calm down because I'm crying and hyperventilating so much. Once I'm at a calm level I pick up my bag, put on my shoes and leave. Is he still alive? I don't really know, but I'm not sure how to make him any more dead than he already is, so the condition he's in now will have to do.

My plan for what to do afterward has been laid out in advance by my ride. I take the stairs down to the ground floor, which then takes me out to a rear building exit. From there I hop over the back fence of the apartment block, which is a little tricky in my dress but I'm agile enough to do it, then I walk through a park area to a street behind the complex. From here, I take out the phone in my bag and dial a number. This stupid ancient phone doesn't even store numbers, but I wrote the number I was given to dial on my hand earlier. I punch the numbers into the phone and make the call. I don't say anything, I've been told not to. I just let the phone ring a few times and then press the red hang up button. Less than a minute later, a familiar black van approaches and parks next to me. The door slides open.

"Get in quick." It's a familiar voice, it's the woman who was with the gun dealer the other day.

I quickly hop into the van and take a seat as the van speeds off. The woman looks at me. She's wearing the same all-black gear and mask as last time I met her.

"Took your time. We all thought something had happened to you."

"It was tricky to do, I wanted to do a good job."

"Gun, please."

I pull the gun out of my bag and hand it to her, along with the brick phone. She takes both items and inspects the gun.

"No bullets left. Is he dead?"

"I hope so. I shot him a bunch of times, and then kicked him a lot. He should be."

"If you wanted to make sure, you could have gotten a knife from his kitchen to finish the job."

"Fuck. How did I not even think of that?"

Even though the woman has a mask on, I can see her jaw muscles flex into a smile.

"Don't worry about it – rookie mistake. You're not a professional yet, Hana."

45. A QUICK MEETING

I'm in Mr Park's office, sitting down on one of the visitor chairs. Iseul and Nari are both sitting here with me. Mr Park is sitting behind his desk. He holds up my blue and purple "Show Me Love" dress, the same dress that I was wearing when I shot Yeonggi two days ago. It's a mess - it's torn from where I jumped the fence, and there's red bloodstains all over the bottom half.

"Care to explain the meaning of this, Hana?"

How deep is Mr Park into this? Should I just tell him the truth? I don't know. I look over at Iseul for some kind of guidance. She looks back at me nervously. I interpret her nervous expression to mean that telling the truth could be a problem here. I'd better make up some kind of lie quickly and try to sound convincing.

"When Youngsook came back to the dorms, when she was bleeding a lot, you know, before she went to hospital... I just happened to be practising getting in and out of my costume when she came in, so I had to go and help her. I couldn't exactly wait and get changed while she was there like bleeding and stuff, you know... and then she grabbed me while she was bleeding and the dress ripped really bad, and heaps of her blood got all over it..."

"BULLSHIT!" Mr Park yells.

All three of us jump in our seats.

I bow at ninety degrees.

"I'm so sorry Mr Park CEO, I swear, it's..."

Mr Park slams his fist down on his desk.

"SHUT THE FUCK UP, HANA! Don't dig a deeper hole for yourself than the one you're already in!"

I remain bowing but don't say anything further.

Mr Park continues. "I know that you're bullshitting me, because I had the costumes inspected three days ago, and then two days ago, and then yesterday! So I know exactly when the damage to the costume happened, and it was long after Youngsook went to hospital! Do you have anything to say about that, Hana?"

I'm completely caught in a lie. There's no getting out of this one for me, I'll just have to beg and grovel. I slide back the chair, kneel on the floor, and start bowing at ninety degrees while on the floor. "It's true that I lied! I'm so sorry Mr Park CEO, please forgive my disrespect!"

"I don't know how you got the uniform into this state, and I don't care. However putting the uniform back on the rack as if nothing was wrong, and then lying to me about it when confronted, this is *completely unacceptable*. Do you understand, Hana?"

"Yes, Mr Park CEO!" Oh thank fuck he doesn't care how it happened, that's at least something.

"It's just as well that we personally check on these things daily! We have a video shoot coming up for 'Show Me Love', and we're now going to have to scramble to get this repaired in time, it's going to be very difficult to arrange. Do you realise the expense of this, and the potential expense of delaying the shoot? We have crew, materials and set design that have been booked for months in advance, just for you to go and screw it all up! All these people need to be paid, whether the shoot goes ahead or not! Do you want to be kicked out of the group?"

I remain bowed on the floor, like my life depends on it, which it probably does. "I'm so sorry, Mr Park CEO! I'll do anything to be given a chance!"

"Tomorrow night at 9 o'clock, you present yourself here, and you will be taken over to Blue Tower! You'll be working there tomorrow night!"

I hear Iseul gasp. Blue Tower... she told me that was bad, but she didn't say what it was.

"Get up off the floor Hana, stop being so pathetic. And Nari... you're not off the hook for this either, not for a moment. If it wasn't for your *truly garbage leadership*, we wouldn't be..."

"Mr Park Jeongmin, sir?"

I hear a deep male voice interrupt Mr Park. I look up and nearly have a heart attack. *Police officers. Oh shit.*

"Girls, please leave the room and go back to the gym. I need to have a word to this lady and gentleman."

Myself, Nari and Iseul get up and file out as discreetly as possible, past the two police officers. We walk out of the administration area and into the gym space.

"Hana, I'm so sorry," says Iseul.

"Iseul, what the fuck is Blue Tower?"

Iseul shakes her head.

"Not sure exactly, but it's nothing good."

Nari looks at me. "Don't worry Hana. I won't ask what you did. I honestly really *do not* want to know. The more I find out about this place, the less I like it, so I'll just stay ignorant this time, for my mental health."

"That's good, because I wasn't going to tell your stupid uptight ass anyway." I reply.

"You fucking insolent bitch, do you want to get hit?"

"Screw off, *kkondae*. I'll hit you first!"

Just then, the two police officers come walking out into the gym area, and now I can get a better look at them both. The man is tall, over six feet easily, skinny with short black hair, he looks neat and clean. The woman isn't much taller than me, about Nari's height, and about the same build too, her frame looks muscular. She has smooth heart-shaped facial features and wears her black hair in a bun behind her police hat. They both look at myself and Nari, we do our best to straighten ourselves up and act like we weren't just about to fight each other.

"Hey girls, have you debuted yet?" the male officer asks.

"Working on it!" Nari replies.

Both of them smile at us.

"What's the name of your group?"

"We don't have a name yet! But our debut song is called 'Show Me Love', expect us fondly!"

The two officers then wave to us and walk down the hall and out of the building. Myself, Nari and Iseul all look at each other.

"What the fuck was that about?" Nari asks.

Iseul just shrugs her shoulders. "No idea."

Nari wanders out to the middle of the gym space to stretch out. Iseul watches the police disappear from view.

"Should I be concerned?" I ask Iseul.

"They love us. After we debut, they'll be at our fan signs, probably. Don't even worry about the police. Worry about Blue Tower."

46. BLUE TOWER

"What's your name, little schoolgirl?"

I'm in a dressing room at "Blue Tower" which isn't actually a whole tower, but just a rented out upper floor of a very large apartment complex that's within walking distance of the agency building. There's a whole bunch of chairs here, the walls are lined with mirrors and lights, and there's four other girls here, all dressed in high-class dresses that couldn't be any more different from my crumpled school uniform. They're all pretty in that generic way, they all have variations of that *ulzzang* face that girls who want to be successful for their appearance have. It's the same kind of look that Nari has, although none are as tough-looking as her, or as attractive. The one who just spoke to me, there's no way any portion of her face is still natural. She's amused by my outfit but I can't exactly wear an agency-branded tracksuit in a place like this, and I sure as fuck am not wearing pyjamas which are the only other clothes I have. I'm not going to explain this to her though, it'll become a conversation I don't want to have. I just glare at this bitch. I have nothing to say to her.

This is so fucking awkward and annoying. I hope Iseul comes through with my clothing request soon.

"Well, you're a friendly one," she taunts.

I guess I'd better not start a fight here, I'm already in enough trouble.

"My name is Hana."

The plastic monster woman seems to want a fight anyway, she reaches out one hand and grabs me by the cheek.

"Well listen here, *Hana*, you had better..."

We're interrupted by the ringing of a bell. This means that a new client has entered the foyer.

"I'll deal with you later!" Miss Plastic shoves my face away from her and walks out through the dressing room door to the foyer, the rest of the girls follow. I make sure that I follow last, because I don't know these girls. I'd rather have them in front of me than behind me, and I also want as much distance between myself and Plastic Monster as possible.

In the foyer, the woman who is running this shit-show, a hateful old bag with gaudy white makeup, is talking to the client in hushed tones. He's a very old man with a hunched back, he looks to be well over retirement age. I can't hear what they're saying but it's obvious that she's asking him to pick a girl. He points straight at Plastic Fantastic. She struts up, takes the old man gently by the arm and they disappear slowly down the hallway to a private room together. That's good, it means I don't have to see that bitch for a while, hopefully he's secretly a serial killer and he murders her, but he looks far too old and harmless for that so I probably won't get my wish, what a pity.

I turn around and go back to the dressing room, with the other girls following me. I'm just about to find a chair to sit down and get comfortable in when the bell rings again. I sigh and retrace my steps back out to the foyer. When I get there, the host is talking to another client, a young man, probably about my age, certainly no older than a teenager. He's kind of pudgy and has thick glasses, he's dressed in a casual jumper and track pants. He sees me and *instantly* points to me, with no hesitation at all, he doesn't even look once at the other girls, not even to quickly check them out. My heart sinks. I was really hoping I'd avoid getting picked.

"What's in the bag?" the host asks him. I only now notice that he's carrying a large school bag with him.

"I already showed this to security at the front?"

"Doesn't matter - I still need to see."

He opens the bag up so she can see inside. From where I'm standing, I can't see what it is.

The host gives him a strange look.

"That's... fine. You do you, kid. You can go with her."

I walk up to him just a couple of steps. Do I have to touch him? I'll try to avoid that for as long as I can. He looks a little nervous like he's not going to make the first move, so I just bow and say to him *"Annyeong!"* Maybe if I come across as cute rather than slutty, he'll go slow or at least wait until we get into the private room before he starts inevitably molesting me.

"*Annyeong!*" he replies and bows back, not even moving forward. Okay, he seems like someone who will play nice. He seems very nervous actually.

"Please follow me."

I walk off down the hallway, looking for a vacant room, keeping one eye on the boy as he trails behind me a fair distance away. This place is busy, I have to go down six doors before I finally find a room that's unoccupied.

Inside the room is a cosy hotel setting. On one side of the room, there's a large double bed, with a decorative metal bedhead. Across from that, there's a small kitchen with a microwave, a sink and a fridge, and a couple boxes of disposable paper towels on the bench. A far corner leads to a bathroom and shower. The other near corner is a lounge area with a big fabric sofa, a massive widescreen television on a stand, and some bean bags and pillows. Everything is conspicuously very neat and clean. The only thing that makes this room not look exactly like a high-class hotel is the large metal sign on a stand right by the doorway.

BLUE TOWER - HOUSE RULES

TOUCHING, NAKEDNESS (TOP HALF ONLY) AND MASTURBATION IS PERMISSIBLE

NO PENETRATION OF ANY KIND (ORAL, VAGINAL, ANAL) IS ALLOWED

GUESTS MUST CLEAN UP THEIR OWN BODILY FLUIDS, USE THE PAPER TOWELS PROVIDED

ABSOLUTELY NO BDSM, BONDAGE, EDGE PLAY ETC UNDER ANY CIRCUMSTANCES

ALL ACTIVITIES MUST BE RESPECTFUL AND CONSENTED BY BOTH PARTIES - OR ELSE!

NO MOLKA - WE HIDE BODIES BETTER THAN YOU CAN HIDE CAMERAS

ENJOY YOUR GIRLFRIEND FOR ONE HOUR MAXIMUM - EXTRA CHARGES APPLY - 100% OF TOTAL FEE PER TEN MINUTES OVER OR PART THEREOF

Iseul wasn't kidding, this is going to be a nightmare. How the fuck I am even going to deal with this at all, without killing the boy, myself, or maybe both of us. Any of those three options sound more appealing than having to go through with this. *It's like school again, but regulated, and without even the pretence of maybe someone trying to stop it. How the fuck did I even get here.* I look over at the boy, he's not even paying attention to me. He's walked over to the television and is doing something around the back of it. He's also opened up his school bag, there's some sort of black box in there.

"What are you doing?" I ask.

"I'll just be a moment!"

I sit on the sofa chair and keep watching him, as he runs some cords from the back of the television to the black box in his bag, which he tips out onto the floor. There are also some other devices in there which I immediately recognise. Gaming controllers.

"You want me to play a game?"

He switches on the black box and hands me a controller. "Please!"

Add playing computer games to the exceedingly long list of activities that I haven't had a chance to do in about a decade. I take the controller from his hand. He's carrying a second controller, and with a convoluted series of moves, he faces the television and starts a game up. The huge screen flashes up a logo: VIRTUOUS ASSAULT.

"Have you ever played this?"

"No."

He points to my controller. "You use these to move, forward, backward, sideways. This stick is to look, and this button is to shoot. When you run out of bullets, press down here to reload."

"Sounds cool, who am I shooting at?"

"We'll start with a deathmatch. So just shoot anything that moves. Everyone's the enemy, even me."

"I think I might like this game."

He presses some buttons on the controller that changes a menu, and a whole lot of guns appear on the screen, each with different prices.

"On this screen you can buy guns. Just highlight the one you want, and press the shoot button to buy it. You can only buy a pistol now, but you get more money as you play so you can save up and buy better guns later, like the rifles."

I notice one of the pistols that I can immediately afford looks identical to the gun that I used to shoot Yeonggi with, just a different colour. It even has the same stupid safety switch on it. I decide that this is my gun.

"I like this one here."

"That's not actually a very good gun in this game."

"I just like it. I'm buying it anyway."

I select the gun and then I spawn into some kind of desert area with a first-person view of my surroundings. I move the stick to look up at the sky and end up looking at my feet instead. It's impossible to control.

"What the fuck! Why is this shit upside down? It goes down when I want to go up! What's with that?"

The boy laughs at me. "Give me your controller."

I hand my controller over to him and he quickly scrolls through some menu options, changes something that I don't get time to read, then gives me the controller straight back. I use the stick to make my character look around again, everything now seems more logical.

"That's better, thank you."

"You're an inverter but I guess I'll still talk to you."

I look over at him, he's smiling. He doesn't seem so nervous anymore.

I start running my character around the desert arena, randomly shooting at people. I'm really bad at it, and I get myself killed a lot. I discover that each time I die, I go back to the shop and then I come alive again, and can try to kill people some more. After a while and several defeats I manage to kill one person, then two. I notice that the boy has stopped playing the game himself and is now just watching me play.

"Do you like the game?" he asks, after I've died in the game about two dozen times.

"Actually I do. This is fun, I just wish the gun was more realistic. There's definitely not enough kick when you fire. Also it takes about seven shots to actually kill someone with it, which is just silly, I know it really only takes about two with this gun."

"I agree, I think pistols need to be better in this game. There's no real incentive to buy them. You have a lot of money saved up. You should buy something better."

I think for a moment. "What has a lot of bullets? I need a gun with the maximum amount of bullets."

He points at the screen. "Heavy machine gun. It's expensive so you can't buy it very often, but you haven't been buying anything for several rounds so you can afford it now."

I buy the heavy machine gun and start up another round. I hold down the fire button and the gun spits out bullets everywhere so randomly and quickly, it's hilarious.

I can't really aim it that well but I also can't help but get a few kills just from sheer luck.

I keep playing, the time flies, virtual killing is fun. It definitely doesn't have the satisfaction of the real thing, but it also doesn't have the stress of knowing if it's going to work out or if someone's going to retaliate and cause me real-world harm. Every minute or so I look over and check on this weird boy sitting next to me. I keep waiting for the time he's going to reach over and try to grope me, after all that's what this place is obviously for, but he never does. He plays the game a little but he spends most of his time just watching me in silence, and watching the screen. He's not even trying to inch his way closer to me or anything, other than to help me with the controller from time to time he keeps a polite distance. After a while, a bell sounds. I look over at him.

"I think that's the five-minute warning. You'd better pack up. You don't want to be charged extra."

He suddenly looks sad, takes the controller from my hand and slowly starts packing up his gaming gear. I don't know why, but I actually feel sorry for him.

"Hey... what's your name? You never told me it."

"Jihu." He bows even though he's not really facing me because he's pulling out cords from the television.

"I'm Hana. Hey Jihu, you don't have anyone to game with?"

"Only online, not in person. Never any girls."

I'm curious, I have to ask. "You didn't want to do anything... besides game?"

He replies hesitantly as he finishes packing his bag and stands up. "I like just watching you play. You're pretty good, for a girl, and you know about guns too, that's kind of neat. I hope we can meet again. *Annyeonghi gyeseyo.*"

He bows, then walks out of the room. I exhale deeply in relief. I slowly walk back out and down the hallway, into the foyer and then the dressing room. There are four girls here, all sitting down doing their hair and makeup, I think they're different girls to the ones that were here before, I guess this place really is busy. Plastic Fantastic thankfully isn't one of them. A couple of them stare at me a little as I enter, but they thankfully leave me alone. I sit down in the nearest dressing room chair and catch my racing thoughts for a moment. What just happened was actually fun and not what I expected at all, but I'm sure most clients aren't like that and if I'm here long enough I'm going to have to sexually satisfy some creep. And I'm here all night. I start thinking about possible survival strategies, when I hear the bell - another client. I let the other girls file out into the foyer and I follow them. When I get out to the foyer, my jaw drops. What the fuck?

"You don't work here! You can't be back here!" yells the host at Caitlin, angrily.

"Damn right, I don't work here."

Caitlin smiles and gives something to the host. It looks like a business card. The host looks at the card carefully on one side, then the other. Her expression changes from hostility to compliance. She then bows to Caitlin.

"I apologise, Miss Park."

Caitlin grabs the card back off the host and walks up to me. She's dressed stylishly, in a loose blue cardigan, a white T-shirt that shows a small amount of midriff, and casual pants.

"Hey, Hana. Let's go to a room. Lead the way!"

After taking a few seconds to pick up my jaw from the floor, I walk with Caitlin down the hallway, into the same room that I took Jihu to, and close the door. Caitlin wanders around the room, investigating everything.

"Wow, this is pretty swanky and clean for a knock shop! Oakland would never!"

"Caitlin, how...?"

"Iseul told me you were here, and where it was, so I snuck out and walked over, it's not that far. She also gave me a card, I don't know what it means, but that thing opens a few doors, apparently!"

"Oh my god... can you get me out of here, you think?"

Caitlin stops running around the room and walks up to me, laughing.

"Get you *out?* Hana, I don't think so. I've just booked you for the *entire night!*"

A light bulb goes on in my head and suddenly my fear evaporates. Caitlin's just saved me from a night of being molested by creeps, *and* she's secured a place where we can be together, in complete privacy, with no threat of being disturbed. Here I was thinking all this time she was dumb; she could actually be the smartest person alive. Or at least the smartest person I've ever met. Certainly the smartest person that I've developed feelings for, which I'm pretty sure is now starting to happen.

Caitlin places her arms gently around my waist. I flinch ever so slightly, but the fear gives way to a feeling of warmth and security almost immediately. She speaks softly into my ear while nuzzling up against my cheekbone with her mouth.

"I like that bed, it looks pretty. It'd look prettier with you on it. Should we test it out?"

Caitlin leads me by the hand to the bed, and tips me over gently, I fall backwards onto the quilt. She then straddles me and I wrap my arms around her shoulder blades, we start kissing softly and passionately. I gradually feel my self-doubt rising. I have to say something.

"Why me?"

Caitlin puts a finger over my lips.

"You're kind of crazy, but I guess I like crazy. You're interesting."

"Even if I've done bad things...?"

"You think *I'm* an angel? Don't worry, I know what you did."

"What's *wrong* with me, Caitlin?"

"I'll admit it's a character flaw, but that fucking asshole had it coming. We both saw what he did to Youngsook. A lot of us wish we could do what you did and get away with it." Caitlin starts nuzzling into my neck. "The other girls we dorm with are okay people, I suppose, once you account for the shitty circumstances that we're all in, but I wouldn't touch them even if they *were* lesbian."

"I'm not a lesbian, fuck off!" I reply instinctively.

"Are you sure? Shall we check?"

Caitlin looks down at my torso and starts very slowly unbuttoning the top button of my shirt.

"Let's check it. Exactly how lesbian are you feeling right now?"

My breathing starts increasing rapidly. This is stressful, but I also don't want Caitlin to stop, how do I convey that? I have no idea.

"I don't know..."

Caitlin parts the newly-created gap in my shirt so my collarbone is exposed and kisses my neckline softly. She then very gradually unbuttons the second button from the top.

"How about now? Do you feel more lesbian, or less lesbian than before?"

My heart pounds against Caitlin's hands as she works the second button loose. I feel like my ribcage might explode.

"Maybe a little more..."

She then grabs my right arm from around her shoulders, hikes up her T-shirt and gently pushes my hand against her chest. I involuntarily hold my breath with a mixture of shock and desire.

Caitlin smiles. "How about now?"

I move my other arm tighter around Caitlin and pull her down into me. I want to disappear into her, into this moment, and forget the world.

47. M/V

"CUT! Hana, that's not right, can you do it again?"

"What was wrong *that* time?"

"We need more arm movement please. You need to reach up more."

I look around at the featureless green box that I'm imprisoned in.

"Reach up where? There's nothing up there?"

"Just pretend that you're a ballet dancer," comes the incredibly unhelpful instruction from behind the camera.

I am so over being here. When we first walked into the TV studio yesterday morning, we were pretty excited that we were finally shooting our music video, but now that excitement is gone and all of us just want to go back to the dorms and sleep for a whole day. Only Nari still seems to give a shit and the strain is even getting to her, she's been grumpy as fuck for the last few hours and stares at me with dagger eyes from behind where the cameraman is sitting because I'm not getting this dance or whatever it is right. Youngsook is deeply regretting coming back from the hospital yesterday and is off sulking somewhere with

Caitlin and Iseul, I don't blame her as she's still in a fair bit of pain. Even Shu's unshakeable *aegyo* has taken a hit and she's sleeping off her fatigue on the hard floor in a far corner of the studio. Of course she can sleep there just fine, even in a place like this with about three dozen staff running around doing fuck knows what and yelling at each other. None of the rest of us have gotten any sleep at all since yesterday morning, we've either been dancing and miming to our song, or waiting around for crews to get their shit together so we can dance and mime to our song. Once this scene of mine is done hopefully that's it and we can all fuck off. I ready myself in the starting position with my arms outstretched in front of me, standing on the platform, ready to twirl up on cue.

"Three... two... one... action!" yells the cameraman.

I do the twirling move again where I turn around and outstretch my arms, to something, I don't fucking know what. It feels so stupid. I guess they're going to make it look good in editing or whatever, but nobody's told me the context, they're just telling me to do the twirling thing, so I have no idea how to even make it look.

"CUT! Hana, make a fucking effort, please!"

I relax my body and groan. "What was wrong *then?*"

"You look like you'd rather be in bed," the cameraman complains.

"No shit, that's because I'd rather be in bed! We've been doing this for a day and a half straight, this is fucked!"

"Hana, at least try to make an effort, then we can all get out of here!" Nari yells from somewhere behind the cameraman.

"I'm sorry, it's just really hard to fake giving a fuck. I'll keep trying I guess, let's go again." I ready myself in the starting position and nod to the cameraman to count it down.

"Three... two... one... action!" he yells.

I do the twist move again, and turn around. There's no way what I'm doing can't feel idiotic. I'm so over it. What do they even want?

"CUT! Hana, that was rubbish! What the fuck are you even doing?" The cameraman yells at me in frustration. I'm frustrated too, so he can get fucked.

"I don't fucking know, what the fuck am I even *supposed* to do? This is stupid! What am I supposed to even be? Why am I doing this?"

Nari steps up. "You're supposed to be an idol, Hana. Why not act like it and get it done."

"Yeah, thanks Nari, how motivating. I can barely stay awake here, fuck."

Nari turns to the cameraman. "Can't we just edit all her shitty takes together or something? There's got to be some useable footage there, right?"

The cameraman shakes his head. "No, we have to get this done. Hana, we're starting, get ready again."

I look down and wait for the cameraman to tell me to start again.

"Hana? We're starting, get ready. Come on."

Oh, he already told me to start just then. That's right. I nod and assume the starting position.

"Three... two... one... action!" he yells.

I start twirling and look up at the ceiling. I keep spinning, trying to do my best. The spinning speeds up, and then it slows down. Is this how it's supposed to go? I look up at the ceiling, trying to focus. It's weird how the ceiling looks a little different to before. It's brighter all of a sudden, and the lights have changed. I try to reach up my arms like I was told to, and my right arm hits something solid, it feels hard and cold to touch, like a metal rail. My left arm won't lift up at all, something's stopping it. I look down at my left arm, there's a plastic tube going into it that's stretched tight and is preventing my movement. I look over at where the tube goes, it's attached to a transparent bag with some clear fluid in it that's hanging on a metal stand just out of reach. I look around and see two rails on either side of me, and I realise that I'm in a hospital bed. I guess something happened to me, although I don't know what, I just remember twirling and now I'm here. Where did the time go? I sit up in the bed slightly, and look around, before I realise that the bed is already slightly inclined in a semi-sitting up position, so I lie back down again. Ijun is here, dressed in her usual school uniform, and playing with her phone. She notices my movement and looks over at me.

"*Annyeong.* How are you feeling?"

"What happened to me?"

Ijun moves her eyes back to her phone and talks softly. "You collapsed during the video shoot."

"Where are the others?"

"Back at the dorm. You will go back there soon also, once that bag runs out."

Ijun points to the bag of fluid attached to the tube which comes from my arm. There's not a lot of liquid left inside there, so I guess I won't have to wait very long.

"What's the bag for?"

"Intravenous drip, electrolytes. Replacing your bodily fluids. You were severely dehydrated. Bastard son of a bitch, fuck!"

"Did I say something wrong?"

Ijun scowls as she taps something on her phone.

"Sorry, it's just the game."

Ijun puts her phone down and looks over at me. I look back at Ijun. I feel like I should try and make conversation since I'm stuck here until this drip comes out of my arm.

"Your school uniform is nice. What school do you go to?"

"Dadang."

I know Dadang, it's a well-known rich bitch school, very prestigious and exclusive. Only the very wealthiest families send their girls there. I guess Ijun must be the CEO's daughter, there's not many other people who could afford to send their kids to Dadang.

"Is it good there?"

"The classes are okay, but everyone hates me. They know I'm in the family of Mr Park, so nobody talks to me, they are too scared."

"That's so silly. It's not your fault that you're his daughter, you can't help it?"

Ijun's look suddenly sours, and she glares at me.

"I am *not* his daughter!"

Oh shit. What? I feel incredibly awkward.

"I'm so sorry, Ijun!"

I bow slightly while sitting up, although the reclining position of my bed makes this difficult.

Ijun holds her right hand up. There's a large jewel-encrusted ring on her ring finger. I gasp.

"You're married?"

"I have to wait a few more months to be married, so it's legal." Ijun stares at the ring. "At that time, I will probably get another one of these."

Ijun's facial expression lightens a little, she doesn't seem cross at me anymore. I don't know how to react to this. I have a lot of questions, but I don't really know anything to ask that would be appropriate and not potentially get my ass booted out of the group so I just sit and look at the ring in silence. Ijun twists her arm around as she inspects the ring. The jewels glisten as they reflect the bright fluorescent glare of the hospital ceiling. I stare at the refracting light as my thoughts wander and I gradually lose consciousness again.

48. HALCYON

The group is lined up in the gym, we're in our usual standing positions. Mr Park and Ijun are both here. Mr Park is holding a clipboard and Ijun is standing with him. We were told specifically *not* to wear our agency gym gear today, or our performance dresses, but we weren't told why. Of course I'm wearing my school uniform because I have no other options. Everyone else has taken the opportunity to get styled up, because after the months of bland and torturous training we all believe a big announcement is coming. After all we just finished shooting our music video a few days ago, so they will no doubt release it soon. I've been busy checking the other members' clothes out, because I'm thinking of what clothes I want to buy for myself when I get the chance. Caitlin's wearing the same cardigan she wore in Blue Tower, but with a pink miniskirt and a different shirt that's a golden colour and has criss-crossing patterns. Nari has really gone the extra mile, she wears a black men's-style jacket, a knee-length black skirt and a glittery buttoned jumper with a white dress shirt underneath. It's a weird combination that somehow looks stylish, the sort of clothes that probably wouldn't work for anybody else but Nari. Shu is wearing a frilly summer dress, all pink of course. Youngsook has a black, much simpler and plainer version of the same type of thing Shu is wearing, no doubt she's dressing for low maintenance comfort because her injuries are still healing and they make it difficult for her to get in and out of clothing. Iseul wears a grey sweater with a blue beret and a matching blue short skirt, I guess she's going for a cute look but I know way too much about Iseul now to consider anything about her cute. Iseul's outfit looks like the one that would work the best for me out of what everyone has on, but then I don't know if I'm all that "cute" either. I guess murdering people doesn't make me very *aegyo*.

Mr Park smiles as he looks us over. "As you know, soon 'Show Me Love' will be released, and you will make your debut as pop idols. Since you are making the transition from trainees to idols, we have some announcements to make. The first one is your group name, which is Halcyon."

We all look at each other.

"What's a halcyon?" asks Shu.

I'm relieved that Shu asked this question because I don't know what it means either, better for her to look dumb than me. Mr Park starts looking down his clipboard in that slothful way that teachers always do when they don't know the answer to a question that a student asks and they have to look it up, he very obviously doesn't know either.

"Halcyon... is a word characterized by happiness, great success, and prosperity. It is used to describe an idyllic time in the past that contains fond memories. It's been chosen as a name for the group to add a nostalgic feel, in keeping with our warm retro-inspired theme of youth and returning the world of music to a more joyful time."

I nod, pretending to know or care about anything that Mr Park just said. Mr Park flips his clipboard around, showing a piece of paper with a pink square on it.

"In keeping with this theme, our team colour is nadeshiko pink, as indicated here."

"Yay!" shouts Shu as she bounces up and down. Why did it have to be pink. I don't give a shit about the colour itself, I'm just against things that make Shu this happy. I do my best to ignore her.

"The official name for the fans of Halcyon will be decided by fandom vote after debut, we are still finalising the process for this. We are now going to lift certain restrictions that were necessary during your training period. You no longer have a ban on using mobile phones and the Internet."

Everyone cheers. Ijun is carrying a small sack, she brings it around to us and holds it out in front of each person in the group. Everyone reaches into the bag one by one and retrieves their electronic devices, the ones that were confiscated when we first joined the agency. When Ijun gets to my position in the line-up I just put my hand up to indicate refusal so she can move on - I never had an electronic device to surrender initially. I look at the others as they examine their phones, they're all smiling. I watch Caitlin, who immediately takes the back cover of her phone off and extracts the SIM card.

Caitlin notices me looking at her. "This thing's old as shit now, I need an upgrade."

Mr Park continues. "You will be required to use your devices from now on to adhere to our new social media policy. You must use your device for promotional purposes. You are all to be allocated public social media accounts. These must only be used to promote the group activities, and you are to make at least one post per day on these accounts, as well as post any content that we request you post. All use of these accounts will be measured and monitored, and any posts deemed not to be in the group or company image will be removed. You are not to use private messaging of any kind on these accounts, or change any of the user profiles or passwords. All existing confidentiality provisions in your contract must continue to be adhered to at all times. Ijun will give you the credentials to these accounts tomorrow."

Well, I guess I'm screwed.

"Mr Park CEO, but what if I don't have a phone?"

I suddenly feel something tapping my right armpit. It's Caitlin, prodding me with her phone.

"Take it, it's yours."

I grab Caitlin's phone and wave at Mr Park, indicating my question is void. "Er... never mind, sorry to bother!"

Mr Park continues to address the room. "Tomorrow we will be releasing your teaser pictures to the world, and then the teaser videos for 'Show Me Love' will appear the following week. So today we have decided to allow you to have a day of freedom. Once you are recognised to the general public, you won't be able to go anywhere in public easily, so please enjoy today to do as you wish, just be sure to return to the dorms by lights out. To facilitate this, we have decided to give..."

Suddenly Mr Park stops talking. His gaze looks far away, like he's looking somewhere behind us. I turn around, the female police officer from the other week is standing behind us. My heart jumps.

"Mr Park Jeongmin sir, can I please have a quick word with you?"

Mr Park walks through our line-up, in the gap between myself and Nari, and up to the police officer. They start speaking in hushed tones. The conversation seems polite enough. I continue to watch them. Eventually, the police officer pokes her head out from behind Mr Park and looks straight at me.

"Hana, please step into the outdoor park area over there, and I'll have a quick word to you in a moment. I just need to check some stuff off my list, it shouldn't take more than a few minutes."

"Yes, Miss officer!"

I try to sound as compliant and helpful as possible so hopefully I don't seem too suspicious. Although maybe that just makes me sound more suspicious? Can police officers tell if you're guilty just by your voice? I then walk over to the sliding glass doors and move through them into the yard. I sit down on the bench but I'm full of nervous energy, so I stand up again and start doing some stretching to try and ease the tension in my body. Half a minute later, the officer opens the door and walks into the park area.

"Hello Hana, I'm Constable Yoon Nabi, please take a seat with me on the bench."

She sits down on the same bench where Caitlin has smoked an entire greenhouse worth of marijuana over the last few months. I swear that I can smell the slightest hint of a residual weed smell whenever I sit on this bench lately, hopefully Nabi can't detect any of it. She then taps the other side of the bench with her hand, inviting me to sit. I walk up and slowly sit with her.

"Hana, I need to tidy up my case notes, and I just need some help. I'm investigating an incident concerning a Mr Lee Yeonggi. Do you know him?"

I nod. "Yes, I went to his apartment one time."

"Yes, we saw you on some camera footage entering the foyer of his complex on the night that someone shot him."

My heart does a double-jump. Have I been caught?

"Why did you go there, Hana?"

I figure that if I make my story as honest as possible, and try not to lie until I have to, I'll come across more authentic.

"I was having some career issues, he offered to help me enhance my career. He asked me to visit him."

Nabi pulls out a small notepad and starts taking notes. "Okay. Do you remember how long you stayed?"

"It wasn't long. Ten minutes, maybe less."

"What did you do there? Was he helpful?"

"No, not at all. He just talked, he said he was going to help me, but I think that was an excuse to get me in his apartment because he just talked about himself for a while and then he tried to pick me up. He offered me a drink but I didn't drink it, I think it might've been spiked. He said some inappropriate things. I felt uncomfortable with the situation, so I left quickly."

"He let you go?"

"I was quick, I didn't give him a choice."

Technically, not a lie.

"We have footage of you entering the building, but nothing of you leaving, I thought you might've stayed there a while?"

"No, I just took the stairs. After what happened I didn't feel safe in the lift, and I had lots of nervous energy. I took the stairs down instead and they took me out the back way, it made me feel a little better. After something like that happens, I like to feel like I'm in control of my movements, you know?"

"I understand. Did you see him again later that night?"

I shake my head. "No, I never went back there. I didn't feel safe, there's something really creepy about that entire apartment block. I hope I never have to go there again. You never know what danger is around the corner in a place like that."

Nabi finishes taking notes and folds her notepad up.

"I'm sorry to hear that you had a bad experience, Hana. Thank you for helping us with our case."

Wait, that's it? I'm not getting arrested?

"Is everything okay? Do I need to do anything?"

"It's fine, we have everything we need now, we won't need to contact you again about this incident, you can put it safely behind you."

This doesn't feel right somehow.

"Are you sure you don't need me for anything else? I really want to be as helpful as possible."

Nabi puts a hand on my shoulder, smiles at me and gives me a small wink.

"Don't worry about a thing, Hana, really. Just leave it to us. Girls look after girls."

49. CHRISTMAS

"Hana, you haven't even picked anything out yet!"

I spin around, looking at the racks and racks of clothes, in all directions. The sheer number of choices here is overwhelming.

"I don't know when I'll get to do this again! What if I get the wrong thing?"

"Maybe what you need to do is eat first. Your brain might work better with some food in your stomach. We can eat what we want today! Let's go outside and keep walking down the street until we find something good!"

Caitlin walks towards the glass double doors of the department store and I quickly follow. We exit out onto the concrete path and take a left turn. The street is busy and the line of shops extends forever, there's no way we can visit it all. I resolve to do my best to see as much of it as possible before time runs out or my legs give out, whichever comes first.

Caitlin points to a small stall further up the footpath.

"Fried chicken! That's it, we're going there! Fuck yes!"

Caitlin sprints up to the fast-food stall and starts jumping up and down. I'm not in a sprinting mood because I'm still so overwhelmed by everything and I want to take it all in, but I hurry after Caitlin as briskly as my attention will allow. I sit down at an outdoor table in front of the fried chicken stall while Caitlin waves at the cook and presents her plastic card.

"Hey mister, can I get a couple buckets please."

A minute later she sits down with me, a paper bucket of fried chicken wings in each hand.

"Merry Christmas!"

I grab a bucket from Caitlin and place it in my lap.

"It's not anywhere near Christmas?"

"Total freedom, we get out of the building finally, I got a new phone, we all get social media access, we can eat whatever we want for a day... tell me it's not Christmas again, go on!"

I bite down on a chicken wing.

"Objectively it's not Christmas."

Caitlin says nothing, she just leans forward and grins at me. Meanwhile the taste of the fried chicken floods my mouth, it feels amazing.

"Okay... this food is pretty damn good. It could be Christmas. I guess I'll try to keep an open mind about it."

I start greedily taking more bites out of the chicken wing until it's nothing but a bone.

"Have you seen the others?"

"Who gives a fuck, I hate them all."

Caitlin takes a bite out of a chicken wing and talks with her mouth full. "You do not! You're such a liar. I know you at least have the hots for Nari."

"Am I that obvious?"

"You do things that piss her off on purpose. I can tell, I'm onto you!" Caitlin waves her chicken wing at me like a teacher, telling me off.

"I've got to admit, when Nari gets mad at me and pins me down, it's pretty exciting. She's too violent though. I don't like violence. Why does she have to be like that."

Caitlin starts laughing and rocking back and forth in her chair. "*You? You* don't like violence? Oh my god, listen to yourself!"

"Okay, okay... I'll qualify that. I like it when I do violence to others, but I don't like it when it's the other way around. I mean, that makes sense, right? I don't like being hit by Nari because she's tough, she knows how to hit, that shit fucking hurts. I'd like to hit her though; it upsets me that I would never beat her in a fight."

"You do like Nari at least a little though. There's more like there than hate."

I think about it while I devour more chicken wings.

"That plastic face is sexy, and she knows her stuff, but her personality is crap, she's such a fucking freak for rules and overachievement. I can't believe she's jogging right now, like, what the fuck is that? We all split up and went shopping, she went jogging. She finally has a day of freedom from this crazy training and wants to just find a new way to torture herself. I respect her desire to do well but she's too much. Can you imagine having a girlfriend like that?"

Caitlin laughs and puts her feet up on the table.

"You don't hate Youngsook either."

"Yeah, she's alright. She's a pretty nice person actually. I have time for her."

"She just wants to sing. It must be hard for her to put up with five talentless losers in her group and yet be constantly told she's the one who's not good enough."

"Do you know that she cuts?"

"No way, serious?"

"Yeah, on her thighs, where nobody can see. Smart, actually. Wish I'd thought of that back when I was cutting... but then maybe not. Thighs would hurt more, I think. She must have some crazy pain tolerance."

"Damn. We've got to look after her and make sure Nari doesn't get to her too much. Just like we need to make sure *you* don't get to Shu too much." Caitlin points another accusing chicken wing at me. "Shu's a nice girl. Save your hatefulness for the people who've earned it."

"Hey *gyopo*, get your feet off the table!" yells the cook behind the fast-food stall counter, interrupting us.

Caitlin looks over at the cook.

"I paid for the food? It's an outdoor table, I'm sure it's had worse things on it than feet?"

"Get your feet off!" he repeats.

Caitlin stands up and grabs her chicken bucket. "Oh fuck this place, let's eat and walk."

I stand up as well. "Where to?"

"I don't know, let's just keep going down this street until we find some interesting shit."

We walk for another couple of minutes and finish off all the fried chicken, when soon Caitlin slows her walking pace down as she walks past a shop front.

"Oh wow, this looks so cool, we're totally going in here! Let's go in!"

Caitlin grabs me by the arms and playfully pushes me through the shop entrance before I even get a chance to see what kind of store it is. Inside the store the atmosphere is really quaint, with a shiny wooden floor, funky modern decor and artfully arranged shelves. I'm not sure what's being sold here though, there's a lot of little statuettes, although some of it seems like cosmetics or hair care products. Nothing looks quite familiar.

"I like this one, do you think this would work for you?"

Caitlin grabs a pink object that looks a bit like a hair-curler, but it's not quite the right shape. She flicks a switch on it and it makes a buzzing noise.

"What the fuck is that thing?"

Caitlin starts laughing at me.

"Oh, you don't know? I'm definitely buying it then!"

"But what is it?"

"I'll be right back! I'll just get this paid for. Feel free to look around, maybe you'll like something!"

Caitlin can't stop giggling as she skips off in the direction of the counter. I walk around to look at the items, and start to read some of the labels on them. The purpose of this store gradually dawns on me and my face turns bright red. Caitlin walks back to me with a big smile on her face, carrying a paper shopping bag. I look at her while covering my red cheeks with my hands.

"I can't believe you pushed me into here! I feel so shameful!"

"Hana, you're so hilarious. You can dispense endless amounts of violence and hostility, but somehow a stick that vibrates a little is crossing a line."

I stop and think about what Caitlin just said. She's right, of course. I wish I could be more carefree and socially uninhibited like her, and less violent, but I'm not sure if I'll ever be any of those things. Maybe she can teach me, or maybe she can't, I don't know if that's even a thing that's teachable, but I'd like her to continue to try. I have a feeling that she probably will. This realisation doesn't mean I don't feel completely awkward right now though.

"Okay, I'm a hypocrite. Can we please get out of here and go buy clothes now?"

50. SMS

It's late. I'm in the dorms, playing with my new phone, which is actually just Caitlin's old phone but that's fine, it's still new to me. Even better, I'm in a different set of pyjamas, one of many new pieces of clothing I was able to buy on our first and possibly last day of freedom for a while. Even better still, I'm watching the final "Show Me Love" video, which was released only about half an hour ago. Everyone else is sitting up in their bunks, doing exactly what I'm doing; playing the video over and over again on their devices. The new song isn't available on streaming services yet and we're not promoting it right now either - Youngsook has to heal a little more first before we can get on music TV shows - but the debut is in full social media swing with press releases and articles galore on all the big sites.

"The video looks great, you look amazing, Caitlin!" exclaims Shu. For once she's saying something I actually can agree with. We all look outstanding but Caitlin's look is the best by far, and the video editor made sure that she got plenty of screen time.

Youngsook smiles while she plays with her latest present, a vape. Nari gave it to Youngsook as a way to apologise for being so harsh during training, and also to help Youngsook quit smoking. "I can't believe they used my voice for nearly all of it."

Iseul nods at Youngsook. "I know, all that re-recording of *my* voice over and over again... just to please the pervert producer, they had *no* intention of even using any of it! You and Shu are the only two people who even got their voice on it."

Nari looks annoyed. "Fuck, they left in the part where I missed the hand movement after the first chorus! We specifically reshot that part of the dance to edit out the mistake and they didn't even remember to fix it!"

I start looking at other related videos that are appearing. Someone's already done a "line distribution" video, which shows exactly how many vocal lines are allocated to each person, so I watch it to see what they come up with. The video mistakenly assumes that the person who the camera is focused on while miming is also the one actually delivering the lines, and as a result from most lines to least, the video wrongly breaks it down to Caitlin - Nari - Shu - Youngsook - Iseul - me. If only the people who made this video knew that despite what person appears on screen at any given moment, it's actually Youngsook for the whole thing except the bridge. I scroll down to the video comments:

Of course Caitlin gets the most lines, she's the prettiest

They really pushed the foreigners and Nari out there and screwed the rest of them, didn't they

Justice for Hana

Someone get Hana and Iseul their compensation

The comments are amusing, but also misguided and not worth taking seriously. They don't understand at all. I'm not upset about being in the video the least, the editors had no choice but to put me last given that I couldn't stick it through to the end of my solo part shooting, and I'd rather not look at myself or have lines anyway. It's completely fine for me to be less popular. I'm not in it for the fame or exposure, I just came here to try to find a lifestyle that is actually liveable, I just wanted to live somewhere where I can be allowed to exist. I look around the room and realise that despite the incredibly harsh conditions of training, and the fact that we rarely all get along, these five girls have still given me the closest thing I've ever had to a home. It's far from perfect, but it's still the best home I've ever had.

I keep looking for other related videos to watch. There are already some "reaction" videos out but I skip those. There's also a "Show Me Love M/V - explained" video, so I take a look at this instead. For ten minutes straight, some computer-voiced narrator picks apart the video scene by scene and comes to the astoundingly tedious revelation that the song is about showing people love. Or something. I wasn't really listening and tuned out halfway through, the computer voice is so monotonous that I couldn't even pay attention. In fact I don't really know what the song's about myself, nor do I really care, after all I didn't write it or even have anything to do with it, really.

Suddenly my phone vibrates. One new message. I take a look.

Caitlin: Speaking of showing people love, we can't hide it from the ones in the group who don't know forever, can we? Since our debut is around the corner, should we tell them?

I have a better idea. I start texting back.

Me: I'm not in the mood for speeches and bullshit. I'm in the mood for you. Just come down here, pin me down and fuck me. I want to make Nari's homophobic ass as uncomfortable as possible. Fuck me until she leaves in disgust, and then don't stop. I want you.

Caitlin jumps down from her top bunk. "Did that clown really say the song was about showing people love?"

"Yeah, brain surgeon, hey." I laugh. I feel my heart rate increasing because I know what's coming, I just don't know when Caitlin is going to kick it off.

"Showing love should be right up your alley, you lesbians," Nari snorts.

"I'm not a lesbian, fuck off!" I reply.

Caitlin takes that as her cue, she suddenly ducks down into my bunk, dives on top of me and starts kissing me passionately without saying a word.

Predictably, Nari starts freaking out. "I knew it! I knew you two were dykes! Oh my god I don't want to see this! Can't you two sluts do this fucking sick crap in private?"

"You can leave the room anytime, Nari."

Caitlin smiles as we continue to kiss each other.

"You fucking degenerates!" Nari screams as she jumps down from her bunk and storms out of the room. "I can't believe now I'm in a group with fucking lesbians AND drug addicts AND gangsters..."

I hear Nari stomping off, who the fuck knows or cares where, probably to the gym space to torture herself with a few hundred star jumps or whatever it is she does for fun. Iseul also jumps down from her bunk and walks out.

"Bye you two, I'm going to follow Nari and make sure she doesn't jump off a bridge. We still need a leader!"

"I'm going too!" says Youngsook, clearly conscious of wanting to give us space. "Oh, um... congratulations on your relationship, bye now!" Youngsook rushes straight after Iseul.

The only other person left in the room is Shu. I look over at her, she's fallen asleep with her phone in her hand. I'm not worried about it; she'll be out until the morning for sure.

I turn my attention back to Caitlin.

"Well, Nari wasn't very happy."

Caitlin starts undoing the buttons on her pyjama top with one hand, and mine with the other.

"Making Nari unhappy is pretty easy. These are nice pyjamas by the way, good choice. I hope you won't be offended if I remove them."

I smile back at Caitlin.

"I'll get over it."

GLOSSARY OF FOREIGN LANGUAGE TERMS
USED IN THIS BOOK

aegyo – acting cute, can also describe someone who acts cute or makes cute expressions.

ahjumma – an informal term for an older lady.

annyeong – an informal greeting used among friends, etc.

annyeong haseyo – a standard greeting used in general polite company.

annyeong hasimnikka – a very formal greeting which is rarely used, generally used only when meeting someone very important for the first time.

annyeonghi gaseyo – a formal goodbye, when you are staying and others are leaving.

annyeonghi gyeseyo – a formal goodbye, when you are leaving and others are staying.

gaoli bangzi – a Chinese ethnic slur for Koreans.

gyopo – a term which technically refers to native Koreans who live overseas, but is often also used to refer to non-native Koreans brought up overseas who are living in Korea, especially Korean-Americans. Not necessarily a derogatory term depending on context.

iljin – organised school bullies that operate like small criminal gangs, known for engaging in extreme violence, underage smoking/drinking and other criminal activity.

jjangkkae – a Korean ethnic slur for Chinese.

kkondae – an insult used to describe an older person who enforces their experience and opinion on younger people in a condescending way - "when I was your age" etc.

mannaseo bangapseumnida – a very formal version of "nice to meet you".

molka – revealing/sexual video or photographs recorded in secret and without consent, usually with hidden cameras or when the subject is unaware/unconscious.

nugu – literally "who?", a derogatory term for an artist or group with no fame who is considered to be a "nobody".

sillyehamnida – a formal request for attention, a very polite version of "excuse me".

soju – a popular Korean alcoholic white spirit, similar to vodka and gin but typically lower in alcohol percentage by volume. Much like vodka and gin, *soju* has a neutral flavour, is sold in both pure and pre-mixed flavoured varieties, and is often used as a mixer with soft drinks and other beverages. Many brands are sold cheaply, it is the preferred drink of juvenile delinquents and *iljins*.

trot – a conservative style of Korean pop music that was popular before the current wave of Korean idol groups, hip-hop and independent rock bands. Trot music is still popular especially among the older generations in Korea.

ulzzang – literally "best face", a look that is popular in Korea among women, the stereotypical *ulzzang* look consists of large eyes, smooth and fair skin, large eyelashes, a heart-shaped face with narrow cheekbones, a thin mouth and a thin nose, *ulzzang*s may possess some or all of these traits. Naturally born *ulzzangs* do exist, but the look is often achieved through combinations of makeup, various cosmetic modifications, and/or plastic surgery.

wangtta – those socially ostracised in the Korean school system and marked as victims of organised bullying by Korean *iljins*. *Wangtta* are often subject to a variety of bullying methods including but not limited to: taunts, threats, physical violence, sexual violence, extortion, blackmail, and being forced to perform subservient tasks for *iljins*, these tasks are known as 'shuttles'. Once the relationship between *iljin* and *wangtta* is established, coercion is often not needed as a climate of fear keeps the status quo in place. Those who associate with students marked as *wangtta* are also targeted, reinforcing the ostracism.

yeoboseyo – a greeting which can be formal or informal, it is used exclusively for phone conversations.

The story of Shin Hana continues in

LOVE LIGHT

Coming in 2024

ABOUT THE AUTHOR

KPOPALYPSE is a musician and music industry veteran from Adelaide, Australia, and he has been writing about Korean pop music, music industry and fan culture since 2012 at kpopalypse.com. He was the first writer to publish completely unedited and raw tell-all interviews in English with people who had been through the gruelling and highly secretive Korean idol training system. He continues to advocate for artist rights and a progressive, pro-sexuality, pro-critical thinking view of Korean popular culture.

Made in the USA
Middletown, DE
04 March 2023

26183110R00239